HAVE I TOLD YOU LATELY

BETH MORAN

B
Boldwood

First published in Great Britain in 2025 by Boldwood Books Ltd.

Copyright © Beth Moran, 2025

Cover Design by Alice Moore Design

Cover Images: Shutterstock and iStock

The moral right of Beth Moran to be identified as the author of this work has been asserted in accordance with the Copyright, Designs and Patents Act 1988.

All rights reserved. No part of this book may be reproduced in any form or by any electronic or mechanical means, including information storage and retrieval systems, without written permission from the author, except for the use of brief quotations in a book review. This book is a work of fiction and, except in the case of historical fact, any resemblance to actual persons, living or dead, is purely coincidental.

Every effort has been made to obtain the necessary permissions with reference to copyright material, both illustrative and quoted. We apologise for any omissions in this respect and will be pleased to make the appropriate acknowledgements in any future edition.

A CIP catalogue record for this book is available from the British Library.

Paperback ISBN 978-1-80483-379-7

Large Print ISBN 978-1-80483-380-3

Hardback ISBN 978-1-80483-381-0

Ebook ISBN 978-1-80483-378-0

Kindle ISBN 978-1-80483-377-3

Audio CD ISBN 978-1-80483-385-8

MP3 CD ISBN 978-1-80483-386-5

Digital audio download ISBN 978-1-80483-384-1

This book is printed on certified sustainable paper. Boldwood Books is dedicated to putting sustainability at the heart of our business. For more information please visit https://www.boldwoodbooks.com/about-us/sustainability/

Boldwood Books Ltd, 23 Bowerdean Street, London, SW6 3TN

www.boldwoodbooks.com

For Joy Taylor
The soul is sweetened by the wise counsel of a friend

1

Sometimes, the tiniest thing can kickstart a chain of events that changes everything. For me, that dull Sunday morning in June, it was the simple act of sleeping through my alarm. Or rather, sticking one arm into the chilly air outside my duvet, whacking the button so hard the clock bounced off my bedside table, and promptly falling straight back to sleep.

I was dreaming. Of golden fields and summer skies. Turquoise butterflies dancing amongst the wildflowers as I strolled past. The hazy heat and sense of all the time in the world felt like oxygen to a soul I hadn't even realised was gasping for breath.

When I finally jolted awake, it took a few seconds to process that the jarring noise was my phone ringing. Head still too foggy to feel more than a vague twinge of trepidation, I fumbled to answer it.

'Hello?'

'Emmie? Emmaline? Are you okay?'

'Yes. Who is this?' I croaked, squinting in confusion.

'It's Barb.'

I scrabbled up my pillow to a semi-sitting position. Why on earth was Barb from the Travel Shop calling me at this time? At any time, for that matter. The only calls I'd got in the past month – make that six months – had been a reminder to book a dentist appointment and some scammer pretending my laptop had been hacked.

'Yeah, so I got your number from Jonny in the office. Like I said, we're wondering if you're okay. Only there's a queue starting to form, and you know what Mandy's like without her coffee.'

A queue? What was she talking about?

'We thought we'd better check if it was a problem with the traffic. Or maybe you were ill, or your van had broken down or something?'

'Um, no. I'm not ill.'

'There's not an emergency?'

'No.' Leaning over the side of the bed, I found my clock, only then registering the hint of daylight peeping around the edge of the blackout blinds.

I stared at the display as Barb carried on chattering about how it was unheard of for me to be late, and she hoped I didn't mind her calling, but they were starting to worry.

Six-fifteen.

What? How had this happened?

And why was I still slumped here, Barb's words buzzing in my ear like a mosquito, instead of fixing it?

Eventually, she paused for breath, and I managed to form the kind of answer I hoped would make her stop.

'I'm okay. Something came up, but it's sorted now. I'll be there by eight.'

'Eight?' Barb exclaimed, prompting a sudden increase in background babble. 'Maybe try for a bit earlier, eh? Security will never forgive you for causing a caffeine-withdrawal riot.'

'The food court sells coffee.'

'I'm going to pretend you didn't say that.'

I hung up, made a feeble attempt to flip back the duvet and found that, despite my being hideously late, my limbs refused to get up. I lay there, immobile, for what felt like eternity.

I tried to remember if this had ever happened before, vaguely recollecting one time as a teenager when my mother said I'd best stay at home, after a night throwing up, more to avoid passing on my germs to customers than any concern for my well-being. Even on my days off, I woke before six.

I didn't know whether to be more worried about oversleeping, or how it had left me paralysed, as if someone had slipped lead weights into my duvet cover during the night.

The most I could summon up was a prickle of fear about why I seemed to feel barely anything at all.

Eventually, after what turned out to be only about ten minutes, the guilt of what Mum would have said if she'd found me like this was enough to propel me out of bed, and into action.

* * *

Parsley's Pasties had been a fixture of the tiny Sherwood Airport for over three decades. My mother, Nell Brown, had run it for nearly all of that time with rigorous efficiency and seemingly unfailing stamina. That was, until she'd suddenly stopped twenty months ago, crumpling to the floor the second she'd shut shop for the day, as if her own death had to fit around the business. After two weeks to mourn, which was probably thirteen days longer than Mum would have approved of, I had donned my green apron and got on with being solely responsible for providing incredible coffee and mouth-watering pasties. These drew staff from every inch of the airport, along with the regular travellers who knew that queuing up at our unassuming kiosk was worth risking a late boarding call.

Since then, I'd continued opening up for business six days a week, fifty-one weeks a year, only taking time off because certain things couldn't be ignored any longer, like getting my catering ovens serviced and replacing my worn-out shoes.

From Wednesday to Monday (Tuesday being the quietest day for flights) I rose at four-thirty, took a precious five minutes to drink a latte and then hurried to the garage attached to the house that Mum had converted into a professional kitchen. After deftly filling dozens of pastry circles and crimping the edges closed, I showered and donned the Parsley's uniform of black trousers and white T-shirt while the first batch baked. I'd then transfer them into Mum's ancient van, kitted out to keep the raw pasties cold and the baked ones warm, and head to the airport, opening the kiosk hatch at six on the dot.

This morning, figuring that I'd have missed the early business travellers, and still feeling somewhat disconcerted that I wasn't especially bothered about the rest, I settled for half the usual number of pasties. I clambered into the van with a mug of black coffee and tried to care that I'd opted for an extra squirt of deodorant and ten minutes of staring into space instead of a shower.

By the time I'd driven the six miles to the airport, then tackled the rigmarole of staff security, it was seven-fifty. As I hurriedly wheeled hot and cold catering trolleys over to the far corner near the second gate (there were only two) people started following me, as if I were the Pied Piper of Pasties. Reaching the kiosk, they automatically formed a not-so-orderly queue in front of the closed serving hatch.

'Give me five minutes,' I pleaded, ducking through the side

door as people I'd served for years started jostling and yelling their regular orders while waving their bank cards or iPhones about.

Ignoring the sweat now gathering in unwashed armpits and behind my bent knees, I unloaded the baked pasties onto the hot plates and the rest into the fridge, flicked on the oven and coffee machine and spent another couple of minutes going through the process of preparing to open up.

Gregory, a manager in the main office, poked his head in the side door.

'The usual please, Emmie, with a flat white and two apple and custards for Karen. You missed her break time.'

'Two?' Parsley's pasties weren't small. Karen usually ate half in her early morning break and saved the rest for lunch.

'Yeah, said she needs to stress eat after the panic about you not being here.'

'It's just a pasty! She could have gone to the food court and got a cooked breakfast. You all could!' I raised my voice in exasperation, causing Gregory to widen his dark eyes in surprise. Me getting snarky happened about as often as I slept in.

'Sure you're feeling all right, Emmie?' He furrowed his brow. 'You look a bit... not quite yourself.'

No. I was not at all sure.

I paused for a moment, wiping a strand of blondish-reddish hair that had escaped my ponytail out of my eyes, the effort of lifting my hand to my head almost as hard as getting out of bed had been.

'I guess now isn't a good time to mention that you still need to sign the lease.'

There hadn't seemed to ever be a good time for that, since Gregory's email two months ago informing me that the rental agreement for the kiosk ran out at the end of June, i.e., two weeks from today. He'd assured me it was the same contract that Mum had agreed to three years earlier, but I wasn't going to sign anything without reading it properly. I just needed to find the time to do that. For some reason, that never seemed to happen.

'Blummin' heck, Emmie. You look like crap. What did you get up to last night?' Barb asked, joining Gregory in the doorway. 'Oh, and the usual, when you're ready.'

'Yep. I'm about there.'

Only, instead of opening up, the second they both disappeared, I found myself sliding to the tiny oblong floor, one hand still clutching a chocolate-sprinkles shaker, staring at my distorted reflection in the fridge door.

All I could think about was that dream. Those fields. The wide-open sky and fresh, summer air that were a world away from the artificial lights and windowless space where I spent most of my life.

A pounding on the hatch snapped me back to reality.

A reality where a gathering crowd of customers were rapidly replacing their relief at my appearance with impatience that they still didn't have what they wanted.

In the end, what got me up was the horrible thought that if I didn't, I'd end up being fussed over. Someone would probably manhandle me to a comfy sofa and insist upon me explaining what was wrong, how I was feeling. They might even fetch Graham, the airport medic. Before the end of the day, everyone would know that Emmaline was not okay, and they would all want to know why.

Even if I could answer their questions, I recoiled against anyone else being privy to what I was starting to fear might be a mental breakdown, or a stroke. Maybe the onset of dementia?

When one of the air-stewards had started acting out of character, it had turned out to be a brain tumour.

With that thought chasing the remnant of the dream away, I got up, smoothed out my apron, stuck on my mother's polite-yet-professional smile and, as I'd been doing since I was thirteen years old, I got on with it.

2

I knew exactly how many pasties to prep in order to sell out between three and three-fifteen each day, factoring in airline schedules and fluctuating seasons. Today, on top of my arriving with less stock than usual, the initial queue had more than compensated for my delay, creating a buzz that meant the handful of regulars waiting for the two-forty-five to Amsterdam were gutted to find I'd only got two pasties left.

'Are these one of each?' an older woman who always flew out on Sundays and returned on Thursday asked, pointing an immaculate scarlet fingernail at the counter.

'Yes. One Sherwood, one vegetarian.'

'I'll take the veggie, please. And a large cappuccino with extra sprinkles and a shot of caramel.'

I was already placing it into a paper bag. She always had the parsnip and white Stilton pasty, despite the younger man who often travelled with her trying to persuade her to go for the meat option, a venison and minted mushy pea recipe Mum had developed on the basis that it was both local and the most environmentally friendly meat.

'She's not a vegetarian,' he often told me, rolling his eyes. 'Just refuses to believe that anything else could be as tasty as this one.'

'I don't care if the venison is better,' his colleague once scoffed. 'I live on salad and grains all week to offset the calorific pleasure of this feast. Why risk it?'

Today, he went as far as to put a hand on her arm as she reached up to take her purchase. 'Come on, Cathy, you know I've gone vegan this month. Are you seriously going to make me hunt down a prepacked plant-based sandwich in here?'

Apart from Parsley's, the only places to get something to eat were the food court on the other side of the building, which didn't do takeaway, or the Travel Shop, which by this time of day was probably down to a flabby cheese and tomato wrap and a couple of cheap sausage rolls.

'And what is a vegan, however superficial they are about it, going to do with a Stilton pasty?' Cathy asked.

'Damn.' The man's face fell. 'It's got cheese in it?'

'That's what makes it so delicious.' She smirked, opening the bag for a deep sniff.

'You don't have any other options?' he asked me, despite already knowing the answer because we only had three flavours on the menu, and, even if the custard in the cinnamon apple pasty had been dairy-free, we now had only one pasty left.

'Sorry. They do a good soup in the food court, if you've time.'

We both glanced at the clock on the display board. He didn't have time.

Mum had considered it revolutionary to put a vegetarian option on the menu, back in 1990 when she'd opened the kiosk. It had taken years to persuade her to stock soya milk.

'I don't suppose you have any gluten-free?' another man asked as Cathy's dejected colleague slunk off muttering about finding a packet of crisps.

'Sorry, this is the only one left. It's normal pastry,' I said, as if gluten-free were ever an option.

I was getting asked questions like this more and more often, I mused while cleaning up a few minutes later, simultaneously trying to scrub away the strange numbness I'd woken up with. Mum had been adamant that sticking to three recipes, done well, was key to our success. Broadening the menu would only compromise the quality. And it wasn't as though I needed to attract more customers. Apart from the horror of the pandemic, business was always enough to keep things ticking over. More recipes meant more work, which I simply didn't have the time or the energy for.

And yet.

Had any of my reluctance to get up that morning been due to feeling a teensy bit bored with facing the same routine for the squillionth time? Had sleeping through my alarm, not simply doing what I'd always done, been enough to awaken a tiny part of me that wasn't sure this was actually what I wanted to be doing for the rest of my life?

I couldn't help wondering if there was another reason I kept putting off signing a new three-year lease.

Every day, I watched up to a thousand strangers jet off to far-off places. And while the short-haul flights from our tiny airport were not that adventurous compared to many, when the most exotic trip you've undertaken is a long-weekend in Whitby, getting on a plane to anywhere is a prospect beyond thrilling.

But that was a fantasy, of course. My life was here. Parsley's was my legacy, and I owed it to Mum to put as much effort in as she had. Most of the travellers at Sherwood Airport were heading off on business, anyway. Probably to boring meetings, trying to fix nightmarish problems or drum up more sales, because they didn't have the luxury of hundreds of customers walking right past them every day.

Besides, Mum and I were the type of people who valued routine. Just like Cathy. When you'd figured out what works best, why risk changing it?

Nell had told me about her cousin – my birth mother. How she'd spent her short life staggering between trouble and disaster. In and out of prison along with the rest of our sparse family. How when the cousin had turned up high on goodness knew what and handed over a tiny baby and a plastic bag containing three nappies and a tub of formula milk, Nell had known the only decent thing to do was take them.

She'd learned how to be a mother through checking out every parenting book in the library, discarding the new-fangled nonsense, and incorporating the remaining advice into a regime based on common sense and practicality, all while continuing to run the kiosk.

It had worked, as she'd often used to remind me. I'd grown into a sensible young woman with a faultless work ethic, one capable of being entrusted with a thriving business when the time came. Any genetic tendency towards criminality or chaos had been suppressed thanks to cutting off all contact with Negative Influences (by which she meant my aunt and grandparents, my mother having died a year after relinquishing me), and building our new family of two on the foundation of self-discipline and integrity.

Still, I'd grown up with the ghost of my birth mother hovering over my shoulder, especially in those adolescent moments when I'd dared to dream about a life more like the ones that the girls at school had enjoyed. Shopping with friends at the weekend, hobbies in the evening and even going away in the school holidays, rather than forever braising venison or peeling parsnips.

'Make-up?' Mum had shaken her head in disgust the one time I'd asked if I could spend my meagre earnings on some eyeliner.

'That only leads to trouble. Do you want to throw away everything I've taught you for a few minutes of frivolity with a boy? It only feels good while it lasts, Emmaline. The consequences are a whole other matter.'

What I'd actually wanted was to see if I could make my eyes look mysterious and cool like the most popular girl in school, Jodie Mayfair.

Now, fourteen years later, I thought about this as I flicked off the kiosk lights, locked the door and headed straight over to the Travel Shop. I was twenty-six. Mum had died almost two years ago. Why was I waiting for her permission to do anything any more?

* * *

After my detour to the shop, I found my usual table in the food court. This table was rarely busy, partly because the food-court offerings consisted of an all-day breakfast that looked as if it had been sitting on the lukewarm counter 'all day', and a 'hot special', rotating five variations of greying, greasy minced beef. There were also a few sandwiches and snacks and the spicy lentil and vegetable soup. Which was delicious.

Six days a week, I treated myself to soup, a warm bread roll and a slice of flapjack with a pot of tea before setting off for home. Today, Blessing, who was working the afternoon shift at the Travel Shop, hurried over to join me.

'What's all this, then?' She eyed the bag of make-up that I'd bought from her only minutes earlier. There'd been a family waiting to pay for a pile of miniature toiletries, so she'd not been able to grill me at the time, but I wasn't surprised that she'd made use of the *back in 5 minutes* sign that was highly frowned upon by all levels of airport management, and followed me straight over as soon as the shop was empty.

I shrugged, concentrating on my lunch. 'I've run out of a few bits. Mascara and stuff. I know it's more expensive here, but I can't seem to get around to it on my day off.'

'Emmaline Brown. In what decade did you run out of mascara? Because the only non-natural thing on your face since you started working here is the occasional smear of icing sugar.'

Mum had started me working at Parsley's on weekends and school holidays the day after my thirteenth birthday. Blessing had been sixteen and a month into her Saturday job, so she'd naturally gravitated towards me as the only other teenager employed at the airport. Since we'd both gone on to work full-time, she'd become the closest person I had to a friend here. Which meant that since Mum died, she'd been the closest person in my life full stop. However, our occasional lunchtime chats about whether Arjun in Security was ever going to confess his love to Helena in Duty Free, or the trials of her ever-expanding family, were still a long way from me sharing a potential existential crisis.

'Maybe I wear make-up in my free time. When I'm going out somewhere nice.'

'What, to the wholesalers? Or are you checking out a fit librarian as well as all those holiday books?' She eyed my bag. I sometimes read a travel guide while I finished my flapjack.

I ate another mouthful of bread. She was right. The library was the highlight of my social calendar.

'If you've got yourself a date, you'd better tell me about it.'

I shook my head, neck prickling with embarrassment at the intimate turn the conversation was taking, while at the same time sharply aware of the shyly smiling, rugged face that had popped into my head.

'I don't have a date. Barb told me I looked like crap this morning.'

'Yeah, well. If you're taking Barb's advice then you'll have to spend way more than forty quid.'

Barb took both her role as unofficial beauty-counter consultant and her staff discount seriously. The rumour around the airport was that she'd once worn so much metallic eyeshadow, the metal detector had gone off when she'd walked through Security. Blessing joked that her manager liked to demonstrate the shop's full range of make-up – all at the same time. In contrast, the only make-up my friend ever wore was a swipe of electric-blue eyeliner that perfectly matched her uniform. She constantly complained about the cheap tunic she had to wear, but the truth was, the way that she tucked it over her curves made it look effortlessly stylish.

'Gregory said I didn't look like myself.'

'He said that?' Blessing frowned, peering more closely at me.

I didn't add that I didn't feel like myself, either. Not ill. Just odd.

'Honestly? And I say this as your airport bestie – you look knackered.'

I put down my spoon. How could I be knackered when I'd had an extra two hours of sleep this morning?

'You've looked worn out since losing Nell,' she said, squinting in apology for the bluntness. 'Which is understandable, when you're grieving. But it's been nearly two years and lately, it's got worse. I mean, if it's just your outside that's tired, then I can recommend some creams and things to help. But is it more than that? Are you as exhausted as you look? When was the last time you had a proper holiday?'

I sat back. Blessing, unlike Barb, was rarely rude. I trusted her opinion more than anyone's. I closed my eyes for a second, to see if I could tune into my body and figure out if this was what it was trying to tell me.

A good few seconds later, when my eyelids were protesting at the very idea of opening again, I had my answer.

'Never.' I moved my bowl to the side and picked up my flapjack. 'I've never had a proper holiday. I spent a week off in January deep-cleaning my kitchen and going for a smear test.' I took a large bite, acknowledging the irony that realising how tired I was had energised me for the first time all day. 'I'm so tired I've been too tired to even notice. I guess I need to start going to bed earlier. It's not like I can take any time off when we're about to hit the high season.'

Blessing gave me a pointed look. 'You think that's the answer? Buy some make-up to hide your bags and go to bed even earlier than your current time of, what, nine-thirty?'

'I didn't buy the make-up solely to hide my eyebags.' I tried to hide behind the chunk of flapjack, because this whole conversation was making my skin itch. 'I just wanted, I don't know. To try something different. See what it was like to be a bit different.'

'What, different from mini-Nell?'

That made me smile. Mum had been five-foot eleven and thirteen stone of hard graft. I was eight inches shorter, and at risk of being blown over if I walked too close to the air-conditioning vents. Despite that, we shared strawberry-blonde hair, green eyes and heart-shaped faces.

'They do say a change is as good as a break,' Blessing went on. 'Maybe trying some new things, having more fun, will help.'

I nodded. 'That's a good idea. I'll think about it.'

'We can start this evening.' She gripped my hand, dark eyes gleaming. 'I finish at seven. How about I head over and do you a makeover? I can show you how to put that stuff on without ending up like Barb. We can brainstorm some other things to help you feel less awful.'

I balked at that, still getting used to the idea that I might be feeling at all awful. But while a large part of me wanted to fob Blessing off – I had to prepare a fresh pot of mushy peas, water my plants, read a book, sit about feeling pitifully lonely – the part of me that had woken up with the scent of summer sunshine in her senses wanted to try something reckless.

'I'll message you my address.'

3

After finishing my pot of tea, I wheeled my trolleys back to the van and drove home, stopping at the tiny supermarket in Middlebeck, the village nearest my cottage, to grab appropriate makeover snacks. That then sent me into a near panic attack over whether to go for crisps, biscuits or ice cream, something more substantial like pizza or fancier like cheese and crackers. In the end, I threw them all in my basket along with bottles of wine, gin and lemonade.

'Having a party?' The fifty-something cashier, who liked to describe herself as a 'local character', asked, loading up two bulging bags. 'Bit of a change from your usual healthy crap.'

'Um. Something like that.'

'Ooh – I know, you just got dumped!' She winked at the teenage boy waiting in the queue behind me. 'Break-up snacks.'

I almost retorted that if I had, then I'd hardly appreciate her announcing it to the whole shop. But then the thought flashed into my head that, if I'd been dumped, at least I'd have had a more recent boyfriend than William, who I broke up with on my twenty-first birthday after a lecture from Mum about priorities.

I mean, don't get me wrong, I had been on dates since then.

Three, in total, with Stefan from the wholesalers. All in the month after Mum's funeral, and all about as ill-judged and awkward as the cheap black heels I'd tottered about in at the wake.

Instead, I mumbled something about having a 'girls' night', and gave a watery smile that became a tentative grin when I realised that this was sort of true.

* * *

I had a couple of hours to mush the marrowfat peas I'd soaked overnight with fresh mint leaves and lemon juice, ready the other items Parsley's was running low on, shower and flap about making sure the house was tidy.

The last one didn't take long, given that the whole cottage consisted of five rooms, which had all been tidied and cleaned the day before. Which was fortunate, as choosing what to wear for the first time Blessing had seen me out of uniform since Mum's funeral took me forever. However many times I scanned my wardrobe, aside from my work clothes, there were still only the three pairs of jeans I'd ordered online and kept despite them hanging off my hips, four T-shirts in varying shades of dark blue, depending upon how faded they'd become in the wash, a grey cardigan and navy jumper, plus a black dress that looked as if I'd borrowed it from one of the stuffiest *Apprentice* candidates.

Surprise, surprise, I opted for my least saggy jeans and bluest T-shirt, jazzing things up with the cardigan and some stripy socks that Gregory had given me in last year's secret Santa.

By the time Blessing arrived, I was debating whether to hide behind the sofa and pretend not to hear her knocking.

The section of brain that was still able to think rationally forced me to go and let her in, Parsley's Pasties smile firmly in place.

'Woah. What's up?' Blessing asked, wheeling a small suitcase into the living room. She'd swapped her work tunic for a black calf-length leather skirt and metallic jumper with matching ankle boots. I wondered if I should have worn the funeral dress after all.

'I'm fine,' I squeaked.

'Girl, you are not fine.'

'This is just... the first time I've had a friend over to my house.'

Blessing studied me carefully for a long minute. The gentle expression on her face was about the only thing preventing me from running upstairs and locking myself in the bathroom until she went away.

'I hear you. After a shift surrounded by strangers rushing about, constant noise, Gavin droning on over the tannoy every thirty seconds, I'm straight in the bath, earplugs in, eye mask on. My sisters have learned that to interrupt me risks death by exfoliation. If I could come home to a quiet house, I'd never ask anyone over.'

'Yeah. Most nights, I'm prepping for the next day, visiting the wholesalers and stuff anyway.'

'Nell didn't really believe in a social life, did she?'

'Time off is for the lazy or feckless.'

She plopped onto the sofa. I forced down the prickle of anxiety caused by her taking my usual seat.

'Anyway, that's why I'm here, isn't it? So both of us can get off the Sherwood Airport Travelator of Endless Monotony. I'm thirty in a few months. Still sharing a bunk bed with my littlest sister. Maybe if I was a bit more like Nell, I'd have my own place, too.' Blessing caught herself. 'Sorry, was that totally tactless? Living alone because your mum died is nothing to be envious of. Crap. I've said something stupid again...'

'No, it's fine.' I missed Mum, but nothing like I'd used to, and had heard enough about Blessing's two sisters and three brothers to appreciate my own space.

She didn't look as if it was fine. I almost told her where the bathroom was, in case she wanted to hide in there for a bit. Instead, I asked if she wanted any food.

'What have you got?'

I bobbed my head a couple of times. 'Might be easier to say what I haven't got… or at least just show you.'

I led her through the tiny, decrepit kitchen where I made hot drinks and prepped my evening meals, into the sparkling chef's kitchen where the real magic happened.

'Wow.' Blessing did a slow spin, taking in the stainless-steel worktops and appliances, the pots of herbs on a shelving unit positioned to soak up sunlight from the huge windows, and the top-of-the-range equipment arranged to maximise the space. My mother might have balked at paying over a pound for a tube of toothpaste, but when it came to her kitchen, no expense had been spared.

'This is where miracle pasties are born.' She opened one fridge to find stacks of large tubs containing various fillings, then the one beside it, full of raw ingredients. I hovered nervously behind her, feeling not dissimilar to if she was going through my underwear drawers or bathroom cabinet. 'Is this evening's choice of food pasty or pasty, with a side of pasty?'

'No.' I took the giant wheel of Stilton cheese out of her hands and carefully pushed it back on the shelf, before closing the fridge door. 'The last time I ate a whole pasty was for school packed lunch.'

'Understandable, I guess.' She nodded, picking up my favourite chef's knife and inspecting the blade.

'Besides, I make the pasties fresh every morning, so there won't be any more until tomorrow.'

'Really?' She surrendered the knife to my outstretched hand and wandered over to the herbs. 'I never knew if that was just something people said: "freshly baked today".'

'This is what I've got.' I gestured to where I'd neatly laid out the food I'd bought on a worktop, causing Blessing to brush off the rosemary leaves she'd just crushed in her palm and come to take a look.

'Ooh. Okay. This is quite a feast. I grabbed a burger on the way over, so I hope you didn't get all this just for me.'

After I fobbed that question off, we decided to take a couple of bowls of crisps for now and put a pizza in an oven for later.

'Right. Let's get down to business,' Blessing said, once she'd taken a seat in Mum's armchair and opened her suitcase. 'I've got a few foundation testers. If we go even a shade too dark, you'll look orange.'

She handed me a tiny tube, the shade of which was named 'porridge'.

'Try it on your jawline.'

I opened the lid and squirted a blob onto my finger, then dabbed it on. Blessing looked up from where she'd been sorting through other packages in the case, then glanced at me, her eyes widening for a second before the previous look of compassion took over.

'You've never done this before.'

I shrugged. 'I've worn lip gloss a couple of times.'

Reaching over, she gently smoothed the blob across my jawline. With a start, I realised it was the most physical affection I'd had since Stefan gave me a clumsy hug and peck on the cheek on our final date.

'Hmmm. That's not quite it.' Oblivious to the tears now prickling behind my eyes, she busied herself finding another colour – 'let's try Arctic hare' – and applied it to the other side.

'That's better.' She glanced around the living room. 'Where's your downstairs mirror?'

'I haven't got one.'

She narrowed one eye. 'Then how do you check if you look okay? You have to keep running upstairs?'

I shrugged.

'That explains why you're the skinny one. Okay, go and grab one from upstairs and I'll show you how to use primer.'

'No... I don't have one, at all.'

'You can't not have a mirror. Even if you literally don't care about your appearance, what if you get something in your eye or have a weird bump on your chin? What if you need to...? I don't know. How do you even know what your own face looks like?' She shook her head in bewilderment.

'There's one fixed on Mum's bedroom wardrobe. If I need to, I use that.'

'Right.' Blessing started packing pots and creams back into the suitcase. 'Lead the way.'

'Um, it smells like the pizza is ready.'

We ate the pizza sitting at the tiny table in the cottage kitchen, Blessing explaining different products to me in between shaking her head at my woeful mirror situation. I didn't bother pointing out that since Mum had died, her mirror was my mirror now. I was too busy trying to find a reason why we couldn't go upstairs. The only one I could come up with was the truth, so I went for that one.

'I'm not sure about us going in Mum's bedroom. It feels like invading her privacy,' I blurted, once Blessing got on to something called finishing spray, so I figured I was running out of time.

'You never go in there?' she asked softly.

'Well. I do sometimes use the mirror.'

'Have you sorted out her things yet?'

I shook my head.

'Okay. I guess everyone is ready for that step in their own time. I thought it was extreme when my auntie threw all Uncle Derek's possessions in the wheelie bin the day after his heart attack, but then we found out he'd been having an affair with the guy who jet-washed the bin, so it made a lot more sense.'

'It's not that I'm not ready. I just… don't know what to do with it.' I shook my head; that wasn't quite right. 'Not her clothes and toiletries, but the personal things. Presuming there are any, of course. This is Mum we're talking about.'

'You can keep whatever you want to.' Blessing took hold of my hand. It felt so lovely, a tear finally slipped out and rolled down my cheek.

'She wasn't my birth mum,' I said, my voice hoarse. 'I was her cousin's daughter. Mum left me everything in her will, but… I don't know. She never spoke about her family, apart from passing comments about what lowlife criminals they were when she was lecturing me about something. My birth mother died when I was a baby, so I never had to worry about who she was or whether she'd ever come back for me. But what if I find something with Mum's possessions?'

'Something proving your family were as terrible as she said?'

'Or the complete opposite.' I sighed. 'You knew Mum. She was uncompromising. Everything was right or wrong, good or bad. No excuses and no second chances.'

'So, you might have a lovely pair of grandparents somewhere, their dodgy days long behind them. An aunt who'd love to meet the niece who's her biological granddaughter. You might have a whole family waiting to love you.'

I couldn't speak, but Blessing knew what I was thinking.

'And every time you look in her mirror, which I'm guessing isn't often, you think about whether the evidence is buried in that wardrobe, behind it.'

'Something like that.' I sniffed.

She dropped my hand and leant over for a proper hug. 'Well, that explains why your T-shirt is on back to front.'

Blessing fetched the rest of the snacks, waiting until three quarters of the chocolate-chip cookies were gone before asking whether I wanted to finish the makeover, keep eating or brave a look in Mum's bedroom while she was there to provide moral support.

'I don't really want all those layers on my face. Even that bit of tester felt weird. But could you show me how to use the mascara and lipstick, maybe a bit of eyeshadow, while we finish the cookies?'

'Emmie, I've eaten two of those cookies.'

'What?'

She laughed. 'I'm not judging. I had a burger on the way here, remember? But I don't hate discovering that underneath the cool, calm exterior is a real-ass woman who feeds her emotions with chocolate.'

'That's the thing,' I said, although it was hard to decipher because I'd somehow ended up with another cookie in my mouth. 'I don't eat stuff like this. I don't wallow in my feelings. I'm usually too busy to think about them.'

Blessing handed me the last one in the packet. 'Here. You've got some catching-up to do.'

* * *

Blessing stayed for another hour, fetching a spare mirror from her car before showing me the right shades to complement my

Arctic-hare complexion, and how to add a 'healthy glow' rather than 'Barb vibes'. We then moved to the kitchen so I could make up batches of sweet and savoury pastry for tomorrow's pasties while Blessing messed about with my meat thermometer.

'Do you have anything else needs doing tonight?' she asked, while helping me wrap the pastry so it could be stored overnight in the fridge.

'Not a lot. I didn't make as many pasties today, so have plenty of fillings for tomorrow. I'll water the herbs and that's about it.'

'What do you do in the evenings, apart from food prep?'

'A couple of times a week, I go to the wholesalers. I clean the ovens, check up on stock. Sometimes have time to do some admin, accounting, that sort of thing.'

Blessing frowned. 'No, I meant apart from work. What do you do for fun?'

'Oh.' This conversation was reminding me why not having friends outside the airport was a good idea. Apart from when they hugged me, said kind things, taught me new skills and helped me wash up, of course.

'I don't get much chance for fun in the evenings. I'm usually in bed not long after nine, so I can get up at four-thirty.'

Blessing waited; she wasn't letting me get out of this.

'I read. I might go for a walk in the summer. But really, running your own business doesn't leave a lot of time for fun.'

'Hmph. Sounds like exactly the type of thing Nell used to say.' She handed me the giant ball of pastry. 'Or not exactly. Didn't she used to say, "Running your own business doesn't leave *any* time for fun. Fun is for loser wimps"?'

'She did not say that!'

'Actions speak louder than words.'

We walked back into the living room, where Blessing collected her things, insisting I keep the mirror. She then came to a stop, holding my front door half open.

'You said earlier today that you wanted to try being someone different. I've been friends with you for thirteen years, and this must be the first time you've tried anything new. You eat the same lunch, tie your hair up with a beige bobble, wear the same ugly style of shoes that Nell wore. And while I love you as you are, I can tell one thing is changing. I think underneath your endless hard work is a woman who's growing unhappy with the person her mother insisted she should be and becoming exhausted by a life she never had any choice about. A fun evening with a friend is a start, but mascara isn't going to solve this. You need to pick one of those places you're always reading about, and go there. Forget Parsley's Pasties for a couple of weeks. A couple of years if that's how long you need to decide whether running a pasty stall is what you dream of doing for the next forty years.'

'I can't just up and leave,' I stammered.

'Plan it, then. How long have you got left on the kiosk lease? If it's ages, there must be a get-out clause.'

I didn't dare tell her it was up in two weeks. She'd have gone upstairs and started packing my suitcase.

'If I'm not open for business, I don't make any money. I can't afford that.'

Again, this was not entirely true. While Parsley's made enough to keep me going day to day, I had also inherited a hefty lump sum from Mum. I was saving it for an emergency, as I knew she'd want me to. Another pandemic, or a kitchen fire that for some reason wasn't covered by insurance. I could become seriously ill and need months off to recover.

'You dragged yourself in two hours late with half your stock this morning. Carry on along the Sherwood Airport Travelator of Monotony and you might find yourself falling off the end. Into a complete breakdown.' She stepped out into the darkness, walking down the path to the narrow road that led up to my cottage, only turning back when she reached her car. 'Are you happy, Emmie?'

For the second time that day, I had to squeeze back tears. 'What's that got to do with anything? Being happy isn't the be-all and end-all.'

Oh, my goodness. She was right. I had turned into my mother.

'No. But it's something. One of the most important things. If you aren't even happy, if you can't even look yourself in the mirror, then what's the point?'

* * *

The second Blessing's car disappeared into the night, I raced upstairs, flinging open the door to Mum's bedroom, and marching over to the full-length mirror that formed one of her wardrobe doors.

'There,' I told the part of myself that had refused to get out of bed that morning. 'Happy now?'

No. Not happy.

And in that moment, standing there, looking at my same old ponytail and faded T-shirt, smoky-grey smudged around my eyes, I accepted that I'd forgotten what happiness felt like.

I took a deep breath and opened the wardrobe door.

4

I knew that Mum's wardrobe was in pristine order because I'd opened it once before to find her one dress to pass to the funeral directors. The only clothes that remained hanging up in here were five perfectly ironed work T-shirts, two pairs of black trousers, two navy, three grey T-shirts and a shapeless grey trouser suit. Her jumpers, cardigans and other clothes would be in the chest of drawers. In the bottom of the wardrobe were an empty handbag, a blanket and a pillow still in its packaging. On a high shelf were a pair of brown sandals and black brogues. I fetched the chair from the corner of the room and stood on it so I could find what else was up there. A hairdryer, small suitcase and a bright-green hat that I'd never seen before. Then, behind that, I found a cardboard storage box, about the size of a shoebox but much sturdier.

I slid it off the shelf and placed it on the bed, which I'd made up with Mum's clean bedding at some point, for no reason other than I didn't know what else to do with her sheet and duvet cover.

Setting the lid to one side, inside I found a large spiral shell.

Next to this rested a dried posy. The flowers appeared to be on the brink of crumbling as I rested them carefully on the lid, but looked like a mixture of forget-me-nots, daisies and one tiny sunflower. Beneath this was a tidy stack of envelopes, tied with a blue ribbon. When I removed those, I found a photograph in a plain wooden frame.

It was Mum.

With a man.

I'd have guessed their ages at late thirties, maybe early forties. They were standing outside an Italian restaurant. Mum was laughing, which was surprising enough, gazing into the man's eyes, but what shocked me to the core was the wedding dress.

Who knew how long I sat there, staring at the photo, comparing the bouquet in the picture with the flowers I'd carefully lifted out of the box? I turned on the bedside light, in case the extra illumination would prove that, no, this wasn't my man-scorning mother. Maybe it was my birth mum, or my auntie. It couldn't be my grandmother (biological great-auntie) as the dress was pure 1980s floof.

But there was an unmistakable brown birthmark on her forearm.

I briefly wondered whether this was a costume. But the look on both their faces was as genuine as it got. Besides, Mum would never have kept a posy from a fancy-dress party, decades ago.

That brought me back to the envelopes. The first one was handwritten to Nell Brown, with no address.

The obvious way to learn more would be to open the envelope. But my mother had been so private when it came to her past. I'd assumed this was down to both her lack of sentimentality and her deep disdain for her family. It had never crossed my mind that she could have been hiding a whole other life.

A sudden thought hit me. Had she lied about everything? About me? If Mum had been married, then maybe this mysterious, conveniently deceased cousin was a lie, too. Could Mum be my biological mother? Was this man, her husband, my father?

Although Mum hadn't actually lied about this. I couldn't recall her telling me that she'd never married, never been in love. I'd concluded that for myself. And I'd seen my birth certificate enough times. The named mother was Kennedy Swan, the father unknown.

So, if this had nothing to do with me, did I have the right to pry into it? These were personal letters. Love letters, potentially. After the events of the day, my brain was in no fit state to decide something like that. I pictured what she'd have to say about it, and let her decide for me. Returning the contents of the box, I put it back on the shelf and went to bed.

* * *

After a brief battle with the urge to bury my head under the duvet and pretend pasties had never been invented, I got up only a few minutes late on Monday. Blaming my grouchy mood on the hours I'd spent churning over the revelations inside Mum's box instead of sleeping, I did my best to plough on as usual.

Gregory firmly plonked a large envelope on the counter when he came for his breakfast. 'I'm presuming there's something wrong with your emails, because I can't think of any other reason why you've still not signed the lease. Here's a paper copy. Read it when you have your soup and call me if you've any questions.'

'Mum may have known this inside out, but I'm in charge now. A responsible business owner would take the time to study it properly,' I said.

'If you've not had time to read a twenty-page document in two months, then you need to seriously question your life choices,' Gregory said, laughing at his own joke. 'A responsible business owner would make the time and get it done.'

* * *

Blessing came over to the kiosk before her shift started at two o'clock, leaning up against the hatch to take a good look at me once I'd filled her travel mug with coffee and handed her a pasty.

'Mascara and dusky-rose lipstick. Subtle, yet effective. I bet no one's said you look crap today.'

I swapped my Parsley's Pasties smile for a real one.

'Thanks for coming over last night.'

'Getting to nosey about the mysterious Brown house while showing off my make-up prowess? The pleasure was all mine. Although, next time we hang out, we're going shopping. That blue T-shirt made your skin tone appear way more porridge than Arctic hare, and I have a feeling the rest of your wardrobe isn't much better.'

'It's no better,' I started to reply, before Blessing, who had turned to check the time on the airport display board as she picked up her purchases, gasped.

'Hello!' She whipped her head back, eyes wide with glee. 'What a perfect day for your secret lover to appear.'

'What?' I instinctively craned my neck to scan the trickle of travellers wandering about the concourse, embarrassed anticipation flooding my pale cheeks.

I didn't have to ask who I was looking for. Blessing had been teasing me about Pip Hawkins since she'd caught us chatting back in September. Not that she knew we were on first-name terms. I'd been doing my utmost (and, it would seem, failing miserably) to pretend her comments about my crush were a puerile joke.

I had one real friend. No family. The only other men in my life were Stefan at the wholesalers, Dev the butcher and Gregory.

Of course I had a crush on the lovely, slightly awkward agricultural student who stopped to chat to me at the start and end of every term. (He'd assured me he was a mature student. I wasn't blushing about a teenager.) I thought about Pip far more often than was reasonable. To see him now, a week before his university broke up for the summer (yes, I'd checked the dates), on a day when there weren't even any flights to the Isle of Siskin, the tiny island in the Irish Sea that he called home and everyone else who lived there called simply 'the island', had my insides flapping like a flustered chicken.

He wore his usual outfit of heavy lumberjack shirt and dark T-shirt, hands pushed into cargo-trouser pockets, but there was no sign of the tatty rucksack he always took as a carry-on.

'His hair is incredible.' Blessing sighed. 'Do you think he'd let me stroke it if I asked nicely?'

Pip had, in my unqualified opinion, perfect hair. Thick and glossy, so dark it shone indigo, it curled over his brow in a way that made your hand itch to smooth it out of his Celtic-blue eyes. He was a couple of inches above medium height in heavy boots, with the lean, robust frame of a man who'd spent his whole life working outdoors.

But none of those things were the reason I'd fallen hopelessly in crush with him. 'Nothing is more beautiful than kind,' Mum used to tell me, and it turned out she was right.

* * *

A few weeks after Mum died, I was still reeling, alongside getting to grips with the business and living with the vast, aching hole where she used to be. On a particularly bad day, starting with a flat tyre and including someone demanding a refund because they'd discovered they didn't like mushy peas, splashing scalding-hot coffee down myself and running out of soft drinks because I'd forgotten to stocktake, I was now facing a customer threatening to sue me for causing his brand-new wife's itchy, swollen face.

'Look at her!' he demanded, grabbing her arm and pulling her closer to the hatch.

Two flights had recently landed, with another one due to take off in an hour, and the kiosk was about as busy as it got.

'You can't deny she looks hideous!'

My frazzled mind was scrabbling like a hamster on a wheel, unable to reach an appropriate reply.

'It does seem quite uncomfortable.'

What she looked was upset. Whether more about the splotches, or her husband's response, I couldn't tell. 'But I'm not sure what that has to do with me.'

'She's allergic to cinnamon,' he spluttered. 'I spent thousands on this honeymoon, and you've ruined it.'

'She had an apple pasty?'

'Well, duh! Have you got another explanation for why she's puffed up like a bullfrog?'

'How absolutely awful.' I turned to speak to his wife, feeling terrible about the tears trickling down her ballooning cheeks. 'I'm genuinely so sorry this has happened, but the menu clearly says cinnamon apple custard.'

'I didn't read the menu, though, did I?' the man yelled. The queue behind him had divided into those taking a nervous couple of steps back, and the people irate enough about the hold-up to press forwards. 'I asked you if the pasty was custard, and you said yes.'

'Look, mate, we've got flights to catch,' a large man waiting to be served interrupted. 'If you've got a complaint, write an email.'

'And, what, I'm just hanging around at the airport for a laugh? We all have flights to catch. Are you going on honeymoon to a five-star hotel in Santorini, chauffeur-driven private tour included? No? Didn't think so.'

'Even more reason for you to send an email later – the Santorini flight is boarding.'

'Um, we don't have a flight to catch?' a tanned young woman said, although she didn't sound too sure about it. 'We just landed.'

'Yeah, but our train leaves in fifteen, so we still need to get our coffee, if you don't mind,' her friend chipped in.

'If I don't mind?' The man's face had turned almost as red as his wife's. 'Would *you* mind? Going on a holiday of a lifetime with a face like that? What about the photos? She's going to scare our future children, if we ever dare show them.'

'Dude, your flight is boarding,' the large man repeated. 'Get out the way, yeah?'

'If I miss my flight, I'm adding it to the lawsuit.' The man pointed at me. 'Two and a half grand.'

'Love, if I were you, I'd leave him to argue and get on the plane without him,' someone said to his wife, patting her arm in sympathy.

'What are you going to do about poisoning my wife?'

'She's not going to do anything. It says cinnamon in the menu. If your wife has an allergy, it's up to you to check,' someone called from the back of the queue.

'Yeah, but the law says you have to display all potential allergens,' another person added as the line rapidly descended into chaos.

'It is displayed!'

'Look at her, though – poor lass just got married.'

And so it went on.

In my panic, all I could think was how much I needed Mum,

and how she'd have sent this man packing and restored order before I had time to pour his wife a free coffee.

Then, out of nowhere, an angel in a lumberjack shirt waded through the jostling crowd and interjected himself between the kiosk hatch and the angry man.

'Stop,' he said, shaking his head in disbelief. 'Look at your wife. She's in pain and upset and instead of offering comfort, you're humiliating her. You need to apologise for your horrible mistake, then make it up to her with the holiday of a lifetime.'

The man gaped for a couple of seconds, until the large bloke spun him around. 'Look at her, mate. This isn't helping.'

'I did ask you to check the menu,' the poor wife whispered, as though she wanted to shrivel into a crack in the floor.

'Come on, I'm getting the same flight as you,' a regular customer called Joanie said, linking her arm through the wife's. 'We can still make it if we're quick.'

'If they let her on. She looks like she's got leprosy,' someone muttered from what used to be the queue.

'Ignore them.' Joanie started hurrying towards Gate One, dragging the wife with her. 'I've got antihistamines in my bag. We'll soon have you sorted.'

'Can we get our pasties now?' Barb called.

The husband had been twisting his head between me, the agitated crowd and his wife, until someone made up his mind for him with a firm nudge towards Gate One.

'I've got two minutes until my break is over,' Barb trilled. 'Pop my usual in a takeout bag, would you, Emmie?'

'Hang on, I was next!' Someone attempted to shove her out of the way, and for a dreadful moment, it looked as though a brawl might break out after all.

'Right, the fastest way to deal with this is for you all to get back into a queue, wait your turn and speak one at a time. If you're in a hurry, try the shop instead.' As soon as he'd said this, the man who had come to my rescue slipped around to the kiosk door and opened it.

'My sister's café has a machine like this, so I can serve coffee and put pasties in a bag, if you do everything else.'

'Yes please,' I said, still shell-shocked.

Fifteen minutes later, we handed the last person their order and I leant forwards, hands braced on the counter, head hanging low.

'Here.' I was still trying to gather myself back together when the man held out a hot chocolate, covered in a thick layer of cream and sprinkles.

I straightened up and took it from him with a weary smile.

'I'd offer you a pasty but there's only apple and custard left, and, well… I thought that might be too close to the bone.'

He had a strong island accent, the gentle mishmash of Irish and Welsh with the blunt vowels of Northern England that we heard often in Sherwood Airport, as it was the only place that flew to Siskin.

'It's listed in the menu as "cinnamon apple and custard".' I sighed, pressing an arm against my clammy forehead.

'Don't let it bother you. That man was what we islanders call a nerk.'

'What's one of them?'

He smiled. 'Look it up in a Siskin dictionary and you'll find a picture of him.'

'Thank you so much. You literally prevented a riot. And please don't let me keep you. You must have somewhere to be.'

'Nowhere that can't wait.' He gave a self-conscious shrug, sipping from his own cup. 'Are the customers often this difficult?'

'People can get pretty stressed out when travelling. Normally, Parsley's helps them calm down, instead of making it worse. I've been working here since I was thirteen so I've handled plenty of snarky customers. It's just... been a bad day. A bad month. I'm not as resilient as usual.'

He hesitated for a moment before replying. 'When I've been here before, there's been another person... your ma?'

I nodded, the near-constant lump in my throat starting to throb. 'She died.'

'Hence the bad month.' His face creased in sympathy.

'And my reduced capacity to cope with bullies.'

'I'm so sorry.'

I nodded, unable to say any more. We finished our drinks, I served a few more customers and then it was time to shut up shop.

'Thank you. You really didn't have to stay.'

He smiled. 'I enjoyed it.'

'Are you here on holiday or business?' I asked as I wiped down the counter.

'I'm starting a part-time master's degree in Smart Agriculture.' He ducked his head a little, eyes flashing up at mine then back down as he bent to sweep up a few stray pastry crumbs. 'Meaning I'll be back and forth every few weeks for the next two years.'

'Oh!' I suddenly remembered the pasty that I'd set aside for him earlier. 'Here. On the house, of course. And any time you're here between six and three, there'll be a free pasty with your name on it.'

'Oh, wow.' He closed his eyes, mouth already full of flaky pastry and rich filling. 'I'd forgotten how good these taste.'

I felt a thrum of pleasure watching him savour what were, in my opinion, exceptional pasties.

'I'd better head off, though.' He glanced at the concourse clock. 'There's a welcome drinks thing later.' He finished eating and picked up the scruffy rucksack he'd left on the floor. 'I'm Pip, by the way.'

'Emmaline.'

I thanked him again for the millionth time, and he left, striding across the airport in the same way I imagined he traversed the wide-open fields of the island.

I mean, how could I not fall for him?

* * *

'Hey, Emmie.' Pip ducked his head, a shy smile at the corners of his mouth.

'The Siskin flight is tomorrow,' I said, wishing my own smile could be as subtle.

'Yeah. Um. I'm flying home on Thursday.'

'Oh. Okay.'

Blessing leant her arm on the counter, eagerly observing this stilted excuse for a conversation.

'So... you were just passing?'

'Aye...' Pip flushed. 'No. I'm finishing off my final project. The deadline is Wednesday and it's reached the point of sheer torture. I mean, getting out there and carrying out the research – grand. Sat in my stuffy bedroom trying to explain it on paper – nightmare. So. Yeah. I had a sudden pasty craving that made it impossible to concentrate. I knew only one place could fix it.'

'You knew only one place could fix it free of charge, you mean?'

'It's cost me the same in bus fares as half a dozen Greggs pasties.'

'Yet still he came.' Blessing smirked, causing Pip to jerk his head around in surprise.

'Oh, this is my friend, Blessing, who works at the Travel Shop,'

I said, with a pointed look that wasn't difficult to interpret as *behave!*

'Nice to meet you. I'm Pip.'

'Yes. I know.' She gave both of us a totally unsubtle waggle of her groomed eyebrows. 'I have to get to work.'

'Here.' I slipped one of each variety into a bag and handed it to him. 'That'll hopefully power you through to the deadline.'

'Thanks. Can I get a coffee, too? I'll pay for it, of course. Or make that two, if you have time for a quick break?'

I dismissed his bank card with a wave, still debating whether I had the courage to join him when a crowd of travellers started pouring through the arrivals door, some of them making an instant beeline for Parsley's.

'Maybe another time?' I asked, cheeks flushing.

'Well, I was going to mention that. This is my final term. So, Thursday is my last flight. Until graduation, in December. Although, the thought of no Parsley's is making me seriously question whether to come back for a PhD.'

The Thursday flight to Siskin was at ten past five, so Pip would probably be checking in around the time I closed up.

'Oh. Okay. I could see you then for one last pasty? And a box to take home, of course.' Pip always bought a couple of extras for his family. I hadn't asked whether that family included a wife or a girlfriend. 'We can eat in the food court if I buy lunch there.'

He waited for me to serve a customer before replying.

'Perfect. I'll see you then.' Pip started walking away, grinning as he waved the bag at me. 'Thanks for saving the day.'

'Good luck with the project.'

'Oh, my goodness.' Blessing laughed, slipping out from where she'd been eavesdropping behind an oversized baggage sign. 'Day one of the new Emmie and you've got yourself a date.'

'It's not a date,' I protested, although my fluttering heart refused to believe me. 'It's a goodbye snack with a sort-of friend.'

Blessing opened the jar of mini marshmallows on the counter and helped herself to one.

'Yet another reason to book that holiday, then, hey? There's, what, three thousand people living on that island? You're sure to bump into him at some point.'

5

It was when I stopped off at the wholesalers on the way home that the idea floating around my head solidified into action. Once I'd loaded up my trolley with cheese, parsnips, flour and other necessary ingredients, a sign caught my eye beside the marrowfat peas.

The lentils were on special offer. I ate lentil soup six days a week so had no desire to eat more at home, but what about in a pasty? Was it time to see if I could bake a vegan recipe as tasty as the other varieties? I checked the price and decided it was worth a go, quickly searching online for lentil stews, curries and pies before doing another round of the warehouse, adding potentially useful items like mushrooms, sweet potato, almond milk and different spices.

'What's this?' Stefan asked, having blatantly elbowed the woman supposed to be on the checkout out of the way so he could serve me. 'Trying a new recipe?'

'I thought I'd see if I could come up with something.'

'Well. It's your business now; time to put your own stamp on things, be your own woman,' he said, nodding his head in approval. 'Speaking of trying something new.' He stopped to clear his throat. 'If you're ready for that sort of thing, the Jolly Outlaw has started a pie and peas night on Thursdays. You get a free pint of beer and a pudding. Only a tenner. We could, you know, give it a try.'

'Oh! Um. Thank you for the invite, but I really have enough of that sort of food all week. You know, pastry, meat and peas.'

'Ah. I hadn't considered that angle. I thought it would be your sort of thing. Not too much your thing. Ha, ha.'

I picked up a bottle of olive oil and offered it to him, in the hope he'd hurry up and finish scanning so I could get out of there.

'They do pizza on Fridays, or steak special on a Monday?'

'That sounds lovely, but you know I'm usually busy prepping in the evenings.'

'Come on, Emmie. You have to take a night off some time.'

'You're right.' The need for some proper nights off was becoming a constant ache in my weary bones. 'But, to be honest, we tried dating and it didn't work out, so I'm going to say no.'

Stefan looked up at me, forehead furrowed. 'I thought we didn't work out because you were still mourning Nell.'

I opened my mouth, ready to agree politely. And then, I don't know, maybe the dusky-rose lipstick took over for a second. Maybe it was down to this weird mood I'd been waking up in. I looked Stefan straight in the eye and told the truth.

'I was, but I also realised that I'm not interested in us being more than friends. Sorry.'

'Right. Okay. Good to know, I suppose.'

I then had to stand there while he painstakingly scanned the remaining mountain of food. Once I'd returned to my normal, unassertive self, I might have to find a new wholesaler.

* * *

I soon forgot the ludicrousness of being sort-of asked out twice in one day as I began work on a new recipe. By ten-thirty, I was too tired to trust myself with a sharp knife, so I grabbed a few hours of sleep and started again first thing on Tuesday morning. By the time I'd mixed, tasted, adjusted and eventually perfected a vegan pasty I was proud of, the sun was setting behind the trees beyond the kitchen window. I'd eaten enough samples to not bother stopping for meals, but I'd totally skipped on my usual day-off activities of washing clothes, cleaning and shopping for my weekday evening meals. My library books would be late for the first time ever. Gregory's envelope remained unopened.

* * *

I cleared up and headed upstairs, but perhaps unsurprisingly found myself too wired to sleep after what had been, for me, a momentous few days. After thrashing about in bed for a while, I gave up, finding myself in Mum's bedroom without even thinking about it.

I removed the box from the wardrobe and, after another brief inspection of the photograph, picked up the letters. Wearing make-up to work had been a tiny step of rebellion. Trying a new recipe had been more like full-on mutiny. Mum had gone, creating a gaping crater where my family history, my past, my identity should be. She'd left me totally alone and I hated it, but I didn't have to stay that way.

I carefully untied the ribbon and opened the top envelope. Inside, I found a handwritten letter.

4 August 1985

Dear Nellie,

I just wanted to say I had a great time yesterday. Normally I hate the Sunflower Festival. I can't stand all the mainlanders flying in with their litter and loud comments about how 'quaint' or 'cute' we are. Let alone the farm gates left open, discarded cigarette fires and the drunken louts scaring my cattle. Can you believe someone tried to ride Parsley, our bull, like a bucking bronco a couple of years ago?

Anyhow, this year, all the noise and the nuisance has been worth it, because I met you. Talking at the picnic, walking along the headland – I can't stop thinking about it. About you. You're the most interesting woman I've ever met. I hope that doesn't scare you off, because the thought of you flying back to the mainland and never seeing you again is what scares me.

The truth is – and now I've started I may as well tell the whole truth – no one has ever made me feel the way I did with you. Is there any chance you felt the same? You made it clear you value independence, but for thirty years, I also believed I wasn't made for marriage. I'm wondering if that's because I was made for you.

Could I see you again, before you leave? Or if not, have your telephone number or address in Nottingham, so I can call or write to you there?

I'll be at the farm all evening, and tomorrow. I won't call in at the Grand again, but Daisy will deliver a note if you ask her.

With faith, hope and love

G x

I read the letter again, more slowly, then a third time, because my brain still couldn't believe what my eyes were seeing. Mum would have been thirty-seven. She was forty-nine when she became my legal guardian. I knew she'd worked in various restaurants before starting Parsley's Pasties in 1990, but that was about it.

At this point, all I'd learned was that a man spent the day with her, and asked to see her again. Although the stack of other letters suggested she'd said yes, and if I kept on reading, I'd surely find out. And could Parsley the bull be a coincidence? With a wry shake of my head, I reminded myself that nothing my mum did was happenstance. Let alone the name of her beloved business.

It was nearly one in the morning. My whole body was reminding me I had to be up in three and a half hours. The thought of staying awake and reading the whole stash, abandoning Parsley's for the day, felt like an even worse betrayal than snooping through Mum's old love letters.

Certain that I had found the man in the wedding photograph, I decided to allow myself a day to process that before I delved any deeper. I honestly didn't think I could take any more bombshells just yet.

6

The spicy lentil and sweet potato pasties sold out within three hours. Admittedly, I'd only made a dozen, but what I'd not accounted for was how many customers relished the opportunity to sample a new flavour. The verdict? Well, the security manager, Tim, who held as much disdain for a meatless meal as my mother did for high-heeled shoes, came back for seconds. He'd only bought the first one because his assistant manager dared him.

I skipped lunch at the food court, as, unable to face any more lentils, I'd decided to go home and make a sandwich, get an early start on the prep for Thursday and then possibly read another letter before it got too late. As I pushed open the main airport door, a woman was struggling on the other side. She had a baby in a pushchair, a bawling child around four or five swinging off one arm and a large toddler flat out on the sopping wet concrete, as rigid as a dead slug.

The toddler was wearing nothing but a filthy T-shirt, socks and a Superman cape.

The automatic door wasn't working so I stood and held the other door open for a few seconds, in case she managed to miraculously find a way to get three children, a pushchair, four cabin bags and a giant stuffed panda to go through them.

'Thank you,' she muttered, starting to nudge one suitcase towards the door an inch at a time.

'I'm not going!' the oldest child screamed. 'I won't leave Sausage and you can't make me!'

As she yanked down with all her strength, her mum let go of the pushchair, the bags hanging from the back causing it to tip over and catch the leg of a man in an expensive suit trying to dodge past.

The only one of them not crying now was the toddler. I dashed over to right the pushchair, lifting a rucksack onto one shoulder and hurrying back to the door to prop it open again.

'It's no good,' the woman said with a jerky sob. 'Boarding closes in two minutes. We'll never make it.'

'Hooray!' the girl shouted, letting go of her mum and punching the air with both arms.

The next plane to leave was for Vienna. If Leandra was on the gate as usual, then it might not be too late.

'No, not hooray!' I said, loudly enough to get her attention. 'Your mum has organised you a lovely holiday, and from the looks of things, she really needs it.'

'She should have brought Sausage, then!'

'Isobel, darling, I told you, you're not allowed to take snakes on a plane.'

'Yes, and I told you that's a stupid rule because corn snakes aren't even venomous and I could have hided him in my shorts and no one would have known.' Isobel stuck both hands on her hips, thrusting her pointy chin forwards.

'Corn snakes don't like strange places. He'll be much happier in his own tank with all his favourite things and lots of lovely crickets to eat.'

'I don't care. I'm not going and neither is Oscar!'

'Okay. Fair enough,' I said, my head scrambling. If I'd spoken to my mother like that, she'd have stuck me in Sausage's tank for the duration of the holiday and force-fed me crickets. 'But now you're here, don't you want to go to the special room and see the aeroplanes take off?'

Isobel's eyes narrowed.

'You even get to go through the secret special supervillain detection machine. And your shoes and bags and everything else have to go through the X-ray scanner in case you're sneaking in a bomb or a corn snake.'

'Do they ever find a bomb?'

'I heard a villain might be sneaking a bomb through this very afternoon. I work here, so I would know.'

I steered the laden pushchair through the doors while the mum grabbed the bags, encouraging Isobel to see if she could find the secret scanner. The second Isobel gave a decisive nod, saying, 'I think it might be that way,' Oscar sprang up and ran past all of us, his bare bottom bobbing.

Due to everyone else having boarded, and the next flight not being due for another three hours, we had a clear run to the gate. Strictly speaking, I shouldn't have been allowed with them, but Kamal and Kaleb worked enough early-morning shifts to simply wink as they waved the best source of caffeine in the airport on through.

* * *

'Nah-ah.' Leandra, who was about to head onto the plane, looked at the bedraggled, half-dressed, tear-smeared family and folded her arms. 'Boarding closed five minutes ago.'

'Come on,' I said. 'You're not on the plane yet. It'll hold things up by only another couple of minutes.'

She waved a hand at the bags. 'That pushchair needs to go in outsized baggage.'

The woman grabbed her baby out of the seat, wrenched the bags off the handles and kicked the pushchair so hard, it crashed into the nearest bin.

'Please, I can't tell you what it's taken to get us here. We're going to see their grandparents for the first time since Lola was born. I can't afford to book another flight, and I really, really need this break.'

'Five minutes late, Leandra.'

Leandra pointed to the clock. 'Six.'

'And yet, you're still not on the plane.'

'I want Daddy,' Oscar whimpered.

'You know Daddy can't come because he's shooting bad guys in his big army tank,' Isobel said.

That caught Leandra's attention. Her son had completed his basic army training a few weeks ago, and she was terrified about him getting deployed.

'He's in Somalia,' Isobel's mum said. 'It's not the easiest, managing all this while he's away.'

Leandra sighed at how quickly she'd caved, then waved them on through, grabbing two bags as they passed. 'That child needs a nappy on before he sits down, though.'

I was turning back the way we came when someone pressed something into my hand.

'It's probably nothing, but I don't have anything else. If you get lucky, promise me you'll take a holiday of your own.'

I spun around to see the mum beaming at me.

Before I could respond, she'd sprinted back through the door that led to the aeroplane.

I opened my hand, finding a creased lottery ticket.

'Okay,' I mumbled, 'I promise.'

An easy promise to make, when sure I wouldn't have to keep it. I stuffed the ticket into my trouser pocket and hurried home.

* * *

That evening, as I chopped, stirred and seasoned in the kitchen, my thoughts kept drifting upstairs to the box. Taking this as a sign that I was ready for the next letter, once everything was ready, I procrastinated a bit longer by changing into pyjamas, sticking on the load of washing that I should have done the day before and vacuuming the living room, then retrieved the box. This time, thinking it might help me feel less as if Mum's ghost was judging me, I took the stash of letters downstairs.

Settling into my spot on the sofa with a mug of decaf tea and a plate of cheese and crackers left over from Blessing's visit, I carefully opened the second envelope. This one had been posted to Nell Brown, at a Nottingham suburb.

6 August 1985

Dearest Nellie,

Is it too soon to write? I know we agreed I would call, but there's always a queue at the telephone box, and I prefer to speak without whoever's next in line spreading my words across the island quicker than a blaze through the barley fields. I tell you, I'm feeling that frustrated at Da's resistance to anything modern. Nothing gets me accused of mainlandering like my request to install a phone. You'd have thought I'd dumped a pile of pig manure in the living room when I bought a television for the farm. Da reckons they're for 'people with nothing better to do than sit about watching people with nothing better to do than act like utter clowns.' I moved it into my bedroom so I could watch the test match in peace.

Besides, I wanted to try writing something down. Words spoken can blow off on the wind and be forgotten.

If this is the start of forever, whatever I say deserves to last.

And after that rambling introduction – what can I say? Except that yesterday was almost perfect. I say almost, because at the end of it, we had to say goodbye, which was harder than I could have imagined a week ago.

With every passing minute, I grow more convinced that this is that indescribable, mysterious force which others name 'true love'. You'll have noticed I'm not one for grand words, but I understand now why good men will abandon their duty, cast off all common sense and attempt the foolhardiest of feats for a mere woman. Because to them, there is nothing mere about her. She is everything. You, Nellie, are everything, now. I find myself aching for some daring quest to not only prove my love, but that I might earn your love in return.

And now I have made an utter nerk of myself, how would it be if I booked a flight to Nottinghamshire?

I will call once I'm certain this letter has reached you, and somehow try to carry on until I hear your sweet voice again.

With faith, hope and love

G x

* * *

I dreamed I was walking through wheat fields again. Only this time, Mum was there. Or rather, the younger version of her, in the wedding dress, pacing along several hundred metres in front of me. No matter how fast I hurried, I couldn't catch her, and when I tried to call out, the sound died in my throat.

I woke several minutes before the alarm, the events of the past few days churning into a vague restlessness that made it difficult to focus. I crimped pasties, skidded the van around corners and dragged the trolleys to the kiosk with an urgency that did nothing to settle my nerves.

At the mid-morning lull between flights, I put on my jacket and left the kiosk, hoping a quick break outside would help me settle. For reasons that were probably all to do with letters and lentil pasties and lunch with a man who was about to leave forever, my eyes kept welling up, and the last thing I wanted was to burst out crying in front of a customer.

It was when I passed the Travel Shop, my agitated gaze roaming the windows, that I noticed the Lotto sign. Stopping, I reached into my jacket pocket and found the crumpled ticket that the woman had given me the day before.

My usual instinct would be to throw it in the bin, but nothing about this week was usual. I pictured vast blue skies, forget-me-nots dancing in a salty, summer breeze and walked straight into the Travel Shop.

Gregory spotted me while I was waiting in the queue, veering inside to talk to me.

'Emmie. I saw the kiosk was unmanned and thought there must have been another emergency.'

'I'm just taking a quick break.'

'Right.' He rocked back on his heels a couple of times. 'Have you had a chance to look at the contract?'

I nodded. 'I read it last night before I went to sleep.'

'And?' His gaze dropped to my hands, as if expecting me to be holding the envelope.

'I haven't signed it yet.'

'Is there a problem? Like I said, it's the exact same terms as the current one. Everyone else has to be open far longer hours, seven days a week. This is the same lease your mum was happy with for, oh, longer than I've been here.'

'Yeah.' I shuffled forwards in the queue. 'I think that might be the issue.'

'Okay.' Gregory looked confused. 'Would it help if we discussed it in my office later on? Because if you don't get this sorted, management will replace it with a standard lease.'

'Not really.'

I knew that the popularity of Parsley's had enabled Mum to wangle a ridiculously good offer, back in the days when it was possible to get away with more flexibility. The problem was me.

His frown deepened.

'But I'll do my best to get it to you first thing tomorrow.'

* * *

'Hey, Emmie.' Barb smiled when I reached the counter. 'It's not like you to be roaming free before three o'clock.'

'Just stretching my legs. Can you check this for me, please?' The Lotto draw had been last night.

I held out the ticket, which she scrutinised with arched eyebrows before scanning it in the machine.

'Not like you to gamble. Were you feeling lucky?' Barb had an amazing gift to make the most innocuous phrase sound like juicy gossip.

'Someone gave it to me.'

'Well,' she said. 'Looks like you owe that *someone* a drink.' She waved the ticket in the air. 'That chime means you've only gone and won.'

'What?'

All the blood in my body plummeted straight to my feet.

'I mean, not the whole thing. But four numbers. That's one hundred and forty big ones.'

'Oh. Right. Great, thank you.'

I gripped the counter for support, willing my vital organs to restart functioning while Barb faffed about, making sure everyone in the shop and whoever happened to be loitering about nearby knew that it was 'someone's lucky day!'

'Here,' she said, preening at the clump of people now waiting behind me. 'Your winnings, madam.'

She then slowly counted out seven twenty-pound notes.

'Congratulations, love,' someone called, prompting a general murmuring of similar sentiments.

'What are you going to spend it on?'

'Knowing this one, she'll treat herself to a food-court flapjack.' Barb snickered. 'Maybe a new apron?'

'What? Young lass like her should be treating herself properly,' an older man said. 'You should do something nice. Buy a new frock or have a night out with your fella.'

'Oh, she hasn't got a fella,' Barb said, sounding as sad as possible while still smirking.

I didn't tell her that I was having lunch with a man in a few hours. She'd be even more brazen about sharing that titbit than the Lotto win.

'Or book yourself a holiday,' the older man's companion said. 'You're in an airport; why not?'

* * *

Why not indeed? I thought, hurrying back to the kiosk. I'd promised the woman who gave me the ticket that I'd go on holiday if I won. What neither of us had clarified was how much money counted as winning.

The notes now safely zipped inside my jacket pocket were enough to buy a flight to somewhere. Maybe even to bring me back again. But not much else.

And yet.

As I got on with placing pasties inside paper bags, serving drinks and handing out napkins, I couldn't help thinking about the other money sitting in a savings account for a rainy day.

It was supposed to be my back-up fund, to be used in a crisis.

But, honestly, with my relentlessly predictable life, these past few days might be as close to a crisis as I'd ever get.

I was still thinking about it when Blessing came over at two, offering congratulations while picking up her regular order.

'We are definitely going clothes shopping now.'

'Can you get much these days for a hundred and forty pounds?'

'You can if you're with me.' She pulled out her phone. 'How about Tuesday morning? If we hit the shops the second they open, we could squeeze in lunch before my shift starts.'

'Yeah...'

'What?' Blessing narrowed her eyes. 'Don't tell me Barb's strong-armed you into one of her mojito nights.'

'No. Ugh. Definitely not. But I might not be here on Tuesday.'

'I know you're not here on Tuesdays. That's why I suggested it.'

'I mean I might not be anywhere here. I might be somewhere much further away.'

Blessing's eyes went round, her coffee mug frozen halfway to her mouth.

'You're going on holiday?'

'I'm not sure.'

'Do it.'

'But what'll happen to Parsley's?'

'Nothing! Small independent retailers still go on holiday. They put a sign up saying, "back on whatever date" and people deal with it. It's not like there's anyone to steal your custom while you're away.'

'I know. But I have two giant fridges full of food and fourteen mint plants to water. The meat delivery is scheduled for tomorrow.'

I stopped to serve another group of customers, and then found Blessing brandishing a napkin in one hand, a blue eyeliner in the other. 'Write it all down.'

'What?'

'Write down everything that needs doing if you go away for a couple of weeks. I have the perfect solution.'

I saw the gleam in her eyes and instantly cottoned on to her plan.

'You're going to house-sit for me?'

'I will even pay you rent.'

'Really?'

She shrugged. 'Mates' rates, obviously.'

I served another couple of customers.

'Who knows? When you come back, I might just stay.'

'Really?'

I loved Blessing, but the thought of her there, in my space, all the time, made my eyelid twitch.

'What do you say?'

'Can I have more than two minutes to think about it?'

'Fine. I need to get to work, anyway.' She checked the time on her phone. 'Let me know after your hot farmer lunch date.'

She stopped then, mouth dropping open. 'Oh, my goodness, Emmie. You're going to the island, aren't you? You're going to buy a ticket to Siskin and have a rip-roaring, heart-thumping holiday romance with Pip.'

7

By three o'clock, my thoughts were still ricocheting between the only practical, rational, doable thing, and the impossible, ridiculous, reckless one that made my legs tremble and my brain feel as if it didn't even know who Emmie Brown was any more.

Then I caught sight of Pip, striding through the airport towards me, and suddenly anything seemed possible.

'Hey,' he said, coming to stop with a crooked smile.

'Hi.'

We looked at each other for a long moment, before being interrupted by someone asking for a coffee. I let them know that we were closed, then lowered the hatch, opening the side door so Pip could wait for me there.

'I heard you got lucky this morning,' he said as I whizzed through the last bits of clearing up.

'What?' I said, flicking off a couple of sockets. 'Has Barb made a banner? I've not heard Gavin announce it on the tannoy.'

'The guy in Security was telling everyone to head over here. Said you'd hit the jackpot and might be offering freebies.'

'Well, that explains why I've been extra busy today.'

I handed him a box of pasties, then shut the door behind me and locked up, explaining what had happened while we headed to the food court.

'Is lunch on you, then?' He smiled.

'Barb reckons I'll splash out on either a flapjack or a new apron.'

'Ooh. Tough choice. What's it going to be?'

I grabbed a tray and started sliding it along towards the soup station.

'I did wonder if there were any seats left on the evening flight to the Isle of Siskin.'

I caught Pip's flinch in my peripheral vision, but by the time I'd steadied the tray and turned back to him, he was peering at the rows of soft drinks nodding his head non-committedly.

'Wow. That's... spontaneous.'

I tried to shrug in a spontaneous, carefree kind of way.

'Great, though!' His eyes kept searching the bottles. 'A great idea. The island is great this time of year.'

'Okay, well, that's... great.' I turned back, flustered by his response.

Was he pleased or panicking? Did I sound like a weirdo who had responded to a casual lunch invite by turning full-on stalker, wedding dress stuffed in my suitcase just in case?

I waited until we were sitting at my table before doing my best to clarify, hoping it didn't sound as if I'd just come up with an excuse while paying for the soup.

'For nine hours a day, six days a week, I watch people head through the doors of Gate Two, wondering if I'll ever get the chance to join them. They fly to three destinations: Belfast, Düsseldorf and Siskin. I spend most of my life surrounded by walls, dreaming of wide-open spaces and a refreshing breeze. The last thing I want is a city break. And I haven't seen the sea since I was fifteen.'

I hesitated before continuing, not wanting to reveal how little I knew about my own mother. 'This week, I found out my mum visited the island before I was born. I don't think she flew anywhere again, so it seemed as good a place as any for my first time.'

'You've never been on an aeroplane?'

I ripped off a chunk of bread roll. 'Every day, in my imagination.' I tore that piece into two smaller ones. 'I've never really been anywhere but here.'

'Well, in my opinion, you couldn't pick a better place to start.'

'You think I should do it?'

'What's the worst that could happen?' He checked his watch. 'Although, is there time? Check-in closes in ten minutes.'

Now that I'd pretty much decided, I simply had to get on that plane. My passport was in my bag, because I used it to get through Security each morning. The bag also contained a pack of tissues, phone, purse, water bottle and a spare hair bobble.

Oh, and perhaps most importantly, in my morning fluster, I'd shoved the stash of envelopes in there. I'd left them downstairs the night before, forcing myself to put them to one side and study the kiosk contract, in some kind of penance for my snooping, then grabbed them on my way to the van. I had no intention of reading them while at work, but some deeper instinct made me want to keep them close.

'Is it rude if I run to the check-in desk and find out?'

'Not if I come with you.'

'You'll have to go back through Security.'

He glanced at the departures board. There were three flights in the next few hours.

'I think I can handle that.'

We grabbed our bags, dumped the trays on the trolley for dirty pots and hightailed it out of there.

* * *

'Here she is,' Ivor on the check-in desk announced. 'The lucky lady! Come to show off your prize?'

'It was a hundred and forty pounds. You won more at the Christmas raffle.'

'Oh.' He folded his arms. 'That's a lot more boring.'

'Which is why Barb didn't tell you the amount.'

'What can I do for you, then? We don't often see a Parsley's uniform this side of the tracks.'

'Is it too late to buy a ticket for the ten past five to Siskin?'

'If check-in is still open, it's not too late. Hang on.' He tapped away on his screen for a minute. 'Your luck continues. We have plenty of space.'

'How much is it?'

He peered at me over the top of orange glasses. 'One two seven for the seat. Do you want to check in a bag?'

'Um. No?'

'A return flight?'

I shook my head. Ivor gave Pip a sidelong glance.

'I don't know what day I'm returning yet. It's just a holiday. I am coming back!'

'Oka-a-a-a-ay.' He didn't sound convinced.

I stood there, my brain freefalling as he booked the ticket and checked me in.

As soon as Ivor handed me the boarding pass, I slammed into reality.

'What do I do now?'

'Head to Security.' Pip led me away from the desk, as a family were now waiting behind us.

I stopped dead a few metres away. 'No. I mean... my house. My business. My life...'

He bent his head to meet my eyes. 'Okay, the first thing to do is breathe. Slowly. Slower. That's better.'

I wasn't in any fit state to explain that his soft blue gaze wasn't helping me regain composure, even if I'd been bold enough.

Instead, I closed my eyes, tuned in to the familiar airport sounds, told myself that there was nothing stopping me from coming back on the first flight tomorrow, and accepted that, however this turned out, I simply couldn't spend another day standing in the same nine-square-metre box, doing the same thing, wondering if there was a whole other life out there, waiting for me.

Besides, I'd made a promise.

'Right.' I opened my eyes again, tried to sound as if I weren't completely freaking out. 'First thing, the Travel Shop.'

I must have hurtled through Security in world-record-breaking time, arriving at the shop breathless and giddy.

'I'm going.'

Blessing straightened up from where she'd been stacking Robin Hood mugs on a shelf, took one look at me, ordered Pip out of there, and got to work.

Fifteen miraculous minutes later, I had a carry-on suitcase that doubled as a rucksack, a large wash bag crammed with miniature toiletries, underwear and pyjamas, two summery dresses, pretty T-shirts, a pair of cotton shorts, jeans and a hoodie saying *Straight Outta Sherwood*, because all the others were at least a size large. Blessing added a bikini and flip-flops, and declared me packed.

I handed her my house key. 'I'll send you a list when I've

calmed down enough to think of one. The cottage is so small, you'll have no problem finding whatever you need. If I leave you the keys for Parsley's, can you take whatever's in the fridge? Oh, and my van is parked in the staff car park, but should be fine for a few days.'

'Yes, brilliant, I'll take care of everything, but we aren't finished yet. You are not running off with a hot farmer in shoes that belong on a nun's car-boot stall.'

'I don't have time!'

'There's no way Ivor is letting that plane take off without you. This is the most exciting thing that's happened around here since that woman tried to smuggle her Pygmy goat through security. Besides, they haven't even announced the gate yet.'

'It's Gate Two.'

'Get in the changing room.'

Despite being modest in size, the Travel Shop clothing section was a revelation, thanks to Blessing being in control of the stock. She found me a pair of wide-legged cotton trousers with a pale stripe, a strappy top and pale-blue jacket that perfectly matched the simple trainers she insisted I needed for travelling.

I didn't recognise myself.

While the other staff member was taking my payment, she handed me a straw hat and a pair of sunglasses.

'A present from me. Now, go. The boarding call was seven minutes ago.'

'Is this the maddest idea ever?'

She gripped both of my shoulders. 'Probably. But it's also the best.'

'Because you get to stay in my house?'

'Go!'

As Ivor's voice boomed over the tannoy, instructing Emmaline Brown to 'get on the frickin' plane!', I scurried across to the gate.

To my horror, but what really shouldn't have been a surprise, cheers and hoots of encouragement echoed behind me. As I skidded to a stop by the desk, Ivor not even bothering to scan the boarding card he'd issued me with less than an hour earlier before shoving me through, two voices rose above the rest.

'Holiday-fling the heck out of that island! Don't come back until you've officially fallen in love, even if that's only with yourself!'

'Emmie, what are you doing? What about that contract? You promised I'd have it by tomorrow!'

8

Stepping from the bustle and noise of my second home, into the relative hush of a half-full, forty-eight-seater plane was enough to send my pulse hammering. I ducked my head, shuffling down the tiny aisle towards the window seat in an empty row near the front.

'Hey.'

Halfway down, I looked up at the familiar, gentle voice. Pip placed a steadying hand on my arm.

'You made it.'

'Yep,' I squeaked.

'It's going to be grand.'

'Mmm-hmm.'

'Can all passengers please take their seats?' Poppy, a regular air stewardess on the Siskin flights, barked over the intercom. Given that the aisle was about ten metres long, and I was the only person still standing, she could have quite easily taken six steps and told me herself.

I hurried past the remaining few rows, apologising as I bumped elbows and ran over someone's foot, then spent another couple of minutes trying to wrestle the suitcase into the overhead locker, which was about two inches too high for me to reach properly, until a man in the seat behind helped me.

I assumed that Poppy ran through the safety instructions, and the pilot introduced himself, but it was all a blur.

I was sitting on a plane.

Wearing stripy trousers.

With a bag of other clothes I'd not owned two hours ago.

I had an hour-long flight in which to a) not die (which I wasn't especially worried about), b) not vomit (which felt distinctly possible) and c) figure out what on earth I was going to do once I got there.

Then we started moving.

And – after I'd been holding my breath for so long, my head spun – so smoothly I had to open my eyes to check if it was ever going to happen, we left the ground.

All my questions, the swirling worries and growing concern that I might genuinely be falling apart, tumbled away, back down to the rapidly shrinking tarmac and cluster of grey buildings below.

I left them behind, lifting my head instead to the fields and forest spread out before us. And, above that, the bright, endless sky.

* * *

Landing on the tiny island runway was not quite so enjoyable.

Although, soaring over the sea, watching the unmistakable, famously bird-shaped outline of the island come into view, curving around the jagged cliff-tops, dipping down above the fields – verdant green, sunshine yellow and, to my heart's delight, shimmering pale gold – took my breath away.

As we circled closer, I ogled at farmhouses tucked amongst the fields, rows of pastel cottages dotted along the coast, and counted two villages, the largest of which, Port Cathan, was designated the capital.

I'd read travel books about all the Sherwood Airport destinations, studying the photographs and soaking up the history and culture of every place I'd imagined one day visiting. But the reality of it was so much more.

I was so busy feeling thrilled that the jolt as the plane hit the ground took me completely off guard. It wasn't only me – there were several loud gasps, exclamations, and one child began wailing as we hurtled down the runway, every one of us bracing ourselves as we were pressed into the backs of our seats.

I squeezed my eyes closed, gripped the armrests and reminded myself that I watched hundreds of people walking off aeroplanes in one piece, every single day.

* * *

'Emmie.' Poppy tapped me on the shoulder. 'Time to get off.'

Prising my eyes open, I found that the plane was already almost empty. While I fumbled to get my seat belt open, Poppy swung my case out of the overhead locker and dumped it next to me.

I gathered my bag, the suitcase and what remained of my wits, and forced my stiff limbs to follow her to the exit, which led into one of those tunnels that took me straight inside the airport building.

Pip was lingering by the end of the tunnel.

'You really didn't have to wait for me,' I said. I'd invited myself onto his flight; I didn't want him to feel obliged to look after some woman he occasionally bought pasties from.

'Best to wait for my bags, though.' He pointed at the carousel taking up most of the room we were now in.

'Of course.' I tried to laugh it off, but it sounded as pathetic as I felt. 'I've never been this side of things before.' Scanning around, I spotted the exit. 'Right. Well. I'd better get on. Thank you so much for the help.' I hitched my rucksack higher on my shoulders, as though preparing to move might make it easier to go.

He nodded, chewing on his lip as he glanced at the carousel then back to me. 'The bus heads into Port Cathan after most flights. If you get off at the main square, there's a couple of hotels that probably have rooms. Otherwise, you can go all the way to the caravan park near Lithin, which has amazing views of the bay. Just avoid the Grand. There's been nothing grand about it since the seventies.'

'Thank you. I'll see what I can find.' My legs were more than a little reluctant to leave the safety of the airport. Or the safety of a friend. I gave myself a mental shake. 'Adventure awaits!'

Then I turned and scuttled through the exit before I could grab onto his arm and beg him to take me with him.

A quick pause to show someone my passport, a detour to the bathroom, a march past a row of vending machines and I hit the double doors leading to the big wide world with as much bluster as I could muster.

I took four steps across the path before coming to a dead stop on the concrete.

''Scuse me, chicken,' a man muttered, his island brogue only adding to my sense of wonder as I hastily moved to the side.

The scene in front of me was nothing extraordinary. A small car park, a bicycle-hire stand, a stall selling drinks and doughnuts.

And yet, everything was different.

The way the light fell on the row of birch trees lining the side of the building. A sparkling mix of silvers and yellows, like an old-fashioned filter on a camera.

The air was heady with salt and sand. And behind it, something wilder, fresher than the earthy richness of my forest.

Even the sounds – seagulls, of course, and maybe the peeping of oystercatchers in the distance. The rumble of a plane, trundling off the runway. Apart from that, no vehicles, no background hum of industrialisation. Instead, as I stood there, my senses relishing this new feast, I leant in and, whether it was a coincidence, or my body was already adjusting to the rhythm of this place, in perfect time with my own breath, I listened to the back-and-forth whisper of the sea.

* * *

The bus stop was easy enough to spot, the large orange sign being only a short distance from the airport entrance. A handful of people were already waiting, so I wheeled my bag over and joined the back of the queue.

'How long until the bus gets here?' a small boy asked, swinging around on the signpost.

'The timetable says two minutes, look.' His mum pointed to the timetable, but he was too busy swinging to read it.

'How long now?' he asked again, a few minutes later.

I didn't catch his mum's answer, as at that moment, Pip, who had clearly been looking for me as he left the main building, returned my tentative wave with a smile and a nod due to dragging two enormous bags past the sign to the long-stay car park.

The third time the boy asked, the mainlanders at the stop were clearly all wondering the same thing. Numerous airport staff had passed us on their way to the car park, which now had only one car and a scooter in it.

'Don't worry, chick. Island timetables are more of a rough guide.' An older man with a strong accent chuckled. 'Connell always gets distracted chattin' to someone or other. No frettin' necessary, he'll be here.'

'Sorry, Bill, but he won't be,' a younger man called over from the doughnut stall, squinting at us from underneath a blue cap. 'He just messaged to say the Landers' cows are blocking Back Road again. Big Lander's mare's birthin' and Mrs L's got the grandkids until Middle Lander's back in port.'

'Ah.' Bill nodded, as if this was nothing. 'Little Lander?'

The younger man adopted a knowing expression. 'Drinkin' with Morrow Taylor in the Grand since lunchtime.'

'Well, that's that, then, isn't it?' Bill checked his watch. 'Connell clocks off at seven-thirty. Not a minute later. Cheers for the heads up, Barnie.'

'I thought the timetable was a rough guide?' A man in smart chinos and a tweed jacket asked, clearly running out of patience. 'He can't stop work on time if he's late because he's been chatting.'

'Not chattin' though, is it?' Bill said, not in the least bit fazed. 'No sane man would consider Lander's wandering cows a fittin' reason to work overtime. Not with a talented cook like Betty putting supper on the table.'

'So, what, he's going to simply abandon the bus on Back Road and leave us all stranded?' the woman accompanying the man exclaimed.

'Oh no, course not!' Barnie at the doughnut stand scoffed, causing the mainlander half of the queue to breathe a collective sigh of relief. 'He'll drop off any remaining passengers and then drive it home.'

'Daniel?' The woman turned to her partner.

'Don't worry, darling, I'll call us an Uber.'

Someone sniggered at the thought of an Uber on the Isle of Siskin.

'Well, do you have the name of a taxi firm?' the mum asked. 'I can't get an Internet signal.'

'That's because there is no Internet signal,' a woman who looked around my age said, rolling her eyes. 'If you want that level of cutting-edge technology, you'll have to come back in 2026.'

'There's no Internet?' Daniel's partner asked, jaw dropping in distress.

'Of course we have Internet!' someone else replied. 'It's just mostly dial-up. A few buildings have Wi-Fi, but there's no mobile broadband, 4G, anything like that.'

'What's dial-up?' the boy asked.

His mother pressed a hand against her chest. 'I'm not really sure.'

'A taxi firm?' Daniel asked, sounding increasingly frustrated.

'You could try Taylor's taxi,' Bill said. 'Let me see now...' He pulled out an ancient Nokia phone and slowly clicked to the address book before carefully reciting a landline number.

Several people started frantically waving phones about, trying to get some reception.

'Probably not worth bothering, though.'

Daniel shook his head. 'Would that be because Taylor's taxi is driven by Morrow Taylor, currently drinking in the Grand with Little Lander?'

Bill simply smiled.

'So, what do we do?' the mum asked.

'I'm going to purchase myself a cup of tea and a doughnut and sit upon that bench over there until my good friend Barnie packs up his stall and is free to give me a ride home.' Bill gave a nonchalant shrug. 'You can do whatever you like.'

There was a moment of general fluster and outrage until one

of the women interrupted, holding both hands up as she positioned herself in front of the stop and loudly introduced herself as Daffy.

'Don't panic. My fella's on his way in our van. Insurance allows nine in the back. Not a soul more. With cattle on the loose, we ain't taking no chances. So, first spot for you, Heather. Who else needs a lift?'

By the time the various islanders had wandered off or joined Bill at the doughnut stall, there were nine of us still trying to sort out who got a ride in the van. Two retired couples, the mother and her son, plus Daniel and his partner. And me.

'It's fine. I'll figure something out,' I said, my nerves jangling in protest.

'Are you sure?' one of the older men asked, eyeing up Daniel with a scowl. 'A female travelling alone at night, in a strange place?'

'It won't be dark for hours,' Daniel's companion retorted. 'It's our wedding anniversary. We're not splitting up. Besides, we've got a gourmet three-course dinner booked for eight at the Grand. We're not missing it.'

'At the Grand?' The corner of Daffy's broad mouth twitched. 'We most certainly can't have you missing that.'

She turned to me. 'Tell you what, I'll send Rozzo over once he's finished his shift. It'll only be a couple of hours. He finally passed his test this week so he's looking for any excuse to get his moped out.'

'No, honestly, I'll be fine,' I protested. I'd have rather slept at the airport than get on the back of Rozzo's moped.

'I really must protest about this...' the elderly man interrupted.

'She said she'd be fine,' Daniel snapped.

'I will.' I nodded vigorously, in the hope it might help me

believe it. 'I love travelling. And adventures like this make it so much more memorable.'

'Where are you staying, dear?' one of the women asked.

'Oh. Not far...' I waved vaguely in the direction most of the cars had left in, just as a van careened around the distant corner.

It choked, rattled and screeched to a halt in front of the bus stop, and a man who looked like Daffy's male twin waved at us through the open window. 'Get in then. Said I'd run an eye over Big Lander's mare after dropping you lot off.'

To avoid further awkwardness, I walked back to the food stand and pretended to look at the doughnuts. There were three left, each looking like the scraggy scrapings of dough from the bottom of the mixing bowl.

'Sorry. We're closed.' Barnie stuck both hands in his jeans pockets and pressed his mouth in a thin line.

'Okay, no problem.'

It certainly felt like a problem. I was teetering between anxious and afraid. All I'd eaten in hours was half a bowl of soup and my water bottle was empty. I was seriously contemplating sleeping in an airport doorway, and my first ever trip to anywhere was rapidly descending into the disaster my better judgement and late mother would both have predicted.

All I wanted was my cottage, my cosiest blanket and a hot cup of Darjeeling tea in my favourite Hattie Hood rabbit mug.

'Woah, I'm joking!' Barnie burst into a grin. 'As long as a customer remains on the premises, Barnie stays open.'

I didn't warn him that this customer might be there all night, too busy trying not to cry.

'What can I get you?'

'Tea and a doughnut, please.'

'Here you go, chicken. On the house. You look like you could do with it.'

He slipped all three doughnuts into a paper-bag with a wink.

'You brought a mug?' He nodded to the sign that read, *Siskin is a disposable-cup-free island*.

I shook my head.

'Sorry, can't serve you a drink without a mug.'

'That rule must impact your trade.'

He grinned, reaching under the counter and plonking an Isle of Siskin travel mug next to the till. 'A fair few thirsty people walk through those doors. After waiting around for Connell, eight quid for a mug with a free tea or coffee thrown in and everyone's a winner.'

'And to think I thought offering thirty pence off if customers bring their own mug was innovative.'

The free doughnuts seemed less of a generous offer, now. I got my phone out to pay, then remembered that, with no broadband data, I'd need to dig out my bank card.

'Right then, Billy-boy,' Barnie called. 'Last customer served, time to get this scooter on the road.'

I turned to check and saw that we did appear to be the only people left. The final car had gone.

'I don't suppose there's a car-hire place?'

What kind of airport didn't have a car rental?

Barnie took off his blue cap, ran a hand through his blond curls before donning a red one, and ambled over to the bike-hire stand.

'At your service, madam. How can Barnie's Bikes help you today?'

9

Twenty minutes later, I was wobbling along the main road into Port Cathan while cursing my stupid need to help random strangers in airports, lottery tickets, the suitcase-rucksack, which I now suspected Blessing had topped up with rocks, Lander's cows and most of all my hare-brained idea to jump on an aeroplane without bothering to take *a single day* to book somewhere to stay, or research how to get around the island, or anything at all whatsoever.

I tried being mad at Pip for helping me get here, instead of talking me out of it, but that was a lot harder than being cross at a random bunch of cows.

Every few minutes, a vehicle rumbled past, one driver hollering at the 'mainlander' hogging the narrow lane.

When a few minutes later the road started to curve upwards in what appeared to be a gentle slope, but felt to my burning thighs like the side of a mountain, I gave up, levering my stiffening limbs off the bike.

Barnie had assured me that Port Cathan was three miles away,

'Eighteen minutes if you're not a regular cyclist. Twenty, max, if you're massively unfit.'

I checked the time. It was eight-fifteen. The longest twenty-five minutes of my life, and no village in sight. The urge to keep going, with the hope that at the end of this hell I'd find a comfortable bed, a shower and a hot meal, battled with the exhaustion dragging at every bone in my body, and the fear that when I arrived at the village things might somehow get even worse.

I settled the argument by awarding myself a five-minute break, wheeling the bike off the road and sinking onto the damp, grassy verge.

Leaning back on my hands, I closed my eyes and once again became aware that I was somewhere utterly *other*.

More birdsong, a distant lowing that I decided must be Lander's herd on their way home and, of course, the gentle rhythm of waves breaking.

Opening my eyes, I caught the first hints of evening pink and gold shimmering around the sun, now hovering above the field beyond the road. I guessed at least an hour until it set, but the air carried the coolness of a summer night, and the light had softened with the lengthening shadows. I hauled myself up and did a full three-sixty, taking in the fields on either side, one full of half-grown wheat, the other a grassy meadow. A few hundred metres back from the road sat a stone farmhouse, surrounded by a large barn and several outbuildings, all encircled with a white fence. Up ahead, a small thicket prevented me from seeing how far the road still stretched, but the treetops almost glowed beneath the waning rays.

A rabbit suddenly scampered out from the hedgerow, bolted across the road and disappeared into the wheat. I spied a bird of prey circling over the far side of the meadow.

This place was beautiful.

I sank back onto the verge, the weariness of a very long day prompting me to consider finding a soft patch of grass, wrapping myself up in my new clothes and sleeping there, when a truck came chugging out of the thicket and down the hill.

I attempted to adopt the pose of a non-lost tourist who knew what she was doing, but it came to a stop anyway.

And, in what might possibly have been the best moment of my life so far, the door opened and Pip sprang out.

'Hey.' He stuck his hands in his pockets, squinting due to the sun being behind me.

'Hi.'

'You decided to cycle from the airport?' he asked, his tone uncertain. Because clearly for the sweat-soaked, dishevelled woman now slumped by the side of a near-deserted road, cycling three miles uphill with a wheeled rucksack was not a wise decision.

'The bus never turned up. The road was blocked with cows.'

He grimaced. 'Why Big Lander trusts his eejit grandson with live animals is one of the island's great mysteries.'

Holding out one hand, he helped my aching legs to a stand. 'Did no one offer you a lift?'

For a thrilling, electrified second, Pip carried on holding my hand after I'd stood up, before suddenly dropping it as if realising I was the crank who'd jumped on a plane and followed him home.

'Not that hiring a bike isn't a perfectly good solution, of course. It's a lovely wee cycle. Just a braw thing to do after a full day at work and your first ever plane ride. I'd be too focused on finding somewhere to stay. But then, I don't do so well when it comes to winging it.'

It didn't need to be said that I wasn't doing that well, either.

'Places in Daffy's van were in high demand. I wasn't about to leave a child or an elderly person stranded.' I rubbed at one of my sore arms. 'She did offer me a ride on Rozzo's moped, but, well...'

Pip cringed. 'Rozzo celebrated his sixteenth birthday last week by devouring his girlfriend's "special brownies", then driving his new moped through Port Cathan wearing nothing but a helmet, hoping it would disguise his identity.' He picked up my bag. 'At the very least, you'd have wanted to disinfect the seat.'

'Is anyone on this island normal?'

He laughed then. A full-on, deep rumble, his teeth flashing as he opened the truck door. 'This is normal. It's you mainlanders who're the strange ones.'

'Are you stealing my bag? Is that normal island behaviour, too?'

He slammed the door and moved to pick up the bike. 'I'm doing what I should have done two hours ago.'

He placed the bike in the back of the truck, then turned to face me, hands on hips. 'I didn't want to make you feel uncomfortable. I'm a random guy who buys pasties from you every now and then, and while here, it's totally *normal* to offer a complete stranger a lift if they need it – as Daffy demonstrated – I've spent enough time on the mainland to know that women there can feel nervous if a man invites them into his truck. I wasn't sure what the honourable thing was, so I wimped out of asking.'

'You're not really a random guy any more.'

He sighed, rubbing one hand through his thick hair. 'I don't feel like one but I wasn't sure if you felt that, too. Once I got home, I stopped overthinking it, realised that, after having lunch with me, if you thought I was a potential creep then you'd have flown to Belfast instead. Or at least got the Siskin plane tomorrow. So, I came to find you. Just in case.'

'You didn't know about the bus, but you still came to find me?'

He gave a sideways glance. 'Have I gone and made it creepy now?'

It was my turn to laugh. 'Pip, look at me. I am very much in need of rescuing. If Rozzo rocked up naked on his moped, I'd have probably said yes at this point.'

I dared to let my eyes meet his for a moment longer than any mainlander woman would consider normal. 'Besides, I followed you. If anyone's sounding the creep alarm, it's clearly me.'

* * *

Pip had reversed the truck and was heading back up the hill before I thought of the most important question.

'I was too relieved to see you to even ask where you're taking me.'

'I could make some joke about my lair, or where I stored all the other girls, but I'm genuinely trying to be reassuring...'

'Kind of too late now you've mentioned it anyway.'

'Yeah. If it helps, though, I'm not taking you to my farm.'

I swatted away the ripple of disappointment with a sensible mental finger wag.

'My sister Lily has converted one of our old barns into a B&B. I didn't mention it earlier because she's not officially open for another fortnight, and, as well as being clueless about what's appropriate when it comes to talking to women I haven't known my whole life, I'm also horribly clued up about how my sister will react to me mentioning that I know a woman. Let alone asking if she can stay in her not yet open B&B.'

'But you're going to ask her anyway?'

'I already did. When I panicked about not picking you up, I called the Island Arms to see if you'd got there safely. They're fully booked for a mainlanders' wedding, which has the knock-on effect of the other decent hotel also being full.'

'I could have stayed at the caravan park.'

'I'd be very happy to drop you off there. I'm sure there's space. But the caravan park shop closed at six, and the family who run it are so stingy, you won't even get a teabag, let alone milk or sugar. Lily used to run a café that officially served the best breakfast on the island. If you stay with her, it'll be worth it. And she said you can stay rent-free for the weekend if you show her how to make your pasties.'

It took me another half-mile before I dared to ask the next, obvious question.

'How *did* she react to you asking if a woman can stay?'

'I told her the hotels were full, so she was fine.'

I was so flustered at the very thought of what Lily might be assuming, let alone the exhaustion, the wild events of the day, I blurted the next question before my common sense could intercept it.

'No. I mean, does she think I'm... *your* woman?'

Pip almost swerved off the road.

He cleared his throat, keeping his eyes firmly ahead. I braved a glance and saw that his cheeks looked as warm as mine felt.

'She knows who you are.'

'The person you buy pasties from.'

Another pause. 'Exactly.'

* * *

We soon reached Port Cathan, winding along the seafront where the harbour displayed boats ranging from dinghies, through fishing boats to a sleek superyacht. On the other side of the road, I counted four cafés, two hotels – including the distinctly non-

Grand – a few touristy shops and an art gallery. Bookending all these were a row of pastel-painted terraces and some larger cottages with brightly coloured window boxes and picket fences.

'It's like something out of a film,' I said, taking in the crowded patio outside one of the cafés.

On the far side of the harbour, we drove past a beach, lit up with solar lights, and a group of people sitting on camping chairs around a firepit, watching the sunset dance upon the waves while dog walkers wandered closer to the water.

'While I admit that Harbour Road does maintain a sheen that mainlanders love, on the other side of those houses is the real village. There's the village store, Tenneson's Farm Supplies, the community centre, school and the fish-market.' Pip grimaced. 'Put it this way: the harbour is busy this evening because the wind is blowing in the right direction. Although plenty of the people living along here have got used to the smell. Mainly because they can't ever get it out of their clothes.'

The road then veered inland, winding back uphill until, less than twenty minutes after we'd set off, we turned down a one-lane gravel track for a couple of hundred metres, pulling into a driveway with a sign that I could just make out through the twilight as *Sunflower Barn*.

I grabbed my case from the back seat while Pip lifted the bike out of the back of his truck, assuring me that it was the best way to get around the island.

The red front door was set underneath a porch trellis, which had a baby honeysuckle making its way up one side. Instead of using the brass knocker, Pip opened the door and walked straight in.

'Hello?' he called, prompting a woman to shoot out of an oak doorway on the other side of the spacious square hall.

'Shush!' she hissed, waving both hands at him. 'I've finally got

Beanie down. If I have to read about that mole one more time, I'm going to dig myself a flippin' tunnel in the garden and live there.'

'Still obsessed?'

The woman, who I presumed must be Lily, hurried across the hall and threw her arms around him. 'It's not natural for anyone to know that much about moles. Let alone a three-year-old girl. It certainly shouldn't be keeping them up an hour past their bedtime.'

She caught herself, peeling herself away from Pip as if suddenly noticing the stranger in her house.

'Oh, you must be Emmaline.'

Her face, framed with the same dark hair as her brother, only pinned in a messy bun, lit up as she stepped forwards to give me a hug. I noticed then the pregnant bump beneath her loose T-shirt.

'My friends call me Emmie.'

'Emmie it is, then.' She stepped back, the pale-blue eyes beneath thick, dark lashes dancing between me and Pip. 'I'm Lily, Pip's biggest sister. Come through and make yourself cosy. You must be dying for a drink. Pip, will you take Emmie's bag up to the yellow room? It's got a daisy on the door.'

I followed Lily into the kitchen, a gorgeous space with appliances to rival my garage and a huge, purple table near a sliding glass door at one end. Beside that was a corner sofa, television and a mountain of toys.

'This is Malcolm, my husband. Malcolm, this is Pip's *friend* who spontaneously jumped on his plane when she heard he was heading home for good, and so is going to be our pre-launch test guest.'

Malcolm, a bear-like man with a shaved head and hearty beard, gave a non-committal nod from where he sat at the table absorbed in paperwork. An older child, sprawled on the sofa reading a Malorie Blackman novel, sprang to a sitting position, her book forgotten.

'You're Uncle Pip's girlfriend?'

Oh, boy.

'No. Just a friend.' I resisted the urge to reverse out of there.

'But you're the pasty girl he's always going on about when he comes home?'

'Um. I do sell pasties, yes...'

'Only a matter of time, then.' She flopped back, lifting the book to her nose again. 'You're smaller than I expected. But a lot prettier.'

'Oh?'

What had Pip said that made her think I wouldn't be pretty?

Never mind that – *Pip had been saying things about me?*

She turned her page. 'Well, you look nice. And he's... Pip.'

'Are you being rude about your uncle?' Lily scolded. 'To his new friend?'

'She can see what he looks like. And if anyone mentions pasties, he goes quiet and awkward like Barnie when he's trying to tell Auntie Violet he loves her.'

Lily spun around, a kettle in her hand. 'What? Are you talking about Barnie Cork?'

'Or what, all the other, non-existent Barnies living on this island?'

'When did he tell Auntie Violet he loves her, and why on earth did no one tell me?'

'I said he *tried* to tell her, Ma.' The girl rolled her eyes, still reading. 'He always gets shuffly and stammery when she talks about how she wants to go travelling. Then he starts going on about all the reasons she should stay. Apart from the biggest reason, which is him being in love with her. Do you people notice nothing?'

'We notice that it's nearly nine o'clock on a school night, and you're not in bed,' Malcolm said in a lilting Welsh accent. 'If you spent more time concentrating on your own business rather than snooping into other people's, you might not have another after-school correction tomorrow.'

'Ugh! I was answering Ma's questions. If I'd walked off, you'd have moaned at me again for being rude.' She rolled off the sofa and stomped out.

'That was Flora,' Lily said. 'Twelve going on seventeen. The only child on the island who gets in trouble for reading too much.'

Malcolm got up and took a couple of glasses off a high shelf. 'I know Lily's put the kettle on, but I'm wondering if wine would be more suitable to the occasion. Low alcohol, in honour of those of us gestating a baby or driving home later.'

Before I could answer, Pip appeared in the doorway. 'It's looking great up there.'

He exchanged a brief half-hug with Malcolm.

'Had a good nosey about?' Lily poked him with a corkscrew. 'Not hard to guess where Flora gets it from.'

'Back in April, the upstairs was a pile of plaster dust and rubble. Now it's all, "show Emmie to the yellow room". Of course I had a nosey.'

They carried on swapping banter until Lily handed me a glass of white wine. Malcolm pulled back the sliding door and ushered me outside to a large patio, with two dining sets and a more informal seating area around a coffee table.

'How's the garden getting along?' Pip asked, once we were all settled on the comfier seats. I'd carefully chosen an individual chair rather than one of the sofas. I still felt whisked up in a whirlwind, and sitting beside Pip would have made it even harder to act normal.

'Come on, little brother, we have far more interesting things to talk about than the garden,' Lily said, with a wink in my direction.

I automatically glanced at Pip, our eyes catching before his darted away again.

'Yeah. I was going to see if I could catch Mammaw, but now I'm wondering if it's safe to leave Emmie alone with you.'

Lily spun towards him so quickly, she sloshed wine over the edge of her glass. 'You haven't seen Mammaw yet?'

Pip squirmed on his seat like a naughty schoolboy. 'She was napping when I got back to the farm, and then I went to find Emmie...'

'Wait. What? Instead of bringing Emmie with you to the farm, you *lost* her?'

Pip turned to me. 'Our grandmother is ninety-one. She's normally in bed by now but will be waiting up for me. Is it okay if I head off, or do you want me to stay and explain to my sister, who has the audacity to accuse me of being nosey, that you're not on the island with me?'

'Of course, that's fine,' I managed to stammer. As embarrassing as this situation was, Pip leaving might just make it easier.

He kissed his sister, drained his glass, threw me the faintest twitch of a smile and left me to it.

10

'I'm sorry.' Lily leant forward, not looking especially sorry. 'Have you not come here to visit Pip?'

I took a slow sip of wine. It was almost fully dark now. A bat flitted across the indigo sky. Even here, what I presumed to be fairly inland, I could hear the water and feel the faint scratch of salt air upon my skin.

'It's been a very unusual day.'

'Ooh, good. Start from the beginning and tell me all about it.' Lily settled back, pulling one of the throws scattered about across her knees. 'And look – even better.'

Malcolm, who had lingered in the kitchen, appeared carrying an enormous board covered in cheese, slices of crusty baguette, grapes and other fruit.

I was so hungry that I overcame my politeness and filled a plate before reciting the events of the day.

'So,' I finished, after another round of cheese and second glass of wine, 'I have no idea how long I'm staying for, or what I'm going to get up to. My only plan is to sit on the beach and read my mum's letters.'

'And you've no clue who the man is?'

'Only his initial.' I wasn't ready to share that yet.

'You might have figured out that everyone knows everyone here. If it's a C or an L, then it might not be straightforward, but if it's, I don't know, an F or a V, then I could be introducing you by tomorrow evening.'

'Did he give anything else away?' Malcolm asked. 'About his occupation, or whether he lived in a village or on the coast? His family?'

I took a moment to consider how to answer. I'd not come here with the intention of finding this man. I still had no idea how the story ended for him and Mum, whether he really was the person in the photograph, or if he'd turned out to be someone unkind, or even dangerous. There had to be a reason my mother developed such a bitter attitude towards men and marriage.

'Not really. But I've only read a couple of the letters.' I put my glass on the table. 'Um, if you don't mind, I've been awake since four-thirty. I think I might head to bed.'

'Of course.' Lily heaved herself up. 'I'm amazed you've got the energy to string a sentence together after today.'

We walked back to the hall and up a wide staircase that led to a corridor with six doors.

'These doors are the guest bedrooms, although yours is the only one finished at the moment. That door at the end leads to the top floor, where there's bedrooms for everyone you've met plus Jack, our six-year-old, and Beanie.'

She opened the yellow-room door, and I followed her in.

'You're my guinea pig, so let me know if there's anything obvious missing, broken or that isn't quite perfect. There's a hot drinks station and mini fridge, towels and a robe, spare blanket in the wardrobe in case it gets chilly... breakfast is whenever you like because we aren't officially open yet. Oh, and this is the login and password for the Internet. It's patchy at best, but we've dial-up downstairs if you need it. Anything else I've forgotten?'

'I can't think of anything.'

I'd never stayed in a B&B before, so had no idea.

'Great. My number's on the notepad by the bed. Message if you need anything – day or night. Treat this as if you're a paying customer, because you are. I used to run a café so I know the value of secret family recipes.'

She slipped out, almost shutting the door before flinging it open again and coming back to squeeze my arm.

'I'm so glad you're here. My brother hasn't looked like that in a very long time. It's lovely for him to have a... friend.'

* * *

I waited for her footsteps to disappear downstairs, then changed into my new pyjamas before settling on the bed with a decaf tea and a home-made brownie from the refreshments tray. A small bedside lamp bathed the room in a gentle glow. Like the rest of Sunflower Barn, it was styled with simple décor that oozed quality. Mum had always scoffed about spending money on fripperies like cushions or pictures. A house was meant to be functional. Who cared what it looked like?

Me, I realised as I compared Sunflower Barn's clean lines with my battered old bedroom. It made me feel peaceful. Soothed. And, given how my life had tumbled into a rabbit hole, I appreciated that more than I'd thought possible.

I replied to Blessing's numerous text messages while I sipped my tea, answering her questions and sending anything helpful that my frazzled brain could think of. I logged into the Wi-Fi, then typed a reply to Gregory's email reminding him there were ten days before the contract ran out, and I was on my first holiday ever so please back off. Then, instead of pressing send, I deleted it, deleted his email and fetched the stash of letters from my bag.

12 November 1985

My Dearest Nellie,

The storm last week brought the telephone wires down. Lorcan Davies will hopefully have them up and running before this letter reaches you, but I couldn't wait to let you know that I've booked my flights. Da is not pleased, but Richard says he's happy to keep things ticking over for a week. Bucky will lend a hand if anything untoward happens, but I'm sure Da and my brother will be grand.

I'll be landing at midday on 27 March. I can't believe I'll have gone a whole seven months without seeing your face (or kissing you!) but the photographs help – thank you for sending them. I'd be wondering if last summer was a foolish dream if it wasn't for hearing your beautiful voice every Sunday. Speaking with you is like a drink of water from Liath Spring after six days labouring in the dirt. I'm afraid that knowing I'll be with you in March could make the days drag even slower. But I'm a farmer and, even as my heart bursts with longing, patience is in my bones.

Besides, there's plenty of work to keep me occupied. Ma wants a new greenhouse for her spring seedlings, on top of everything else. Da is slower every year, although he'd rather blame the tools or the weather – his sons – anything but admit he's growing old. Which again brings up the same arguments about investing some money into making the farm easier. If it was up to him, we'd still be harvesting with a scythe.

Anyway, I'm rambling again.

All this was simply to tell you that I'll be in Nottingham before you know it.

And I love you.

And will think of you and miss you every minute between now and then.

Entirely yours,
With faith, hope and love
G

I lay in the luxurious bed for a long time that night, gazing at the sliver of moon through the window. My thoughts tossed up and down like a dinghy from Port Cathan harbour out on the Irish Sea: Mum. The kiosk. How Barnie had the audacity to charge a pound for those mutant doughnuts.

I thought about change. How terrifying it had always seemed. How exhausting it was proving to be.

And yet, like when doing anything momentous or significant – climbing a mountain, building a house, or childbirth – I imagined, because I'd never come close to doing any of those things – for the first time in longer than I could bear to remember, I felt properly, wholly alive.

The last thought, before my mind gently drifted into the harbour of sleep?

I had talked, and laughed, and sat in a truck beside Pip.

I was in his sister's house. *He'd come to find me.*

His family seemed to believe Pip liked me, as more than a friend.

Could I dare to believe it too?

11

After waking at the decadent hour of six-thirty, I scrolled through my phone for a few minutes until the Wi-Fi vanished, made another cup of tea and pulled up the armchair to admire the view out of the sash window. The yellow room overlooked a long lawn, dotted with fruit trees. There were two hammocks, more chairs, a complicated climbing frame and, in one corner, a chicken coop. Beyond the back wall were fields, which I guessed were part of Hawkins Farm, owned by Pip's family. A herd of cows were meandering along a hedge, and on the horizon behind them glistened a thin, silvery ribbon that I realised, with a flush of delight, was the sea. I looked for any sign of a farmhouse, but there were trees blocking the view on one side, and a cluster of cottages on the other.

Just after seven, Malcolm ambled down the garden, a small child in a mole onesie holding his hand, a slightly older boy dressed in shorts, wellington boots and a cowboy hat walking next to them. The boy, who must have been Jack, reached up to open the door on the chicken coop, and, after a little encouragement, five black and white hens trooped out. Malcolm had a brief tussle with Beanie over whether she needed his help to scatter a carton of food (Beanie won), and they left the birds to their pecking and scratching.

Deciding it was probably breakfast for humans as well as chickens, I took a blissful shower in the en suite wet room and selected the rose sundress that Blessing assured me complemented the strawberry-blonde tones in my hair. What she hadn't mentioned was that it had straps instead of a proper back, and only reached halfway down my thighs. For a woman who lived in cotton trousers and a T-shirt, I had to fight feeling as though I were heading to breakfast with strangers half dressed.

* * *

The scent of scrambled eggs and coffee greeted me at the kitchen door. Malcolm and the girls were sitting at the table eating, while Lily stood at the stove, supervising Jack prodding the contents of a frying pan, an apron over his bare chest.

'How did you sleep?' Lily asked, her face a mix of eagerness and trepidation.

'Brilliantly.'

'The bed was comfy?'

'It was wonderful.'

'Room wasn't too hot or cold? Because I forgot to show you where the thermostat is...'

'It was just right.'

'What about the shower? And did you try the brownie? Because it was a newish recipe and some people find them a bit stodgy...'

'Ma!' Flora groaned. 'Stop with the interrogation. Emmie's only just got up.'

'Well, yes, and are you sure the bed was okay? Because it's still very early to be up when you're on holiday. Oh, my goodness, was it us? Did we wake you thumping down the stairs like a rhinoceros stampede?'

'Everything was perfect,' I said, a little too loudly because this barrage of questions was making me break into a sweat. 'It was like spending the night in a cosy corner of heaven. Honestly. And the brownie had precisely the right amount of stodge.'

'Really?' Lily promptly burst into tears, blotting her face with her apron while Flora came to help Jack scoop eggs onto a plate of toast.

'Here, Mother. Sit yourself down and eat some eggs. They're good for baby.'

Flora steered her mum over to the table, Jack following with the plate, and Beanie hopped off the bench and pulled out a chair for her.

'Mammy gets tired because she's getting everything ready for the grand opening *and* growing a baby,' Jack told me, blue eyes solemn, cowboy hat tipped back over blond waves.

'Sometimes, the baby makes her cry, but she's not really sad,' Beanie added, climbing back onto the bench.

'Well, if there's anything I can do, I'd be happy to help,' I said, startling myself as the words popped out.

'Be careful what you offer,' Malcolm said, eyes twinkling as he helped his youngest daughter push the last bit of egg onto her fork. 'We're reaching the point where we might just take you up on that, and there's a heck of a lot to do. You could end up staying longer than originally planned.'

* * *

While eating poached eggs that Jack proudly informed me had

been laid by, 'Pecky. No, Clucker. Or that one looks like maybe it was from Mrs Scratchy,' Lily asked what I had in mind for the day.

'Pip asked me to let you know that he'll be in the chicken barn most of the day, but there's a "welcome home" family meal for him this evening, and he'd love you to come.'

I briefly weighed up the embarrassment at being introduced to Pip's whole family alongside getting to see him again. No contest.

'Fantastic.' Lily grinned. 'I'm heading into the village this morning, so if you don't have other plans then we could shop for pasty ingredients, get baking this afternoon and bring some along to the meal?'

'Had you considered that Emmie might not want to spend the first day of her holiday making pasties?' Malcolm asked, loading the dishwasher after reminding the children to bring him their empty plates. 'And by that, I mean have you forgotten you'd promised to help finish painting the lilac room?'

'Och.' Lily dismissed that with a wave. 'It's only a small room; you'll be fine without me.'

'Will I also be fine doing both school runs, picking Beanie up from nursery and chasing up those forms for your da, as well?'

Lily furrowed her brow, looking startlingly like her youngest daughter, who was currently sitting on the floor, struggling to stuff a water bottle into a tiny bag.

'There's a long list of things to do in the next two weeks, my love.'

'I know that.' Lily sighed. 'Okay. I suppose Emmie should spend the first day of her holiday out of a kitchen.'

'We could buy the ingredients this morning, and then I'll help you paint?' I suggested. Very aware that, not only was I staying with these people I didn't know for free, the prospect of an empty afternoon made my skin itch. 'We could bake tomorrow.'

Malcolm gave his wife a look that clearly said there was no way their first guest was getting roped into painting.

'How about you come with me to buy the food now, and then enjoy Port Cathan while Malc and I paint? I can pick you up when I get the kids from school.'

'Perfect.'

* * *

We drove four miles back to the village in Lily and Malcolm's bashed-up seven-seater car, dropping Flora and Jack off at their school and Beanie at the nursery next door, and then headed to the farmers' market. I was slightly anxious about trying to source ingredients somewhere other than the wholesalers and butcher I was used to. Logic told me that I knew the recipes well enough to improvise if needed, but it had been drilled into me from birth that, when it came to Parsley's Pasties, deviating from the exact formula was sacrilege.

It was easy enough to find good-quality flour and fat to make a dozen pasties. Lily then impressed me by bartering down the price for the vegetables and herbs. The first obstacle was venison.

'We don't have deer on the island,' Lily explained as we scanned the meat stall.

'We could try beef?' I suggested, stomach clenching.

'Not happening. I'm not having my sisters gloating over my inferior pasty-making skills. We're doing this right.'

She had a quick back and forth with the butcher, throwing in various pointed remarks about how she'd be purchasing plenty of bacon and sausages from him soon enough, eventually agreeing on a price for him to ship some venison over from the mainland in the next few days, with a minimum order that made my eyes water.

'That'll make a lot of pasties.'

'No worries, I've got a huge freezer. Besides, they really won't last that long.'

The next issue was white Stilton. While the delicatessen had two of the blue varieties (impressive enough, given that official Stilton had to be manufactured in one of three East Midlands counties), there was none of the far rarer white – i.e. mould-free – Stilton.

After an extensive tasting session, I persuaded Lily to use a creamy Lancashire cheese combined with some crumbled feta as a substitute.

'I think this combination might even be better than the Stilton,' I said, with the growing realisation that, while Parsley's pasties were downright delicious, food had changed a lot in the past couple of decades. I made a promise to myself that when I got home, I'd spend more time experimenting with different flavours.

We loaded the food into the car once Lily had finished haggling for everything else on her original list, and then she pointed me in the direction of the seafront, swapping numbers with the promise that, if she didn't hear from me, I'd meet her by the school gates at three-thirty. By the time I'd strolled to the harbour, it was nearly eleven.

I watched the boats bobbing up and down for a few minutes, but found the weight of several empty hours pressing on my shoulders far more stressful than if I'd been neck-deep in food-prep, admin piling up around my laptop.

Feeling lonely was nothing new. The scary part was feeling lost. Adrift.

Not geographically – although being somewhere so different was a challenge.

I felt lost in time. It wasn't so much that I didn't have ideas about what to do, more that, without a clear structure, I was overwhelmed at where to even begin.

So, try what you know works, I told myself, after far too long dithering on the verge of panic. *Make a schedule.*

I crossed the road and headed for the nearest café with outside seating, called Toasty. The three other tables on the wide pavement were all full of people with local accents, causing a ripple of satisfaction that I'd probably found a decent place to start.

I ordered tea, a slice of gooey fudge cake for now and a panini for a later lunch, aiming for holiday-indulgence despite my stomach being full of eleven varieties of cheese, and by the time the waiter brought it out, the tension had begun to subside as I typed out a schedule on my phone notes app, including window shopping in the tourist shops and a couple of hours on the beach.

I had no idea what to do on a beach for two hours, especially with no Internet, but while browsing in a tiny charity shop, I decided to buy a book, and then stopped at a souvenir shop selling beach towels. My confidence growing by the second, I settled down to read the first few pages.

The next thing I knew, I was waking up to find the tide lapping at my ankles while a labradoodle gobbled my sandwich.

'Oh, my goodness, I'm so sorry,' the dog owner cried as she ran over, although her face was contorting in a way that made me think she was trying not to laugh. 'Pigeon can't resist mozzarella.'

I scrabbled to my feet, rescuing one trainer from an incoming wave as she yanked the dog away by its collar and clipped on its lead.

'Is that your book?' the woman asked, pointing at the novel now bobbing about on the waves.

Before I could tell her that it didn't matter, it had only cost a pound and the first chapter had sent me to sleep, she'd stripped off her maxi dress, handed me Pigeon's lead and was wading in.

She looked stunning, thigh-deep in the water as she reached for the book, droplets shimmering on her toned arms, honey-blonde highlights cascading down her back. Somewhere around my age. I imagined she spent her days off surfing or sailing around the headland, not cleaning her already clean house and reading books about places she'd never been to and never would.

'Here.' She splashed back out, shaking her barely damp hair like someone in a shampoo commercial before handing me the soggy clump of paper. 'The least I could do. I'm so sorry this naughty boy ate your lunch. Say sorry, Pigeon!'

Pigeon said nothing, the look on his face implying that he was more proud than sorry.

'The tide comes in up to the post.' She pointed at a wooden sign clearly stating, *High Tide*. 'But mainlanders are always leaving their stuff on the beach while they go off swimming or whatever, and next thing they know, their phone and keys are halfway to Wales.'

Grabbing my towel, she started vigorously rubbing her legs. 'I've never seen anyone lose their stuff while sat right next to it, though. Were you half asleep?'

'Fully asleep, actually,' I said, trying not to cringe. This woman was a goddess. So utterly relaxed in her own skin, which perhaps wasn't surprising considering how gorgeous it was.

'Ah.' She dropped the wet towel on the sand and took Pigeon's lead back from me. 'You're lucky he only got your sandwich, then. This rascal ate my dad's wallet once, because there was a stick of chewing gum inside it. Thankfully, not the kind that's poisonous to dogs.'

She began walking back towards the edge of the beach, her dress draped around her shoulders like a shawl. 'Are you coming?'

In the spirit of my new, wildly spontaneous life, I decided that I was, slipping on my trainers and stuffing the towel into my bag as she chattered on about the dog needing surgery, but her dad's bank card being ruined from the toothmarks.

After leaving the beach, we crossed over and strolled past a few shops and the Grand hotel before she ducked down a side street, stopping at a tiny hole-in-the-wall food outlet, briefly pausing in her current tale about a local who lost their wedding ring in the sea and then found it inside an oyster shell three years later, to order three lobster rolls.

'Here,' she said, once she'd handed one steaming bread roll to me and another to Pigeon. 'If I'm replacing the sandwich, it might as well be with the best food in Port Cathan.'

I was halfway through my first bite – savouring a whole new burst of flavours – when she stopped nibbling hers.

'I'm Celine, by the way.' She grimaced. 'Not a traditional island name, but my ma's mad on *Titanic*.'

'I'm Emmie.'

She went completely still, the edge of the roll held up against her mouth.

After what felt like an excruciatingly long second, Celine sprang back to life as if someone had un-paused a film.

'Oh, my goodness. You're Pasty Girl.'

'Um, what?'

'Iris – Pip's sister – said you'd followed him over here.' She resumed nibbling. 'I mean, at first we all thought he'd brought you home to introduce you to the family. That would have caused major drama, for obvious reasons. Crushing on someone who served you a coffee is one thing, but returning with a mainlander in tow is serious business. So, big sighs of relief all round when he explained you'd invited yourself.'

'I didn't follow Pip,' I mumbled. 'Me visiting the island has nothing to do with him.'

'Oh. Well, that's even better, then, isn't it?' She dabbed at her lip with a corner of the dress still draped around her shoulders. It was a little disconcerting having this conversation with someone wearing an orange bikini. 'It did seem a bit extreme. We were worried it might escalate into a restraining-order situation.'

I didn't ask if it was Pip who'd told Iris that I'd invited myself here because of him. I wasn't sure I could bear to hear the answer.

'The thing with Pip, he's so lovely. Always helping some needy person out. You wouldn't be the first woman to take it the wrong way.'

'I didn't take it the wrong way.'

'Of course you didn't. I'm sorry for implying otherwise. Now I've met you, it's obvious you'd never do anything so bonkers. Apart from falling asleep on the beach when the tide's coming in. That was not a sensible move.' She giggled, then squinted up at the sky as if searching for something. 'Anyway, time I was going. It was fascinating to meet you, Emmie. I'll probably see you around. Come on, Pigeon.'

Being a mainlander who can't tell the time using the position of the sun, I dug my phone out of my bag and saw that it was probably time I started walking to the school. I'd napped for maybe an hour and a half and had managed a good few hours the night before, but it felt as though years of exhaustion had caught up with me.

I read two texts from Blessing as I started back along the seafront.

> People are RAGING about no Parsley's. Someone threatened to sue the airport for emotional distress and the food court crumbled under the pressure of more than two customers at once. Also, Gregory asked me to say you need to reply to his email, asap, and remember you can't be closed for more than ten days without permission from the airport director.
>
> Speaking of which – any idea yet when you'll be back?

I paused on a bench overlooking the sea and sent her a brief reply saying that, no, I didn't know yet, and not to worry about Gregory; I'd contact him. I then composed a draft email to Gregory telling him that I still had nine days to sign that contract, I'd do it when I was good and ready and him hassling me wasn't helpful.

I didn't bother to save the draft, knowing that once I'd logged into the Internet back at the B&B, I'd no longer have the guts to send it.

12

We were nearly home by the time Lily had heard all about Jack's animal project, spelling test and how Jamie had wanted to swap lunch but he didn't want to because Jamie had raisins instead of a brownie, so Jamie had thrown a raisin that hit Kendra in the eye, and so it went on. The second he'd left the school gates, he'd ripped his polo shirt off and stuck on the cowboy hat squashed in his bookbag.

Flora's day was 'Whatever,' answered with the disdain perfected by all tweenagers. She then dropped the sneer to ask what I'd been doing.

'I mean, apart from the hideousness of shopping with my mother. I bet she haggled over every penny, as if we're paupers scrabbling for a crust of bread.'

'The reason we aren't paupers is because your mother knows how to negotiate a decent bargain,' Lily replied. 'You'll be wishing you had my negotiating skills when reading time gets cut again due to more rudeness.'

'We're going to the farmhouse so there'll be no reading time anyway,' Flora scoffed, before catching her mum's face in the rearview mirror and hastily adding, 'Sorry for being rude about how embarrassing your haggling is.'

'It wasn't at all embarrassing,' I said, twisting around in the front seat. Lily was positively easy-going compared to my mother. 'My mum used to bring her own kitchen scales to the wholesalers because she was convinced the cheesemongers were dodgy. It wouldn't have been so bad if she was right. But they matched up perfectly every time.'

'Your mammy sounds weird,' Jack said.

'She was pretty unusual, yes. But her fierce business skills helped create the best pasty company outside Cornwall, so it was worth it.'

'What did you do this afternoon, then?' Lily asked.

I described going to the café, which they agreed served irresistible cakes, and how my decision to read a book on the beach ended up with losing both my lunch, and the book, but gaining a lobster roll, thanks to the dog's owner, Celine.

'She seemed to know your family,' I added.

'That's because there are three thousand and forty-one year-round residents on this piffling island,' Flora said. 'We all know everyone else. In far too much detail. You literally can't fart some days without the entire population smelling it.'

'Maybe your stinky farts!' Jack giggled, causing Flora to reach over and tickle him until he squealed.

'Celine was at school with Iris,' Lily explained, slowing to turn onto the lane leading to the barn.

'Iris is your younger sister?'

Lily nodded. 'Ma had me, Violet and Pip in three years, then Iris four years later. Surprise fourth babies turn out to be a family trait. It's also probably worth you knowing that Celine has the classic best-friend's-older-brother crush.'

'Right.' That put a different slant on our conversation.

'And while we're talking about it, because I don't want you to be on the back foot, and because my brother clearly likes you, as do I – given the limited dating pool, he and Celine used to go out.'

'Is it overstepping if I ask if they were serious?'

'Celine started prepping for the role of farmer's wife with her toy stuffed sheep. Most people assumed it was inevitable. They had a few casual dates once he was back from his first stint at uni and she was old enough for the age gap not to matter, then were in a proper relationship for about a year before he left for the master's degree. They broke up when he realised she was deadly serious, and he wasn't ready for that.'

'She told him that if he didn't ask her to marry him soon, they were totally done, for good this time, and she'd find herself a man who wasn't so effing scared of a real relationship,' Flora said, holding up her hands to convey the drama.

'Excuse me?' Lily barked as she pulled to a stop by the side of the house.

'What? I said effing. *She* said the whole word!'

'Are you really Harriet the Spy in disguise?' Lily sighed.

'It's not like there's anything else happening on this prehistoric lump of rock.' Flora might have sounded sullen, but I spotted her helping Jack undo his seat belt and making sure he'd not forgotten his goose collage.

* * *

Beanie appeared at the top of the stairs as soon as we entered the house, Malcolm dashing after her to retrieve the lilac-covered paintbrush and strip off her spattered smock. I went to shower off the sand while everyone else trooped into the kitchen for snacks and general chaos. It was fair to say that hearing about Celine had been a drawing pin in the rapidly inflating balloon of foolish notions I'd been harbouring since Monday. I wasn't here chasing after Pip. If anything, I was searching for clues about my mother. But I had been dreaming about him for almost two years. I'd never expected those dreams to come true, until he'd strolled up to the kiosk a few days ago. Now Blessing, and Ivor at the check-in desk, Lily and even that stupid lottery ticket had made me believe that amazing things were possible, even for someone as unamazing as me.

Celine and Pip had broken up because he hadn't been ready to commit. But he was older now. He'd made it clear that he wanted to settle on the island, run the farm one day. There was the beautiful Celine, who'd been eager to be Pip's wife her whole life, and here was me, a mainlander, who had no idea what she wanted. And, even if she did, neither the courage nor the freedom to go after it.

* * *

'No,' Lily said firmly, when I slunk downstairs an hour later. She'd changed into a khaki linen jumpsuit that showed off the gentle curve of her bump and was now sitting at the outside table, reading a recipe book. I'd swapped into the second dress Blessing had selected, which had puffed, off-the-shoulder sleeves, a fitted waist and tiered skirt in dark cream, covered in tiny leaves and flowers. It felt perfect for ambling through summer meadows or milling at a party with a glass of gin and tonic.

'You aren't wimping out and staying here by yourself because my brother's ex-girlfriend made some snide comments.'

'I never said she made any comments.'

'You didn't have to. Celine is fine, but when it comes to Pip, she's completely irrational. And you aren't letting her win.'

'Win what?' I asked, sinking into the chair opposite her.

'Win at bullying you into missing a fun evening because she's scared you'll snag her island farmer.'

'I don't think she was trying to bully me.'

'Did you feel bullied?' She poured me a glass of iced water from a jug on the table while I considered that.

'I'm so out of my comfort zone here, it's easy to feel intimidated.'

Lily's face softened. 'Do I intimidate you?'

I shrugged. 'Beanie intimidates me.'

'It's so long since I've spent any time on the mainland, I forget what it's like to be somewhere full of strange rules without the unwritten rulebook.'

'You also make me feel very welcome, and as relaxed as it's possible for me to be, given this is the first time I've stayed in a different bed since I was fifteen.'

She sat back, surprised. 'And you managed to sleep?'

'Better than I do most nights at home.'

A satisfied grin spread across her features. 'I'm sorry. This is a soul-baring moment, but you just made my B&B dream come true.'

'Mammy, are we going yet?' Jack asked, tumbling through the door into the garden. 'I'm so-o-o-o hungry and Grammie said she's making pot sausage. Emmie, do you like pot sausage?'

'I have no idea,' I said.

'But once Jack has put on his shirt, you're coming to try it, aren't you?' Lily asked gently, nudging my foot under the table. 'Because if I turn up without Pip's friend, I'll get sent straight back to fetch you. And I'm not making my brother sad on his second night home.'

'I'll go and get ready.'

'Ugh.' Jack slumped onto the floor. 'I might be so starving I've died by then.'

* * *

It turned out we were cycling to the farmhouse, Beanie on a seat behind Lily and Jack in one of those tag-a-long bikes attached to his dad's.

Unsurprisingly, it didn't take long for me to end up trailing behind. After turning off a dusty path onto the side of a large field, Flora dropped back to cycle alongside me.

'Everyone's going to want to talk to you, but if you're nervous, you can hang out with me, if you like,' she said, glancing over to where I was starting to sweat.

'That's really kind of you, thank you,' I managed between huffs.

'It's not, actually. I love my family but I've been hanging out with the same people every single day my whole life. How is that preparation for my future? I need information about the real world from a real person, not just dumb books from the mobile library.'

'Flora, the island is a valid part of the real world. Way too many mainlander kids spend most of their time stuck in the fake world of social media or online gaming, anyway.'

'Ugh. Don't get me started on that. Can you imagine what living on an island with virtually no Wi-Fi is like? I have to wait until boarding school until I'm allowed a smartphone. Sharing the family PC is not the same.'

'When do you start boarding school?'

'Thirteen. Which means by the time I get there, I'll already be just another island freak who doesn't know anything about anything that actually matters to people my age. I'll be stuck being friends with the same old equally clueless kids. So I'll keep knowing nothing and being no one in a never-ending circle until my only option is to crawl back here and live on Hawkins Farm until I die.'

'I know it might be hard to imagine, but I do understand. If anything, I'm jealous you get to go to boarding school. I got my first phone for my eighteenth birthday, and I might as well have lived on an island for all the places I never went to and things I didn't know.'

'It's not hard to imagine at all. It's why I'm talking to you, because it's obvious you have the same problem.'

With that statement lingering between us, we bumped along the hedge in silence for another minute or two. At this rate, I was going to leave this island best friends with a twelve-year-old.

'What are you hoping for, in your future?' I asked, keen to think about something other than my social inadequacy.

'If I could choose, then I'd be an intelligence officer to start with.'

'Wow.'

'Then, I'm thinking politics. Or a pathologist. Wouldn't it be cool to figure out how people died?'

'You're not interested in working on the farm?'

She scoffed. 'I might have to get interested. My aunties and uncle aren't producing another heir any time soon.'

'Are they all single?'

'Auntie Iris is engaged to Hugh. He's a vet. They wanted to get married in August, but Ma was supposed to be organising all the food and then the oops baby happened, so with having to get the B&B ready as well, they've postponed it.'

'When is the baby due?'

'October.' She stopped her bike to point out a family of rabbits hopping amongst the grass. Really, it was worth stopping to simply breathe in the view. A rainbow of pink, blue and yellow wildflowers danced in the gentle breeze. I caught the faint whiff of bonfire smoke and cow manure mingling with the salt air. Beyond the edge of the field, the ribbon of Irish Sea was sparkling periwinkle. I wasn't sure I'd ever get bored of taking in the breadth of the sky – clear, wild blue from one horizon to another: such a contrast to the forest back home.

'Anyway.' Flora pushed herself off again. 'Auntie Violet is single because she loves Barnie, but he's solid islander, and she wants to travel. And Uncle Pip should know if he loves Celine or not by now. The farm's future is in jeopardy unless I step up.'

'I'm starting to appreciate why you're so invested in your family's romantic lives. But what about Jack or Beanie? They might want to be farmers.'

'Jack might dress like a cowboy, but he's scared of cows. And the only animal Beanie's interested in tunnels under the ground. Besides, would you entrust prize cattle to someone with a name like Beanie?'

We both burst out laughing until my front wheel started wobbling, threatening to topple me into the corn.

'It is unusual.'

'She's supposed to be Rosemary, like my grammie.'

'Are all the women in your family named after flowers?'

Flora nodded. 'That's an island thing.'

'Is Beanie an island thing, too?'

'No.' Flora shrugged. 'It just sort of found her one day, and stuck. Look, there's my potential future prison, right there.'

We both stopped again as the path began to slope downwards, revealing a large stone farmhouse halfway to the sea.

To one side, a herd of cows clustered underneath a huge chestnut tree. Below that, a short distance from the farmhouse was a spacious yard containing a tractor and other machinery, various-sized outbuildings forming a border on three sides, and an enclosed field full of small trees that Flora told me was where the forty thousand chickens roamed free.

'Come on,' she called, accelerating ahead as she freewheeled down the slope. 'I can smell the sausages from here!'

* * *

We propped the bikes up against the side of the house and I followed everyone through a wooden side-gate to a garden at the back, already regretting my decision to be brave and come along. When I saw the groups of people helping themselves to drinks from the long trestle tables, sitting in deckchairs or hovering near the enormous barbecue, the urge to flee only grew.

About two dozen heads swivelled towards us as Lily and Malcolm called hello, adult conversations fading into potent silence as the younger kids ran to play with two chocolate Labradors while Flora joined a couple of girls sprawled on a blanket.

'Come on, let's get the hard bit out of the way,' Lily murmured, linking her arm with mine. 'Stop them speculating.'

She led me over to the table, where two women with the same dark hair as Lily and her brother were sitting with glasses of wine and a giant bowl of crisps.

'Iris, Violet, meet Emmie.'

'Pasty Girl!' Violet beamed, patting the bench beside her. She was more angular than her sisters, with short hair curling over high cheekbones that accentuated grey eyes. She wore white, baggy combat trousers and a red crop top that managed to look both comfortable and dressy. 'Come and sit down, tell us everything. We're dying to hear what antics our darling brother got up to on the mainland.'

At that point, a man appeared with a tray of drinks.

'Ladies.' He sat down beside Iris, kissing her on the top of her head before handing Lily a lemonade.

'This lady has a name,' Iris said, pointedly. 'It's Emmie, and she's about to tell us all Pip's wild student secrets.'

Iris's wavy hair reached almost to the waist of her flowery smock dress. She had blue eyes, like Lily, and Flora's sardonic smile.

'Emmie, this is Hugh, who I'm hoping to marry at some point, despite him spending more time with animals than me these days.'

Hugh handed me a glass of wine, raising a thick, sandy eyebrow. 'She's pretending to sulk because I had to cancel a day of wedding preparations to save a mare and her unborn foal from dying.' He gave his fiancée an unashamedly adoring glance. 'She's a farmer. We both know full well that if I'd chosen invitations and centrepieces over the horse, she'd have called off the engagement.'

Iris poked her tongue out at him.

'Anyway,' Violet said, 'back to Emmie telling us about Pip before he comes to find her.'

'Where is he?' Lily said. 'He's meant to be the guest of honour.'

Violet screwed up her face. 'Celine is showing him her "welcome home" present.'

'What's that – a tattoo of him riding Basil?'

'Basil is our black bull,' Violet told me.

'A scrapbook,' Iris said, wincing.

'Of what?' Hugh looked horrified. 'Pictures from when they were going out?'

'Pictures, ticket stubs. A dried flower from the bouquet he gave her. And not only from when they were going out. It starts with the programme from a school nativity.'

'That's even worse than a tattoo,' Lily said.

'I know.' Iris sighed. 'I tried to talk her out of it, suggested she got him a nice bottle of something, or a book. But she's decided the best way to get him back is to show she means business.'

Violet eyed me over the rim of her wine glass. 'Maybe she should have baked him something.'

As my face heated up in embarrassment, Pip and Celine emerged from the farmhouse's French doors, causing a flurry of shouts and whistles. Pip had swapped his usual checked shirt for a plain olive-green one, his cargo trousers for faded jeans.

My heart leapt even as my stomach shrivelled at the sight of him with Celine.

She wore a tiny white dress with a floaty skirt and sandals. A portion of her wavy hair was twisted into a braid around the crown of her head. She could have walked straight off a photo shoot for a countryside magazine.

'Celine giving you a proper island welcome home, was she?' a younger man standing beside Barnie called.

Pip gave him a sharp stare, before breaking into a grin as Jack and Beanie dived at his legs, balancing on a foot each while he dragged them over to our table, the dogs prancing alongside them.

'Sisters. Hugh.' There was a microsecond-long pause when his eyes met mine. 'Emmie. I'm glad you could make it.'

I tried a smile as the children detached themselves and he eased in beside me on the bench. 'Well, I did have to cancel a few other things, but, you know. I heard the pot sausage was unmissable.'

'I told her!' Jack announced, before he and Beanie raced off again.

'Here.' Celine arrived, handing Pip a bottle of beer before squeezing in on his other side. I edged as close to Violet as I could, but his hip still rested against mine, the situation continuing to be lovely and awful at the same time.

Pip twisted around slightly to face me. 'How have you enjoyed your first day on the island?'

'It was really nice.' Nice. *Not exactly scintillating conversation, Emmie.* I tried harder. 'I had a haggling lesson from Lily at the farmers' market this morning over pasty ingredients, then spent the afternoon exploring Port Cathan.'

'You're making pasties already?' His eyes gleamed. I had to look away.

'Hi, Emmie.' Celine leant forwards to offer me a smile. 'I presumed you wouldn't be coming this evening, seeing as your trip has nothing to do with Pip. What changed your mind?'

'Lily invited me,' I mumbled.

'Oh, my goodness,' Celine continued, clearly uninterested in my answer. 'Pip, you should have seen the pickle Emmie got into earlier. She only went and fell asleep on the beach, right by the shoreline when the tide was coming in. All her things washing out to sea and she didn't even notice. The first she knew of it was when Pigeon helped himself to her panini.'

She burst into giggles, head gently bouncing on Pip's shoulder.

'Pigeon ate your lunch?' Pip didn't reply to Celine, but he didn't move away, either.

'I bought her a lobster roll, it's all good.'

Lily, who'd been chatting to Iris, leant across the table to get her brother's attention. 'Hey, why don't you introduce Emmie to Ma and Da?'

'Ooh, yes,' Iris added. 'Mammaw makes it her personal business to vet every newcomer to a family occasion.'

'Would you mind?' Pip asked me.

Would I mind leaving the awkwardness of the Pip sandwich? I moved so quickly, I nearly knocked my glass over.

As we wandered over to the barbecue, Pip bent his head towards mine. 'I hope Celine wasn't rude. We used to go out, years ago, and she can get a bit protective.'

He wrinkled his brow when I didn't answer. 'Ah. She was rude. I'm sorry.'

'She wasn't rude, just… protective is probably the best word for it.'

'Anyway.' Pip straightened up as we approached a man who was clearly the source of the Hawkins siblings' dark hair. 'This is my da, Gabe. Da, this is Emmie.'

For a second, it looked as though Gabe was going to smile, say hello, do any of the normal things a person did when introduced to someone. But when he looked at me, he froze, his mouth hanging open as a blob of fat dripped off the barbecue tongs onto his trousers.

'Da?' Pip said, loudly, causing Gabe to jump.

'I'm sorry,' Gabe said, his voice hoarse. 'You look very much like someone I used to know.'

'Oh?' Apprehension skittered up my spine. It was my turn to go still.

'Yes.' His eyes welled up, head shaking slightly as if he couldn't believe his eyes. He waited for his son to be distracted by someone else coming over to say hello, then bent towards me so that no one else could hear. 'Her name was Nellie Brown.'

13

Before I could recover myself, a plump woman with a flyaway silver bob hustled over, handing Gabe a platter of raw burgers.

'The pot sausage is all ready to go.' She slid her arms around Pip's waist and gave him a squeeze. 'I'm still pinching myself that you're home.'

'You'd think I'd been off into space, not an hour's flight away. I was always going to come back after two years. You know the main reason I went was to help the farm.'

'The mainland has a habit of convincing people to change their plans. And it doesn't matter how far you go; I can never quite settle when one of my children is off the island.'

'Well, I'm here now, so you can relax and enjoy the party. This is Emmie, who makes the pasties. She happened to be visiting, so Lily invited her along. Emmie, this is my ma, Rosemary.'

'I didn't know you knew Lily.' Rosemary gave a surprised smile as she unwound her arms from Pip and shook my hand.

I let Pip explain how I'd ended up at Sunflower Barn, Gabe's revelation still reverberating through my head.

He'd started transferring the burgers onto the barbecue, but while I watched him, he glanced up at me, the intensity in his eyes removing any trace of doubt that I'd stumbled upon the G from the letters. I tried to recollect the photograph, and while I couldn't be sure it was him, it certainly could be. Gabe was tall like his son, his frame wiry. His face had that tanned, craggy look resulting from a life spent outdoors in the elements. He had a thick beard, trimmed with grey, and the deep lines around his eyes implied he smiled often.

Once the burgers were sizzling away, Gabe called over to a man sitting alone at a table. 'Richard, would you mind watching the food for a few minutes?'

That confirmed it – G had spoken about a Richard in one of the letters.

Richard shook his head in resignation, but picked up a crutch with each hand and hauled himself up. In contrast to most of the men, who wore smart shorts or cotton trousers and shirts, Richard wore tatty brown cords and a beige T-shirt. He was broader than his brother, his beard more scraggly, but had the same piercing eyes.

'Emmie, would you like another drink?' Gabe asked, the faintest tremble of nerves lurking behind his question.

'Yes, please.'

'I'll fetch it,' Rosemary offered.

'No, my love. You've got enough to do. And my brother has far too little. Let him do this for me.'

I don't know how I made it to the drinks table. Avoiding the alcohol, I took the nearest soft drink. Gabe grabbed a bottle of beer, but instead of returning to the barbecue, gestured with his head towards a pond in the corner of the garden.

Neither of us spoke until he'd stopped by a bench and we sat down.

'You're related to her, aren't you?' Gabe asked, his voice soft enough not to be overheard. 'If the resemblance hadn't given it away, your reaction would have.'

'I'm her daughter.' I took a sip of lemonade, hoping it might ease the nausea threatening to rise up the back of my throat.

Gabe nodded. 'I thought you must be. Although, I'm somewhat stunned. She was always so adamant she never wanted a child. I mean... no offence. She clearly changed her mind.'

'No, you're right. She didn't, really. But then, I arrived, and she was never going to shy away from her responsibility.'

'That's true.' He glanced at me. 'If I may ask... how is Nellie?'

'She died almost two years ago.'

Gabe fell against the back of the bench, his face appearing to fold in on itself for a few seconds, before he straightened up, rubbing a hand over his beard.

'Do you mind telling me what happened?'

'It was sudden. A brain embolism.'

'I'm so very sorry. That must have been tremendously difficult.'

I swallowed hard, remembering the constant ache of raw grief.

'How did you know her? I... I found some letters. From a G.'

Gabe blinked a few times. 'I can't believe she kept them.' He shook his head. 'But yes, they were from me. They will explain better than I ever could who we were to each other.'

'I've only read the first three. I won't keep going if you'd rather I didn't.'

He dropped his gaze to the pond, clearly deep in memories. A school of tadpoles were trying out their new legs, wriggling amongst the water weeds.

'Did she tell you about me?'

'She never spoke about her past, or her family. I don't even know if she had any real friends.'

'That must be hard, if it's just you now.'

I nodded. 'That's partly why I came. Not to dig up anything, but I thought being here might help me process some of it.'

It seemed a ridiculous coincidence that I'd stumbled across G on my first full day here. But there were three thousand people on this island, narrow that down to the right age and gender, and how many of them were farmers, and it would probably be more unlikely for me *not* to bump into Mum's mystery man at some point.

'Did you know she named her business Parsley's?'

Gabe looked at me blankly.

'It was the name of your bull. You mentioned it in the first letter.'

He furrowed his brow. 'Parsley? I should remember that. It sounds about right, though. We've always named them after herbs and such. I'd never have guessed, given what happened.'

'Oh?'

'Read the letters. They should fill in some gaps. And if you call in another day, I'll find the ones she sent in return.'

'She wrote back?'

His mouth twitched. 'Not half as often as I wrote to her. But there's one or two.'

'That's so kind of you. Thank you.'

'One more thing, if you'd be so kind.' He stood up, slowly. 'Would you mind not mentioning to anyone what you read there? Especially Rosemary or my children. This is a close community, with long memories. It wasn't an easy time for my family, and I don't want to dredge up old pain.'

'Do you think anyone else will recognise who I am?'

We started slowly walking back to where people were now serving up dishes of food.

'If my mother was much younger, then possibly, but her

memory's not so good these days. And no one else will have known Nellie's face like I did.'

'Do you still think about her?'

He gave me a rueful flick of his eyebrows. 'Read the letters.'

* * *

We joined the disorderly queue loading up with food. Pot sausage, it turned out, was hot-dog sausages smothered in fried onions and peppers and a smoky home-made ketchup, topped with a layer of crispy sliced potatoes and melted cheese. I helped myself to a generous spoonful and added some salad and a piece of fish, which Gabe insisted I sample due to it having been freshly caught that morning by his neighbour.

'Come and sit with Mammaw.' Pip was waiting at the end of the buffet to lead me to a round table positioned in the shade of the house. Richard was there, along with a couple who introduced themselves as Iris's fiancé, Hugh's parents, and the ninety-one-year-old grandmother.

'Mammaw, this is Emmie, who makes the pasties,' Pip said. 'Remember I told you she's here on holiday?'

'I certainly do remember,' she replied, her accent so strong, I had to concentrate to decipher the words. Despite her age, she appeared at least as tall as her granddaughters, with straight shoulders beneath a woollen cardigan and a determined tilt to her pointy chin. 'But did I forget you describing what a looker she is?'

Pip winced. 'No, I didn't happen to mention that.'

'You seem familiar.' She craned forwards to where I'd gingerly sat down beside Pip. 'Have you been to the Island before?'

'I haven't, no.' I glanced over to where Gabe had found a seat with his wife.

Mammaw narrowed her hooded eyelids as she stabbed at a tiny piece of fish. She didn't look convinced.

'Maybe you've seen me at Sherwood Airport, where I run my pasty kiosk? All the island flights land there.'

'Only time I've left Siskin is on a boat. And that would have been long before you were born. Is she replacing that other one, then, Philip? I thought I saw her still sniffing around.'

'Mammaw...' If Pip slumped any lower in his chair, he'd disappear under the table. 'Celine is only a friend. You know that.'

'Are you sure she knows?' Richard said in a rough voice, his eyes on the plate in front of him.

'Emmie is here on holiday. I've not brought her home to meet the family.'

'What do you call this, then?' Mammaw tipped her chin even higher.

Pip closed his eyes briefly, then hunched over his plate, picked up his burger with both hands and took a large bite.

'Did he warn you about this?' Hugh's mum, sitting on my left side, said with a humorous twinkle. 'Don't mind a word Aster says; she's a born troublemaker.'

Aster carried on eating her fish, a satisfied smirk on her face.

The table chatted about this and that, whether it would rain any time soon, Lander's cows escaping yet again, the market price of crab. It was hard not to keep searching out Gabe. My stomach was still knotted up from discovering who G was. At one point, Celine drifted over, but when no one offered her a seat, she left again. As the sun began to sink below the house, someone started strumming a guitar, and within moments, people playing a violin and bodhran had joined them. Rosemary handed Richard an accordion, and as he played, he sang a slow sea shanty, his voice blending with others to create a haunting sound that carried us away from a lovely garden bathed in late-evening sunshine to misty coves, murky depths and foam spraying against a fishing boat's prow as it braved the wild, blue yonder.

When they upped the tempo, a few people got up and began a whirling sort of jig including plenty of kicks reminiscent of Irish dancing.

'Aren't you going to invite your guest to dance?' Aster asked, her knuckles tapping out the rhythm on the tabletop.

Pip looked at me with a shy smile, his eyebrows raised in question.

'I wouldn't know what to do,' I said. Even the younger children were seamlessly spinning amongst the adults, flicking their shins up in near perfect time.

'I can lead you.' Pip held out his hand.

The only time I ever danced in public was when Blessing dragged me onto the dance floor at the airport Christmas party. I usually lasted for about three excruciating pop classics before pretending I needed a wee.

But that was the old Emmie, who stuck to the recipes and always arrived at work on time. Who allowed a stifling combination of fear and duty to control her every move.

I wondered if the evening's bombshells could have blown old Emmie to smithereens.

Could I do it? Could I dance? Risk making a fool of myself in front of Pip, his family and the woman determined to win his hand?

But right now, that hand was being offered to me. How could I resist it?

We slid into the wide circle of dancers, me gripping onto Pip as if my life depended on it. Feeling someone else take my other hand, I turned to find Gabe beside me. It made sense that Pip would position me next to someone I'd already met, but it didn't help in my attempts not to stumble. As the bodhran thumped a furious beat, we stomped and spun, I was passed from one hand to another, around and in and out of the circle but always returning to Pip's flushed cheeks, glowing gaze and firm grip.

'Okay?' he asked as the tune came to an end with a final flourish, the circle breaking apart to clap and cheer and bend over with hands on hips, gasping for breath.

I nodded, my own lungs heaving, but as the band struck up the opening notes of the next reel, Pip leant close to my ear and suggested we take a break, asking if I'd like to see more of the farm.

We had to move well away from the raucous dance floor before it was quiet enough to ask if it was okay for him to abandon the party.

He scanned the garden, those guests not dancing all deep in conversation, or, in the case of Iris and Hugh, entwined in a hammock, rocking gently beneath the emerging stars.

'No one will miss me.'

I didn't think that was completely true. Celine was talking to Lily and Violet, but her head was twisted in our direction. For obvious reasons, I wasn't about to point that out.

Pip led me across the lawn to the pond, winding around the side to a gate leading into a meadow beyond.

'Are we going to need a torch?' I asked, aware of the lengthening shadows. 'You know where you're going, but I'm only a mainlander, remember?'

Opening the gate, Pip waited for me to walk through then came alongside me. 'It's fine; we're following a proper path.' He then paused. 'But I hadn't thought about you feeling uncomfortable going for a walk with me if it gets dark... We could see if anyone else wants to come?'

'No, it's fine,' I replied, quickly. Any nervousness at being alone in the deepening dusk with Pip had nothing to do with feeling unsafe. 'As long as I don't accidentally step off the edge of the cliff and drown.'

'Nah,' Pip said, with a playful grin. 'You'd smash to bits on the rocks before you had a chance to drown.'

'That's okay, then.'

His smile softened. 'I'll keep you safe, don't worry.'

I absolutely believed he would. But, for all sorts of reasons, that made it impossible to relax.

We wandered along the edge of the meadow, on a dry, dusty path sloping gradually downwards towards the coast. Pip showed me the neighbouring fields where the cows and Basil the bull lived, weather permitting.

'They're grass-fed, so need more space, but the produce is worth it.'

'You use the calves for beef?'

'We do.'

'Do you eat it yourself?'

He frowned. 'I'm a farmer, Emmie. I wouldn't raise cattle if I wasn't prepared to consume the products. Although...' he ducked his head, sheepish '...that doesn't mean I don't take myself off for a wee cry every time we send them to the abattoir, mind.'

'What else do you farm?'

'Free-range chickens, we've a small pear orchard that goes to Siskin cider, and a few different vegetables and grain depending on the season, crop rotation, that kind of thing. Oh, and the sunflowers for the tourists. We do pick your own through August and most of September. It's humiliating how much profit that makes compared to the crops we harvest ourselves.'

We reached a stile at the end of the field, and he took my hand to help me down, as the far side was swathed in shadow. To my secret delight, as we began descending a steep path made up of broad, sandy steps, he didn't let go.

'We hear a lot about farmers struggling to make ends meet. Is it the same on the island?'

'For some. Most are coming up with ways to make it work, though, like with the sunflowers. We'll have more breathing room once the bed and breakfast is running. Lily will pay the farm a share of the profits, instead of taking out a mortgage. Intensive farming has never been an option here, so it's always been a careful balance between a business that's viable now and sustainable long-term.'

He chatted for a while about some of the ideas he'd picked up from his master's course about Smart Agriculture, occasionally breaking off to point out a landmark, a nearby dwelling or a wild animal enjoying the dusk.

Even with my limited understanding, it was clear that farming was fraught with difficult choices, further complicated by the whims of Irish Sea weather, and mainland food fads.

What was also clear was how deeply engrained this life was in Pip, and how passionately he cared about ensuring his family legacy survived for generations to come. I understood how a family business was about so much more than earning a living.

'You must have missed it while you were studying.'

He laughed. 'I didn't miss the early starts or the long days. I was also happy to forgo the biting winds and endless autumn drizzle. But when I walk across our land, knowing that all of it has been built by my ancestors' hands. Glancing up at the sky and instinctively interpreting the shade of blue or smear of grey. The song of the sea and looking out across 40,000 square miles of open water. Aye. I missed it. Here.'

We went through another, small wooden gate, beyond which the path turned sharply to the right, and there, only a dozen broad steps below us, was a tiny cove, inky waves lapping against the pale crescent of sand.

'Is this part of the farm?' I asked, slowing down to take it in. The sun had disappeared below the horizon while we walked, leaving fading streaks of rose-gold above the furthest stretches of water. To one side, rockpools glinted. Directly overhead, more stars had begun to appear.

We slipped our shoes off, sinking into sand that was cool and damp. Pip opened a storage box tucked against the rocks and brought out a picnic blanket, a bottle of Hawkins perry cider and two plastic glasses.

'Did you plan this?' I blurted, my heart accelerating. 'Is it something you do with all the mainlander women?'

Pip looked at me in mock horror. 'What, offer them a tour of the farm and then lure them down here, ply them with cider and then… and then I don't know what, because you're the first mainlander I've brought here. Any island woman knows full well what lies at the end of the path.'

'A bottle of cider and a blanket?'

'Usually a bonfire, or a cricket match. Maybe some crabbing in the rockpools. Ma and Da generally keep a stash here this time of year. If we'd been lucky, there'd have been crisps or biscuits too.' He smiled. 'If I'd planned it, there'd have been strawberries and fine wine, not farm leftovers.'

We settled on the blanket and Pip poured the cider. A gust of wind off the water made me shiver, so he slipped off his shirt and draped it around my shoulders, leaving him in a short-sleeved, white T-shirt.

'Now you'll be cold,' I said, taking a sip.

'Nah. Once you've slept out here in March, a June breeze is nothing.'

We sat for a while, admiring the picture-perfect view. Beside me, Pip's forearms rested on his bent knees, his glass catching the shimmer from the half-moon now sailing above our heads. It was wonderfully still, yet my body was far from peaceful, due to being deliciously, painfully aware of the proximity of the man next to me, close enough to feel his body heat and catch the faint tang of barbecue smoke.

It was undoubtedly the most beautiful, thrilling, nerve-jangling moment of my life.

After a while, I found the courage to sneak a glance to the side, and found him gazing at me.

'Sorry.' He jerked his head forwards, blinking rapidly as he shifted on the blanket. 'I still can't believe you're actually here.'

'Tell me about it.'

'Any idea when you'll be heading back home?'

'There'll be a hefty fine if Parsley's isn't open next Sunday, unless I get permission from the big boss, which isn't likely considering my only excuse is a stunning view and great company.'

I didn't add that the fine was starting to seem worth it.

14

After chatting a little longer, I was unable to suppress my third giant yawn, so we tidied up and started the trek back uphill. When I got my phone out to use as a torch, I found a text.

'Lily says they're heading home, so they'll leave the door unlocked for me. That was just before ten, so almost twenty minutes ago.'

'I'll cycle back with you,' Pip said.

'You don't have to,' I protested. 'This is meant to be your big night.'

'The party will be winding down now. This is a late night for a farmer. I can either hang about watching everyone clear up, feeling guilty because there's no way they will let me help, or I can do something useful, and see you safely to the barn.'

'That's very kind of you. But given the state of my cycling in the daylight when I didn't have half a bottle of cider sloshing around in my system, I will be pushing not riding the bike. It'll take a lot longer.'

'I'm in no hurry. If you're not going to ride it, leave the bike. I'll drop it over in the morning. Hang on, I'll let Ma know so she doesn't send out a search party.'

'Won't this make things even worse?' I asked, after he'd sent the message and we continued on in the direction of the barn instead of turning towards the garden.

'Make what worse?' Pip asked, puzzled.

'You being with me, instead of at the party. Walking me back. Your family are already convinced there's something going on between us.'

Pip stopped, turning to face me. After an embarrassed moment, I dared to look up at him.

'Isn't there?' He gripped the back of his neck with one hand, and I realised I wasn't the only one feeling nervous.

'I... I don't know.'

'Okay. Well... would you like there to be?'

'I...' I stalled, wanting to say yes more than anything. Except, how could I, now I knew something huge had happened between Gabe and my mum? 'The past couple of days have been a lot. Brilliant – but very disorienting, for all sorts of reasons. I could decide that while I'm being reckless, why not go all out, have a holiday romance? But I'm not quite my old self right now. And I'm not confident enough in this new Emmie to know whether it's something she'll regret.'

Pip looked steadily at me, his brow furrowed. 'I wasn't referring to a holiday romance.'

My heart plunged into the pit of my stomach. *Had he been talking about friendship? Pasty making?*

'Emmie, I really like you. I thought that clumsy excuse about craving a pasty last week made it obvious. I know my family are making daft assumptions. My life is here, yours is over there. But whatever this is, whatever it could be...' He stopped, shaking his head as he glanced away, then turned back again. 'I'm not the kind of man who messes about with mainlander flings.'

'So what did you mean by something going on, if we don't want a holiday thing? Neither of us have time for anything long-distance.'

After a long moment, he sighed. 'I don't know what I meant.'

'Well, that's that then, isn't it?' I said, my hammering pulse protesting otherwise. Here I was, standing in the moonlight, listening to the man I'd been dreaming about for two years tell me that he liked me, and I was somehow talking him out of anything going on between us. 'There's nothing going on.'

* * *

We were nearly back at the barn when Pip spoke again.

'I hope that doesn't mean we can't hang out as friends.'

'Of course!' I said, cringing at how keen I sounded. 'I'd love to see more of the island while I'm here, if you have time to show me. Plus, you've got to try Lily's pasties.'

'And I'll drop the bike back tomorrow.'

'I'll come and get the bike.'

'Are you sure?'

'I'll enjoy the walk.'

It was the only decent excuse I had for returning to the farm, and I was desperate to ask Gabe for Mum's letters.

'Tell you what, come at lunchtime and I'll show you the best spot on the island.'

'You won't be working?'

He grinned, broadening his accent as he replied. 'Sure, us island men need to eat. I'll pack us a traditional island picnic.'

'Okay. One o'clock?'

To my disappointment, we'd reached the barn driveway.

'Perfect. I'll say goodnight here, if you don't mind. I'd bet Basil's horns on my big sister spying on us from her bedroom window.'

He looked up at the attic and blew a jaunty kiss before giving me a wink and a nod that made my breath catch, then he disappeared into the night.

* * *

Every muscle in my body groaned with exhaustion, but thoughts were fizzing about in my head like fireworks. I got ready for bed, mixed a hot chocolate and reached for the letters, safely stored in the bedside table.

This time, I could picture the man who had written it, hear the words as if he'd spoken them out loud in his measured rumble.

Meeting Gabe had changed everything.

4 April 1986

My darling wife, Nellie

(or at least, you will be by the time you read this)

I write this letter sitting at your friend Christopher's kitchen table, counting the minutes until we meet at the register office, and our real life can begin.

The last few days have been like paradise on earth. I'd thought that nothing could beat waking up to the island birdsong, watching the seals playing in the waves while I drink my tea. But now I know better. When you smile and hand me a mug of coffee, it's like being greeted by an angel.

And now I get to share every morning with you, for the rest of my life.

A simple man like me can't find the words to express how grateful I am. I only pray that I can make you half as happy.

You try not to show it, but I know you're worried about my family, what they'll think about all this. Fear not, my angel, they will surely love you once they get to know you. And don't fret about the farm. If that work doesn't suit you, there's always a café or hotel in need of good staff. Who knows, maybe one day you could open a wee restaurant of your own?

What I mean to say is – whatever the future brings, we will have a good life, because we will be together. I willingly lay the independence I guarded so fiercely at your feet, and admit I cannot live without you. Nellie Brown – Nellie Hawkins! – I will do whatever it takes to make you as blessed to be my wife as I am to become your husband.

And now I must stop wittering because the taxi is waiting.
With faith, hope and love,
Forever and only yours,
G

* * *

The flood of panic when I woke up on Saturday and the clock on the wall said ten past eleven was instinctive. I leapt out of bed, hands tugging at my hair as I cursed myself for oversleeping, bewildered as to how it had happened. What would Lily and Malcolm think at me getting up so late? I'd have to skip the mug of tea I'd hoped to enjoy in bed, jump in and out of the shower rather than washing my hair…

And then I stopped. Closed my eyes. Breathed. Reminded myself where I was.

This was meant to be a break from all of that.

I had nothing to do and nowhere to be until I met Pip for lunch.

Literally, the only things I had to do between now and then were drink tea, eat breakfast and get myself ready.

The panic subsided to a functional level, but not enough to stop me hurrying downstairs only fifteen minutes later, a lifetime of busyness snapping at my heels.

'Emmie!' Jack announced when I appeared in the kitchen, dropping the aeroplane he'd been playing with. 'Mammy said we had to wait for you to help us collect the eggs. I was starting to think you were going to sleep for one hundred years like Sleeping Beauty.'

'Jack!' Lily looked up from where she and Beanie were baking at the kitchen worktop, Beanie wearing a home-made paper mask that I suspected was meant to be a mole. 'Emmie's on holiday. I told you, she can sleep in for as long as she likes.'

'All I'm saying is I'm glad she got up now because waiting is boring.' Jack had already slipped on his left Croc.

'You're going to have to wait even longer, I'm sorry to say. Emmie is a guest of Sunflower Barn Bed and Breakfast, so she gets breakfast.'

'I can help with the eggs first,' I said.

'Nonsense. How would that be us testing out the system?' Lily dusted off her hands on a cloth. 'You can either sit outside, or in the dining room, madam. Which would you prefer?'

'I'd prefer not to be called madam,' I joked before I could stop myself.

'Great!' Lily hurried around to a large whiteboard hanging up on one wall and wrote, 'Do not call guests madam. Is miss any better?' She stuck the pen in her mouth and chewed on it for a moment. 'I can't afford to insult the mainlanders by getting these things wrong. It's so long since I've been over, I forget all the cultural stuff.'

'I'm not offended. It's just a bit formal. And implies I'm either old or married. Miss is only really for teachers or naughty children. I think a welcoming, homely place like this would do better with someone's name.'

'Emmie, I'm very pregnant. I already have three kids. I can't be trusted to remember my own name, let alone anyone else's.' She gave me a side-on look. 'You are Emmie, aren't you? If not, I'll have to stick with Pasty Girl.'

'Emmie, Emmaline, Hey You. I really don't mind.'

'Mammaw called her "Pip's New Girl",' Jack said. 'You could try that.'

'That's not really a solution when it comes to other guests,' Lily said, frowning at the whiteboard.

'Yeah, we can't assume he's going to date *every* woman who stays here now he's ditched Celine,' Flora said, lolling on the sofa with a different book.

'Um, he's not dating me,' I pointed out in a tiny voice.

'Yet.' She smirked.

'Ever,' I said, gaining courage, because these rumours were torture. 'I'll be back on the mainland soon. It's not practical for us to date when we live so far away from each other. Especially when neither of us get much time off.'

Flora shook her head, eyes gleaming behind the book. 'Was it practical for Elizabeth Bennet to fall in love with Mr Darcy? Bella to insist she married Edward? Romeo to romance Juliet?'

'Romeo and Juliet both ended up dead, so…'

Lily grinned. 'Well, putting aside whether Pip and Emmie are going to admit they're in love and start dating for the moment; there's eggs to collect, and breakfast to eat. So, *Emmie who is not Pip's girl*—'

'Yet,' Flora, Jack and Beanie whispered all at the same time.

'Would you like to have breakfast outside or in the dining room? Oh, and how would you like your eggs?'

I ate my scrambled eggs on home-made sourdough toast outside, hoping the tranquil view would enable me to regain composure before setting off to meet my never-would-be-boyfriend for a picnic lunch that wasn't in the slightest bit a date.

15

Rosemary opened the farmhouse door, looking very different from the night before in denim dungarees patched with random swatches of fabric, a Breton T-shirt and frayed bandana keeping her bob out of the way.

'Oh, Pip's friend.' She gave a broad smile. 'We weren't sure how long you'd be staying. Not many self-employed folk can shut up shop and take a little jaunt without very good reason. Unless you have someone managing the restaurant while you're gone?'

'It's a kiosk, not a restaurant, so I work by myself these days.'

'Right, well, how very lovely to be able to come and go as you please, without anyone else moaning about it.' She gave me a nudge with a knowing chuckle. 'The last holiday Gabe and I had was our honeymoon, and he spent the whole four days fretting about the animals. I think he missed them more than the children when they were away at school. Still, such is a farmer's lot. Wed to the land, wife a mere mistress.'

'Maybe you can take a break now Pip is home?'

'I wouldn't hold my breath. Violet and Iris have been godsends, but Iris will be helping Hugh's parents with their horses once she's married, and Violet was always more of a sailor than a farmer. Gabe would be the last to admit it, but he's slower than he used to be. Even with Pip, there's a lot of catching up to do. To be honest with you, Emmie, I'm not sure how much longer we'd have been able to carry on without him. It's hard enough scraping a living these days. Not having our son to help shoulder the burden doesn't bear thinking about. Anyways.' She rested a hand on my arm. 'Here's me waffling on. Were you here to pick up the bike?'

'Yes. Although I was hoping to say hello to Gabe, if that's okay?'

Rosemary squinted one eye. 'Oh?'

'I'm looking for a new egg supplier and he offered to give me some advice.'

It was the best lie I could come up with on the spur of the moment.

'Right. Well. Violet's sorting the eggs today. Gabe is picking strawberries. Across the yard, past the cowshed on the right and you'll see him.'

'Thank you.'

'I'll leave the bike by the far gate for when you're done. And don't let Gabe drone on too long about those chickens. He forgets that not many people are obsessed with farming like him and Pip. Not when there's the bonniest island in the British Isles to explore. Take the bike, have some fun. You should make the most of your time here.'

'Thank you. Pip promised to show me a nice picnic spot, so I'll pick the bike up after that.'

'Did he now? How lovely. I suppose the north fence will wait until another day.'

She said goodbye and I left, trying to ignore the twinge of guilt about stealing Pip away from his responsibilities so soon after he'd arrived.

* * *

I took the short walk to the farmyard, grateful for Lily's insistence that I brought wellington boots as I skirted the worst of the mud while passing the pungent cowsheds – empty in the summertime – out the other side to where a short path led across a scrubby stretch of grass to what must be the strawberry patch.

'Ah, hello.' Gabe straightened up from where he was picking fruit in one of the middle rows, alerted by the dogs bounding up to greet me. He took off his cap, wiped the sweat off his forehead, replacing it with a streak of dirt, and picked up the container he'd been using to collect the strawberries.

'Not the best crop we've had, but they're more for pleasure than business. Don't tell Rosemary that, mind. She's very proud of her award-winning jam. Lily used to charge twenty pence extra for it in her cream teas, back when she was running the café. Here.' He plucked one of the larger fruits and offered it to me, giving a nod of satisfaction when I took a bite, releasing a burst of juicy sweetness that made my taste buds tingle with pleasure.

'No substitute for freshly picked.' Gabe held out the carton, and I couldn't resist accepting one more.

'It seems a waste to turn them into jam.'

'Oh, plenty enough are used fresh. We supply two of the cafés and the greengrocer's stall. Lily will be serving them with pancakes once she's open. Those too small, mishappen or whatnot will be jams, pies, sauce. Nothing wasted. Nor frozen, if we can help it, apart from ice cream. Here. Take these back to the barn with you.' He pulled a carrier bag out of his jeans pocket and filled it with a generous handful, which I tucked inside my bag. 'But before you go, the letters.'

We walked back to the farmhouse, Gabe pointing out what the different buildings were used for as we went. He pointed to one a short distance away from the farmyard, surrounded by relatively clean paving slabs, rather than muddy gravel.

'That's the Old Barn, the first Eber Hawkins built, back in 1746, after the great famine. Before then, Hawkinses were subsidence farmers, growing, fishing and hunting just enough to survive. But Eber had a dream, to leave something more for his children. All fourteen of them. He was the first to think beyond the next winter. Planted potatoes, beans and wheat. Gambled his fishing boat on a game of dice and won two horses, and three cows. By the time his son, Conan, took over, they had a herd of twenty suckler cows and the most sought-after bull on the island.'

'And now you have all this,' I said, loving the stories of the Hawkins history.

'Aye. But now it can too often feel like we're heading back to pre-Eber days. Scraping through one harvest to the next. It's the only reason Pip talked me into this fancy master's thing. I remembered how my father, Aster's husband, drove me to distraction with his refusal to move with the times.'

'Change isn't easy.'

'No, but I decided it has to be easier than watching my stubborn pride destroy what Eber started, and everything the Hawkinses have built since.' He waved a hello to his wife, hanging out wet washing in the garden, all trace of the previous night's revelry vanished from the lawn and patio.

'I told her I wanted your advice about free-range-egg suppliers,' I said as he opened the kitchen door and we slipped off our boots, the Labradors waiting patiently while he wiped their paws with a threadbare towel.

'Very good. As long as they've got the Lion Code, RSPCA and all that, you'll be grand.'

'Brilliant.'

'If Rosemary asks you about it, tell her I rambled on so long, you stopped listening.' He led me through the kitchen into an office space, where piles of papers covered a desk made from an old door. Unlocking a filing cabinet, he flicked through various folders until pulling out one labelled, *Relocating sewage tank*.

'It was the most off-putting title I could think of.'

Opening it up, Gabe pulled out a stash of papers, in the middle of which was a plain brown envelope, which he held out to me.

'I presume you want them back?' The way he gripped onto the envelope for a brief second before allowing me to take it was enough of a clue.

'Yes. If you don't mind. And if you have any questions, well… I'm always more than happy to discuss chickens, eggs, cows and crops with those who're interested.'

'Thank you.'

'There you are.' Rosemary appeared in the doorway. 'Have you finished picking the strawberries already? Because there's a plate of party leftovers waiting for lunch.'

'No, my love. I'll head back over after this delicious lunch you've prepared.' Gabe gave her a tender smile, waving at the filing cabinet. 'I wanted to find the name of that new breed of layers Pip was talking about. It's not too far from Emmie. They grow some plant that makes the yolks darker, if I recall correctly.'

He carried on mumbling as we walked back to the kitchen and Gabe took a seat at the table beside Aster, who had opened up a sandwich and was scowling at the contents.

'It's you.' She gave me a dismissive glance. 'Back already?'

'I came to ask Gabe's advice about chickens.'

She gave the food a sniff before folding the bread down again. 'Must be keen.'

That was enough to make me want to crawl beneath my chair and hide, but Aster wasn't finished. 'Just mind out, Philip is an island farmer. He'll not be happy anywhere else. Forget chickens, try asking Gabriel's advice on that.'

She looked up, eyes cool as they assessed me. Finally, after a small, satisfied nod, she focused back on her sandwich.

I didn't want to think too hard about what that nod meant. Gabe merely smiled wryly as he shook his head. 'Emmie's not here to steal Pip away, Ma. And even if she was, he's got no intention of abandoning the farm. Don't fret.'

Aster took a large bite of her sandwich. She wasn't the one fretting here.

I was declining their offer of a meal for the third time when the front door banged open and a moment later, Pip appeared, the dogs dancing around his legs as though this were his grand homecoming, rather than two days earlier.

'Just in time for lunch,' Rosemary said. 'I've got your favourite cider chutney.'

'Ah, sorry, Ma.' Pip eyed the plate of meat, bread and salad on the kitchen worktop and put an arm around his mother. 'I've picked up a hamper from Dahlia's.'

'Ooh, hark at you. Two years at an English university and now you're shopping like a tourist. Those hampers cost a lot more than my leftovers. Caroline told me they decant cheap, imported factory produce into fancy packaging and stick on a sprig of garnish to make it seem posh.'

While his mum was talking, Pip spotted me lurking in the doorway to the office. His sudden enormous grin was impossible not to reciprocate, despite how it caused Rosemary to abruptly stop talking as Gabe carried on eating, seemingly oblivious.

'Have you been waiting long?' He checked his watch. 'It's only quarter to.'

'I was asking your dad about egg suppliers. I'm thinking of getting a new one.'

'Oh.' Pip looked slightly taken aback. 'You could have asked me. I know a lot of Nottinghamshire farmers.'

'Of course you do – I don't know why I didn't think of that. It was more some general advice really, rather than specifics. I mentioned it last night, so Gabe offered to have a chat next time I was here.'

'Right. Well. If you give me a couple of minutes, I need to change.'

Pip disappeared, and after a minute of hovering while Gabe and Aster ate and Rosemary topped up Aster's drink and offered her husband more chicken, another pickled onion, a slice of fruit cake, I mumbled an excuse and went to wait outside in the sunshine, donning my trainers instead of the boots.

'Sorry if that was awkward.' Pip reappeared a short while later, his muddy cargo trousers and grimy shirt replaced with a pair of grey shorts and pristine, pale-blue T-shirt. 'As far as island mothers are concerned, there's no greater insult than spurning their home-cooked meal for something shop-bought.'

He held up a small picnic basket.

'I suppose she wants to spoil you after being apart for so long.' We began walking in the opposite direction to the day before, back towards the strawberry patch, only this time weaving around the side of the yard rather than straight through it. 'I would have been happy with leftovers. The food last night was fantastic.'

'High praise indeed from the owner of Parsley's.' Pip smiled. 'I'll be sure to pass your compliments to the chefs.'

He paused as we reached a stile, allowing me to go first. Anticipating some rugged terrain, I'd worn shorts rather than a dress, and it was the right choice. As we wound towards the edge of the cliff, frequent gusts whipped my hair out of its ponytail and flapped my new top. However, after about ten minutes of this, our conversation limited by the whistle of the wind and me having to concentrate on the narrow stony path, we turned a corner, curving around a slight hillock, and within seconds, I was looking at paradise.

Pip spread a blanket out at the base of the slope that was sheltered from the wind but not the sunshine, and we settled down to soak it in.

The grass around us was thick with flowers – I recognised willowherb, buttercups and the daisies and forget-me-nots from Mum's wedding bouquet – butterflies and bees dancing amongst the blossoms. Rather than a cliff-top, here the land sloped more gently down towards a wide strip of pale sand, beyond which lay the shimmering sea.

'Watch.'

Pip pointed to the sea on one side, taking hold of my shoulders and turning me slightly when I couldn't find what he was showing me, moving the arm that was pointing to only an inch from my jaw.

'Oh!'

I saw it then, a flash and a splash, then several more.

'Dolphins?'

'Porpoises. See the nose is blunter than a dolphin? If you want to spot a dolphin, we can walk to the northern coves another time. If you want to see a whale, we need to use the boat.'

I felt a warm glow at Pip's suggestion that we'd have more days like this. Combined with his hand, still resting gently on my shoulder, the proximity of his chest to my back, it did a good job of rattling my resolve to avoid a short-term something with him.

We watched the porpoises frolic through the waves until they disappeared into the distance. When Pip moved away, it felt as though the sun had gone behind a cloud.

'We'd better eat. I don't want Da thinking I've picked up slacker habits from you mainlanders.'

The hamper was full of food that definitely didn't taste mass-produced. Separate pots of tomato, potato and prawn salads, crusty rolls still faintly warm, which we smothered with salted butter and a crumbly cheese. A thick wedge of crab quiche and then tiny, tart raspberries served with a mini tub of clotted cream, washed down with cloudy lemonade. We were talking and laughing the whole time and, putting the location and the company together, it was, without a doubt, one of the best meals of my life.

Usually, I shied away from people asking me personal questions – it wasn't as if I had anything much to share beyond making pasties. The older I got, the more acutely I realised that most people viewed hearing about my odd upbringing with morbid fascination rather than genuine interest.

Given the insular nature of his own life, the solidarity with which Pip listened to my descriptions of Mum's uncompromising ways, sharing his own island stories, and the impact they had on his time at boarding school in return, made talking to him not only comfortable, but uplifting and at times even joyous.

Who knew how much a, 'Me too!' or a 'You think that's bad...' could mean?

I even found myself telling him what little I knew about my birth mother, which he responded to with such sincerity, I wept.

We spotted an osprey swooping, emerging from the sea with a fish glistening in its beak, and watched a family of rabbits. An older couple walking with a pair of red setters were the only people, except for yellow-clad figures on fishing boats and ferry passengers waving on their way to Ireland.

Sticky Formica tables, strip lights and LED screens felt like relics from a distant time.

'Ah, I have to go,' Pip said eventually, checking his watch. 'I can leave the blanket if you wanted to tarry a wee bit longer?'

'No, I'll come now.' I had a stash of letters in my bag, and needed to match them up with the others before I started reading.

We were quiet for most of the walk back. I couldn't guess Pip's thoughts, but hoped they might in some ways echo mine.

It seemed they did, when he paused by the farmhouse door.

'I have to get changed, then meet Da in the fields, if you're grand making your own way back from here?'

'Of course. Your mum said she'd leave the bike by the far gate. Is that the one near the pond?'

'Aye. That's it. Well. Enjoy the rest of your day, Emmie.' He looked away, hand gripping the back of his neck, which I was learning meant he felt nervous. 'I had a bonny time.'

'Me, too.' If *bonny* meant *the best two hours of my life so far*. 'Thanks so much for taking me.'

'So... would you maybe...? Sunday afternoons, we usually head to the beach. I mean, Lily's probably already mentioned it. I wouldn't want you to feel obligated to spend your whole time here with the Hawkinses... but, well. We swim, chuck a ball around. Light a bonfire when it cools down. You'd be very welcome, if you don't have any other plans.'

'That sounds amazing. I'd love to, thank you.'

He grinned, a twinge of pink blooming beneath the farmer's tan.

'Lily's bound to invite you too, so you don't have to bother about coming as Pip's girl.'

There was a part of me starting to feel more bothered that I *wouldn't* be her.

16

I floated across the lawn, waving my fingers at the tadpoles in the pond and nodding hello to a pair of ducks. The bike was where Rosemary had promised, and I grabbed on with gusto, looking forward to sailing back along the path to Sunflower Barn.

It took me a couple of seconds to notice that the handlebars were damp. Sticky, I realised as I snatched my hands away. I sniffed them, only to recoil in horror.

I had no idea what that stench was, but I imagined a dead fish had possibly been involved.

I dug through my bag for a tissue to try to wipe it off, then checked the rest of the bike. The saddle was splattered with the same liquid. Using the remains of my water bottle, I did my best to clean off the worst of the mess, but the lingering smell still triggered my gag reflex if I bent too close.

My buoyant mood evaporated. I wheeled the bike home, the return journey seeming far longer than it had previously, and not simply because it was alone and uphill.

Lily was heading out to pick the kids up from a birthday party when I arrived back.

She started to ask how lunch had been, before coming to an abrupt stop, whipping around and promptly vomiting in the nearest bush. I hastily wheeled the bike back to the furthest part of the drive, then fetched a glass of water and a napkin from the kitchen.

'What fresh hell *was* that?' Lily spluttered, gratefully accepting the water. 'Smells like you fell in a pile of rotting fish guts, then tried to wash it off in the septic tank.'

'It was on the bike when I came back from lunch. I wondered if an animal had sprayed on it.'

Although that wouldn't explain why it was only on the handlebars and saddle.

'No animal I've ever come across.' She frowned, giving a tentative sniff from the safety of several metres away. 'Where had you left it?'

'Your mum wheeled it to the far gate. Maybe someone walking along the footpath tipped something over the hedge?'

'No islander would have done that.' Lily looked pensive for a moment before shaking it off with a shrug. 'Must have been a tourist. Perhaps they found an old bottle on Minke Beach and decided to empty it out.'

A bottle of gone-off embalming fluid? And again, it didn't explain why they'd omitted to get any on the crossbar or wheels. But I didn't have the same unquestioning faith in islanders as my host. I lived in a village. I knew how feuds and petty grievances could fester. Maybe someone had been offended about not being invited to the party? What I also knew was that it was a rental bike on Hawkins Farm. On the off chance this had been intentional, it surely didn't have anything to do with me.

* * *

Malcolm left for a run shortly after Lily.

'I'll not be back for a couple of hours.'

'Wow. That's a decent run.'

He winked, stretching out his hamstring. 'To the Island Arms. Three miles each way. Lily's messaged to say the kids are happy, so they'll be stopping out a while longer, too. If you go out, leave the key under the purple shell.'

'I was planning on sitting in the garden for a bit.'

'I was planning on visiting for a stag weekend and heading back to marry my lass in the valleys. This island makes a mockery of plans.'

I accepted his parting offer of a glass of wine – it was well into the afternoon, and I was on holiday, after all – and tried to pretend I didn't feel like a complete imposter, reclining on an outdoor sofa in my shorts and sunglasses, then opened up the brown envelope.

Three smaller, plain white envelopes were inside.

Disappointing, considering Mum's box had contained nine. Unsurprising, considering the likelihood of her writing any letters at all.

I opened up the first one and scanned it for a date.

Seeing her precise handwriting, using the thick, black pen she'd insisted upon writing with right up until she died, triggered a tidal wave of grief and homesickness that threatened to suffocate me.

Pressing the letter against my chest, I forced my gaze towards the climbing rose, fixing on a bee buzzing amongst the yellow and peach blooms that were already open. Breathing in slowly, I focused on the blend of aromas – warm grass, the chicken coop, wine and pollen. Gradually, as my breathing settled, I tuned into the hen's comforting clucks, an aeroplane whirring in to land on the other side of the island, a distant moo.

'Okay. Are we quite finished with the overdramatics?' I lessened the pressure of my hand, as if it made any difference, and took another peek at the cream notepaper, making sure I read only the date.

It was 1988. Two years after the previous letter I'd read from Gabe. I checked the others, but they were both later the same year.

I slipped them back into the brown envelope, reeling from the discovery that they had been communicating for at least four years, and turned to the other pile, unable to wait to read the next chapter in their story.

4 April 1987

My darling wife Nellie,

I had to stop there, take another few breaths and a good slurp of wine. The photograph had made it pretty clear that she'd gone through with the wedding, but to have it confirmed in writing that Mum had been married was still a jolt. I sat for a minute, trying to picture her with Gabe. Laughing, cuddling on the sofa together at the end of a long day. Tucked up in bed. Then again – Pip had told me that he was twenty-nine, so Lily must have been born only six years after this letter.

Was it more accurate to picture them bickering, knocking heads over the million things Mum held her pig-headed opinions on? Blazing rows or days of moody silence?

Either way, Mum being married was still mind-blowing.

A letter for our anniversary, seeing as I'll be up with the dawn again this morning, and quite possibly incapable of forming a coherent sentence when I return. I know this year has been a big change, leaving your city and starting afresh. There must be so much you miss. Supermarkets. Cinemas. Bus stops on every corner. But now Ma and Da's shock has worn off, I hope you are starting to feel more settled. Farm life takes some getting used to, I'd imagine. There's a lot taken for granted when you grow up amongst cows and wheat, riding a tractor before most kids try a bike. But you're doing grand. Better every day. Ma even asked if I could trouble you for your pastry recipe (she couldn't possibly ask you directly – you'll have learned there's no stubborn pride like an island woman's when it comes to her kitchen). And waking up with your strawberry hair spread across my pillow, coming home to the warmth of your arms – well – I don't imagine that unbridled pleasure will ever fade. You, here on my island, my farm – our land, and one day our children's. The only thing that could make me happier is knowing you are as home here as I am. Soon, my love (I know – you'll feel a lot better once the other cottage is finished and you can have your own stovetop!).

Save me an anniversary kiss for when this weary farmer returns.

I shall think of you every moment of the day, and it will spur my efforts so that I can be home as soon as I can.

With faith, hope and love,
Your grateful husband,
G

Like in all Gabe's letters, his devotion shone through every paragraph. But, unlike the others, in between those heartfelt lines, I detected some teething problems for the newly-weds. I could guess how Gabe's family felt about him turning up with a 'mainlander' wife. An independent city girl who would have detested being expected to slot into another woman's household. While the farmhouse was a decent size, I couldn't imagine it was easy for the couple to enjoy much time alone together, either. For a brief, mad second, I wondered what it would be like for me to move into the farmhouse with Pip, while his parents still slept in the master bedroom, Aster in the ground-floor snug that he'd told me about, Richard in an annexe tacked onto the back of the house.

After a lifetime living with Mum's established order, plus two years fending for myself, I couldn't begin to fathom how I'd handle new rules, customs and family dynamics.

Good job you'll never have to, then, isn't it? I reminded myself, hastily stuffing the letter back into the envelope in response to the sound of Lily's car pulling into the drive.

'Ack. Don't tell me Malcolm's gone for a run?' she asked, once Beanie and Jack were playing happily on the grass with a wooden farm and Flora had disappeared upstairs.

'Sorry.'

She shook her head in disgust. 'He gets on at me about all the jobs need doing. Now instead of helping me sort the soft furnishings in the lilac room, he'll be setting the world to rights with his Welsh cronies until I'm far too knackered to hang a curtain.'

'I'll help,' I offered.

Lily narrowed her pastel eyes at me. 'I'm thinking you might actually mean that.'

'I do!' I laughed. 'I work six days a week, and spend my evenings and days off cleaning and sorting out everything else that needs doing. I know I'm on holiday, supposedly learning to chill out for the first time ever, but if I don't pace myself, I'm going to have a serious relapse. You'll find me scrubbing cupboards at three in the morning.'

'Really?' She grinned. 'You wouldn't hear any complaints from me. Except that you're my test guest, and that's not quite the home-from-home experience I'm going for.'

'Come on,' I said. 'I promise I won't mention it in my review.'

Lily grabbed my hand, which I then used to help haul her up. 'Oh, my goodness. You're going to write a review?'

'Best breakfast on the island,' I said, with a nonchalant shrug. 'So far, anyway.'

'Don't try the Copper Pot by the ferry port. That used to be my café, and they've stuck with all my recipes.'

* * *

By the time we'd hung the curtains, made up two single beds and plumped cushions, hung pictures and arranged knick-knacks to Lily's satisfaction (until it all looked stunning, in other words), the younger kids were growing fractious, hens needed putting to bed and Flora was rootling in the cupboards for supper.

While Lily plonked Beanie and Jack in the bath, Flora and I shooed the chickens back in the coop then made bubbling cheese on toast, smothered with cider chutney. We scattered the strawberries I'd brought back over bowls of traditional island honey ice cream, and poured mugs of thick, creamy hot chocolate.

I made it through another Flora inquisition on mainland life, doing my best to channel Blessing as a far more typical example of English culture than me, but before long we were chatting about how she was considering journalism as an alternative to intelligence – 'I'm not sure I can be bothered with being bossed about' – and she was providing examples of all the latest island scoops.

'So, the word on the Lithin promenade is that Barnie was seen in the gallery.'

'Okay.' I matched Flora's body language, leaning forwards

across the kitchen table as she took a triumphant bite of toast. 'I don't know what Lithin promenade is or why it matters that Barnie was in the gallery. Is he a secret art lover?'

Flora rolled her eyes. 'Lithin is the other village. Well, it's barely that, to be honest. It's got like three shops that are any use and then the promenade, which is all tourist stuff. Most of the houses are holiday lets so it's the most boring place on earth in winter. Anyway, the gallery may sell paintings, but none that Barnie could afford, even if his cousin did paint half of them. But it also sells jewellery.'

'Aha.' I nodded. 'Engagement rings?'

'I don't suppose he's after a shell necklace for himself, now, is he?'

'I didn't think he and Violet were even going out.'

'They aren't. But around here, that doesn't make much difference. Not when you've grown up knowing every tiny little thing about each other. It doesn't take much dating to decide if there's going to be any chemistry or not. And Auntie Violet is ramping up the travel plans now Uncle Pip's back. If Barnie's smart – which is up for debate, to be fair – he knows it's a grand gesture or nothing at this stage.'

We carried on chatting for a while longer, then a sheepish Malcolm arrived home, hastily taking over with the bedtime routine while Lily helped herself to the last slice of cheese on toast and Flora went to read in bed.

'So, have you found out any more about your ma's mystery man?' Lily asked, almost causing the ice cream I'd just swallowed to refreeze in my gullet.

'Um. Not really. I've only read a couple more letters.' I scraped at the remains in my bowl, despite suddenly feeling nauseous. 'I know they definitely married and lived on the island at some point.'

'And you still aren't ready to reveal the vital initial?'

I shook my head. 'I'd rather read to the end of the story first, if that's okay.'

'Of course it's okay. It's your story. Ach, you only met us a couple of days ago, which is plenty long enough to learn what a bunch of gossipy old tattletales we are around here.' She got up to put the kettle on. 'You're coming to the beach tomorrow, aren't you? Pip did ask?'

'Um. Yes.'

She nodded, pleased with herself. 'I thought as much.'

'But can I come as your guest, not Pip's?'

Lily turned around and leant back on the worktop, arms folded across her bump. 'I don't know why you two are faffing around about this. It doesn't take Flora's spy skills to see that you're sweet on each other.'

Knowing what a bunch of gossipy old tattletales they were, I decided the best way to deal with this was to be honest. Lily could then let everyone else know, and at the very least, they could stop grilling me on the subject.

'I've lived in the same place, done the same job and pretty much nothing else for my whole life, so anything different is a big deal. I'm not used to dating, and I've done more socialising in the past two days than in the previous six months. I'm not going to be able to keep anything casual, or a bit of fun. While I can't deny that I like your brother, I don't want my first proper holiday to end in a broken heart.' I tried to lessen the over-sharing with a laugh, but it came out more like a strangled cry for help. 'I might never find the courage to get on a plane again.'

Lily came to sit down, kettle forgotten, her face creased with compassion. 'Pip wouldn't deliberately hurt you, Emmie. Or play with your feelings. But I can understand why you don't want to start something when his life is here, and yours is on the mainland.'

'Thank you.'

She patted my hand. 'Having said that, no life is set in stone. Ask Malcolm. I for one would not be complaining if Parsley's Pasties relocated.'

17

Sunday morning, I awoke to find the sun beaming through my window and a rapid tapping on the bedroom door.

'Emmie,' Lily pretend-whispered, loud enough for me to hear her clearly through the solid layer of oak. 'Are you awake?'

I padded over, glancing at the clock to see it was only eight-thirty, and opened the door. 'Has something happened?'

'Yes.' Lily was fizzing with excitement. 'Logan at the harbour messaged to say the meat's arrived on the morning ferry. His wife, Jennie, is heading to North Cove to visit her grammie who's taken a fall, so she's dropping it off on the way.'

'Great.'

'It will be here in approximately seventeen minutes.' She looked me up and down, bouncing on her swollen toes. 'Will you be ready? It would be amazing if we can have some pasties baked in time for the beach.'

'Give me twenty. And maybe time for some breakfast?'

'Eggs, bacon, pancakes?'

'Toast is fine.'

She gave a determined nod. 'I'll do an egg and throw on a couple of rashers.'

* * *

I ate breakfast in the garden. I would have stayed inside, due to an early-morning chill still lingering, but every available clutter-free surface was rapidly filling up with ingredients and cooking equipment. Lily was itching to get started, and I was itching to have a quiet moment to eat my egg and bacon on toast before we embarked on a marathon baking session.

She shooed the children and Malcolm off to Siskin Church – still a regular part of most islanders' weekends – and sat waiting with such simmering anticipation that I forwent the second cup of coffee I'd been hoping for, and we got to work.

It had been twenty months since I'd stood shoulder to shoulder with another chef, and I'd forgotten how helpful it was to have someone to pass the salt, form a two-woman production line or simply share in the quiet contentment of chopping a mini mountain of vegetables.

Lily was a focused cook, saving any conversation for intelligent, informed questions about flavours or technique. When the pastry was chilling, venison stewing, peas mushing, we stood together at the kitchen table with the vegetarian ingredients and began working out how much of the different cheese to add.

The simple act of tasting, discussing, tweaking a little, before repeating the process until finally agreeing on the perfect quantity, was another new experience. Having someone to share this with made my chest ache with the loneliness of both the past couple of years, and the decade prior to that, where it had taken months of conniving to get any of my suggestions heard. Even then, they'd never been discussed, merely announced as if they had been Mum's idea all along.

There should have been freedom in running things by myself but, up until creating the new vegan pasties, all I'd done was carry on enforcing the old rules and routines. Nevertheless, I tried not to be too harsh on myself – making changes to a successful business was a lot of responsibility for a twenty-six-year-old whose biggest decision prior to that had been whether to wear blue or black socks on her day off, or which book to check out of the library. Of course I would struggle to find the confidence to make any changes alone.

But having someone else to say, 'Do you think that's too salty?' or, 'I agree, the third version is the best,' was a revelation.

I briefly wondered whether Blessing might like to swap her turquoise tunic for a Parsley's uniform. Then I remembered how she'd manhandled my kitchen contents (pausing in my mixing to send her a reminder to water my herbs) and decided that an unsuitable co-worker would probably be worse than continuing alone.

At two-thirty, I carefully lifted the final tray out of Lily's huge oven.

'Wow. They look and smell so much better fresh,' Lily said, dreamily, gently poking a perfectly golden crust.

'That's why I bake most of them once I get to the kiosk, with each batch small enough to sell out within a couple of hours.'

While they were undoubtedly tastier fresh, these looked like the best pasties I'd made without Mum. It turned out teamwork really did make the dream work.

'Can we have one?' Jack asked, popping up in between me and his mum, Beanie squeezing in with him.

'I told you, these are for the beach. By the time we get there, they'll have cooled down enough to eat.'

'But I'm too hungry to ride my bike,' he protested.

'I'm hungry. I want one too,' his sister echoed, standing on tiptoes so her huge, round eyes could see what she was missing.

'Did you not both eat cheese and ham sandwiches, an apple and a giant pretzel an hour ago?'

'Exactly!' Jack said. 'A whole hour ago.'

'Moles eat half their own body weight in a day,' Beanie announced.

'Good job you're a girl, then, and not a mole. The sooner you both get ready to go, the sooner we can get there and you can try one.'

Less than five minutes later, Lily was loading two cool boxes full of pasties in the car. She was driving to spare her swollen ankles. The children were lined up in the hall, accompanied by several tote bags, a football and two giant stuffed moles. Beanie was clutching a hamster inside one of those plastic balls they run about in.

'No to Digger and Dirt. Definitely no – make that never – to Mister Whiskers. Hamsters are not allowed at the beach,' Malcolm said.

'He's not a hamster. He's a hairy-tailed mole so that means he can come,' Beanie sang happily.

'Jack, have you got a shirt in there somewhere?' Malcolm asked, ignoring her.

'Nope.'

'Stupid question, I suppose. Have you at least got sun cream on?'

'Flora did it.'

'Great. Now once you've put on your surf shoes, we can go. Moles can't come to the beach, either. Put him back in his cage, now.'

'Cowboys don't wear shoes.'

'I think you'll find they do. Otherwise, what happens when they step in a cowpat, or on a rattlesnake?'

'Do not. They wear cowboy boots.'

'You haven't got any boots, buddy. Surf shoes or nothing.'

Jack marched to the front door. 'Nothing.'

'No, I mean you can't go if you don't wear shoes. Beanie, put Mister Whiskers in his cage.'

'Not going, then.' Jack plonked himself down, arms folded, chin jutting from beneath a miniature Stetson. Beanie put the hamster ball down, the occupant making a break for the kitchen, and tipped herself upside down in her brother's lap.

'Well, that's a shame. I thought you wanted to try one of Emmie's pasties.' Malcolm shrugged, picking up one of the larger bags. 'Auntie Violet has made crackle cakes for the bonfire.'

'Crackle cakes!' Beanie flipped upright and grabbed one of the surf shoes that Flora had picked up from the shoe rack, attempting to wrestle it onto Jack's bare foot. 'Let's go!'

While Flora bent to help her sister, Jack's resolve clearly wavering as he lifted his leg to make it easier, Lily returned, instructing her youngest daughter to return the hamster to his cage in the living room while we loaded up the car.

I was sorely tempted to ask if I could ride in the car along with Beanie, but didn't want to appear like a feeble mainlander, so it was back on the rental bike.

'Ew.' Jack wrinkled his nose as he and Malcolm passed me. 'Flora, did you fart again?'

Flora overtook me next. 'Ugh! The only way a fart could smell like that is if someone's eaten a dead dinosaur first. Unless...' She gave me a curious glance over her shoulder. 'Is that what English farts smell like?'

'No!' I said, with enough force to sound suspicious. 'Something gross got on the bike yesterday.'

'Why didn't you clean it?'

'I did.'

Then Malcolm had a go, with bleach, and then I tried again.

'Here.' Malcolm had paused so that I could catch up, then he reached across with a plastic bag. 'It won't stop the bike stinking, but hopefully means it won't get absorbed by your dress.'

'It might be too late for that.'

'Ah, well. We can always sit you upwind.'

18

Lily had said that the weekly beach afternoons were generally family only. I realised, making my way down the last set of steps to the sand, the rental bike left well out of smelling distance, that 'family' had a loose definition on Siskin. As well as various Hawkinses, plus Hugh, all busy setting up cricket stumps, seating and other activities, I spied Hugh's parents, who I'd met at the party, Barnie and another young man who must have been his identical twin. A gaggle of children who didn't seem to belong to anyone were running in and out of the waves with the farm dogs and Pigeon, which inevitably meant Celine was also there, looking resplendent with her beach waves, bikini top and cut-off shorts as she batted a volleyball to no one in particular.

'Oh. It's you again,' Aster said, eyeing me up and down like a cow at the island auction. 'Are we inviting mainlanders to everything now? Is she coming for Christmas?'

'Ma.' Gabe gave his mother a warning look as he handed me an iced tea.

'I'm only asking.' She waved a hand in resignation. 'If Lily is going to bring all her guests to our private, family afternoons then

I'd like to be warned in advance so I can decide to stay at the farmhouse and clean out the chickens instead.'

'Come on, now, Mammaw,' Malcolm said, kissing her hello. 'I thought I'd convinced you that we aren't all bad.'

'Did you, now?' She sniffed in reply.

I'd said hello to a few people and now stood awkwardly, debating how to ask where Pip was in a way that wouldn't arouse any more suspicion, when a small motorboat chugged around the rocks on the far side of the cove, Pip sprawled out on one side, Lily perched on the other with Beanie, and Richard steering.

'Is that Richard's?' I asked Malcolm as the boat pulled up to a tiny wooden dock half hidden behind some boulders.

'It belongs to everyone. The farm's boat, really,' he answered as we wandered over to help unload the cool boxes and bags. 'Most families have at least one.'

'Do you and Lily?'

'We have a couple of surfboards, if that counts.' He took Beanie and put her down before offering a hand to help her mum, who lifted her maternity maxi-dress out of the way with the other hand as she stepped out of the boat. 'All our spare cash has gone into children or the businesses, so we settle for borrowing this one for now.'

Once Lily had moved to the side, Pip helped his uncle clamber off, then hopped out himself before walking over to the end of the dock where I stood waiting.

'Hi.' He smiled, sticking his hands in his shorts pockets. 'You look nice.'

'Oh. Thanks.' I looked down at the shorter, rose-pink dress I'd worn a few days ago, as if I'd not tried on everything in my holiday wardrobe before selecting it, hoping my face didn't look quite as sappy as that compliment made me feel.

'It's okay to say that, seeing as we're friends?' he asked, forehead creasing. 'It's not overstepping?'

'I don't think so. I mean, I don't mind.'

It might be hard to mind now every time he *didn't* say it.

'Well, that's good enough for me.'

He fetched the cool boxes and passed me one, while Malcolm and Lily unloaded the rest of the items from the boat and we carried them over to a pop-up shelter.

'I don't believe this.' Lily groaned, opening up one bag to find a very agitated hamster, still in its plastic ball. After scolding Beanie with the promise that the next time she brought her pet on an outing, they'd leave him there, she tasked her children with building an enclosure where Mister Whiskers could roll about in the shade, using rocks, driftwood and whatever else they could find. Lily then poured herself a drink and took a seat on a deckchair, nodding for me to sit beside her.

'That poor animal has been with us, what, six weeks? I can't believe he's survived that long,' she said, shaking her head while biting her lip in a way that implied she was desperately fighting a belly laugh. 'These are ninth-generation farm kids. Eber Hawkins will be face-palming in his grave.'

She tipped her sunhat down over her nose and shuffled lower in the seat. Approximately thirty seconds later, Jack was tugging on her arm.

'Mammy! Mammy! Maaaaa!'

'What?' Lily replied from behind the brim of her hat, her voice resigned.

'You promised we could have the pasties when we got to the beach. We got here *hours* ago, and I'm so hungry I really, really, really need one. Right now, Mammy!'

'Is Mister Whiskers safe?'

'Yep.'

Lily tipped the hat back to see where Flora and Beanie were busily arranging a long black branch.

'Beanie and Flora are watching him, so he *is* safe,' Jack argued.

'Go and help them finish off, and I'll get the pasties ready.'

Unlike the previous few days of clear skies, this afternoon, the streaks of cloud drifting above our heads made a warm pasty the perfect accompaniment to the intermittent sunshine and fresher breeze.

Everybody had at least one, so the cool boxes were soon empty.

'That was divine,' Violet said, wiping her fingers on a napkin. 'Emmie, are you sure you won't consider setting up a franchise at our airport?'

'Excuse me,' Barnie, sitting beside her on a blanket, huffed. 'Are you trying to do me out of business? I really don't need the threat of any competition right now.'

'If you learned how to make a half-decent doughnut then Parsley's Pasties wouldn't be a threat,' Violet teased.

'You said my doughnuts tasted like a dream holiday in food form.'

'True. But they *look* like a bad day at work.'

'Ouch.' Barnie winced. 'You know how I said I like it when you're honest with me? Scrap that. Lies are fine when it comes to my food.'

'Could you ship these over?' Hugh asked, finishing off his second helping. 'Maybe Barnie could sell them on his stand, so they'd be no threat to his dough-blob business.'

I shook my head. 'They'd have to be transported frozen, then baked here. It wouldn't be cost-effective for a business my size, even if I did have time to make enough.'

'Shame,' he mused. 'These would be perfect for our wedding.'

'Oh. My. Days.' Iris, sitting beside him, grabbed his arm. 'I was thinking the exact same thing.'

'Really?' I looked up in surprise. 'They're not exactly fancy.'

I'd never been to a wedding, but on films and TV-show weddings, people ate classy dishes with at the very least a knife and fork, not a pie specifically designed to be eaten with your hands.

'If you hadn't noticed, we're not that bothered about fancy around here,' Violet said.

'Besides, tasty beats fancy any day,' Iris agreed.

'We wouldn't have to bother with plates,' Hugh added.

'We'd still have plates,' Iris said sternly. 'People might want to put their pasty down while they pose for a photo, or tell the bride how gorgeous she looks.'

'That's a grand idea,' Pip said, smiling. 'Given that the only islander who won't charge ridiculous tourist rates for catering got herself pregnant at the worst possible time.'

'I have apologised for that,' Lily retorted. 'It wasn't planned.'

'Yeah, we gathered that by Malcolm's face when he announced it.'

'All the decent places are booked up anyway,' Iris went on. 'Even if we wait two years, they insist on hosting the entire reception on site, which costs another fortune, and is pointless when we'd rather use the farm.'

'Is that settled, then?' Hugh asked, turning from Iris to me. 'We're expecting about eighty people. Is that doable in Lily's kitchen?'

'What?' I must have lost track somewhere, because surely Hugh wasn't asking me to cater his wedding. 'I have to fly home on Friday at the latest, so I can be ready to reopen on Sunday. Otherwise I get a fine and could lose the lease. Same if I miss any more days in the next twelve months.'

'What are you doing on Thursday?' Hugh asked Iris.

'I was planning on helping your ma with the new gelding, but I guess I'm getting married instead.'

'Um. What?' This must be a joke.

'Can you get everything ready for then?' Hugh asked me, before suggesting a price that seemed more than reasonable as I quickly calculated the cost of eighty pasties and added a generous discount.

'I... I suppose so. But can *you*?'

Iris shrugged. 'We've got outfits and rings already. The bridesmaids are sorted. The wine and other drinks are stacked in the back barn. Someone can arrange a few flowers and I'm sure Richard's band will be free. What else do we need?'

'How about the means to actually get married?' Rosemary, who due to sitting a short distance away hadn't joined in until she came to fetch Gabe another pasty. 'You know, a legal ceremony, signing the register, trivialities like that.'

'Arnie, are you around on Thursday?' Iris called over to where the man who looked the spitting image of Barnie was chatting with Richard.

'They're twins?' I whispered to Pip, while Arnie brushed the pastry crumbs off his shorts and ambled over. 'Arnie and Barnie?'

Pip grinned. 'Barnaby and Arnold. His ma and da didn't twig until they got old enough for nicknames.'

'I've got a couple of meetings in the morning. Why?'

'Will you marry me?'

Arnie laughed. 'I'm not sure what my wife would say about that.'

'I'm serious. On Thursday. At the church.'

'Did you notify the registrar within the past year?'

'November.'

'Are you still planning on Hugh being the groom?'

'She'd better be,' Hugh chipped in.

'Then it would be my pleasure. Talk to Linda about the music and whatever else.'

'Thanks, Arnie. You're the best minister on the whole island.'

'No bother.' He squeezed past them, took the very last pasty and gave me a wink as he went back to his seat. 'I'm the only minister on the island.'

'Oh, is two o'clock okay?' Iris called after him.

'Perfect. Gives Linda time to vacuum up after the toddler group and put some chairs out.'

'You all got that, right?' Iris shouted, standing up so everyone on the beach could hear. 'The wedding's back on – 2 p.m. ceremony, then food and dancing in the Old Barn.'

She leant down to take Hugh's hand. 'Come on, phone reception is rubbish here, and we've got a load more people to invite. I'd probably better make a list or something too.'

The beach reverberated with the news as Iris and Hugh gathered their things and left. I was still slightly in shock.

'They're seriously going to organise a wedding in four days?' I asked Pip.

'Looks like it. Although, like they said, most of it's already done.'

'I take longer than that to work up to a big food shop.'

It was incredible to me that someone could make such a momentous decision with such apparent ease. Hugh and Iris hadn't even discussed it. Where were the planning, the spreadsheets, the agonising discussions, the headaches?

'I guess I'm staying until Friday, then.'

Pip smiled, a blush creeping up his face. 'I guess so.'

* * *

Aside from a few more snipes from Aster, it was a perfect afternoon.

I played cricket for the first time, discovering that I could hit a ball a decent distance, but was a hopeless bowler. I built a sand church with Beanie and a couple of Hugh's nieces, and we conducted weddings with a shell for the bride and a dead crab for her groom, until his legs fell off. I sat and watched boats sailing past, enjoying the kiss of sunshine on my bare skin, and listened to the blend of excited chatter and more serious conversations.

I talked to Pip. And when I wasn't talking to him, I automatically tuned in to where he was, what he was doing, including joining in Celine's volleyball game, and investigating rockpools with Jack.

I also couldn't help continuously searching out Gabe. The man who would have been my stepfather, if things had turned out differently. The only man my mother ever loved – or even liked. Despite Pip having told me that Richard was the older brother, as the one who ran the farm, Gabe was clearly patriarch of the Hawkins family, and he carried the honour with easy grace and calm composure. I surreptitiously watched him chatting to every single person on the beach, dividing up the teams for games, ensuring the children were being safe in the water, checking Aster had a comfy seat and enough to drink.

'Pip said that you do this most Sundays,' I said to Lily, who spent most of the afternoon snoozing, in between rescuing Mister Whiskers from repeated escape attempts.

'When the weather's good enough. If it's wet, we don't bother, and if it's cold, we only last a couple of hours.'

'I thought farmers were supposed to work all the time.'

'They've worked all week. And this morning. An afternoon off is hardly an indulgence.'

'Yes. I just... this is *really* off.'

'What do you mean?' She sat up and twisted around on her deckchair to look at me properly.

'I spend my afternoons off cleaning or catching up on jobs.'

Lily screwed up her nose. 'Then how is that off?'

I thought about that for a minute. 'I don't know.'

'When do you catch up on doing nothing?'

'Today?'

'Are all mainlanders like that?'

I considered what Mum would have said about the kind of mainlanders who sat about at weekends, doing what she called 'nothing' and I was starting to realise other people called 'resting', 'recuperating' or 'enjoying themselves'.

Her answer to this question would have been, *All decent, hardworking, responsible ones are.*

For the first time, I was seriously questioning whether she was right.

'I don't think so.'

'I was going to say. No wonder you're all stressed out and anxious over there, if you don't know how to take time off.'

'Now it looks as though I'll be spending my time off baking pasties,' I said, smiling, because honestly I had got so much from these past few days, I was happy to give something back. Busy and frantic was my comfort zone, after all.

'Baking pasties, and hopefully helping me sort some decorations? I know Iris is all for keeping it casual, but it's not every day my baby sister gets married and moves to the other side of the island. I want to make up for letting her down with the catering.'

'Whatever you need, I'd love to help.'

* * *

As the afternoon mellowed towards evening, a small bonfire was lit and Rosemary handed out hot dogs to anyone who could squeeze one in. The children, now huddled in sandy towels with damp hair plastered on rosy cheeks, roasted marshmallows as Richard led the adults in a round of haunting sea shanties, depicting wild tales of smugglers, shipwrecks and women driven half mad with grief, waiting for their lost sailors to come home.

Eventually, as the warmth of the day began to dissipate, the family started to disperse. When Richard readied the boat just before nine o'clock, there was a small queue of people opting to avoid the climb back up the cliff, so Pip offered to walk instead.

'Are you heading up now?' Rosemary asked as she shook the sand off a blanket. 'Your father needs you in the chicken shed tomorrow while he shows Hugh that sick calf.'

'I know.' Pip took the other end of the blanket and helped her fold it before placing it in the storage box. 'But I'm going to stay a bit longer.'

Rosemary furrowed her forehead, opening her mouth to reply. She then paused as she caught his stance, arms folded, shoulders set, a myriad thoughts flitting across her face before she simply sighed.

'Well, you're a grown man. I suppose you can decide what time you go to bed.'

'I am, and I can.' He leant forwards and kissed her on the cheek. 'I've missed a lot of island sunsets over the past two years. I'm going to savour this one.'

Rosemary glanced over to where I was gathering up plastic glasses and putting them in a bag. 'You'll be wanting breakfast?'

'Yes, Ma.'

'Porridge will be ready at six.'

19

It was another hour before the egg-yolk sun finally sank beneath the distant waves. Pip hadn't asked if I wanted to stay with him, but he'd left two chairs out, and handed me a glass of cider, so I took it as an invitation.

We'd sat mostly in silence, and I'd treated it as another learning opportunity in being still, doing 'nothing'. I tried not to view savouring the sunset with a man whose presence made every nerve hum as a task to tick off my never-ending mental to-do list. I almost managed it, too.

'Four days until you go,' Pip said, when he finally stood up and stretched. 'Any plans for how you'll make the most of them?'

I restrained from suggesting I spent them trailing around after him, or grilling his dad about my mother, instead mumbling something about baking, helping Lily with the barn and whatever she had in mind for wedding décor.

'You should visit Hugh's stables. Jasmine does horse rides for the tourists. They pass the best place for dolphin spotting, and by the Siskin Stone.'

'I've never ridden before.'

'They've got horses well used to novices. And she's bound to do it for free, given the scandalously cheap price Hugh offered you for Thursday.'

'I'll think about it, thank you.'

I instructed myself not to mind that he hadn't suggested coming with me. Pip was a farmer. He had a life to be getting on with, including whatever needed doing with forty-thousand free-range chickens and their eggs.

We slowly walked back up the path, which was easier this time because I felt more adapted to the island terrain and so less cautious. Still, Pip took my hand in the shadowy stretches, and helped me over the stile where I'd parked the bike.

'Do you want to leave it at the farm again?' he asked, nodding at the bike, his nose giving a puzzled twitch.

'No. I'll ride it back.' I hadn't told him about the horrible smell, because I didn't want him to feel bad about it happening on Hawkins land, so while I definitely wouldn't risk leaving the bike exposed again, I also didn't want him to walk me back alongside it. The moon had appeared between the clouds, and was full enough to mean I'd see at least something of the track back to the B&B. Besides, every hour I spent with Pip, my feelings only grew deeper. Many more sunsets on the beach and moonlit walks were going to make leaving Siskin with a broken heart unavoidable, whether we kept things friendly or not.

'Are you sure? I can walk with you to the far gate.' He did a rubbish job of hiding his disappointment, but I nodded firmly.

'Thanks for a wonderful day. I'll see you around.'

I clambered onto the bike and did my best to minimise the wobbles as I lumbered down the path, knowing he'd be watching.

'Take care in Clover Field,' Pip called after me. 'The gate can be stubborn, but the cows will still be out so double-check it's shut.'

By the time I'd reached Clover Field, a cloud obscured the moonlight, so I wheeled the bike instead. I squashed my nerves at navigating a field of half-tonne beasts alone in the dark, and hurried to the other side with no incidents, giving the gate a rattle to ensure it was closed before using the glow from the barn now up ahead to navigate the rest of the way.

The ground floor was empty, so I tiptoed upstairs, opening the yellow room door as quietly as possible before dumping my bag on the chair, opting for the soft bedside lamp and clicking on the kettle while I jumped in the shower.

I added a splash of milk to my decaf tea and took an absent-minded sip as I walked over to the bed.

My brain interpreted the smell a second before the taste hit my tongue.

I'd have smelled it the second I poured it if the room weren't full of steamy lavender from my shower. The milk was beyond sour. My initial thought, apart from utter disgust, was confusion that it could taste so awful and not be set like Greek yoghurt. I peered at the mug, spotting a couple of flecks of yellowy-brown yuckiness. When I took the milk jug back out of the mini-fridge and inspected it, it appeared fine until I gave it a stir, the subsequent odour sending bile rising up my throat as I lifted out the spoon, now covered in thick, nasty goo.

After braving a tentative sniff from a safe distance and analysing the goo under the lamp, the only possibility I could come up with was that it was a big dollop of bird poo. I tried to recall the droppings in the chicken coop, but couldn't remember clearly enough to identify whether this was the same. Besides, all bird poop could look identical, for all I knew.

I rinsed out the mug, my scrunched-up face turned away, and then investigated the kettle, other mug and plate, neatly wrapped cookie and everything else on the refreshment tray or in the fridge, running through different possibilities of how the milk jug had become contaminated. It had clearly been refilled since I'd last made a drink that morning. Had Lily or Malcolm left it near an open window, or on an outside table, and a bird had somehow, freakishly, managed to poop in the mug without them noticing?

Or, perhaps, a chicken wandered into the house at some point during the day. Except that we'd been cooking all morning, and someone would have noticed a chicken strutting about. Malcolm would have shut the birds in the coop as soon as they all arrived home.

I wondered whether I could ask Lily a few innocent-sounding questions about when she'd replenished the milk, or where she did it. Whether a bird had got in the house at all.

I briefly wondered whether to show her the jug and ask her straight out if she could figure it out.

One thing stopped me.

It was the second unexplainable, revolting thing that had happened in the past two days.

While I had initially brushed off the bike-juice as nothing to do with me personally, I couldn't confidently dismiss this as an accident. Which meant it was a deliberate act of nastiness that I was meant to discover.

The mounting fear at the thought that someone would direct such a sinister act of animosity towards me was enough to send me running to the bathroom.

Once my stomach was horribly empty, my throat raw, I went over the rest of the room inch by inch, trying desperately to work out who had had the opportunity to sneak in and deposit the poop. It had to be someone who'd arrived at the beach after us, or knew that I'd be staying on after they'd gone. Unfortunately, that ruled out only Pip – it could be any of these other near-strangers, whose values and customs I had barely begun to understand.

That inevitably led me on to motive. I thought about how Celine had dragged Pip away from our conversation to play volleyball, going all out with her teasing and hair-tossing.

There was also Aster, who had made several rude asides about me. And what about Gabe? Did he harbour resentment about whatever had gone awry with Mum, seeing my sudden appearance as the perfect chance to exact revenge?

Richard, while I was trolling through potential suspects, had ignored me completely. Did he share Aster's misgivings about mainlanders?

Then there were all the others. I couldn't ignore the fact that Lily and Malcolm had the best opportunity. Perhaps it was one of the kids, playing a hilarious island-style prank, and I was getting all worked up for nothing. The bike was simply a coincidence.

I tried to circle back to believing that Clucker or Pecky had snuck in and left a present behind in the milk jug when no one was looking. I needed to at least check the carton in the kitchen fridge in the morning.

But my intuition wasn't buying it.

Feeling more alone than at any other moment in my lonely life so far, I brushed my teeth until my gums bled, flicked the lock on the bedroom door and checked under the covers one last time before sliding into bed.

Unable to think of any other way to try to settle my frantic nerves, knowing that there was at least some chance I would find an answer there, I reached for the letters. I was grateful that the next one according to date was written by my mother. With the taste of that tea still lingering in the back of my mouth, I needed the comfort of her familiar hand.

11 January 1988

Gabriel,

While it may be considered cowardly to hide behind a letter, you yourself have said that writing words down can be the safest way to make sure they are taken as meant, and not misheard. Besides, I have waited up every night this week hoping you would ask me how I am, or would simply take a proper look and so notice what is happening to your wife.

You haven't asked, so a letter it is.

My darling husband, while my love for you is as sure and as strong as the day we married, I have failed as your wife in making your dream come true.

I am not happy here. I am, in fact, more miserable than I thought possible. I have tried (surely you have seen how hard I have tried?) to be a capable farmer's wife, a dutiful daughter-in-law. A true islander, in spirit if not in blood.

I simply cannot do it.

Your family hate me. The island women scorn me.

Those infernal chickens wish to thwart my every move.

I don't know what I detest more: the weather or your mother ordering me about like an incompetent child, saddling me with tedious, loathsome tasks and then complaining when I don't complete them with the skill or speed of someone born here.

I resent how all you have left for me is exhausted dregs after yet another long, lonely day.

Gabriel – I married you to share a life together. We speak less now than when limited to a weekly phone call.

I think I must go home, before this farm destroys any trace of the woman you fell in love with.

My question is – will you come with me?
Nellie

I wept as I read the letter. Picturing my strong, proud mother feeling isolated, belittled, so thoroughly out of place, made my heart ache. She'd been thirty-seven before she'd dared to risk it all for love. And perhaps it was no wonder she never took a chance like that again. After four days on the island, I could only imagine how brutal it must have been to have the Hawkinses' rejection as a permanent housemate. I wondered whether she'd encountered doctored mugs of tea, or worse.

Despite my raw emotions, I felt compelled to read another letter, unable to settle until I knew Gabe's reply, and trusting that it wouldn't make me feel even worse.

12 January 1988

My dearest Nellie,

There would only ever be one answer to your question:
Yes.
I would go to the ends of the earth for you, my love. Your doubt on this matter is proof that I am the one who has failed.
(Although, I must help Da with the calving, first.)
With faith, hope and love
Your wretch of a husband,
G

Comforted that, at this point, Gabriel had chosen Mum over his family and the farm, and she'd still had someone on her side, I tucked the letters back in my bag and turned off the light.

20

I gave up my pitiful attempts to sleep once the first rays of dawn illuminated the crack between the curtains. Still feeling squeamish about the refreshments in my bedroom, I showered and dressed in shorts and a T-shirt and quietly tiptoed downstairs to the empty kitchen.

After several sniffs and swills of the milk carton in the fridge, I made a mug of tea and slipped outside to sip it on the patio. It was impossible not to feel at least slightly better, soaking up the soft magic of an early-morning summer garden. I distinguished at least four different bird songs, accompanying the distant neigh of horses. The air was fresh like Eden, and dewdrops still quivered on the foliage. I luxuriated in the stillness, doing a better job each morning of shaking off the urge to get on, get going, get busy, replacing it with a sense of peace that, right now, my only task was to enjoy the moment for as long as I wanted to.

A plane buzzed overhead – the early-morning flight to Sherwood Airport. I could picture the rows of business travellers, maybe older children who'd been home for the weekend heading back to school, the stragglers from last week's wedding returning to the bustle of mainland life.

Did I miss waiting for them, pasties warm, coffee brewing? Knowing how almost every moment of my day would unfold, enveloped by safe and familiar?

I took another sip of tea. Considered the stinky bike, the poopy milk. Weighed this up against picnics with Pip, sea shanties and sun-soaked beaches, and decided that no, I didn't. Not one second of it.

It did, however, prompt me to check my phone and email.

More messages from Blessing, that I replied to with a phone call that I politely ended once she started grilling me on why I hadn't snogged the hot farmer yet. Another email from Gregory, unable to hide his irritation behind the professional business-terminology.

I typed a brief reply to say that I hadn't forgotten about the lease, and would sign by the deadline at the end of the week. I also informed him that the kiosk would remain closed for ten days, as permitted in the current contract (even as I wondered why on earth Mum had bothered with a clause allowing her ten days off, when the most she'd ever taken was two). I deleted it, then took another look at the wide, open sky before retyping it and pressing send.

By the time I'd done this, the children were up and asking if I wanted to help them let the chickens out, and Lily had loaded smoked salmon and cream cheese onto toasted muffins, joining me back on the patio with a notepad and pen to discuss the plans for Thursday's marital feast.

I was doing my best to concentrate on answering her questions, while at the same time building up the courage to ask her about the milk, knowing how mortified she'd be, when her phone rang.

'Morning, Da.'

Her cheery expression froze.

'What?' She stood up and started pacing down the garden, making it impossible to hear what she was saying, even as the brisk tone made it clear that it was serious.

After less than a minute, she hung up and came to stand on the opposite side of the table to me.

'The Clover Field cows got out during the night.' The welcoming B&B smile had been replaced with a hard mask.

'Oh no, that's awful. Are they back safe now?'

Lily gave a terse nod. 'Thanks to Sean Munden catching sight of them on the way to his fishing boat. Too late to stop Jackie ripping her shoulder open, though. Da will have to make the call once Hugh's looked her over.'

'Make the call?'

'Whether it's worth saving her or not.'

'What?'

'This is a farm, Emmie. Our livelihood. They aren't pets.'

I sat back, having no idea what to say.

'The gate was left open,' she added, with a brief glance at me as she folded her arms.

My stomach nosedived.

'You cycled home alone last night. Pip warned you to check the dodgy gate.'

'I did. He did,' I stammered. 'But I checked the gate. It was shut. I rattled it to make sure... Lily, I'm so sorry... I honestly thought it was shut. It *was* shut.'

I'd been so paranoid about leaving it open. I knew, with absolute certainty, that I'd left it closed.

'Someone else must have gone through after me,' I said, sounding pathetic even to my own ears.

Lily closed her eyes for a brief second, then opened them again as she sat down, still refusing to meet my frantic gaze.

'Look, it's not entirely your fault. Pip shouldn't have left you to it. I mean, you couldn't have known the seriousness of not securing it properly.'

'No. That's not true.' I leant forwards, desperate to convince her. 'I might be a mainlander, but I live in the countryside. I know how important it is not to leave a gate open. Even if Pip hadn't warned me, I've have made sure it was closed. But he did, so I checked it even more thoroughly. Lily, I know you don't know me that well, and have no reason to believe me, but I promise you that I shut the gate.'

'Maybe you checked the other gates, but forgot the Clover Field one,' she said, a tear sliding down her face.

'The field nearest to here. With the big tree in the corner. The other side of it has far gate, leading to the farmhouse garden. I definitely checked that one. I double-checked every one of them.'

Lily tried to shrug it off. 'However it happened, it's done now.'

She began collecting the breakfast things, calling to the children to check their school bags were packed.

'There was something wrong with the milk in my bedroom,' I blurted.

Lily looked at me, her face creased in disappointment. 'Well, so. Shall we call it even?'

* * *

I stayed seated at the outside table while Lily and the children finished getting ready and left for school, wishing I could vanish altogether but too distraught to move. A minute or so after they'd gone, Malcolm came to find me.

'Don't fret yourself,' he said, placing two large, frothy coffees on the table. 'These things happen. And Hugh messaged to say the damage is minimal. Jackie will be fine in a few days.'

'But I didn't do anything,' I said, doing my best to look him in the eye. 'I know I shut the gate.'

'Emmie, no one doubts that you *believe* you shut the gate...'

'No.' I shook my head, firmly. 'I checked it. The latch was down. Someone else must have used it after me.'

'Someone ignorant enough about farms to leave it open?'

I winced at the implication I was that ignorant.

'A tourist could have ended up on the path, walking back to the caravan park from Port Cathan.'

'If they'd taken a few wrong turns in the dark, then I suppose it's not impossible.' Malcolm sighed. 'But like I said, these things do happen. It might be better to apologise and move on rather than keep protesting your innocence.'

'Lily is really upset with me.' I slumped back, despondent.

'She was a lot more upset with me when we lived by the café and I didn't shut the coop properly. We lost three hens to a polecat.' He took a slow sip of his own drink. 'She's stressed about the opening in two weeks, the wedding, kids. Money. And while I'd sooner swim with the basking sharks than risk saying it to her face, she's always resembled something of a polecat herself when chock-full of pregnancy hormones. One of the upsides of living on this "lump of rock", as Flora calls it, is that we know all too well each other's mistakes. You learn it's not worth holding a grudge when there's no escaping each other. She'll be fine by lunchtime.'

'I really hate you all writing me off as a hopeless mainlander.'

Malcolm raised one eyebrow. 'Those who'll think that already thought it. There's nothing to be done about them.'

'Do they still have that opinion about you?' I asked, Mum's letter still on my mind.

'Why do you think I'm opening a B&B and not sorting eggs or planting cabbages?'

'Does "they" include Gabe?'

Malcolm smiled. 'Gabe won't let me near his animals because I'm an accountant. He's happy enough to let me look over his books, mind, and sort the endless paperwork that lords it over modern farming. He gave me his blessing to marry his eldest daughter. Aster and Richard haven't spent any real time off the island, so are more, shall we say, *traditional* in their views. Mind you, we can both be grateful Gabe's old da is no longer with us. Forget traditional, he was downright xenophobic.'

Malcolm had reassured me to the extent that I almost told him about the milk jug. It seemed entirely possible that if it had been deliberate, the saboteur might have left the gate open too. Even better, he could have a perfectly logical explanation for the milk, in which case, I could stop freaking out about it.

However, I was also aware that a couple of days ago, I was potentially Pip's unhinged stalker. I felt nervous about arousing any more suspicion. And if someone genuinely had it in for me – most likely, their goal was to drive me back to the mainland, although it seemed an extreme reaction considering I was only here on holiday – then perhaps it was better if they didn't know I was onto them.

For the next hour, I instead argued back and forth with myself about whether to buy a ticket for the next plane out of there.

I was still staring at the airline's online shopping basket when Lily and Iris blew through the front door, all smiles and excited chatter about the wedding.

'Are you sure it's still okay for me to stay and do the food?' I asked, because remaining in this strange place and taking on something as important as catering a wedding would be difficult enough as it was. If I spent it riddled with nerves, it would surely end up a disaster.

'Did Lily make you feel bad about the gate?' Iris threw her sister a stern look. 'Did she happen to mention the time she flooded the barn, ruining half the oat crop? Or when she stole Granda's old tractor in a fit of temper and crashed it into a stone wall?'

'Well, what about when you snuck out for a romantic night in the hayloft with Hugh and set the place on fire?' Lily retorted.

'That's precisely my point,' Iris replied. 'We've all made stupid mistakes, Emmie. While you might not be an expert on farming, you're a genius pasty maker. Let's get planning.'

By the time we'd finished discussing pasties and drinks and opted for cake and definitely not Barnie's doughnuts for dessert, I crossed Lily and Iris off the list of people who might want to drive me away. Maybe I was being naïve, but I'd once again experienced the thrill of collaborating with people who were both genuinely enthusiastic and respected my skills, and I loved them for it.

* * *

I went into Port Cathan with Lily to buy the available ingredients and order the rest, after which she declared it lunchtime and insisted we stop for fishfinger sandwiches at the harbour, served from the deck of a revamped fishing tug.

'Right, working lunch,' Lily said, as we sat on a bench close enough to the Island Arms to use their Wi-Fi. 'Now the food is under control, we can cover some of the other details. What's your experience with flower arranging?'

'Um, none.' I didn't mention that the only flowers I'd bought – or received – had been a modest bouquet for my mum's funeral.

'Okay. No problem. How about centrepieces?'

As Lily rattled through the rest of her list, it became clear that I was not a woman of many talents.

'I can follow instructions,' I added, hoping to redeem myself. 'And I'm used to working long hours. I might not be very creative, but I don't mind being treated as a dogsbody.'

We finished our sandwiches and Lily sent me some links on her phone.

'I was thinking something like this, for flowers. Though I don't know where we'd get enough, at such short notice. The island preservation committee will fine us if we pick anything wild.'

I had a look at the images of intricate bouquets and garlands.

'Iris doesn't strike me as a very extravagant person.'

Lily snorted. 'She's planning a wedding in four days. That says it all.'

'So why not keep it simple? How about an iris on the end of each pew?'

'The church has chairs, not pews.' Lily narrowed her eyes thoughtfully. 'But that makes it easier – we can tie them on with a ribbon. We'd need quite a few, though. I can't imagine the flower stall has time to order enough in.'

'Okay, so how about every other row, you do a lily, or a posy of violets? I don't know what asters look like, but you could include those, too.'

'They're really pretty.' Lily, her excitement growing, showed me a picture. 'And apart from lilies, we can get all of them in purple. We'd need to include some rosemary sprigs, too. Daisies, for our other grandma, and Jasmine for Hugh's ma. But, Emmie, this is brilliant. Iris will love it.'

Now we'd settled on what to me was an obvious theme, the creativity flowed, and by the time Lily needed to pick up the children, we had enough doable ideas for the reception décor, too.

'I know this is all fairly simple, but are you going to manage it by yourself?' I asked, aware that Lily couldn't stop yawning as she drove us all back to Sunflower Barn. 'Could Violet help with anything?'

'Violet will be prepping the Old Barn with Pip and Da. Once the junk is cleared out, it needs a sweep, scrub and all the broken boards sorting. Then they need to collect and set up a load of borrowed tables and chairs. Uncle Richard's helping Lester Drum make a bar, so he'll have no time either. But Celine's a bridesmaid, she'll help, and we can ask Ma and Jasmine. Aster's fingers are too stiff to tie ribbons, and I wouldn't trust her up a ladder, but she can still bake better than anyone on the island, so I'll ask her to do the cake.'

'And to think people spend years planning a wedding.'

Lily smiled. 'Me and Malcolm had a barbecue in the back meadow, bring your own chair and a bottle. People thought we were showing off because we ferried in an ice-cream van and some of Malcolm's family were very unimpressed with the Portaloo.' She sighed, dreamily. 'It was a fantastic day.'

'I'm having pot sausage at my wedding,' Jack announced from the back seat. 'With a hundred million sausages. And chocolate cake.'

'Sounds great.' I turned around to face him. 'Who are you going to marry?'

Jack frowned. 'I don't know yet. Not any of the girls in my school. They're all way too annoying.'

'What about me?' Beanie asked.

'You can't marry your own sister,' Flora said, patting her sister's pudgy knee.

'Then what about... Emmie?' Beanie said, face lighting up at the very thought.

'Nah,' Jack said. 'Even if she wasn't so old, she loves Uncle Pip. Everyone knows that.'

'Emmie, do you want to marry Uncle Pip?' Beanie squeaked in excitement.

'Um...'

And there it was. Sitting in this car, with Pip's gorgeous, funny family, my pleasantly sun-kissed face enjoying the salty breeze through an open window...

Even if I was still haunted by a tampered refreshments tray – how could I look a three-year-old girl in the eye and say no?

* * *

I spent most of the afternoon setting peas to mush in Lily's largest pans, and filling up the slow cookers she'd borrowed from various neighbours with the extra venison we'd not used the day before, adding the other ingredients we'd bought that morning. I'd then do another batch after the rest of the meat arrived in a couple of days. Once everything was simmering nicely, I left Lily and Malcolm painting another bedroom while Flora kept half an eye on her brother and sister in the garden, and went for a walk.

After initially setting off towards the farm, I then deliberately turned in the opposite direction to Clover Field and headed inland. This led me through the orchard's symmetrical rows of pear trees, then alongside a meadow with warning signs informing me that on the other side of the stout fence was Basil, the bull. I walked for nearly an hour. Frequently slowing to an amble to take in the scenery, admire a patch of wildflowers or the sun dancing through the leaf-canopy.

It was on the other side of a small copse of deciduous trees that I discovered it. Breaking cover from the shadows, I found myself at the edge of a large field. Blinking a few times in the sudden glare, I suddenly realised.

A vast field of ripe winter barley. Golden ears rippling in the late-afternoon sunlight like gentle waves. Above it, from one horizon to the other, clear blue sky, the only blemish a distant bird of prey hovering on an air current. And, as on every inch of this island, the ever-present susurration of the sea.

It was the place I'd been dreaming about. A location so irresistible, I overslept for the second time ever.

As I continued along the footpath between the crops and the hedge, I laughed out loud at the butterflies dancing alongside me. Turquoise, like my dream, as well as a rainbow of reds, oranges, vibrant yellow and palest green.

Little over a week ago, this had been a fantasy inside my worn-out head. And while I marvelled at how I had ended up here, the truth was it had been simple. A £127 ticket for an hour-long flight.

The hard part would be going back.

* * *

Fearing I might end up wandering around in circles, when I'd completed a circuit of the field, I headed back along the way I'd arrived. It was almost five, and the children had asked if I'd help them make pizza for dinner. Reaching the orchard, I spied a figure under one of the trees, head tipped back, looking at the branches. As I moved closer, I realised it was Richard, leaning on one crutch, wearing the same brown corduroy trousers as every other time I'd seen him, paired with a scruffy checked shirt.

'Been scoping out the land?' he asked, still squinting up at the tree, lined face mottled with flickering shadows.

I paused a couple of metres away. Richard gave the impression of being the kind of man who didn't pass the time of day with strangers, and his odd question added a hint of menace to the orchard's hushed gloom.

'Just a walk to the barley field.'

In a silly way, I was hoping my knowledge of crops would prove I was a country-girl, not a clueless mainland urbanite.

'Shut the gate?'

'There wasn't a gate...' I stammered, before noticing the curve at the corner of his mouth.

'Hmmm.' He rubbed a hand over his bedraggled beard.

'Although, I did make sure the Clover Field gate was secure last night.'

'If you say so. Your mother would argue black is blue, to save looking a fool.'

He turned towards me, that beady stare like a gun pointing at my chest.

I couldn't speak. Every muscle had frozen.

'Don't seem so surprised, girl. I got eyes. Best thing she did was swallow her pride and run back home. Even if it nearly cost us everything when my brother went with her.' He turned back to the tree. 'No good can come of you poking that old bees' nest.'

He bent forwards, prodding the trunk with his crutch, clearly signalling that the conversation was over. I waited another moment while my body remembered how to move, then scurried past, thoughts freewheeling faster than the gulls above my head.

21

'Perfect timing,' Lily trilled, coming out of the kitchen to find me taking off my muddy trainers. 'Bases are rolled out, sauce is ready. All that's left to do is choose your toppings.' She turned to go, before twisting around again, as if she'd remembered an afterthought. 'Oh, and Pip asked if you fancied helping at the Old Barn afterwards. What with chasing down the cows this morning, and waiting for the vet, they've not made much progress and Violet is feeling the pressure.'

I was tempted to decline, opting for a long bath and an early night instead. While I was used to physically busy days, so much emotional upheaval on top of a rubbish night's sleep had left me drained and jittery. Richard's cryptic comment had only added to the chaotic swirl of the milk jug, Mum, escaped cows, wedding plans, my future plans and the business that I'd temporarily abandoned at who knew what cost.

The reasons I chose to accept were firstly because I was clearly being blamed for them being so behind, and so helping out was the least I could do. Secondly, while the situation with Pip should have added yet another layer of stress and uncertainty, in reality, the thought of an evening clearing out a filthy barn of junk with him felt more soothing than a bath, or a glass of wine in the garden. I acknowledged that right then, I needed to be with a friend. And, perhaps more importantly, I ached for my mother's steady presence. Spending time with the man who had loved her felt like the next best thing.

* * *

Cycling over to the farm after helping clear up dinner, I found Pip with Violet and Gabe, lugging a huge piece of machinery out of the Old Barn's double doors.

I was hovering at a safe distance when Rosemary appeared at my shoulder.

'Ach, Emmie, you really shouldn't be here.'

I felt a stab of paranoid panic that she was angry about the gate until she nudged me with a twinkling smile.

'This is your holiday. It's bad enough that my family had the cheek to strong-arm you into cooking for a wedding – they forget that the rest of the world has those things you call "boundaries". But dragging you over here to help with this mucky mess really is taking liberties. This surely cannot be your best offer for an evening out?'

I didn't know how to answer that without either confirming that I was, indeed, a bit of a loser, or implying that their beloved island was somehow lacking in things to do. Instead, I mumbled something about repaying Lily for letting me stay. Rosemary shrugged, smiled and led me to a patch of the nearest wall of the barn, which was covered with – oh boy – about a thousand bird droppings, and pointed out a scrubbing brush and a metal bucket with a pair of rubber gloves draped over the rim.

'Well, if you're determined to help, then this is the safest job for a newbie. Make sure you wear the mask and gloves. You can catch nasty infections from breathing in the dust.'

I almost asked if you could catch them from drinking it in a mug of tea too.

* * *

The light was fading by the time I put down the brush, satisfied that the wall was now worthy of a wedding reception. I'd worn half the bristles off and refilled the bucket from an outside tap more times than I cared to count.

I pulled off the mask and gloves, wiped my grimy forehead and stretched out the kinks in my back as Pip walked over. Apart from a quick hello, we'd both been focused on our different tasks – or, in my case, at least pretending to be – so this was the first time he'd spoken to me properly since I'd arrived.

'You must be ready for a drink.'

'A cup of tea would be bliss.'

'Will blackberry wine do instead?' He held out a Coca-Cola sized bottle of dark liquid.

'Needs must, I suppose.'

He clinked his bottle against mine, and we perched on the side of a rusty water trough that was almost as filthy as we were. Rosemary had disappeared to make Aster's supper a while ago, and not returned. As Gabe went to help Richard check the chickens were safely abed, Violet came to say goodnight, grabbing a bottle from Pip's bag to take with her.

'Thanks for your help, Emmie. I cannot imagine how my little brother persuaded you to spend a Monday night scrubbing bird crap off a barn wall, but I'm very grateful.'

'To be fair, I didn't know scrubbing crap would be involved.

But really, it's the least I can do,' I mumbled as she ruffled Pip's hair and left.

'Did you come and help because you felt obliged to?' Pip asked, twisting around to face me. 'When Lily invited you to stay, she didn't expect anything in return.'

'Maybe. But she didn't expect me to injure one of your cows, either.'

'That's why you're here?' Pip asked, his forehead creasing with concern. 'Emmie, no one blames you for what happened.'

'That's not true. They might forgive me, but your family definitely blame me. And I feel especially horrible about it because I know it wasn't me.'

Pip looked at me steadily through the dusk. 'Ah. I can see why that's worse.'

Him not questioning my conviction, gently pointing out that I must be mistaken, because there was no other explanation, made my throat constrict. Being believed – *trusted* – gave me the courage to explain.

'Growing up, forgetting something or making a mistake that proved I was unreliable – *irresponsible* – was nearly unforgivable. Mum would respond with this crushing mix of disappointment, disgust and bafflement. Like, "Why would you do this, Emmaline? I don't understand why you chose to let us down. I thought you cared about Parsley's", or our home, or my education, or whatever else it related to. She'd not outright punish me, but I'd have to complete pointless, petty tasks until I'd "earned her trust" back. When I was about eight, she made me clean every black speck off all our huge oven shelves because I got absorbed in a book and the dinner burned. It took hours. Another time, I had to write out the instruction manual for our dishwasher by hand when I used the wrong setting. Scrubbing the barn wall would have been right up her street.'

'So, you learned not to forget things.'

'Yes. To listen and follow instructions to the letter. I have a lot of flaws. But saying I'll do something and then a few minutes later not doing it isn't one of them.'

Pip stretched out his legs, the movement causing his bare arm, still warm despite the night air, to brush against mine, goosebumps rippling up my skin.

'Sounds like your mother could have made a good Siskin farmer. The punishment should not only fit the crime, but every other crime you might have committed.'

I flinched before I could catch myself.

'Maybe if she'd been allowed to run things. Unlike me, she was far better at giving orders than following them.'

Pip pointed out the long-eared bats swooping in and out of the eaves above us, and the conversation eased into lighter topics. Mum had always scorned therapy as for the weak-willed, or attention-seekers. As I sat here, the relief of having shared something painful and personal with what I hoped was a genuine friend – as if a secret shame had been wiped clean – was what I imagined it must feel like.

As Pip walked me home – not because I might leave a gate open, he was clear to point out, but in case there were more tourists wandering about who might cause similar problems I could otherwise get the blame for – I couldn't help wondering what else my mother had been wrong about.

I could have felt angry with her. I probably did, somewhere below the grief and the thrill of realising that I didn't have to pretend I agreed with her any more.

Most of all, since I'd opened that box of letters, when it came to my mother, I simply felt sad.

* * *

4 April 1988

My sweet Nellie,

Another anniversary – two years I have had the joy of being your husband! – so time for another letter. While you've made it clear there won't be any children who might one day get to read our love story, perhaps there will be nieces and nephews to enjoy these letters instead. And you mustn't mind the comments from Da. Richard will inherit the farm – it's his job to produce an heir! I chose you, and your happiness will always come first.

A lot has changed in a year, hasn't it? Now you're the one working every hour God sends, while I feel my way through the concrete and brick jungle that is Nottingham. I'm grateful for a few days of work, but for the most part, it seems the only person in this city who isn't frantically rushing from one important matter to another is me.

It turns out I had taken for granted living in a place where everyone knows who you are and all about your business.

But listen to me moaning on more like a farmer discussing the price of beef than a grateful husband writing a love letter to his bride!

Let me try again:

The other night, you asked if I miss the island, and my immediate answer was of course, it was my home. But from the first time we met, my home has been with you, and you are more beautiful to me than a thousand Siskin sunsets. You are my family, now, Nellie. Our love is the land in which I cultivate a life I am forever grateful for. My harvest shall always be your smiles, your touch, your trust.

I will meet you from work this evening, if I don't get lost on my way to the restaurant!

With faith, hope and love
G

* * *

I woke up on Tuesday morning to my first island rainstorm. I'd been vaguely planning on doing something touristy, like cycling to the smaller village, Lithin, or booking a slot on a boat that did whale-spotting tours. Instead, I spent the morning helping Lily assemble shelving units for the guest living room while Malcolm uploaded pictures of the completed lilac bedroom to the website and across their social media.

Either side of picking the children up from nursery and school, we peeled, chopped and sautéed enough parsnips for twenty pasties (just about every parsnip on the island, given the season) and prepared the rest of the vegetarian ingredients ready for the Stilton delivery on Wednesday. Lily was in almost constant contact with her sisters about the wedding. They were arranging the church service, entertainment and the other details as if they had all the time in the world and none of it really mattered anyway.

'Oh!' Lily exclaimed, after reading a message about borrowing wine glasses. 'We forgot a hen do. Or, what do you call it? A bridal shower! Which one would be best, do you think?'

I looked up from stirring a giant pan. 'I don't know the difference. To be honest, I've never been to either.'

Lily looked to the other mainlander in the room, who beetled his eyebrows in thought.

'The amount of alcohol involved, mainly. Alcohol, tacky props and the likelihood of a stripper turning up.'

'Which one is that?'

'A hen night.'

'Right, let's go for a bridal shower.' Lily nodded vigorously before going blank again. 'So not much booze, no props and no stripper. What *does* it have?'

'Depends on the bride in question.' Malcolm shrugged. 'I think the only essential ingredient is cake.'

'Sounds perfect.'

'But really, the chief bridesmaid should be sorting all this out.'

Lily called Celine, who created a group chat, *Bridal Parteeeee*, and by the time we were washing up, ten women had accepted an invitation to meet at Lily's old café, the Copper Pot, at seven that evening for drinks and desserts.

'Violet says we need an activity,' Lily read out. 'But Celine is working until six so won't have time to sort anything.'

'We could do something crafty,' I offered. 'Make bunting for the barn, and the other decorations? It saves us trying to do them all.'

'That's perfect.' Lily beamed. 'You're a wedding genius, Emmie. I'll ask everyone to contribute fabric for the bunting. We've got that ribbon from the market, and plenty of sewing machines between us. We just need to make sure Fern has a different job, like serving the cake, because she can't sew a straight line.'

'What about bringing some fabric that reminds them of Iris, or will remind Iris of them?'

'Oh, that's even better! An old dress or something.' She glanced at the pile of pots and vegetable peelings that used to be the kitchen. 'We'd better get moving with all this if we're going to be ready for seven, though.'

'I don't mind finishing it while you're there.'

'I'm going to pretend the brains behind this whole thing didn't just suggest she might not be coming.'

'Are you sure? I don't know how Celine would feel about that.'

And I didn't want to find a hair in my cake, or gob of spit in my wine glass. Even worse, I was paranoid about what nastiness I might discover when I got back here.

'How Celine feels is irrelevant. This wedding is only happening because of you. And don't worry.' She patted my arm. 'She knows I know what she's up to. I'll make sure she behaves herself.'

22

We arrived at the Copper Pot half an hour early, Lily retrieving the key from an ornamental kettle hanging by the door. By the time the others started to arrive, we'd pushed a load of the wooden tables together to form a craft station, and I was arranging cakes onto platters while Lily set out various drinks.

Celine was the first through the door, carrying a sewing machine as well as a full carrier bag dangling from each forearm.

'Hey, Lily!' She beamed, before hesitating when she saw me. 'Oh, Emmie. No one told me you'd been roped in as waitress. That's so kind of you to help out. Means us island gals can have a real proper catch-up.'

'Emmie's here as a guest,' Lily said, in a no-nonsense, mum voice.

'Oh?' Celine said, sounding distracted as she started setting up her sewing machine next to Lily's. 'I thought we agreed that, with it being so last minute, we'd stick to family and close friends only.'

'Family, close friends and the woman who saved the day by giving up her holiday to cater the whole damn thing with four days' notice,' Violet said, who'd appeared in the doorway as Celine was speaking.

'Yes, of course. Sorry, Emmie, no offence.' She scanned the room for a plug socket. 'I mean, I'd have expected you to be spending the evening with Pip, rather than a bunch of strangers.'

'We aren't strangers!' Lily snapped. 'Celine, are we going to have to ban you from talking to Emmie like we did with Poppy after Pip took her to the school Christmas disco? We all know you want to marry my brother, despite him ending things two years ago, the main reason being that every other half-decent farmer who's remotely in your age bracket is already taken. But Pip will make up his own mind about who he wants to be with, and you making passive-aggressive digs at his friend won't do you any favours.'

Whew. I buried my head in the bottom of the fridge. These island women didn't beat around the bush.

They reminded me of my mother.

'Besides,' Jasmine, Hugh's mum, added, having arrived right behind Violet, 'we might be old-fashioned around here but this isn't some sort of medieval tournament where he's forced to pick one of you. From what I heard, all that poor man wants is to focus on his farm. Take the hint, Celine, have some self-respect.'

Ouch.

'Okay, so firstly, even if I am still interested in Pip, it's nothing to do with how old he is. Little Lander and Craig Kelly are much closer to my age.'

'That's why I said half-decent,' Lily muttered.

'And secondly, me and Emmie are friends. I wasn't making a dig because I know her and Pip will never be a thing. She's only here a few days and knows nothing about farming. Hardly credible competition given my and Pip's history.' Celine glanced at

Jasmine. 'Not that this is a competition, of course. I only said what I did because we're the worst at being cliquey when we get together. Anyone who hasn't grown up knowing the old stories and silly in-jokes is bound to feel like a bridal-shower gooseberry at times. I mean, Emmie, can you even sew?'

'Um, yes. I can manage bunting.'

'Oh.' Celine looked taken aback. 'Did you bring fabric?'

'Flora, Jack and Beanie donated an old item of clothing each,' Lily said. 'They didn't want to be left out, so Emmie will sew their flags.'

'Well, that's perfect, then, isn't it?' Celine trilled, with nothing in her expression to suggest she'd been called out for being mean, or that the comments about her and Pip were embarrassing or unwelcome. I couldn't help thinking about the milk jug, though. I could believe that Celine trashed my rented bike and bought me a lobster roll, without batting an eyelid. Breaking into my bedroom at Sunflower Barn, however, still seemed excessive.

As the evening wore on, I tried not to feel like a bridal-shower gooseberry – or like someone who was being secretly targeted by an unknown enemy.

It helped that, in the modest-sized café, at least one Hawkins sister was always close by, and more often than not, they remembered to explain the in-jokes and whisper essential backstory to the increasingly outlandish tales of life on a tiny island, including what sounded like an alarmingly unsupervised stint at boarding school. However, while Iris's friends were perfectly nice, after brief exclamations about how they couldn't wait to try my infamous pasties, it was only right that the attention was all on the bride to be and celebrating twenty-five years of female friendships. It was tempting to wish I'd had the option of spending the evening with Pip, rather than 'a bunch of strangers', but the truth was, as the women laughed, teased, sewed and played a rowdy game identifying who said different quotes about either Iris, Hugh or both of them, what I really wished was that I hadn't reached twenty-six having never experienced anything like it.

It was reminiscent of the moment I'd walked out of Siskin airport into the salty air and clear skies of the island and felt as I'd been birthed from an aeroplane womb into a whole new reality.

While so frighteningly new and *alive*, this was something I ached to understand, to be a part of, to belong to.

It was when Celine turned up the volume to Madonna, the girls' night staple that spanned the Irish Sea, and Violet grabbed my hand, dragging me onto the tiny space they'd designated a dance floor, that I finally acknowledged quite how empty my life had been, and that whatever happened when I returned to the mainland, I would never – I *refused* to ever – be the same.

We were on the floor, rowing back and forth to 'Rock the Boat', when the café door opened and a man burst through wearing a checked suit and a yellow cap.

'What the hell?' Iris's friend, Fern, yelled into the sudden silence as Celine flicked off the music.

'My thoughts exactly,' Violet said, expression grim as she squeezed out of the line on the floor and clambered to her feet, brushing the dust off her velvet flares and scanning around for her platform trainers.

'Barnie, this is a bridal shower,' Lily said, not unkindly. 'Invitation only.'

'I know.' Barnie lifted up the cap to wipe his clammy brow. 'But I was with the lads, and Hugh, in the Island Arms, and they all got to talkin' about love, and marriage, and how the right woman can tame the wildest heart, and, Violet, I couldn't bear it any longer.'

Violet folded her arms, glancing up at the ceiling as though summoning the strength to hear out a drunk, desperate man's declaration. 'What couldn't you bear, Barnie?'

'You not knowing that you've tamed my wild heart.'

Eight women tutted as one.

'Are you going to tell him, or shall I?' Iris asked her sister.

'It's your bridal shower, of course I'll do it.' Violet sighed. 'It's probably my fault for not spelling it out earlier.'

'Tell me what?' Barnie asked, face swivelling between the sisters.

'Are all men this clueless?' another woman, Holly, asked me. 'Or is it just islanders?'

'Tell me what?' Barnie was rigid.

A day ago, I would have been surprised that Violet didn't take him outside, or in the back kitchen, or at the very least into a corner before answering him, but I was rapidly cottoning on to the fact that privacy and discretion weren't how islanders did things.

'Barnie, I have not tamed your wild heart.'

'You have! Honestly, Violet, I knew it as soon as—'

'Are you going to listen or what?'

Barnie nodded mutely.

'Your heart is as wild as a milky mug of cocoa. It's literally island-shaped. And even if it wasn't, you know I have zero interest in taming it. You can't allow yourself to get carried away by Connell's cider-fuelled ramblings.'

'How do you know it was him?'

'Please. He's given that speech so many times, his own wife is sick of hearing it.' Jasmine groaned.

'Then you turn up here, disrupting Iris's special night, and expect me to suddenly change my mind. I know you, Barnie Cork.

I fell for your oversized, mushy island heart after you lent me your best pencil on our first day of school. But my heart *is* wild, as you know all too well. And, unlike Connell, I will not tame it for anyone. I will not submit my dreams to a man's, put them to one side for a distant day I hope might eventually come, once all his plans have been fulfilled and our babies grown, by which time, my elderly parents will expect me to be taking on the farm. I will not settle nor shrink myself to fit in someone else's safe world. Not even yours, Barnie. You are the best person I know. You make me laugh like no one else, and you know exactly how to dry my tears. If anyone could make me stay, it would be you. But you also allowed me to see who I really am. To dare to live free. I will miss you more than I can bear to think about.' Violet paused to wipe the tears pouring down her face. 'But I'm not destined to be the wife of a man who lives for his doughnut stand.'

'I live for you,' Barnie croaked, his own eyes spilling over.

Violet paused for the briefest of moments.

'Goodbye, Barnie.'

'You're really going?'

'Once my new niece or nephew is safely here, I'm leaving.'

'Well, I guess that's that, then. Arnie's waiting outside.' Barnie pulled off his cap, used it to blot his face then turned to go.

'Will you dance with me at the wedding?' Violet blurted.

Barnie paused, one hand on the door. 'Since when have I danced with anyone else?'

We all sat there, in our line on the floor, until the door closed and the sound of a car pulling off faded into the distance. Violet stood to one side of us, face crumpled.

'Does that mean Barnie's fair game now?' Fern asked. 'I wouldn't mind working on his doughnut stand.'

'Can somebody please pour my sister a drink?' Lily asked through gritted teeth. 'And help me up. And tell Fern that she'd better wait until Violet is a good few thousand feet in the air before making another comment like that unless she wants to be pushed off Lithin cliff.'

'Celine?' Iris said, with a note of steel in her voice.

Celine flicked to an ABBA song, we turned down the lights, turned up the volume and danced our wild hearts out.

23

A combination of farmers, café owners and a pregnant bridesmaid meant the festivities concluded by eleven. Lily and I were dropped off by Taylor's taxi, which had squeezed enough women into a seven-seater car to surely invalidate any insurance. While Lily paid the teenage babysitter and secured her a lift in the taxi, I made a drink of mint tea in the kitchen and padded up to bed.

By the time I'd checked every inch of the room, then checked again, I dared to hope that everything was as I'd left it. Given that Celine and Richard were both accounted for that evening, if anything had been amiss, that would have implicated Aster as the only other person who seemed to dislike me.

I decided instead that the most sensible conclusion was the obvious one – the incidents were unfortunate coincidences, which I'd try not to let taint my remaining time here.

I was about to treat myself to another letter while I could still keep my eyelids open, when my phone pinged with three messages in quick succession. They were from an unknown number.

> How long before Pip gets fed up with pasties?
>
> Because anything else he'll want from a wife, island women can do better
>
> Keep your hands off him and spare both of you the embarrassment

I was shaking so hard, it took three attempts to get a screenshot. I sat propped against my headboard, attempting to sip my tepid tea until the panic galloping through my bloodstream started to slow down and my brain unscrambled itself into a few distinct thoughts:

I now knew that the bike, the milk, probably the gate, were not coincidences.

I also knew why – someone wanted to scare me away from Pip.

Despite nothing romantic happening with him, outside my own fervent imagination, someone was feeling mistakenly jealous and threatened enough to take some seriously bizarre action.

Did this mean they were dangerous? Unstable? Or just especially determined to marry him?

I might have wondered whether this person, who knew Pip far better than I, had seen, heard or been told something that implied Pip might be more interested in a serious relationship than the ease with which he'd accepted our need to stay friends had implied.

But then again, given that this person had made disturbingly little effort to hide her identity as being Celine, I readily dismissed this. The Hawkins sisters had been clear that when it came to Pip, she was irrational.

At least now I had actual evidence, and so could do something about it other than conduct endless inspections of the yellow bedroom and avoid being alone on the farm. I would show Lily in the morning – if nothing else, she could corroborate the sender as

Celine, or else fill me in on any other women harbouring a secret obsession with her brother.

After a long time going round and round how things would play out over the next few days, I reached for the escape of another letter. The first one was more of a note so I ended up reading the next one written by my mum, too. It heartened me to remember that I was a Brown. Competent, capable and utterly unflappable. Or at least I knew how to pretend to be.

As with the previous few, there was no address on the first envelope, simply, 'Nellie'.

4.00 p.m.

Nellie,

I've called the restaurant three times and got no answer. I'll try again from the station, but if I wait for you to come home, I'll miss the last train. There's been an accident with the new combine. Richard is seriously hurt. They're airlifting him to hospital in Wales but he might not last the night, so I'm going straight there.

I love you,
G

10 August 1988

Gabriel,

I have given up waiting for you to call (or get a phone installed in the farmhouse!). I know this harvest must be even more gruelling than usual, with Richard still in hospital, and your mother with him, but could you perhaps spare me a two-minute phone call to reassure me that you have not also been crushed beneath the combine? You know I cannot rely on your father to inform me should anything happen to you, his loathing of me having only intensified since I 'stole you away'.

How is your brother? Did they manage to save his leg? You must all be questioning what to do about the farm. I cannot help wondering about your thoughts on the matter. I suspect that letting go of the land after seven generations may feel almost as bad as losing a leg.

You once said that your home was with me now. But despite your efforts to hide it, I know a part of your heart remains on the island.

What I mean to say is – I appreciate that there is far more at stake than a barley harvest. If you need to stay longer while your family decide what to do, I understand.

Although that does not make missing you any easier.

The flat is as forlorn as the eastern coves in February without you.

Nellie.

* * *

When I came downstairs for breakfast, the children were all eating soft-boiled eggs with buttered toast. Malcolm was packing up lunchboxes while Lily – well, Lily appeared to be self-combusting in front of a pile of boxes.

'Emmie!' Beanie called. 'Do you want an egg from Pecky, Hopper or Pooper?'

'I don't know. Which would you recommend?'

'Not Pooper,' she replied with absolute solemnity.

'At risk of failing the guest trial, would you mind making it yourself?' Lily asked, wringing her hands. 'The rest of the ingredients are here, and I need to figure out where to put them. I knew it would be a lot, but having them here is giving me Braxton Hicks contractions. Plus, the florist called to say that a third of the irises have been crushed in transit, are we okay with carnations instead. Celine has decided the bridesmaids need to perform some choreographed dance down the aisle. The rehearsal for which consists of watching a YouTube thing and a half-hour video call. I'm not booty-popping in church, even without a baby bump. And if this wedding wasn't enough drama, some fiend has left a three-star review on TripAdvisor, describing Sunflower Barn as "meh". If you're going to write a fake negative review for a non-existent trip, why wouldn't you go all out with a one star?'

I was about to reply that three-star reviews tended to come across as worse, as people were more likely to dismiss truly horrendous reviews as being written by picky whiners, but she hadn't finished, yelping, 'And it would be really, very helpful if for one blessed minute, you stopped kicking my bladder!'

'It's not baby's fault,' Jack said, frowning as he scooped out the last bit of his egg.

'Sorry, baby. Sorry.' Lily waved one hand at everyone, the other rubbing her bump. 'It's all catching up with me, you know? Once tomorrow is over with and we can focus back on this place I'll feel a whole lot better, but I honestly think that up until then, one more issue could send me tumbling right over the edge.'

'The edge of what?' Jack asked. '*Into* what?'

His mum shuddered 'Let's just pray we never find out.'

I looked at Lily, checking a packet of venison before squashing it into the fridge, her face pale, hair in a bedraggled bun, a smear of something unidentifiable across her backside.

I left my phone in my pocket.

* * *

After boiling myself an egg and waving the kids off to school and nursery with Malcolm, I helped Lily organise all the ingredients, and then we got to work.

It was going to be a long day of mixing flour and fat, rolling it gently, layering the pastry into perfect flakiness, then adding the fillings and transporting one hundred pasties to the farmhouse where they would be stored overnight in the chest freezers usually reserved for cuts of beef before being freshly baked early afternoon, ready to be served from four o'clock.

It was a blissful distraction from everything else, including not only Celine but the most recent email from Gregory requesting I call him immediately to discuss amendments to the new contract, for example reducing the time allowed for closure from ten to three days.

The very thought of hunkering behind that kiosk all day made my insides wither.

Lily spent most of the day multitasking like a pro, dealing with issues on speakerphone while scooping out ladles of mushy peas, negotiating an even fiercer discount with the florist when they dropped off the decidedly droopy bouquets as the dance video Celine had sent through played in the background.

The last pasty was sealed and glazed at five on the dot.

Malcolm took one look at the piles of dirty pots and trays and sent his wife for a nap in the hammock. When I picked up a tea towel to help with the washing up, he was equally insistent in ordering me out of the house.

'It's another gorgeous day. Tomorrow, you'll be sweltering in the farmhouse kitchen. If that's going to be your last day on this strange little paradise, make the most of this one while you can.'

'Okay...' I stood awkwardly by the sink. 'Have you got any suggestions about what to do? Or where to go?'

'Here.' He pulled out his phone and pointed out a road that

ran straight across to the east coast to the island's second village. 'You can't go without visiting the bustling metropolis that is Lithin.'

'How far is it?'

'About an hour's walk. Or you could cycle.'

'Yeah. It's been a pretty full-on day...'

'Of course!' Malcolm shook his head. 'Walking three miles along a path you don't know, to a place you've not been before, is not a restful evening. Hang on.'

He opened another app.

'The bus will be passing the end of the road in twenty minutes.'

'Presuming there aren't any escaped animals, or Connell gets distracted chatting?'

Malcolm grinned. 'This is our primitive equivalent of live journey app. He posted a photo of himself by the harbour two minutes ago. Looks like it's one of those rare occasions when he's almost on time.'

I took fifteen minutes to hastily shower off the scent of braised meat, swap my shorts for a sundress, brush my hair and pack a bag.

Flora met me in the hallway. 'Aren't you going with Da to the farmhouse?'

'He's insisted I enjoy a few hours off,' I replied, moving out of the way as Malcolm hurried past carrying a box.

'Uncle Pip will be there, getting the Old Barn ready. Celine is helping, too.'

'Yep. I heard her talking about it with your mum.' Of course it had crossed my mind, but the thought of popping up at the same place as Celine made my lungs seize up with anxiety.

Flora folded her arms before catching me off guard with a

conversational curveball. 'Have you decided to stay here forever yet?'

I took a moment before answering, deciding to pretend her question had nothing to do with the previous mention of Pip. 'I can't, even if the island is my new second favourite place in the world. I have a home, and a business back in England. I can't just abandon it all.'

'Hmph.' She wasn't convinced. 'A good job Helen of Troy didn't think that way. Or Arwen.'

'That's not quite the same. They gave up everything for love. I'm only here on holiday.'

As I said goodbye and made my way outside to wait for Connell's bus, I heard her mutter, 'You're only here on holiday? If you believe that then maybe what they say about mainlanders is true after all.'

* * *

The minibus trundled up a few minutes after I'd walked to the end of the gravel drive and found a place to wait by the side of the larger road. Malcolm had assured me there were no formal stops; Connell would pick up and drop off at any point along the route. I held out one arm, just in case, and he came to an abrupt halt directly in front of me.

'Well, you must be Emmie,' Connell said, with a grin that almost split his round face in half.

'Hello,' I said, avoiding looking at the patches of rust, numerous dents and hole the size of a football as I climbed up the steps.

'Pip's pasty girl, everyone,' he announced to the other passengers occupying about half the seats.

'Oh, no.' I turned to face them, my hands contradicting the

greetings, 'oohs!' and knowing nods with a vigorous 'no!' gesture. 'I'm making pasties for Iris and Hugh's wedding, but I'm not Pip's girl.'

'Yet,' someone called.

'Ever,' I said with a rictus smile, but I was pretty sure no one heard me over the sniggers. I scanned the eight or so passengers to confirm that Celine wasn't one of them and pulled out my purse. 'A ticket to Lithin, please.'

'Return?' Connell asked.

'What time's the last bus from Lithin?'

Connell scratched his head. 'I'll probably stop at the caravan park for a quick drink and a natter then be heading back through Lithin 'bout six-thirty. Pass here maybe seven, depending on how busy we are, then on home, for Betty to serve up supper.'

The journey was about three miles, according to Malcolm's map. That was a lot of stops.

It was five-thirty now.

'Single, then, please.'

'That'll be six pounds fifty. Cash only.'

'Oh. Okay.' The shuttle bus to Sherwood Airport covered fifteen miles and was two pounds. Even cheaper, with a frequent traveller pass.

Connell wrinkled up his forehead when I held out a twenty-pound note.

'Sorry, chicken. I don't do change. Ends up causing delays.'

'I don't have six pounds fifty.' I rooted through the handful of coins in my purse, knowing it was nowhere near enough.

'I don't mind taking the twenty if you don't.'

Of course I minded. I was about to back up and find an alternative plan for the evening when a voice called out from the back, 'You can't charge Pip's girl tourist rates, Connell. He'll go mad when he finds out.'

There was a murmur of assent as Connell scratched his head again.

'How about a fresh pasty?' a woman in the front seat suggested.

'Um... I don't carry them around with me.'

'Well, you could always drop one off tomorrow.'

'No chance,' another passenger said. 'She's got the wedding tomorrow. There won't be time to wait around for the bus.'

'What about Friday, then?'

'I'm sorry, but I really won't have the chance to do any more baking,' I said apologetically.

'Slip him a leftover from the wedding, then; no one'll notice,' yet another passenger chipped in.

'Stealing from the bride and groom to pay her bus fare? Is that the type of thing people do on the mainland?' The woman at the front huffed.

'Nah, Pip's a decent fella. He wouldn't be with a lass who'd be stealing from his own family, now, would he?'

I held out the note again, thinking it a small price to pay to end this nonsense.

Connell puffed out some air, sucked in his cheeks and narrowed one eye. I could see how the bus ended up behind schedule.

'Okay. I owe Pip a favour. You can tell him that's it paid.' He raised his voice so the whole minibus could hear. 'One single to Lithin, free of charge, for Pip's pasty girl!'

'About time, too,' a man near the back said as I hurried to the nearest available seat, presuming he was referring to the delay.

'Pip's not getting any younger, after all. His ma and da will be that pleased he's finally chosen a wife.'

I slid down the back of the seat and pretended not to hear the rest of the bus discussing my wifely qualities as we started heading down the lane.

There was no point hoping Pip wouldn't find out I'd not only taken his favour from Connell, but also allowed a minibus to think I was his bride-to-be for the sake of a free ticket. The whole island would probably have heard about it before Connell clocked off for the evening.

Including Celine.

I slid a little further down in my seat and prayed that she loved Iris enough not to sabotage her wedding feast.

24

It soon became apparent how a bus could take so long to cover such a short distance. Every time someone got off or on, which varied between half a mile and a couple of hundred yards apart, Connell would have a chat about where they were heading, where they'd come from or what the last few people had said in answer to those questions. I also realised fairly quickly that no one paid the 'tourist rates'. Some handed the driver a bottle of cider or a piece of cake. Others proffered a tub of cherries, clutch of rhubarb stalks or a battered paperback. One man tried a piece of driftwood, shaped a bit like a fish, but Connell reminded him that he accepted 'useful items only', so the man decided to walk instead.

At eight minutes past six, we pulled up on the one road that made up the centre, and all the rest, of Lithin.

Like Port Cathan, the road ran alongside the coast, with a row of buildings on the opposite side to the promenade. Beyond this were steps leading down to a pebbly beach.

I strolled from one end of the promenade to another, which took about five minutes. There was a small pub and fancy-looking restaurant, but I chose a 'catch of the day' special from the fish and chip shop and found a wall overlooking the sea.

The fish was crisply battered, the chips deliciously squishy and the Siskin sauce had the perfect amount of tang to balance the grease.

While I ate, a dog owner threw a ball into the waves for a pair of collies to chase, children busily constructed a tower of pebbles and a couple wandered along the shoreline arm in arm. The contrast in these strangers to the people I usually observed, scurrying across the concourse to then stand impatiently in a queue, noticing nothing save the departure board or the phone in front of their nose, was stark.

The time on the Isle of Siskin had been a revelation. These farmers and café owners, shop-workers and bus drivers worked hard to make a living, but they also made sure they didn't neglect the 'living' part. Having spent several days adjusting to new surroundings and people, taking everything in, and now this evening on Lithin promenade, I started to think what this newly discovered way of living might mean for me.

Not a grand fantasy like in one of Flora's novels. In the real world, there were contractual obligations, bills to pay, deliveries on order. A houseful of stuff, all I'd ever known, every memory from my childhood. But as I'd learned more about this whole other side to my mum, I realised that pretending I hadn't chosen my current circumstances – the business and the busyness, the famine of friendship and family – was a cop-out. It might not have been easy to go against Mum and open some different doors – to travel, or study. Buy a pair of high-heeled shoes. I'd seen not only with Blessing, but also here, how family expectations impacted lots of people. But the brutal truth was, Mum no longer cared what I did with Parsley's, or the cottage. Besides, she was the best example I'd known of someone who defied expectations, ignored convention and followed her own path, chose her own life and then lived with it.

Those thoughts finally led to me one conclusion, as I sat and watched a fleet of boats bobbing on distant waves, surrounded by children's laughter blending with the chatter from the pub across the street.

A new pasty recipe and a makeover weren't enough.

I was done with working in an airport.

I couldn't spend my days in a giant, windowless, weather-less box any more. I didn't want to be constantly battered by the onslaught of other people's stress as they hurried past.

I wanted to work under the open sky. Or at least somewhere I could look at it.

I wanted more lie-ins and late nights. Long, lazy lunches on my days off.

At the very least, I wanted to try it and see.

I decided I had to do more travelling. Properly explore the wonderful place where I'd grown up. Join a club to learn something completely different and maybe even make some friends.

I owned a house and had a stash of savings.

What was the worst that could happen?

I finished my food, wandered down to the water's edge, and, for the first time in as long as I could remember, I allowed myself to dream.

That night, after managing to snag a lift back to Sunflower Barn in Taylor's taxi, I wrote the most important letter of my life.

I then read two of the saddest.

10 November 1988

Gabriel,

I waited by the phone all morning, yesterday. Whenever else you've missed our scheduled call, at least you've left a message as soon as you can, so when I get home from work, I know you're safe and well. I barely slept a wink all night. Has something terrible happened, or did you merely forget it was my birthday, that you'd promised to call?

I honestly don't know which would hurt more.

I even called the phone box in the hope someone else would answer, and at least tell me you were still alive. I stayed up, listening for the buzzer, in case you'd flown home to surprise me.

What a fool, imagining the farm or your family could spare you for even this, my fortieth birthday.

I know you're working hard. I've experienced how the farm can devour all your time, your energy and every waking thought. But I am your wife, Gabriel. You have said many times that I am your everything.

What emergency arose that is more important to you than me?

Is a broken fence more urgent than my broken heart?

Did your mother ask you to change a light bulb or request a lift to her odious Island Wives club?

I will not apologise for being angry. Unless you are dead or incapacitated. In which case I shall merely redirect my anger towards your family for not immediately informing your wife.

Are you ever coming back to me?

Do you even want to any more?

Nellie

16 November 1988

My dear Nellie,

I'm so very sorry. I know you're angry. But please, if our marriage means anything, if I mean anything to you, read this letter. You know how easily my words come out wrong unless I write them down.

I didn't forget. I woke up with a smile on my face because I knew I'd get to wish you a happy birthday that morning. I couldn't eat my porridge, I was that excited. Like a child on Christmas Eve. A young (old) boy in love.

And then the tractor wouldn't start, so I needed to help Da with that. One of the cows had fallen sick. Ma had already asked me to pick up Richard's prescription if I was heading into the village, and the queue at the chemist was that long. So, it was already late morning by the time I reached the phone box, only to find it broken. On my way to ask James Madden if I could borrow theirs, Lander flagged me down to say an auditor had turned up and I was needed straight away.

I meant to call as soon as I could, to leave a message. But with one thing and another – I won't bore you with the details, I know they only sound like excuses anyway – I simply couldn't. And then it was so late, I was exhausted. I knew you'd be upset, so I convinced myself it'd be better to call in the morning, when I had the energy to talk properly.

Only, Ma was ill – properly ill for maybe the first time in her life, so I had to help with Richard, tend the chickens, wait for the doctor. And before I knew it, it was afternoon, you were working, and I could only speak to your answerphone. I don't even care that the whole island knows about Gabe Hawkins using the Maddens' phone to leave desperate messages for his wife, proving all their predictions about the rushed mainlander marriage to be true.

I know it's not good enough. I hurt you, and I'm that sorry. I can't imagine how you felt, waiting for me to call on your birthday.

I only hope you liked your present.

I'm going to keep calling every day at 9 a.m. until either you answer, or it's Christmas, in which case I'll be seeing you anyway.

I'm sorry.

I love you.

You know the farm needs me right now, but I will be with you as soon as I can.

Yours, in eternal love,

G

That was it. No more envelopes, but still many more questions. Was this incident the deciding factor in their marriage ending? Did something worse, more significant happen, or was it simply a trickle of disappointments and distance that eventually washed away any last trace of hope or commitment to work things out?

One way or another, I had to find out.

25

The morning of Iris and Hugh's wedding, my innate Parsley's alarm clock woke me at four-thirty.

My first thought was a ripple of joy that I'd be seeing Pip that day. I immediately pushed away the dismay that followed, knowing it would probably be the last time I ever saw him. I wasn't going to allow that to spoil the remainder of my island adventure.

My next thought was to check my phone. I wasn't surprised to find Gregory had already replied, the email sent at one that morning. It was a long one. He covered all bases in trying to persuade me to change my mind, including warning that I'd never find another offer as good as at the airport, and would be bankrupt before I'd had the chance to build up a profitable business anywhere else. He also begged me to stay, offering to discuss a rent discount that I knew would make the other vendors riot, and threw in two paragraphs of melodramatic flattery, describing in great detail how the airport food and beverage offering had suffered without me. After a vague threat about the fine for failing to open on Sunday, the final day of the current contract, questioning whether it was even legal for me to back out of renewing my lease at this late stage, he then finished off by stating I could shove my pasties up my own cockpit. I had no idea what that meant, other than writing an email in the middle of the night probably wasn't the wisest idea.

I decided to allow him a couple of days to apologise before I replied. I was aware of the fine I'd have to pay for Sunday, and had enough to cover it in my savings. Instead of opening up on Sunday, I'd spend the day clearing out the kiosk instead.

Now wide awake, I showered, dressed in shorts and a T-shirt – not ideal catering wear by any means, but it was already pushing twenty degrees outside, and I wouldn't survive a day in the kitchen in jeans – and savoured a mug of tea in the garden, with the bliss of knowing that, for the foreseeable future, I could enjoy as many mornings like this as I chose.

I phoned Blessing at five-fifteen. The news about Parsley's would be all over the airport, so I needed to catch her before she set off for the early shift.

'I hope you're calling at this time because you've not been to bed yet,' she croaked.

'I'm catering the wedding today, remember? I think my body automatically clicked back into the Parsley's schedule. I woke up an hour before my alarm.'

'Ugh. I suppose I'll allow it given that you'll be spending most of the day with Hot Farmer. But it doesn't explain why you're calling me.'

'I have some big news.'

'Oh. My. Goodness. You boffed him, didn't you? Did he confess that he loves you? Ask you to be Mrs Hot Farmer?'

'No! None of those things. I told you none of those things are going to happen. It's about Parsley's...'

I hastily explained to Blessing that I was still coming home on

Friday, but I wouldn't be coming back to work. She shocked me by crying.

'I'm changing things up, though. I know it's not the same as seeing each other every day, but if we hung out more outside the airport, we can get to know each other properly, have some real fun.'

'What, more fun than discussing the inspiration behind Barb's latest eyeshadow and blusher combo?' She sniffed. 'What if you don't want to be friends with me now you're a carefree, wild spirit about to embark on unknown adventures, and I'm back to being a saddo sharing an underwear drawer with her teenage sister?' She paused to blow her nose. 'You'll be far too busy to hang out with me. Oh, which reminds me, we've got a family thing on Friday evening so I might struggle to get all moved out after work. When do you need me gone by?'

'Um... how about never?'

There was a long pause.

'Do you mean I can stay? Forever?'

'Well, I hope it won't be forever. Didn't you say you were desperate to get married at some point?'

Blessing squealed so loudly, I dropped my phone.

'You aren't serious?' I could still hear her as I bent to pick it up. 'Are you serious? Emmie, don't joke with me about this. You have no idea. Honestly, if you were joking then now you have to let me stay anyway and never admit you didn't mean it, because if you make me go back now, I'll never recover.'

'I can't believe I didn't ask you to move in with me ages ago.'

'Neither can I. I've only been dropping hints for the past year.'

'It never would have crossed my mind that you'd want to live with me.'

'What, because I'm such a loser?'

'Because *I'm* a total loser.'

'Emmie, what? Hang on. I need to go so I'm transferring you to the car phone.' A couple of seconds later, she reconnected, voice slightly fuzzy from the speaker. 'You own your own house and business at twenty-six, and don't give a crap what anybody thinks. And *you're* the loser?'

'I give a crap what everyone thinks!'

'Then why do you wear those clothes, and... be like you are?'

'Because I give most of a crap about what Mum thinks. No. Scrap that.' I stood up and started walking down the garden. The grass was damp with dew, the birds a full-on symphony all around me. I sucked in a deep breath and made sure I meant what I said next. 'I did care, more than anything, what she thought. But I'm closing Parsley's, so I guess I now care more about what I think.'

'Wowee. Hold the line on *that* thought, Emmie.'

'What?'

'Keep caring most about what *you* think. I mean, when it comes to being you, and what you want. Obviously care about what other people think, too. Like, me, when it comes to my woeful living situation and how much I want to properly be your actual, real friend. But I'm so down with you finally thinking about what you want.'

We chatted a bit more, about Blessing moving the rest of her things over to my – *our* – house, and how I was genuinely very happy for her to have Mum's old bedroom, once I'd got back and emptied it, so we could redecorate.

'Right,' she said. 'I'm nearly at the airport, but before I go, what are you wearing to this wedding? I don't suppose there's loads of clothes shops over there.'

'Definitely not ones that sell catering uniforms. I'm in the shorts and blue top.'

There was a moment of silence.

'You're wearing shorts? To a wedding? Where the man you've been crushing on for two years will be in attendance? I thought you were over trying to please Nell?'

'I am...'

'Then *what the hell, Emmie*?'

'I'm baking pasties all day. What did you expect me to wear?'

'You aren't going to the reception, once all the baking is done?'

'No. I'm not invited to the reception. I'll be too busy clearing up, anyway.'

'Excuse me?'

I was momentarily confused by that response, as it seemed to have an echo, until Lily appeared at my side with another mug of tea, and I realised that she and Blessing had both said the same thing.

'Of course you're invited to the wedding!' Lily exclaimed, before leaning closer to my phone and yelling, 'She is invited!'

'Good to hear it,' Blessing huffed. 'Look, I'm heading to Security. Call me later when you've decided what you're really wearing. No, send me a photo. No – do both. Photo then call. I love you, bye!'

Lily shoved the mug at me so that she could put both hands on her hips and stare me down properly.

'I know you've only been here a week, Emmie. But haven't you figured out anything about how we do things around here yet? You don't need an invitation to the wedding that is only happening because you've stepped in to cater at the last minute. Of course you're coming. The students we've hired to waiter are clearing up. As soon as the last tray of pasties is out the oven, I expect to see you in the Old Barn.'

'I can't... I'm not sure...' I stopped, took a breath. Remembered who I was trying to be now, and decided that I should go, so I would. 'Thank you, that would be lovely.'

'Perfect.' Lily smiled, enjoying the view for a moment before snapping her head around to look at me. 'What *are* you going to wear? If you didn't think you were invited, then you won't have sorted anything. Unless you happened to squeeze a just-in-case outfit into your suitcase?'

'No. I didn't. I have the long sundress I wore the other day, but it's not clean.'

'It's lovely, but not wedding-worthy.' She smiled. 'Not a "finally convince my brother to convince you to at the very least have one night of romance" outfit, anyway.'

'I don't think I want an outfit like that.'

'Yeah.' Lily scrunched up her nose. 'Sorry, but I've seen the way you two look at each other, so I don't think that's true. I mean, he'd be happy to give it a try if you were wearing Mammaw's old dressing gown and wellies, but he needs to know you want him to try, given that, for reasons nobody can fathom, you both pretended you didn't.'

I tried to come up with an argument against this, but I really didn't have much brain power left for making arguments that in my heart of hearts I didn't quite believe in.

Given that this was the new, own-what-you-really-want Emmie, I might as well admit to myself that what I really wanted was a dance, a kiss, or some sort of romantic moment with Pip before I left. Wouldn't it be easier to start my new life, knowing that one of my impossible dreams had already come true?

Lily narrowed her eyes at me.

'Celine probably has something you can borrow.'

'No, I couldn't,' I said, far too quickly. 'I mean, we're completely different sizes.'

'Hmm. I don't think Iris or Violet will have anything that fits you, either. I have one pretty dress, but I've worn it to so many things, everyone will know you've borrowed it. Ooh!' She grabbed my arm so hard, I nearly spilled the rest of my tea. 'I think I have the answer.'

She trotted inside before I had time to ask what, but had to trust that whatever she came up with would be better than crumpled shorts.

The kids had been granted the afternoon off school, but Flora and Jack had to go in for the morning, despite their protests. As soon as Malcolm had set off, Lily and I cycled to the farmhouse to add the boxes of freshly delivered flowers to the other decorations before I headed to the kitchen and Lily took the rest of the flowers over to the church.

The barn bustled like an August Saturday in the airport. Borrowed tables and chairs of various shapes and sizes had been set out earlier, and Rosemary and Violet were now adding brightly patterned tablecloths. Richard and Hugh's parents were following behind with wine glasses, forks and napkins. Others were hanging up the bridal-shower bunting and strings of lights, offloading drinks and more glasses onto a makeshift bar or doing a final sweep of the floor.

I spotted Celine in one corner, arranging photos of Iris and Hugh on a table, along with a postbox for cards and a guest book. Swallowing back the nausea constricting my throat, I wondered whether there was a lock on the kitchen door, and if it would be rude if I used it.

'Could anyone have come up with a better choice of meal for a home-made wedding?'

I turned to find Gabe standing next to me, hands stuffed in the pockets of his jeans, a soft smile crinkling the corners of his eyes. 'When Rosemary and I wed, we thought sandwiches and sausage rolls would keep things simple, but it still left us with a hundred-and-twenty dirty plates. Hot, filling food you can eat with your fingers, no washing-up necessary? Pasties are perfect.'

'I hope they turn out okay. It's always a bit of a risk, using slightly different ingredients and a strange oven.'

'Pah. You'll be fighting off future orders by the end of the night.'

'Well, once people know I'm heading back tomorrow, that should deter any bookings. It'd cost a lot more if I had to include flights and accommodation.'

Gabe nodded. 'Well, we can only see what happens. Although, I'm glad you've not discounted the idea altogether. It'd be grand to have you visit again, some time.'

'I'm not discounting much at this point,' I said. 'I've decided to close the kiosk.'

Gabe raised his eyebrows, his gaze searching my face.

'It's this place,' he said, with a knowing nod as if he'd found what he was looking for. 'Has a way of helping people see things they didn't before. Changes your perspective. Some say it's how the light refracts off the cliff-tops that opens your eyes. Or the sea air, clearing out all the gubbins in your head. Others put it down to pure island magic.'

'Maybe it's all of those things,' I said, kneeling down to unpack a box of irises. 'I think, for me, it's the lack of distractions. Limited Wi-Fi. Less background busyness bombarding me all day. Plus, time to think, and space to be.' I picked up a pair of Lily's scissors and began snipping the ends off the stems. 'I love it here, as I'm sure most people do. Although, I can understand why it wouldn't suit everyone.'

Gabe opened another box, this one with lilies, and joined me. 'Your mother, you mean?'

I nodded, a sudden lump in my throat making it difficult to reply.

'You read the letters?'

'Yes.'

'You probably have questions, then.'

I looked at him, surprised. Gabe had been married to Rosemary for a long time. I hadn't expected him to want to restart the conversation about his first wife.

'I've heard about every remotely interesting happening relating to the past two generations of Hawkinses, plus plenty of stories that aren't.' Gabe's face softened. 'I can't imagine not knowing my family's history, where I came from.'

I thought about Kennedy Swan, my birth mother, and the unknown man who fathered me. Unlike all the other times, I wondered whether I should do something to find out more of her – *my* – story.

'There's a lot the letters don't say,' I replied, dragging my thoughts back to the woman who had been my mother in every way that mattered.

'You're flying back in the morning?'

I nodded, snipping the last stem in the box.

'Let's find fifteen minutes or so later today, then. Now's not really the time or place.'

'Thank you.' It was clear in my voice how much I meant it. If things had worked out differently, perhaps Gabe would have been my stepfather. The thought of his gentle, easy-going nature being there to alleviate Mum's stern severity brought tears to my eyes.

But when I turned away to compose myself under the guise of fetching another box of flowers, I spotted Pip approaching the barn, and I had to appreciate that if Gabe and Mum had stayed together, there'd be no Pip – or his sisters – so things had worked out for the best.

'Hey.' It was embarrassingly obvious how he ignored everyone else and walked straight up to me.

'Hi.' I ducked my flushing face over the new box, fiddling with the parcel tape.

'Philip,' Gabe said, not bothering to keep the amusement from his voice.

'Oh, hi, Da. What can I do to help?'

'Your sister is in charge; I'm only here to do what I'm told.'

'Which one?'

'I've no idea. I daren't ask.'

'Lily?' Pip called. 'What do you need me to do?'

'Those flowers want arranging into ten vases for the tables.' Lily marched over. 'Da, will you help me over here, please?'

'Over where?' Gabe got up, brushed his knees off and tried to work out what Lily's vague hand gesture had been waving at.

'Over anywhere that means Pip and Emmie can have some space,' Lily hissed, loud enough to cause Celine, now hanging photographs near the barn entrance, to stiffen.

'I'm sorry,' Pip said, shaking his head with an embarrassed smile. 'I have tried telling them.'

'Once you islanders make your mind up about something, you really stick to it.' I offered what I hoped was a light-hearted eye-roll in return.

'Yeah,' Pip muttered. 'Something, or someone.'

Kneeling beside him on an old horse-rug, as I snipped and stripped the different flowers of their lower leaves, and Pip arranged them in the vases, that comment hovered between us like a cloud of static electricity. I had never been so acutely aware of another human being's presence (not even when Mum stood over my shoulder the first time she let me roll out pastry).

It felt like the culmination of every conversation we'd had at Parsley's, each sentence treasured like a precious stone. The thrill of racing through the airport, knowing he'd be on the first aeroplane I'd ever set foot on. Him jumping out of his truck to give me a lift to his sister's, the picnic, the walks, all that talking but then the comfort of companionable silence... It all grew into a realisation as glorious as the sunsets we'd watched over the sparkling Siskin sea.

I didn't want to say goodbye to this man.

For the next hour or so, as we quietly got on with our task, I thought about his dad's revelation in the second letter he'd written to Mum.

With every passing minute, I grow more convinced that this is that indescribable, mysterious force which others name 'true love'.

This wasn't a silly crush on the first lovely man to show any real interest in me as a person.

It wasn't a holiday thing.

The way my heart trembled, my skin burned when his arm brushed against mine…

It was definitely not a nice friendship.

Once the thought crept into my head, it was so obvious, I couldn't focus on anything else.

With every beat of my heart, I grew *more convinced*.

I was falling in love with Pip.

Thud, thump, thud.

I love Pip. I love Pip. I love Pip…

The only thing I was uncertain about now was what to do about it.

26

When Blessing phoned as I handed Pip the second-to-last bunch of asters, I couldn't scramble out of the barn fast enough.

'Hey.'

'Hi. Are you okay? You sound out of breath.'

'Yes. No. I have no idea.'

'Tell me.'

I paced over to the nearest fence, then started marching alongside it. 'You called me, you go first.'

'You'll never guess what I've done.'

I stopped. 'It's not something to do with my kitchen, is it? You've not set the house on fire, or killed all my plants?'

'If I had, you think I'd break it to you by asking you to guess? No. It's a good thing! Exciting. And nothing to do with the house.'

'You have a date?'

'Well, yes, but that's not a big deal. Guess again.'

'Please tell me. I've got quite a lot to do today.'

'I've handed in my notice.'

'Wow!'

Blessing had worked at the Travel Shop since she was sixteen.

'Why? What are you going to do instead?' For a panicked moment, I wondered if she would now expect to live with me rent-free, which was okay – I had no mortgage to pay, but I would be living off my savings for now and we had agreed that Blessing would split the cottage bills and buy her own food.

'Help you in whatever you're doing next? I can't make pasties yet, but I can wash up, manage accounts and serve coffee. Compared to you, I'll smash marketing, social media, all that biz.'

'Blessing, I have no idea what I'm doing next.'

'Okay, we can take some time out and travel for a bit instead. Pick up seasonal work. I don't know, but I do know that I'm done with airports. Unless I'm catching a plane. I hate work without you there. Barb's bitchy comments start to really bother me when I can't laugh about them with you, later. A 6 a.m. start is torture without a decent coffee. Plus, Mum said I have to give the car back if I move out and I can't afford to buy one myself. It'll take nearly two hours to get to the airport on public transport.'

'Are you sure this isn't just a bad day? It might not hurt to think about it for a few days.'

'Maybe. Except I got a bit fired up about resigning and told Barb that if she put more effort into what came out of her mouth instead of what she slathered on it, all her staff might not want to leave. Honestly, Emmie. I've been Assistant Manager that long, I'll have no problem finding customer-service work if I need to. I might be impulsive but I'm not irresponsible. I'll still pay my way.'

'In that case, great! I'm glad to have a wing-woman on my journey into the terrifying unknown.'

'Okay, you're super busy, so enough of me. What's your news?'

I'd walked far enough along the fence line that no one else could possibly hear, although I did a good three-sixty scan to make sure.

'I think I'm falling in love with Pip.'

I counted six skittered heartbeats before Blessing answered.

'Emmie, that is not news.'

'It is to me!'

'How many people on that island have made comments about the two of you?'

'Too many,' I mumbled, hunching my shoulders.

'Precisely.'

'Fine, but that doesn't help me. What am I supposed to do about it?'

'Tell him? Kiss him? Ask for his number and if you can meet up when he comes over for his graduation?'

'I don't want to come home,' I whispered. 'Not yet, anyway.'

'So don't! It's your life, Emmie. What did you just say to me? Enjoy the wedding, and then take a few days to think about what's next. Find out what he wants, too. Because he clearly loves you back.'

'You think so?'

'Don't you?'

I thought about this. 'I think he might…'

'And you're going to walk away from that, why?'

'Because I'm a wuss?'

Because I was terrified that I'd end up making the same mistake as my mum, rushing into something I couldn't handle. Or even worse, Pip might think he loved me enough to make the same mistake as his dad, potentially destroying both his relationship with his family and the farm. Then he'd get to know the real, Sherwood-Forest me. The one with an empty past, pitiful present and no clue about the future. And he'd leave again, so all that trouble would have resulted in nothing but a smashed-up heart.

Because if I stayed, I'd have to confront all the weird things that had been happening, and confrontation came about as easily to me as telling a man that I loved him.

'Ah crap, there's a queue of customers and Barb's giving me the evil eyeliner. I have to go. Call me though, as soon as something happens!'

She hung up, leaving me leaning against a wooden fence, head swarming with muddled thoughts.

Pip appeared at the barn door, calling out as he started walking over.

'Everything okay?'

'Yeah. It was Blessing. She's quit her job.'

He came to stand next to me, the fence creaking as he rested his hips against it.

'You look worried about that.'

I kept my eyes on the grass, unable to look at him now every part of my body hummed with the truth about how I felt.

'Not really. I'm more worried that I've also quit mine.'

His head jerked up.

'Oh?'

'The lease on the kiosk runs out on Sunday. I'm not signing a new one.'

'Why?'

I dared a peek at him through my hair. His face shone with hopeful anticipation.

'Pip!' Rosemary was outside the barn, tapping her wrist wildly. 'When you've finished standing around chatting, Hugh says can you meet him at the church ASAP, please. You probably ought to take your suit with you.'

He pushed himself off the fence. 'I'll talk to you later?'

All I could do was nod. Hopefully by 'later', I might have figured out what I wanted to say.

* * *

After a few more minutes completing the reception centrepieces, I helped Lily load up the remaining flowers for the church, and then followed Rosemary to the kitchen. She was showing me how the oven worked when Aster appeared.

'Lily asked if I could give you this.' She held out a dress. 'It's a lend, not a gift, mind. I may not have worn it in decades, but it still fits me.'

In all the activity, I'd almost forgotten about an outfit, and felt touched that Lily hadn't. I accepted Aster's offering with some trepidation – she was in her nineties, although I had to admit, we were similar builds – and held it up to have a proper look.

'Oh!'

'Don't sound so surprised.' Aster frowned. 'I might be an old farmer's wife, but I can scrub up on occasion.'

The dress was lovely. Pale-green satin, with sheer, capped sleeves, a fitted bodice and full skirt that would reach just below my knees.

'I bought it for my husband's funeral. He hated me in black, and this was the same colour as his eyes.'

'It's beautiful. But are you sure?'

Aster's glare was fierce enough to scorch the pasties. 'I wouldn't have said yes if I wasn't sure. It's only a dress. Now, Rosemary, is the cake safe and secure on the middle shelf?'

'Yes.' Rosemary opened the fridge door to show her.

Aster gave a brisk nod. 'You know that's the only place where things stay reliably cool in that ancient thing. I don't know why you haven't replaced it yet.'

'You know we can't afford to replace the fridge until after the Sunflower Festival. As long as we keep things in the middle, it's not a problem.'

'Are you going to try it on?'

It took a second or two to realise she'd switched back to me.

'Ma, do you really think there's time for that? Emmie has a lot to do.'

'You're the chef,' Aster barked. 'Is there time?'

'I think so. I mean, yes. If I'm quick.'

Rosemary showed me to a downstairs shower room, tutting about how the service would be starting in a couple of hours. I could understand her being stressed – having four days' notice to plan for her daughter's wedding couldn't have been ideal.

I slipped the dress on, managed to zip it up and jumped up and down a few times, trying to catch sight of it in the small mirror above the sink. It seemed to fit okay, and from what I could see, it definitely looked better than my shorts, and even worked with my white flip-flops, so I gratefully changed back and Rosemary hung it in the coat closet under the stairs.

If I'd had any lingering suspicion that Aster had been the person trying to ruin my time here, this erased it. If she hated me, then there'd be no way she'd lend me this dress.

'Right, we'll leave you to it,' Rosemary said, shooing me back to the kitchen. 'Everyone's been instructed to keep their phones on today, so any problems, call me or Violet. The numbers are on the countertop, here. But try to avoid between one-forty-five and three because we'll be at the ceremony.' She took a deep breath. 'Come on, then, Ma. Time to get changed.'

'I know full well what time it is. Do you want to check I've brushed my teeth and put clean knickers on, too?'

'Are you sure you can manage this?' Rosemary hovered in the doorway, hands wringing. 'There's still time to throw some sandwiches together. The farmer's market has some lovely pork pies.'

'Please don't worry. I've been doing this since I was thirteen. Go and enjoy your daughter's wedding. The first pasties will be ready at four-thirty.'

'No, we need them served at three-thirty.'

'Really?' Lily had been very clear when she'd shown me the schedule.

'Yes. Iris wants them then. I can ask Lily to call you if you don't trust me.'

'No. Of course. Three-thirty. No problem.'

Rosemary frowned, clearly thinking there might be a problem if I couldn't even get the timings right.

'I just really want it to be an unforgettable day.'

'It will be. And the pasties will be ready on time.'

Iris and Hugh's wedding was certainly a day both I, and the rest of the Isle of Siskin would never forget.

27

I spent the next few hours baking pasties in batches, keeping them warm in the Aga and a mobile food trolley borrowed from one of the hotels. Lily checked in when she'd arrived at the church. I assured her that the dogs were keeping a watchful eye on every crumb. Rosemary messaged seven times. When I failed to answer the seventh message within ten seconds, because I was busy moving pasties from the oven to the Aga, she phoned.

After a brief explanation, met with thinly veiled suspicion, I ended the call thinking that a private-catering business might not be the best career move after all.

So, I wasn't surprised when she barrelled into the kitchen as soon as the first cars started pulling up just after three.

'How's it going?'

She opened the oven door, followed by the Aga and the warming trolley. I reminded myself how I'd feel having a stranger take over my kitchen, and tried not to let my irritation show.

'Any issues?'

'Not since you last phoned fifteen minutes ago, no.'

'Right. I'm sorry. I just want it all to go well.'

'How was the ceremony?'

Rosemary pressed a hand to her chest. 'Perfect. What more could a mother want than for her daughter to marry a fine, island man? No skeletons or last-minute surprises. Two people who understand each other. Understand this way of life and know it's what they want. When Lily married Malcolm, I was that worried about a stranger in the family, I didn't sleep for months.'

'That's wonderful.' I almost sounded as if I meant it. Rosemary must know about Gabe's first wife, and I wondered how much that tainted her view of a suitable partner for her children.

'Two down, two to go!' she cried, giving the Labradors a pet before whirling out of the door.

* * *

At three-forty-five, I left the sanctuary of the kitchen and went to find Lily. I'd timed everything to perfection, but had forgotten that islanders tended to allow a lot more flexibility in their schedules.

It was a balmy afternoon, and most of the guests were gathered on the outside space by the open Old Barn doors. Richard and his band were playing a gentle folk song, the children were occupied with a game of boules on the grass, and everyone else was chatting in small clusters, drinks in hand and smiles on faces.

Scanning around, I spotted Iris and Hugh posing for a photograph under a large oak tree, Celine beside them, but Lily was inside the barn, supervising the makeshift barman. Her lemon maternity bridesmaid dress contrasted beautifully with her dark hair, pinned up with a silk lily, and sun-kissed skin.

'The pasties are ready. I'm worried they'll start cooling down.'

'Oh?' She checked her watch. 'We've still got the rest of the photos to do yet. That's why we said food at four-thirty.'

'Right. But your mum said Iris moved it to an hour earlier.'

'What?' Lily looked confused. 'No. I showed you the schedule. It's not changed.'

'Okay. No problem.' I started to back away.

'Are you sure? Are they going to be ruined? Hang on, let me find Ma.'

Lily followed me out of the barn, but Rosemary was nowhere to be seen, and no one else seemed to know where she was either.

'I can't believe she got it wrong.'

'She does seem a bit stressed.'

'She's an islander woman, relinquishing control of one of the most important days of her daughter's life. You bet she's stressed.' We wandered around the side of the barn towards the house, Lily suggesting Rosemary might have nipped back for something, but Celine caught up with us on the front yard.

'Iris wants you for a bridesmaid photo,' she said, slightly breathless. 'Hey, Emmie. Looks like you've been slaving away, bless you.'

'Hi.' I glanced down at my sweaty T-shirt and resisted the urge to redo my ponytail, hoping she couldn't see me quaking as I forced myself to look at her.

However firmly I told myself that today was about Iris and Hugh, not some preposterous grudge, it didn't make it any easier to stand in front of the woman who was trying to bully me away from Pip and off the island and pretend I didn't know that she must know full well I knew it was her.

Celine looked as gorgeous as I'd have expected in a sleeveless, lemon, A-line dress and strappy heels, the top half of her hair twisted into plaits like a laurel wreath, the rest loose waves. Her smile innocent, if a little tense.

Lily briefly explained the timing issue with the pasties as we walked over to where Iris and Hugh were still under the tree with the photographer, Violet waiting to one side with her nieces.

My heart lurched to see Pip, fiddling with the posy in Flora's hair, in a moss-green suit that fitted perfectly. I couldn't have felt more like a sweaty, scruffy outsider amongst all this wedding finery.

Then he turned towards us, eyes widening in surprise when he saw me. The expression on his face made none of that matter. He looked as though he didn't see the messy hair and rumpled clothes, but the actual me, underneath all of that. And as if he thought that person was as lovely as a bride in her wedding dress.

I could have stood there, gawking back at him, until the pasties had all gone stale. I wasn't sure I'd be able to do anything else, until Celine stalked right up to him and brushed at something that wasn't there on his lapel, breaking the moment.

'Emmie got the times wrong, so we need to hurry up with the photos,' Celine said, once she'd thoroughly wiped off the imaginary whatever it was.

'Um, no she didn't,' Lily corrected. 'It was Ma who told her three-thirty.'

There was a brief discussion, whereby Iris and Hugh happily agreed to one more posed photo with the bridesmaids while Pip rounded up the waiters and I raced back to the kitchen to start serving.

'There we go, issue solved, potential disaster averted,' Lily said, so pointedly that I wondered if she also suspected some sort of interference. As I hurried past the barn, I considered stopping to ask Rosemary if Celine had been the one to tell her the time had changed. No one else had a reason to, and she had the least to lose if the food was lukewarm or dry. However, Rosemary was chatting with a group of people I didn't know, so I decided not to bother opening that can of worms unless I needed to – which I very much hoped I wouldn't.

As I started transferring the first batch of pasties – maybe a few minutes past their peak, but thankfully still utterly delectable – onto a platter, I couldn't shift the sense that something wasn't quite right. The trolley, which I'd positioned ready by the table, was now a couple of feet away. While I wanted to believe that someone probably nudged it as they moved past to get to the bathroom, I would have been naïve not to consider that it might have been moved for more sinister reasons.

With dread pounding in my chest, I broke open a random pasty and checked through the contents, including a good sniff and a quick taste.

'Quality checking, or unable to resist the best pasties in the universe?' Pip asked, appearing in the doorway.

'I don't normally, but timings are never the same in a different oven. And, well, it is a special occasion.'

'You really need an independent opinion, then,' he said, walking over and breaking off a piece, then waving it underneath his nose. 'Hmmm. I'm getting hints of mole, maybe a smidgen of cowboy hat, classic literature, and chicken feathers. Do I detect overtones of interference from my bossy big sister?'

'If you want to be useful,' I said, unable to help laughing, 'you can unload all the veggie pasties from the Aga onto that dish.'

For the next few minutes, we worked as quickly as possible to load up the platters as the waiting staff bore them away to the Old Barn. Even with the door and windows open, it was sweltering work, and, despite having ditched his jacket, rolled up his shirt-sleeves and undone the top two buttons of his white shirt, Pip looked as hot and bothered as me by the time we'd finished. Hot, bothered and that dichotomy of dishevelled-man-in-formalwear that did nothing to help me cool down.

'This is genius catering,' he said, leaning back against the table and wiping his face with his pocket square. 'Twenty minutes of hard graft, but then it's all done.'

'Um, quite a few hours of hard graft over the past few days. And it's not done; there's a pile of baking trays to wash, and the cake needs serving.'

'The cake!' Pip's face lit up at the thought. 'Have you seen it? Mammaw was being all secretive about the design. She finished the icing while we were setting up this morning.'

'It's in the fridge.' Aster had lived up to her reputation as the best cake-maker on the island. The two tiers were decorated with edible sunflowers, a pair of yellowy-green siskins nestled together on the top. The sides were edged with waves of piping to represent the sea, and the overall effect was sweet and yet exquisite. 'I'm under strict orders to keep it on the middle shelf until the cake-cutting in about half an hour, but I won't tell anyone if you sneak a peek.'

Pip opened the fridge door a few inches and winked at me before pressing one eye against the gap.

I turned away with a smile and started filling the sink with hot water.

'Emmie.'

As I flipped back around, it was instantly clear that all trace of jollity had vanished.

'What?'

Face sombre, Pip stepped back to let me see into the huge, old fridge.

'Oh, no.'

It was clear why Aster had been so adamant about her storage instructions. I had to bend down to look properly at the cake, both tiers now crammed side by side on the bottom shelf, right above the vegetable rack. The soft icing around the sides had started sagging, the waves blurring together into a squishy mess. Several of the sunflowers looked as though they were wilting, and the male siskin's beak and eyes had slumped into the melting mass, while the female's head had slipped off entirely.

'Help me move it.'

We shooed the dogs into another room to prevent their inquisitive noses from causing an accident, then, while being careful not to cause any more damage, we slid each tier out and returned them to the middle shelf – that was, after removing a tray of unbaked pasties that I'd left in the freezer as backup in case I dropped or otherwise spoiled another lot.

We wacked the temperature down a couple of degrees and shut the door.

'It is fixable?' Pip asked after a distressed silence.

'We could remove the worst of the flowers, try sticking the head back on the siskin bride. But the waves are ruined. The best option is probably to smooth them all out.'

'How long will it take you?'

I looked at him, stricken. 'I bake pastry, not cakes. We'd have to ask Aster to do it.'

Pip fired off a message to one of his sisters, shaking his head grimly when a reply pinged through a minute later. 'She's gone to sleep off the champagne before the band start up again. But asked if we'd take a photo of the cake once it's assembled.'

I shouldn't have been surprised when Rosemary appeared, just as we were working out where to position the bird's beak.

'Pip, what are you doing skulking about in here? This is your sister's wedding,' she scolded as we spun around, hiding the cake behind our backs. 'Did you even eat one of the pasties you've been going on about for two years? Everyone's wondering where you are.'

'By everyone, do you mean Celine?' Pip asked, grimacing.

'She was one of them, yes.'

'Then there's your answer,' he shot back. 'Her refusal to accept that I'm not interested in rekindling anything between us is hard enough under normal circumstances. Wedding Celine – *Chief Bridesmaid* Celine – is too much. I'd rather deal with the cows on heat. Besides, Emmie needed some help.'

'Hmph. I thought that was why we were paying those students from Port Cathan: to help Emmie.'

'Yeah. This was something else.'

'Oh?' She lowered her eyebrows. 'Emmie was supposed to call me if anything came up. Is everything under control, Emmie, as you assured me it would be?'

Pip and I exchanged a glance, and in silent agreement, moved apart so that Rosemary could see the cake on the worktop behind us. She immediately bustled over.

'What is this? What did you do?' she squawked, hands flapping over the top tier.

'Someone moved it to the bottom of the fridge,' I said, apologetically. 'We found it like this.'

'Why would they do that?' Rosemary was nearly shrieking.

'I have no idea. There was no reason for anybody to be in the kitchen.'

'Except you. Why weren't *you* in the kitchen?'

'You told me the wrong time for the pasties. I was trying to sort it out with Lily.'

'Oh, so it's *my* fault that you left the kitchen unattended, putting the cake at risk?'

'At risk of what?' Pip interjected. 'Someone sneaking in and moving it to a different shelf on the fridge? As you said, why on earth would they do that?'

'I don't know. You tell me why someone would want to destroy Iris and Hugh's wedding cake.'

'I have no idea.' Pip took hold of his mother's hand, trying to calm her down. 'Who apart from family even knows about the dodgy bottom of the fridge?'

'No one! That's my whole point. Is it more plausible that someone deliberately crept into my kitchen and spoiled your mammaw's wedding cake, or that someone – Emmie – forgot about the fridge and moved the cake so that she could, I don't know, fit something else in?'

'No.' I shook my head.

Rosemary looked at me for a long moment, taking a deep breath as her initial consternation readjusted into a semblance of sympathy.

'You have been very busy. I'm sure it was an easy mistake to make in all the confusion and clamour. We shouldn't have left you alone to manage everything, given how different things are here compared to what you're used to.'

'No.' I tried to keep calm, but it was difficult due to the adrenaline stampeding through my arteries. From the moment I'd seen the cake, the possibility that this had been deliberate had been cramping in my guts. 'This is my business. I've baked and served pasties non-stop for over ten years, in a far more demanding environment than this. There was no confusion or clamour. And I didn't open the fridge once. I had no reason to. Let alone move the cake. I would never have dared try by myself.'

'I'm sorry, Emmie, but lying about it isn't going to make things better,' Rosemary bristled. 'We can forgive a serious mistake like this, even if it has wrecked Aster's painstaking work. After all, it's only a cake. But not owning up to it is a whole different matter. It's... shameful. We don't do things like that here.'

'Ma—' Pip protested, but Rosemary cut him off.

'No, Philip. I'm going to tell Lily, then send someone in to slice that up and serve it in pieces. We'll have to explain to Iris and Hugh why they can't cut the cake. And lie to Aster about why there's no picture of what will probably be the last wedding cake she ever makes.' She sniffed, striding back to the outside door. 'As for you, thank you for the pasties, but I think it's time you left us to celebrate with our family and friends.'

'No, Ma,' Pip called, but she'd already gone. Instead, he turned to me. 'Don't go yet. At least, not like this. I'll talk to Lily and make sure no one thinks it was you.'

I must have looked distraught, because he took hold of my hand and clenched it against his chest. 'Promise me you won't go. It'll be easy to work out who moved the cake. Probably one of the waiting staff. Or Violet.'

'Or Celine,' I mumbled.

'Celine? Why would she be in here messing about with the fridge?'

I shrugged, unable to face answering that.

'Do you really believe me?' I asked instead, voice trembling. The whole situation was horrendous.

Pip lifted my hand, kissed it gently, then looked me right in the eyes. It made everything about a zillion times better.

'You learned not to forget things,' he said, softly. 'Catering instructions, especially.'

My eyes filled with tears. He'd taken seriously what I'd told him about Mum.

'Besides, I've seen you running the kiosk with a queue snaking halfway down the concourse. People bellowing their orders, everyone frazzled, a semi-riot over the last cinnamon apple custard. Working alone, in our vast kitchen, must have been a piece of cake in comparison.' He winced, dropping my hand. 'Okay, terrible analogy for now. But yes. I trust you. With this, and just about anything.'

He turned to go. 'Lily told me Aster's lent you a dress. Get changed, take a deep breath, and by the time you're ready, I'll have solved the great cake mystery.'

28

For want of anything better to do, I followed Pip's advice, retrieving the dress from under the stairs and going back to the shower room to change. I could produce nothing more than a hollow sob when, after putting it on, I found one of the delicate mesh sleeves had been ripped away from the seam.

'I suppose mainlanders don't know how to put dresses on without tearing them, either,' I muttered, bitterly.

Sinking onto the closed toilet seat, I dropped my head into my hands and surrendered to the sheer awfulness of my situation.

How on earth had I ended up here?

What was I thinking, freeloading a holiday off a family and then spending the whole week tagging along to things as if pretending to be one of them?

Inserting myself into Pip's life, despite his deranged ex hating me enough to deliberately sabotage her best friend's wedding just to make me look bad. Never mind the bird poop or nasty messages.

How did I convince myself that I was the kind of woman who could handle a strange place, with people I didn't know, no plan whatsoever, and somehow not make a complete mess of it?

After years of bleak loneliness, during the past few days, I'd started to embrace the joy of being a part of something. A way of life where people waded right on into your business, caring meant sharing, and no one questioned that the beating heart of a healthy community was admitting they were better together.

I had genuinely started to feel at home here.

Now, sitting on a cracked old toilet, in a ruined dress that belonged to a woman I felt scared of, while a few metres away, rumours spiralled about my catering incompetence, no doubt fuelled by a person who despised me, I had never felt so alone or longed more to be sitting at my usual food-court table, eating a bowl of lentil soup.

* * *

I'd left my phone in the kitchen, so had no idea how long I sat there, sobbing pitifully, until I was startled by a loud knock on the door.

'All right in there? Or will I have to drag myself to the bathroom upstairs?'

Great. Richard was probably the second-to-last person I wanted to see right then. He was still a footnote on my suspect list – the only other name, now I'd discarded Aster.

'One moment,' I croaked back.

I blew my nose, splashed cold water on my blotchy face and tried to unzip myself, but the awkward hook at the top of the bodice was stuck.

Even greater. Now I'd have to ask a sinister old man who suspected I was here to cause trouble to undo the precious dress his mother had preserved for decades, and I'd wrecked in minutes.

After another few seconds hovering about in case I woke up

from this nightmare, I reluctantly opened the door, my shorts and T-shirt clutched to my chest. My plan was to slip past him and reach my phone, but he had planted himself right in front of the doorway.

'Didn't answer my question.'

'What?'

Richard's gaze remained impassive. 'Are you all right?'

I blinked a few times, eyes darting across the floor between us. He looked less daunting in his crumpled suit and wonky tie. 'Um...'

'There's a rip in your sleeve.'

'I know. I feel terrible. I could say that I honestly don't think it was me, but I've denied so many things over the past few days, I probably already sound like someone with a pathological lying problem. To say I'm dreading what your mother will say is an understatement.'

'What's she got to do with it?'

'This is the dress she wore to your father's funeral.'

Richard scratched his beard. 'We'd best fix it, then.'

I boggled at him, astounded.

'If you'd be kind enough to vacate the bathroom, first, so a crippled old codger can use it.'

After more awkward dialogue, and an excruciating eon where his careworn farmer's fingers fumbled at the hook, hot breath huffing on my neck, I swapped back into my own outfit and trailed after Richard into the office, noting that someone had chopped up and served most of the cake while I was bawling in the bathroom.

He rummaged in a drawer, then handed me a spool of white cotton and a needle. 'Thread this for me.'

'You can sew?'

'Seems as good a time as any to give it a try.' He glanced up, and for the first time, I saw warmth flicker behind his watery blue eyes. I risked a weak smile at what I hoped was a joke.

'Yes, I can sew,' he said as I handed back the threaded needle. 'Skin, mostly. Mine, and plenty of animals'. But every Siskin farmer knows how to patch a hole or mend a tear.'

I suspected the quality of needlework required to sew up a hole in a farmer's jacket was not quite the same as a satin gown. But given my current reputation, at least it wouldn't be me butchering the repair job.

'You're leaving tomorrow.' Richard squinted at the sleeve as he held it up to the light.

'Yes.'

'Probably best.'

He made a bold stab at the fabric, and I flinched.

'Unless… you've reasons to stay that don't include stirring up the past.'

'What do you mean?'

'Reckon you've fallen for my nephew.'

As someone who was entirely unused to sharing my feelings, confessing them to Richard seemed no less bizarre than the rest of this situation.

'I think I might have.'

'Think?' He glanced up, sharply.

'Know.'

'But can you fall for this place? His family? Our way of doing things?' He went back to deftly dipping the needle in and out. 'Pip loves the farm as much as the rest of us. You might persuade him to give it up, if you don't want to stay. But don't try unless you're sure you're worth it.'

Of course I wasn't sure about that. But it really wasn't relevant. Because, secret bully aside, I adored it here. The island, the farm, the Hawkins family. It had been love at first sight. Or, more accurately, at first breath of sweet, salty air.

I had no business, a trustworthy tenant for my house and nothing else to miss.

I wasn't about to try persuading Pip about anything, but I couldn't help hoping he'd be happy if I didn't catch tomorrow's flight.

'We both know how badly it can turn out.'

'What can?' I asked as Richard tied off the thread and flipped the dress back right-side out.

'Mainlander and islander.' He looked at me. 'Your mother and my brother.'

I let out a slow breath.

'How did you know it was me?'

'I told you, I got eyes.'

'She wasn't even my mother. My mum was her cousin.'

'Close enough. Couldn't be a coincidence, strawberry-hair, green-eyed girl turning up here. Talking about her mother. I shared a house with Nellie for a long time. Same mannerisms, way of speaking.'

'And you drove her away again.' My throat constricted at the memory of the letters.

'Not me. I'd nothing against her. She tried hard, no complaining. Was a decent match for Gabe. It was our parents made it impossible, forced her out. All that nonsense about an heir, like she was another heifer to be bred. Backfired on them when Gabe went too, though.'

'You think Gabe shouldn't have left the island? And neither should Pip?'

He shrugged. 'Didn't say that. I just said know what you're asking. Your mother learned that, when it came down to it, Gabe had to put the farm first.'

I accepted the dress from him, running my fingers along the mended seam. It wasn't perfect, but about as close as hand-sewing could get.

'Do you think I could handle it here?'

Richard chuffed. I think it was his version of laughing. 'Don't matter what I think.'

'Then it doesn't matter how you answer.'

'You cleaned the crap off the barn, no grumbling.'

I nodded.

'Yes, I reckon you could be an islander. More importantly, will the rest of them allow you to be?'

I held up the dress. 'Your family have been more than welcoming. I need to talk to Gabe, though. He doesn't want anyone knowing who I am.' I hesitated. 'And whoever ripped the sleeve might make it difficult. It's not their only attempt to scare me off.'

Richard made a dismissive grunt. 'Once that girl knows Pip's made his choice, she'll soon move on. Too much pride to compete with a done deal.'

I sat back, slightly gobsmacked at where a conversation with Richard had ended up. 'I could postpone my flight home for a while, at least.'

Um, what? Was I really thinking about ditching everything I'd ever known for an island I'd never even seen a week ago?

Who was I kidding? Deep down, beneath the sensible, reliable Emmaline Brown, I'd been thinking about this since Pip Hawkins first came to my rescue, almost two years ago.

'I'll let you get changed.' Richard pulled himself up using his cane and started limping to the door.

'Thank you,' I said. 'For the dress, and the advice.'

He looked down at his rumpled trouser leg. 'Reckon I owe you one. Seeing as it was my damn leg wrecked your mother's marriage.'

29

Ten minutes later, dress on, hair brushed and Blessing's make-up lesson put into practice, having brought a few basics with me, I took a shaky breath and gingerly slipped out of the bathroom through the empty kitchen and outside.

I held out little hope that Pip would have identified the cake-wrecker. After my conversation with Richard, Celine was the only name on the list of people out to get me. There was no way she'd have owned up to ruining Iris's wedding cake. But I did have faith in him steering any suspicion away from me.

'Emmie!'

My heart sank as Iris called from the entrance to the barn. It was approaching five-thirty, and the air was warm and bright, with only the faintest hint of the evening crispness to come. Bolstered by her grin, I walked over, only to be yanked into a huge hug as soon as I reached arm's length.

'I've not had a chance to talk to you all day. You look lovely, by the way,' she said, pressing her face against my cheek.

'Well, you look stunning.'

'I know! It's probably not the done thing to admit it, but I scrubbed up okay, didn't I?' She laughed, finally letting me go. Her dress was what Blessing would call 'boho', a simple mermaid style but with flared sleeves and lots of soft lace. Her long hair was completely loose, and when she stepped away from me, I spotted white trainers.

'Anyway, thank you for all your hard graft. The food was perfect. Everyone wants to know how we can persuade you to stay and open up a kiosk here.' Her eyes danced as she nodded to the far side of the barn doors. 'I did suggest that my brother might be the one to talk to about that.'

'Oh?' I was past being coy. If nothing happened with Pip this evening then it would make my decision about whether I got on a flight tomorrow that much harder. I didn't have to base my decision on how he felt, but if he wasn't interested in being more than friends then staying here would be torture. I'd risk becoming another Celine. Speaking of which, now the initial shock of the dress and the cake had worn off, I felt a spark of righteous Brown anger. Hating me was one thing, but taking it out on her friend's cake and Aster's dress was despicable. As soon as the wedding was over, I would tell Pip everything. He'd know best how to handle it.

'Come off it, it's clear as day he's sweet on you. I can't believe he's not made a move yet.' Iris put her hand on my arm. 'Unless he has, and you turned him down.' She gasped. 'Oh, please tell me you didn't. He's a really decent guy. Soppy as anything too.'

As much as I'd been getting used to the islanders' custom of spreading their thoughts out like a buffet, I had no idea how to answer that. To make things worse, Pip wandered through the barn entrance.

'Hey.' Seeing his smile felt like sinking into a warm bath. 'You look... I mean... Wow.'

He shook his head, gripping his neck as his cheeks flushed.

Oh, boy. This man actually might like me.

'Thank you.'

We stood there grinning dopily. If my brain had been able to process a coherent thought, it would have been imagining my life as a farmer's wife – baking at the huge table, picking pears in the orchard, showing my children a newborn calf...

'Oh, for goodness' sake, kiss her already!' Iris cried. 'She's flying home tomorrow.'

Pip jerked back, his expression transforming into one of embarrassed shock.

'Er...' He glanced at his sister, then back at me. 'I mean... is that? Do you...?'

'Um, probably not here...' I waved vaguely at the guests, at least half of whom were now gawking at us, thanks to Iris.

'Yeah. Of course.' Pip ducked his head, spotting the onlookers. 'We could go for a walk or something?'

Before I could answer, a ripple went through the building. Like a domino run, everyone rapidly flipped towards the back of the barn.

'Oops. Here we go!' Iris muttered, clutching onto Hugh, who had suddenly appeared at her side. 'Hey, move to the side, people, so the bride can see,' she ordered.

As the crowd of people parted, it revealed Barnie, down on one knee by the music speakers.

'Oh no,' Pip groaned, quietly. 'We told him not to do this.'

'Don't worry.' Flora popped up next to him, a knowing smile on her face. 'It's not what you think.'

'Violet,' Barnie began, holding one hand aloft in a courtly gesture.

'No, Barnie.' Someone nudged Violet into the empty space in front of him. She clutched her hair with both hands. 'I can't believe you'd do this at my sister's wedding.'

'I'm doing it with your sister's blessing,' Barnie said, sounding a little peeved.

Violet scanned the room until she found Iris, raising both eyebrows at her in a *what the hell?* gesture.

'It's true,' Iris said, cheerily. 'Hear him out, sis. It's a biggie.'

'That's what I'm afraid of,' Violet ground out through a clenched jaw.

As if proving that this was indeed a biggie, Barnie whipped off his blue cap and held it to his chest.

'Go on, Barnie-boy!' someone called, prompting cheers of encouragement.

'Violet, I love you.'

'Yes, I already know that. I love you, too. But you know—'

'Please, let me finish,' he said, firmly. 'I love you, and I want to marry you. Whatever you might think, you mean far more to me than any doughnut stand. Than this island. I only love it here so much because it's where you are. Without you, it's nothing. Without you, *I'm* nothing.'

'Yet all this still means nothing, because I'm leaving.'

'Yes. I know. Which is why I bought you a wedding present.'

Violet took a step back, face screwed up in annoyance. 'Have you bought me a wedding present, for *our* wedding, despite me making it abundantly clear that we are never going to be more than friends?'

'Aye, well. That was before you saw the present.'

Barnie had put his cap back on and was now trying to wrestle something out of his trouser pocket, but what he eventually managed to extend towards Violet was not a ring, as we all expected, but an envelope.

'Go on,' he said, sounding like someone coaxing a skittish horse. 'If you really do love me, the least you can do is open it.'

With no small amount of reluctance, Violet took the envelope, opening up the paper she found inside with an impatient huff. Gradually, as her eyes scanned the page, her body went still, her mouth falling slowly open.

'This is a ticket to Australia.'

'You said you always wanted to go.'

'For two people?'

Barnie shrugged. 'If we're married, I think it's only fair that I come on the honeymoon.'

'You think a fancy holiday is the answer? Barnie, how can I even think about marrying you when you don't listen?'

'It's a one-way ticket,' Barnie blurted. 'I'd have got more, to other places. I know you want to see Thailand, and Peru. Alaska. But I thought it would be more fun to plan that together.'

The barn was so quiet, we could have heard the bats snoring in the rafters.

'You're going to come travelling with me?' Violet was gripping the tickets so hard, I feared the paper would rip. 'What about the stall? The bike rental? You can't just up and leave everything behind.'

Barnie stood, wrapping his hands around hers to steady their trembling.

'I told you. You're my everything.' His voice was soft. 'I mean, that's if you want me to come. You did say you'd miss me more than anything.'

'Of course I want you to come, you daft oaf.'

'And you'll marry me first?'

'Give me your cap.'

Barnie looked confused, but he did what she'd asked.

'There. Coming from you, that's more of a commitment than a ring.'

'Well, if I'd known it was that easy, I'd have saved my money for hotels,' Barnie said, whipping a ring out of his jacket pocket, and holding it out to his fiancée. 'Shall I take this back, get a refund?'

'Don't you dare.'

And then he pushed the ring onto her finger, she wrapped her hands around his neck and they were snogging in the middle of barn surrounded by cheers.

Pip gave me a wry glance, and then caught sight of his mother, squeezing through the crowd to get outside.

'Ma.' He moved across, catching her wrist as she reached the doorway and gently tugging her to a stop. 'Hey, it's okay.'

Rosemary's face crumpled as she fell against her son's shoulder. 'She's really going.'

'We always knew she'd be going. At least this way, she won't marry an Australian and end up settling thousands of miles away. You can trust her and Barnie to keep each other safe, and there's twice the reason to keep coming home.'

She sighed. 'I know she's got to go. And I will be happy for her. But for now, let me weep a wee minute for my child who is leaving.'

'Okay.' Pip pressed a kiss against her hair and stepped back. 'Only a minute, mind. This is Iris and Hugh's day, and they're stopping five miles down the road.'

If I hadn't already fallen for this man, seeing the tenderness towards his mother would have done it. I had so much to learn about love and family, and the thought of discovering those things with Pip sent shivers through me.

The walk – and potential kiss – presumably forgotten, I grabbed a glass of wine and joined the other guests in toasting the new couple, waiting until the gaggle of well-wishers had thinned before moving over to offer my own congratulations.

'Emmie,' Barnie said, offering me a sweaty hug once Violet had turned to chat with Celine, who I'd done a great job of managing to avoid so far. 'Precisely the woman I was hoping to see.'

'Oh?' A prickle of trepidation scampered up my spine. Had Celine done something else to make me appear incompetent? At least Pip was hovering nearby so he would hear it, if so.

'How do you fancy relocating to a new airport?'

'Excuse me?'

'Well, there couldn't be a better person on the island to take on Barnie's doughnuts and bike rental.'

'Maybe one who lives here?' Celine, rudely breaking off from her conversation, said with a tight smile.

'Ah, sure, Pip said he was talking her into staying, now that she's closed down the kiosk in Sherwood Forest. Isn't that what the whole conversation in the doorway was about? That's what inspired me to get on with my proposal.'

'No. It wasn't about that,' Pip said, sounding strained.

'Oh. Well. The offer still stands. Think about it and let me know, aye?'

Barnie turned aside, as someone else came to clap him on the shoulder and kiss Violet on the cheek. Pip glanced at Celine, whose narrowed eyes made my stomach clench like a concertina as I wrestled between fury and fear.

'Excuse us, Celine,' Pip said, politely. 'Emmie and I were about to take a walk.'

'I need a word, Pip, if you don't mind.'

'Maybe later?' he replied, jaw tight.

'I'd really like to talk to you first, before you go off with Emmie. Please. It's important.'

The air in the barn had grown suffocating, making my head swim. It was all I could do not to flee, leaving Celine to spout whatever lies she'd concocted, but Pip was having none of it. He knew Celine better than most. I wondered if he, too, suspected she'd been the one to move the cake.

'I said later.'

He placed a hand behind my elbow, catching my eyes to check whether I was happy to leave before carefully steering me through the clumps of people dancing and out of the oppressive atmosphere, into the glorious evening.

He waited while I closed my eyes and sucked in enough deep breaths of cool air to be certain I could walk without stumbling.

'Are you okay?' he asked, once I'd opened my eyes. 'I'm sorry if that looked like you were an excuse to escape Celine. I would have asked about a walk anyway, but if you'd rather not... You've had a long day.'

'A walk sounds bliss,' I said, straightening my shoulders. 'It's quite stuffy in there. I probably shouldn't have drunk that last glass of wine before eating properly.'

'You've not eaten?'

I wrinkled my forehead. 'Only that earlier bite of pasty.'

'Come on, then.'

I opted to wait outside the kitchen while he slipped through the door, appearing a moment later with two bottles and a paper bag.

We continued to the farmyard, the sounds of music and laughter growing muffled as we skirted around the muddier bits, and headed towards the orchard. Instead of passing through the gate, Pip turned to the side, stopping at the bottom of a huge beech tree.

Nestled in a giant fork where the trunk split into three was a wooden platform.

'What do you reckon? Are you up for it?'

He gestured to the rickety wooden ladder with his chin. I slipped off my flip-flops and wobbled my way up.

'I've never been in a treehouse before,' I said as Pip inserted a thick slice of cheese into a bread roll he'd retrieved from the bag.

'That's a grand way to describe a few rickety boards and a railing.'

I accepted the rough sandwich and took a bite, instantly feeling better as I leant back against one of the giant branches.

'Was it for playing in, or more serious farming purposes?'

'If it had been for farming purposes, Da would never have let me get away with such shoddy craftmanship.' He poked his foot at a wonky nail sticking out of a plank.

'You built it yourself? How old were you?' I shuffled up to allow him to sit alongside me.

'About ten. Iris wanted to help, but I spent more time preventing her from falling off or hitting herself with the hammer than I did constructing the thing, so I mostly snuck out here on my own. Don't worry,' he added, spotting my nervous glance at the joints holding it in place. 'Da checked it all afterwards. It's held steady for nearly twenty years.'

We sat in silence as we ate, Pip opening two bottles of lemonade, a refreshing accompaniment to the early-evening balm. In front of us, we could see over the top of the farm buildings to the house, catching the odd glimpse of people milling around the Old Barn on the other side. Behind us, through a small chink in the branches, the sea shimmered.

'A great place to spy on all the goings-on.'

'If you mean watch out for Da or Richard coming to rope me into herding the cows to a new field, or spreading a heap of muck, then aye, it did the job.'

'What did you do when you saw them coming?'

He laughed, glancing upwards. 'Slipped up there like a squirrel. Or jumped down and hightailed it in the opposite direction.' He paused. 'Not all the time. Or even most of it. I was a typical kid, craving freedom and adventure, but I also wanted to learn as much as I could about how to take care of our land when my time came.'

'Freedom and adventure?' I pulled a wry face. 'I should have built myself a treehouse. It's not as if we were short of trees.'

'Nell kept you busy?'

'Once she'd collected me from school, there was always work to be done. Picking up food orders, prepping. She had me standing on a chair to chop vegetables when I was too small to reach the counter. Weekends and holidays were at the kiosk, lolling on a bench with a book or some colouring. By the time she'd have considered me old enough to roam free around the airport, I was working on the till and cleaning up.'

'Didn't you ever have fun?'

'You're suggesting that peeling bucketloads of parsnips isn't fun?'

He smiled, turning to look at the view stretching out in front of us. It was only a week past the summer solstice, and nightfall was still a long way off.

'I guess we all have our own definition of what's enjoyable.' His voice dropped, and my heart thumped, like a dog wagging its tail. 'But I have been wondering how island life suits you.'

He was sitting side-on to me, with perhaps three inches between us, and I could feel the tension in his body mirroring the anticipation in mine. Slowly, his hand moved across the board and wrapped around my fingers. A flurry of sparks danced across my skin.

'Island life suits me very well,' I whispered, sounding oddly like a Jane Austen character.

'You like it here?'

'I love it here,' I said, daring a peek in his direction. 'I was thinking, if you didn't mind, and it doesn't make me seem like the disturbed stalker your family feared, of staying a bit longer.'

Pip jerked his head around to look at me. 'Only a bit?'

'Well. I haven't got anywhere to stay once the B&B opens next week. Or a job. Any of my stuff.'

He took hold of my other hand, face glowing in the greenish leaf-light.

'You can stay in Iris's old room.' He frowned. 'No, that's too much. But there's bound to be someone with space. Plenty of the holiday homes will do longer-term lets. I mean, if you wanted one. And if you aren't ready to start selling pasties, with your reputation, you could get summer work in any of the cafés or hotels. Lily would probably hire you while she's on maternity leave.'

I swallowed, the reality of what we were discussing suddenly overwhelming.

'You could stick it out until the Sunflower Festival, at least.' He bounced my hands up and down. 'Think about it, Emmie. Sundays on the beach, lunches on the cliff-top. We could take the boat out, spot some wildlife. It'd be the perfect antidote to all those years of slog. The island's even better in July.'

For an enchanting moment, I let a montage of Pip and me dance through my head, where we explored the island together, spent time with his sisters, swam in the Irish Sea and gorged on freshly picked strawberries.

I also thought about Celine, and the potential fallout from me telling Pip what she'd done. But honestly, she was the one in the wrong; surely it wouldn't be so bad that I couldn't enjoy another few weeks here?

As Pip watched me, his face alight with hope and angst, I wanted more than anything to say yes, fling myself into his arms and have that kiss Iris had ordered. To pretend, for a few blissful moments, that it could all work out perfectly.

But then, inevitably, I pictured Gabe. How would he feel about me staying longer? Would he consider it an opportunity to talk about Mum, to bring both of us some closure? Or would he be angry that it risked someone finding out who I was?

Because how could I stay for any length of time and keep something like that a secret? Lily hadn't forgotten that I was here to find out about the person in Mum's letters. She was bound to ask me about it again. Let alone if Pip and I started a romantic relationship – how could I not tell him our parents were briefly married?

As these thoughts pressed in behind my skull, all I could do was grip onto Pip's hands and make sure I didn't move a single centimetre closer to him.

'I would like to stay. But there's a couple of things I need to sort out first.'

Pip gave a careful smile, sensing my hesitation. 'Does that mean you, um, might like me? I asked you, when we were walking home from the beach the other night, but you never answered.'

'Well, I jumped on a plane and followed you from the mainland, didn't I?'

'Emmie, I'm serious. I've been driven half mad the past few days, wondering.' He gave a weak laugh. 'The past couple of years, if I'm honest.'

I took a deliberate, slow breath. Gripped his hands even tighter, and did him the courtesy of looking straight in his eyes.

'Yes. I like you. A lot. All that time I was your pasty girl, you were my hot farmer.'

He laughed properly then, one of shock. 'You think I'm hot?'

'Well, Blessing came up with the name. I... I think you're lovely.'

It was Pip's turn to dip his head, an embarrassed grin spreading across his face as he couldn't resist dropping a hand to grip the back of his neck.

'I think you're lovelier,' he mumbled, one side of his mouth quirking up.

We sat there, the silence between us charged as a sea storm. A gust of wind rustled the canopy of leaves, and somewhere in the orchard, a wood pigeon cooed.

'We agreed not to have a holiday romance,' he said, having to stop and clear his throat before carrying on. 'I know everything is still up in the air, but, given that we're both hoping you'll stay... would it be out of order if I kissed you?'

If my cheeks had grown any hotter, they'd have started a wildfire. I gave the bravest nod I could manage, which turned out to be not brave enough, as Pip still eyed me, waiting.

Unable to trust my voice, I instead leant forwards until he realised what I was doing, and tipped his head to meet mine.

I hadn't been sure about whether New Emmie would regret this, six days ago.

Now, what felt like half a lifetime later, I was certain that my only regret would be if I got on a plane without having kissed Pip Hawkins.

Our lips touched, and for a couple of seconds, we hovered there, in this moment between Before and After, the contact between us as gentle as the whisper of distant waves.

Then, with a rough sigh, Pip slid one hand around my back, pulling me closer, and as the pressure increased, our mouths fitting perfectly together, we tumbled into what I knew, with absolute certainty, was love.

30

The beech branches were swathed in shadows when the repeated murmurs of, 'We have to get back,' and 'Your family will be wondering where you are,' could no longer be swatted away with a breathless, 'I don't care, they can see me any time,' or, 'I've been waiting forever to hold you, anything else can wait.'

'Okay,' Pip said, pulling away and examining my face as though it would be the last time he could look at me, before pulling in for one more soft peck. 'Let's go. You can kiss me tomorrow. I won't make you miss the best part of an island wedding.'

We clambered back down, Pip wrapping an arm around me as we strolled back, the twilight sending chills across my feverish skin.

I hesitated as we approached the Old Barn, the rhythm of the live band pulsating through the darkness.

'I said there were a couple of things I needed to sort out.' I unwound myself from his arm. 'Is it okay if we keep this to ourselves until I've done that?'

I half expected Pip to shake his head, bewildered. Was there such a thing as a Siskin secret? To my relief, he nodded, gave me a light kiss on the top of my head, and said that he'd nip to the bathroom and check on the dogs, giving me time to find a seat and a drink before he followed me in.

Instead of a seat or a drink, I found Gabe, leading Rosemary onto the dance floor, where Richard's band were striking up a folksy tune.

'Emmie.' He beamed at me. 'Are you joining us for an island reel?'

'Maybe later.' I leant closer so I didn't have to shout. 'I know it's not really the time, but in case I don't get a chance tomorrow, are you still able to show me that information we'd talked about?'

Gabe squinted for a moment, wading through the wine and whisky in his system before he realised what I meant. 'Ah, of course. The information. About the things. Of course. Absolutely. Although, I've promised my wonderful wife a dance. How about I find you as soon as it's finished?'

We agreed that I'd go and see if the kitchen still needed tidying up, and he'd find me there in a few minutes.

Wandering back to the farmhouse, I started to busy myself stacking serving platters and scraping leftover pastry crusts into the bin, unable to resist slipping a couple to the dogs, sitting patiently beside it as if offering the perfect alternative to condemning any food waste to landfill. The waiting staff were responsible for clearing up, but I was restless, my head buzzing with love and wonder at the events of the day so far, alongside the thrill and apprehension about how it would end.

As I collected a pile of dirty glasses near to the office door, I overheard Pip talking to somebody. Unable to resist leaning closer, I then caught the clear reply.

My heart stuttered like a panicked bird trapped inside my ribcage.

Celine.

'I've seen the way you look at her, Pip. Please don't deny it. You at least owe me the respect of being honest.'

'I'm not sure I owe you anything,' he replied cautiously. 'In the two years since we broke up, I've always been honest about not wanting to get back together.'

'I know that. But I wanted to be Mrs Pip for a very long time. You can't blame me for holding out hope that you might change your mind.'

'I haven't, and I won't. Now, if there's nothing else, I need to get back to the wedding.'

'Or get back to her?'

'Either way, it's none of your business.'

'Whew.' Celine chuckled. 'You really have spent too long on the mainland. As it happens, there is something else. I wanted to tell you that I'm pleased for you.'

'What?'

'For you and Emmie. Whether or not something's happening yet, it's clearly going to. Or, at least, it should. Like I said, I've seen the way you look at each other.' Her voice lowered so I had to step right up to the door to keep earwigging – which I never would have done, if the woman hadn't been wreaking clandestine havoc. She had a nerve talking about honesty.

'I never saw that look in your eyes when you were with me. I tried to convince myself you simply weren't ready, or were so laid-back, you didn't feel that kind of passion. But I've realised since Emmie showed up, you just didn't feel that way about me.

'I want a man who can't take his eyes off me. Not because I can birth a calf or drive a tractor. Just because I'm me. And I know that will never be you. So, I've eaten a tub of Dahlia's ice cream, dried my eyes and applied for and been accepted on *The Perfect Wife for a Farmer's Life*. Apparently I'm an ideal candidate. We start filming the previews in a few weeks.'

'Wow. Is anyone from Siskin on there?'

'It's shot in Texas.'

'Oh. Okay.'

'Will you miss me, then?' Celine asked, playfully, as I held my breath.

'Um...' Pip sounded doubtful.

'You git.' Celine laughed. 'Come here and give me a friendly hug goodbye. Then go and get that gorgeous mainlander. You were made for each other. I'm honestly trying very hard to be happy for you.'

There was a brief pause while I poised, ready to scuttle back across the kitchen, but Pip had a question.

'Were you in the kitchen earlier, before the pasties were served?'

'What? No. This is the first time I've been in the farmhouse since we left for church. Once we arrived back, I was with Iris organising photos until Lily told me your ma got the timings wrong for serving the food.'

'You didn't tell Ma the time had changed?'

'Of course not.' Celine sounded genuinely puzzled. 'I have the spreadsheet on my phone. When I asked Rosemary, she said you told her.'

I paused, trying to process that. Celine sounded completely believable and she'd also come across as genuine when she'd wished Pip well. It was true that she'd been busy with the photographer when I'd left the kitchen unattended. It would have been virtually impossible to sneak back and move the cake, even if she had been aware of the faulty fridge so had known where to move it to.

Which turned my shortlist of suspects completely on its head.

Did I go back to Richard? Or Aster?

Or did someone else have a serious issue with me being here?

When the kitchen door opened and Gabe stepped in, for a dreadful moment, I wondered if it could be him.

But he didn't need to use underhand tactics to scare me away. A blunt conversation would have been more than enough.

As he smiled, pulling out a chair and gesturing for me to sit down, I hastily scrubbed him off the list. Perhaps our conversation would help me know who really belonged on there. However, before we could start, Pip and Celine came out of the office, both of them startled to see me and Gabe standing by the table.

'Emmie,' Pip said. 'Celine and I were just, um…'

'Pip was telling me that he's fallen for you, and I was wishing you the very best before I leave on my own romantic adventure,' Celine interrupted. 'I really hope you don't catch that plane tomorrow. This man is one in a million. You both deserve the chance to figure it out.'

Too discombobulated to reply, I watched as Gabe made an excuse to Pip about helping me clear up and ordered him back to the barn with the promise that his mother and sisters had missed him.

We waited for them both to leave, then sank into opposite chairs.

'Right. You have questions and I promised you answers, but we'd better be quick about it.'

I took a deep breath.

'Having read all the letters, it's a lot clearer why things didn't work out between you and Mum.' I paused, choosing my words carefully. 'Do you think it would have been different if Richard hadn't had his accident?'

Gabe scratched his beard. 'I don't know. I don't think so. I hated it in Nottingham as much as your mother loathed it here. Perhaps we'd have found a compromise. Scraped together the money for a deposit on a few acres in England. But I doubt it.

Your mother had my heart, but I felt as though another vital part of me was back here. I don't know, my liver, or a good chunk of lung. I was lost. Enfeebled. Certainly not the husband your mother deserved.'

'Could you have made it work if you'd moved out of the farmhouse, converted Sunflower Barn maybe?'

He thought about this.

'We'd have probably lasted a while longer. But your ma, she didn't take to farming. The long, lonely days, out in all weathers. How a year's profits can vanish in a bad storm or the nightmare of a positive TB test. And she was never comfortable with island ways.'

'The slower pace?'

One corner of his mouth curled up. 'Possibly. I was thinking of the, shall we say, neighbourliness.'

'Being oblivious to the very notion of minding your own business?'

'Aye. Gossips, she called the other island women. Busybodies, forever finding fault with those different from themselves.'

'Was that true?'

He sighed. 'Maybe some of them, aye. But she didn't help by acting all proud and pretending she didn't care to be friends with any of them, anyway.'

I nodded. 'That sounds like Mum.'

'It was ludicrous, Da refusing to install a phone so even speaking to each other was a huge challenge while we were apart. How could we keep going like that? I wasn't at all surprised when the letter came asking for a divorce because she'd fallen in love with someone else.' He grimaced. 'Didn't stop it feeling like she'd ripped my poor, withered heart in two, though.'

'What?' I sat back, dumbfounded. Was a letter – the most important letter – missing?

'So, I knew she was set to remarry.' Gabe didn't seem to have noticed my reaction. 'But I must confess that her having a child shook me. She was always so adamant about it.'

The only reply I could manage was a shaky, 'No.'

'She must have known, deep down, we wouldn't make it, and that's why she refused to even discuss children.'

'No. She never remarried. There wasn't anyone else,' I spluttered. 'She didn't change her mind about having a baby. Her cousin turned up on the doorstep one day and left me there. Mum didn't trust anyone else in the family with a child, and she refused to let me go to a stranger, so became my legal guardian.'

'Well, I'll be jiggered.' It was Gabe's turn to be astounded. 'There was no other man?'

I shrugged. 'Not unless she kept another husband a secret, but I didn't find any evidence to suggest that.'

'Then why would she say such a thing? Your mother never lied.'

We sat there in stunned silence, each trying to fit these new pieces into the puzzle that was Nellie Brown.

'I guess we will never know for sure,' Gabe concluded eventually. 'Whatever the reason, it eases my mind a little about you and my son.'

'Excuse me?'

It was astonishingly naïve of me, but I'd never clocked that Pip's dad having been married to my mother might be an issue. Could we be considered ex-stepsiblings, if Mum and Gabe had ended all contact before either of us were born? Was it a problem if in reality, we were ex-step-second cousins?

'He told me the first Christmas he came home about the pasty girl he'd fallen for. I about fell off the tractor when Violet announced he'd only gone and brought you back with him.'

'But you know I came here because of Mum, not Pip.'

Gabe raised an eyebrow.

'Okay. Mum *and* Pip.' I glanced at him, suddenly nervous. 'I've been talking to him about potentially staying here longer.'

He nodded, waiting for me to continue.

'But if I do, if we become proper friends, and I end up spending more time with your family, it feels wrong to keep carrying this secret.'

Gabe took a long, slow breath. 'I understand.'

'It's your secret to tell, so if you don't want it shared, then I'll make my excuses to Pip and fly home tomorrow.'

'It's not a secret that I was married before. Plenty of people knew Nellie, after all. I'm not ashamed of that, or of you being here. But there was a fair bit of ill feeling. Mostly due to misunderstandings, assumptions, and the like. I wouldn't want people putting any of that on you. Or questioning why you're here now.'

'Why would they question it?'

'It is a little odd, my ex-wife's child turning up and staying with my daughter.'

'But I didn't know who she was. I didn't even know you existed until two days before I came here. It was Pip who offered me the room at Lily's.'

'I know that. But not everybody else does. The reaction might not be what you're hoping for.'

I sat back, perturbed.

'I suppose our deciding factor will be how serious you are about Pip.'

'Oh?'

'Are you prepared to chance causing upset, if it means you can stay?'

'Do you think Pip will be upset?'

'Maybe a little, at first. Maybe not, if we can explain it to him carefully. That it was me who insisted on you not telling him.'

I thought about it. Fobbing Pip off with a lie, getting on the plane back home and carrying on as before, never knowing what might have happened if I'd stayed.

Or revealing the truth, and risking him wanting nothing to do with me because of it.

One of those options meant my friendship with Pip would definitely end, along with the possibility of anything more.

The other one meant I had a chance, at least.

A chance of a new life, on this island that I was growing to love.

A new life, with Pip, who I loved even more.

'Will it cause trouble for you?'

Gabe gave a rueful smile. 'Nothing I'm not willing and able to handle. Ah, love. It can't have been easy, losing your mother, no other family to support you, or answer your questions about her. Then the bombshell that she had a secret husband, a hidden past. Whether you stay or not, the least you deserve is the opportunity to tell Pip the truth, share who you really are with him. Let's do it. Only, not on Iris and Hugh's big day. And I'll speak with Rosemary first, if you don't mind.'

We left the kitchen, although Gabe paused as we reached the corner leading to the Old Barn, impulsively pulling me into a hug.

'I hope you know how very much I loved your mother,' he said, voice rough with emotion. 'I meant every word I said, and I'm so sorry that she's no longer with us. Whatever happens next, I'm grateful to have had a chance to meet you, and I hope we get plenty of opportunities to share more about what a blessing it was to have known and loved her.'

'Thank you.'

'Come on, then, I believe my son would very much like to invite you to dance.'

31

'Ah, there you are,' Pip said, his face lighting up as Gabe and I approached a table full of Hawkins family members. 'The band's just taking a cider break, but Jack was hoping you'd join us in a line dance once they're finished.'

'Great.' While my bones were heavy with exhaustion, I was fizzing with adrenaline and anticipation, and there was no way I was turning down the chance to dance with Pip again.

'Did you see Ma?' Pip asked his dad. 'She was asking after you, so I pointed her to the kitchen to see if you'd finished clearing up.'

'No.' Gabe furrowed his forehead briefly, before shaking it off with a shrug.

'Still hanging in there, Mammaw?' Gabe asked Aster, pulling out the empty chair on one side of her, while I took a seat beside Pip, who instantly took my hand beneath the table, causing my insides to melt like warm caramel.

'I was waiting for Pip's girl to come back. I wanted to ask her something.'

'She's not Pip's—' Lily gave an apologetic glance in our direction, before stopping mid-sentence. 'What? Hang on? Are you two...? *Is she?*'

Flora, leaning up against her da, a novel about Robin Hood open about an inch from her nose, pursed her lips, murmuring, 'Keep up, Mother.'

Her uncle tried to look cool, but a grin kept escaping the side of his mouth. Mercifully, we were prevented from being grilled any further by Rosemary stomping up to the opposite side of the table to her husband, arms folded across a heaving chest.

'Are you all right, my love?' Gabe asked. 'Is there a problem?'

Rosemary's hair was askew, her cheeks crimson. She clearly wasn't all right.

'I'm fine,' she huffed. 'No problem that wants addressing in the middle of our daughter's wedding celebration.'

She threw a quick glance in my direction. Any sense of carefree joy evaporated as my whole body braced itself. Something else must have happened to make me look bad. And if it wasn't Celine, busy chatting to Violet and Barnie at the next table, who was it, and what had they done this time?

'Are you sure?'

Rosemary gave a firm nod.

'Come and sit with me, then?'

Rosemary ignored him, twisting her body to face the empty dance floor.

'What did you want to ask Emmie, Mammaw?' Pip asked, breaking the painful silence.

'Ah, yes. Well. I've been trying to work out who she is,' Aster said, nodding briskly in my direction. 'Your hair. Those eyes. The way you hold your hands when you stand. I knew it was familiar. And then I tried your pasty, and it clicked. I've only known one woman who can make a pastry crust so light and flaky, crisp and soft all at the same time. And you? Well, you're like one of those

Russian dolls that would have fitted inside her. Then Lily said your mother lived here, once. It's her, isn't it? You're Nellie's girl?'

'Who?' Lily asked, looking puzzled.

'Nellie!'

'Nellie Brown. Otherwise known as the witch who stole my husband away and tried to destroy the farm,' Rosemary suddenly shrieked, one slender finger pointing straight at me. Our whole table froze.

Most of the people nearby were also jolted into silence as they turned towards the sudden commotion.

'Ma, what are you talking about?' Lily stood up, reaching for her mother's hand, but Rosemary shook it off.

Rosemary was well beyond listening.

'Why is she here, Gabriel? Why have you welcomed her with open arms? How could you disrespect me like that? *What are you doing with her?*'

'Nothing!' Gabe stood up now. 'I've done nothing to disrespect you.'

'What? Sneaking around pretending to talk about chickens?' Rosemary spat. 'I saw you, not ten minutes ago, embracing in the dark! Muttering sweet nothings about how much you loved that shrew, and how you wished you were still with her, not me. Nothing to disrespect me? You've disrespected your children, your farm. All of it!'

'What?' Iris had hurried over, dress swishing. She stared at her father. 'What is she talking about, Da?'

'I did give Emmie a hug outside, yes,' Gabe said, his voice sounding as old as time. 'We'd been talking about her mother, who, yes, was my wife for almost four years, before anything happened between me and your ma. It was an emotional conversation. Nell passed a couple of years ago, and Emmie only recently found out that her mother had been married. Inevitably, she had questions about that, and it was only fair I provided some answers.'

'One of which being that you wished you were still with her?' Lily snapped.

'No! I expressed that I wished she was still here, as in still alive. I said I'd loved her, because I had. Rosemary, you know this. I have always been honest about that with you.'

'Up until last Friday, I'd have believed you, when she turned up and you acted as innocent as a seal pup. If you've always been so flaming honest, why have you been lying about it all week?'

'I didn't want to upset you.'

'Well, guess what: I'm a *bit upset*.'

'I'm so sorry about that, my love. I was going to talk to you about it as soon as the wedding was over. You can understand that today is not the day.' Gabe glanced around the room of gobsmacked guests. 'Now is not the time, or the place.'

'Maybe you should have thought about that before you let her bewitch you, just like her mother. I cannot believe you are falling for the same tricks all over again. Have you asked yourself what she's really after? Apart from a free holiday? Her mother's left her high and dry, so now here she is, wheedling her way into everyone's affections, conveniently falling for the heir to the farm. She's after her share of the land she'll never get to inherit, because you saw sense and left that leech back on the mainland where she belonged.'

'You're wrong,' Pip said, but the hint of doubt in his voice was devastating. At some point, he had let go of my hand.

'Do not refer to Emmie's mother that way,' Gabe said, clearly struggling to remain calm. 'Whatever misplaced gripe you have with Nellie, these accusations are unfounded, unkind, and, more to the point, make absolutely no sense.'

I could only sit there stricken, dying inside. Wishing more

than anything I'd never come here while begging my legs to start working so I could leave.

Rosemary dismissed her husband with a snort of contempt.

'If I'm so wrong, Philip, then what? Is she after taking you away? Robbing our farm of its rightful owner, just like her mother tried to?'

'No.' Pip shook his head, distraught. 'She wants to stay.'

'Hah,' Rosemary scoffed. 'That snooty old cow tried to fool us with that one, too. Lasted less than a year. You think this girl can hack island life? Look at her. We've hatched chickens with more meat on them. Learn from your da's mistake. Mainlander women have no understanding of commitment. No thought for eight generations of Hawkinses, working themselves to the bone to hand something of value on to their children.'

'Please, Ma, try to calm down so we can talk about this sensibly,' Lily said, attempting to manoeuvre her mother away. 'Let's go back to the house, where it's quieter.'

'And leave her with you all? To spin more lies!'

'She can come too.'

'I will not have that girl in my home.' Rosemary's face crumpled as the anger gave way to heaving sobs. 'Not until you admit that she's your daughter!'

'What?' Every ounce of colour drained from Gabe's face. I couldn't look at Pip, who must have felt sickened.

'Rosemary, this conversation needs to continue in the house.' Richard, who had watched all of this unfold with no discernible expression, hauled himself to his feet, unmistakably assuming the authority of the older brother.

With no small amount of fuss and borderline hysterics, Aster and both her sons, Rosemary and her four children trooped over to the kitchen, me trailing dismally behind them, upon Gabe's insistence.

We left Malcolm to round up his children, and get them safely home to bed, while Hugh oversaw the abrupt halt to festivities.

'I'm so sorry,' I whispered to no one in particular, once we'd gathered around the table. 'I've ruined the wedding.'

'If only it was just the wedding,' Rosemary hissed. She had refused to sit down.

'Don't take this upon yourself,' Richard said. 'It wasn't your intention for anyone to find out today. And it wasn't your choice to keep your identity concealed in the meantime. This is why we don't do secrets.'

He scowled at his brother. 'Truth will always come out, usually at the worst possible time.'

'Can we please get back to the slightly more urgent issue of whether Da is Emmie's father?' Violet asked, her face a brittle mask.

'There is no issue,' Gabe said, with a weary sigh. 'Emmie must be younger than Pip.'

'How old are you?' Iris shot at me.

'Twenty-six.'

'There you have it.' Gabe looked at Rosemary, eyes imploring. 'We were married for four years before she was born.'

'And?' Rosemary's rampant fury had cooled to icy rage. 'We all know how you felt about that woman. The mainlander who drove Gabriel Hawkins out of his mind with lust. And who conveniently opened a shop in the only airport that flies to Siskin. I wonder what made her decide to do that? No chance at all of you bumping into each other while off on one of your conferences. Or how about when you insisted on seeing our children to boarding school?'

'The times I took them to school, we got the boat so I could drive their cases over.'

'Are you denying there's any chance this woman is your daughter?'

'Are you seriously implying there's any chance she is? I always knew you were jealous of her, Rosemary, but I divorced her and married you.'

'He can't be her dad – Emmie is adopted,' Pip said slowly.

All the women whipped their heads towards me.

'But you look just like her.' Aster's wrinkles deepened as she leant forwards in her chair to where I hunched on the opposite side of the table.

'Nell was my birth mother's cousin,' I said quietly. Hating the feeling of betrayal that accompanied stating this almost as much as I hated it being true. 'Their mothers were identical twins.'

'Have you got that?' Gabe asked his wife bitterly. 'Or do you have further evidence to substantiate this fictitious affair with a woman who wanted nothing more to do with me?'

'She did, though,' Rosemary blurted. 'She still wanted you.'

'What?' Gabe shook his head, frustrated. 'She wrote to me demanding a divorce so she could marry another fella. While Emmie here informs me the marriage never happened, why on earth come up with a lie like that if she still wanted any part of me?'

Every remaining trace of bluster seeped out of Rosemary like a deflating balloon. She sank into the chair next to Aster's, eyes darting anywhere but at her husband. Or me.

'She knew it was up to her to make the impossible choice. Otherwise, you'd never have let her go,' she almost whispered. 'The only way to convince you to commit to the farm, fulfil your family duty, was if you believed it was for her sake. Either that, or it would prompt you to finally go back and fight for her.'

'Why would you say this?' Gabe said, shaking his head in denial.

'She said it, didn't she?' Aster asked, sounding every second of her ninety-one years. 'In the last letter. The one you never got to see. Is that right, Rosemary?'

Gabe was incredulous. 'She wrote another letter?'

Aster placed a hand on her daughter-in-law's arm, but her eyes were on her son. 'You two had already started courting. She was the most sensible match for you. For all of us. Nellie wasn't a farmer. She hated it here. And then, brazen as anything, she announces that she's not having children. So, she's useless on the farm and useless to the family.'

Gabe gripped the edge of the table with both hands. His lips a thin white line. 'She was not useless to me. She was my wife. And you stole a letter she sent, saying what – that she didn't really want a divorce?'

To my surprise, Aster began to weep. 'I never read the letter. Rosemary was with me when Postie Scott delivered it, and I didn't stop her slipping it into her pocket. I was ashamed of how your da and I treated Nellie. Seeing how devastated you were when you came back without her made me regret how selfish we'd been. But you'd finally started to smile again. To whistle while you drove the tractor, talk sweet nonsense to the calves. What I did was wrong, but I couldn't allow that woman to break your heart all over again. Not when you were so happy with Rosemary.'

'That wasn't your decision,' Gabe said, his words like shards of ice.

'No.' Aster lifted her head, pointlessly blotting the trickle of tears with the back of her gnarly hand. 'But I'm not sorry for it. Look at the life you made, here, with your island girl. Four fine children. Grandchildren. A son determined to carry on our legacy. Are you sorry for it, Gabe? Do you wish I'd made your new love give the letter back?'

'We did it for you,' Rosemary added, finding confidence in Aster's words.

'No.' Gabe banged his hand so hard on the table, the jugs on the dresser rattled. 'You did it for you. The pair of you and Da. For generations of people who have long since gone to the churchyard and don't care a jot whether their farm thrives or falls into ruin!'

'So, you do regret not knowing. She was your first choice, after all. Not me.'

'She was my first wife!' he roared. 'We were still married. And now you dare to force your insane, twisted logic onto Emmie. As if she has anything to do with any of it. The pair of you should be bending over backwards to make her feel welcome, if you've the slightest bit of shame for what you did.'

'I know that,' Aster said. 'Once I'd realised who she was, I thought it was a chance to redeem the wrongs done to her mother. She's in the dress I wore to your father's funeral. You couldn't think I hold anything against her, if I did that?'

'If only Ma could say the same,' Lily said, with a sharp glance at Rosemary. 'Ma? What possible reason do you have now for all this resentment towards Emmie? What Nell did or didn't do decades ago is nothing to do with her. You can't blame her for wanting to come and find out more about her mother's history.'

'You think that's why she's here?' Rosemary asked, with a caustic laugh. 'Or, how about she's here for revenge on the family who hounded her mother off the farm? You don't think she's angry about spending her life in a poky kiosk dishing out the same old food to people infinitely more successful than she is, when if things had been different, she could have been here, adopted into a family with two hundred acres of land?'

'That makes no sense,' Violet said. 'If Emmie was here for revenge, why would she help out Lily and cater Iris's wedding?'

'She scrubbed all the bird crap off the barn,' Pip added. 'She's spent her holiday helping us.'

'Maybe she did those things, while smiling and acting all meek and clueless and grateful. I don't blame you children for being so trusting, seeing as none of you knew how sly her mother could be. But, Gabe, did you not question how all these coincidental accidents and incidents kept happening, once she'd swanned onto the scene?'

Rosemary slowly scanned our faces, eyes gleaming. 'The open gate, despite the fact – or *because* – Pip warned her about it. Mysteriously getting the times wrong for serving the wedding food, and blaming it on me. What better revenge on Nellie's mother-in-law than to spoil the last wedding cake she'll probably get to make? I ask you, who else but this family and her knew about the broken fridge? It couldn't have been anyone else. She said it herself, she's a highly competent caterer and top-notch businesswoman who never forgets a trick. Have you a better explanation? Have *you*?'

She turned her glare on me, and I had to close my eyes to prevent being overwhelmed with the horror of it all. I'd started to realise as we'd made our way to the farmhouse that all the nasty incidents had been Rosemary. Would it come down to the fierce word of a beloved wife and mother against that of a quaking, stumbling stranger?

'I thought not.' Rosemary's triumph was growing. 'You may have been kind enough to lend her your most precious gown, Mammaw. But don't fool yourself for a second that she respects that sentiment. We've seen how clumsy she is, but to damage a dress so well made must have been deliberate. Did you curse our family as you ripped that hole in the shoulder?'

There was a stunned silence. I pressed one hand against my frantic heart, sure it would explode before this ordeal was over.

'How did you know about the torn seam?'

Richard's sardonic voice penetrated the swirl of blind panic clouding my vision. For the first time, a glimpse of fear peeked out from behind Rosemary's defiance.

'Look at it. It's obvious. Her sheer audacity to parade around in a vandalised dress surely proves how much sick pleasure she is deriving from her revenge.'

'I can't see it,' Violet said, sitting beside me. 'Which shoulder was it?'

'The right one. And you can't see it because I repaired it before she put it on,' Richard said. 'If you'd noticed it while it was still hanging in the coat closet, Rosemary, why on earth didn't you say something then? To Ma, if not her.'

'Maybe I know the dress better than you,' Rosemary gabbled. 'I can spot a darned seam, even if Violet can't.'

'But you didn't say it had been mended, only that she was parading around in it ripped,' Lily added.

'You really can't tell it was ever torn,' Violet reiterated, having peered closely as she fingered the fabric while I prayed I wouldn't throw up on her bridesmaid dress.

'You ripped the dress,' Richard said. 'Moved the cake, deliberately told Emmie the wrong time for dinner, and have you really become so poisoned by jealous spite, you risked our precious herd to make her look bad?'

'Better risking an injured cow than losing the whole farm!'

The stunned silence seemed to go on forever.

'You tried to ruin my wedding?' Iris asked, eventually, her voice small.

'Och, of course not. No one who organises a wedding in four days is going to be that bothered by lukewarm pastries and a sagging cake. I was just showing you that she's not capable. Pip – she's not fit to be an island farmer! She can cook the one meat we don't produce on this island, and a half-decent pastry crust. She knows nothing about anything that matters. I had to make you see before you did something stupid like your father.'

'Rosemary.' Gabe spoke her name like a warning bullet being fired.

'You spoiled Mammaw's cake?' Iris asked, choking back a sob. 'And her dress? If you were worried about Emmie, why didn't you just talk to us? Talk to Pip?'

'Because none of you knew who she was!'

'What else did you do?' Gabe asked.

'Nothing,' Rosemary said, but the way she turned her head, hitching her shoulders up as she folded her arms, gave a different answer.

'She soaked the bike I hired from Barnie in something really nasty,' I said.

'Oh, my goodness. Ma, was that you?' Lily exclaimed, screwing up her nose in memory of the stench.

'After I'd come home from the beach on Sunday evening, I found bird droppings in the milk jug in my bedroom.'

'What? Why didn't you say anything?' Lily was wild with anger and disgust. 'You're my test guest and you found bird crap in your milk?'

'I thought it was Celine. I didn't want to cause any drama before the wedding,' I mumbled.

'So, you said nothing while she continued her intimidation tactics at Iris's wedding?' Violet asked, frowning.

'She's Iris's best friend. I felt sure she'd not do anything to ruin her big day.'

'Which turned out to be accurate,' Pip added. He'd been mostly quiet throughout this whole agonising conversation. 'It didn't cross your mind to consider it might be anyone else? That if you told me, I'd take it seriously, and do something to help?'

'Did I lay awake at night, alone in a strange bed, the first time

I've ever been anywhere, and wonder who the hell might have tried to poison me, or make me appear liable for cows being injured? As it happens, I spent a considerable amount of time questioning who I'd provoked to such disturbing levels of hatred.'

'That can't have been easy,' Gabe said. 'Thank you for staying and cooking for Iris and Hugh.'

'It wasn't.' I stood up. 'But being here, how welcome you all made me feel. Getting to know your family, and this incredible island, and the weird, wonderful way you live together on it, made it worth it. But all this stuff about Mum, and what happened with the lost letter, well, that's not something I can hear any more about. There's a lot you need to discuss as a family, that, me being a mainlander, I believe isn't my business. If you don't mind, I'll head back and try to get at least some sleep before my flight.'

Nobody argued, so I grabbed my bag from where I'd left it on the hook of the door what seemed like a lifetime ago, and slunk out.

I didn't know whether to feel relieved or frustrated when Pip caught up with me at the edge of the farmyard.

'You're leaving?'

I waved my hand back in the direction of the house. 'Your mum hates me, Pip. As in, lost all sense of reason, frightening hatred. She snuck into my bedroom and put bird crap in the milk jug. If it was Celine, I could have stuck it out, as long as you believed me. Kept out of her way. But your *ma*? I can't compete with that. Not the way you people love each other. And everyone else will now see me as the daughter of "that woman". Who nearly wrecked everything. Staying here would be challenging enough without that hanging over me, people questioning why I'm really here.'

'I'm really sorry about Ma.' Pip ran an agitated hand through his hair. 'I mean, clearly she needs help. Therapy, or something.'

'In which case, the last thing she needs is me attaching myself to your family like a mainland limpet. How could she – how could any of you – handle me dating her son? And if nothing's going to happen with us, then what's the point? Why would I uproot my whole life to move here, given all the added complications? Having to either avoid you, somehow find a whole different social network on an island of three thousand people, who all know I'm Gabe Hawkins' ex-wife's daughter, or hang out with you, while never getting to hold your hand or kiss you again.'

He tipped his head up to the sky, the moonlight glinting off his tears.

'There's a whole world out there, Pip. Islands, mountains, other cultures... Why would I choose to stay in the one place where I'm viciously not wanted? Please, if you care about me at all, don't make this harder than it has to be. Please let me go.'

I spun around, stumbling through the deserted garden to the footpath leading to the fields, only slowing when it became clear that Pip wasn't coming after me, and I was free to release the noisy, soul-wrenching sobs.

I used my last dreg of energy tossing my things into bags, ignoring Blessing's messages begging for an update, carefully draping Aster's dress over the armchair, crawling into bed in my underwear and finding that, in actual fact, I still had the stamina to cry a whole load more before sinking into a fretful sleep.

32

At some point before I woke at four-thirty, an envelope had been slipped under my door.

I made myself one last mug of tea, curled up in the chair facing the huge window, and watched streaks of pink, gold and lilac sunrise spread across the sky for a long moment before I opened it.

4 April 1989

Gabriel

I don't need to tell you that today is our third anniversary. I can't help wondering whether you have written me a letter, despite knowing that it would surely be full of the pain and anger I've caused.

You may be wondering why I've written one (if you haven't immediately tossed this into the living room fire).

Well. You are still my husband. And, I implore you – I will happily beg, if that would make a difference – that after reading what I have to say, you consider remaining that way.

I have made a hideous mistake, asking for a divorce. Not least because, for the first (and last) time, I lied to you. I lied about falling in love with another man. It took thirty-seven years to find one man I could envisage sharing my life with. Can you really imagine me finding another?

You are the only man I have, and will ever, love, Gabriel. I asked for a divorce for the most cowardly of reasons – fear. I was afraid that you would choose the farm over me. And I was more afraid that you wouldn't. That eventually, you would feel obligated to return to England, devastating your family, betraying your legacy and seething with buried resentment towards the wife who you were bound to discover sooner or later is by no means worthy of that sacrifice. I chose to believe that you belonged on your beloved island. That my love had a lesser claim on you. That even if I retried making a home on Hawkins Farm, we would live out our days in misery.

So, I invented a reason that you would find impossible to deny. You've always valued my happiness above your own, and I knew you would release me to remarry if I asked.

And, yes, a small part of me hoped that my letter would rekindle the fire you once felt. That you would ride in like a knight on a white horse, to claim your bride.

That, somehow, we would find a way to be happy. Or if not happy, then at least at peace.

Of course, that did not happen. You have fields to plough and calves to castrate. More common sense than money to waste going after a woman who has clearly told you she wants someone else.

So here I find myself, on our wedding anniversary, living with the single greatest mistake of my life.

I had spent so long alone, yet was never lonely until I met you.

I had rarely known joy, and yet never once encountered such despair.

I had considered myself to be content, to be enough. Now I am consumed with longing.

If there is any chance you can forgive me, please don't sign the papers. Call me. Call my solicitor. Come to me. Or I will come to you. I don't care what your family must think of me.

I'm not asking for forgiveness now. Merely for you to consider whether it's worth finding out if there is still hope for us.

I love you.

I'm sorrier than I could ever say.

Please give me a chance. Give our love another chance.

I will do whatever it takes.

Your wife,

Nellie

I could not begin to imagine the depth of feeling that had prompted my proud, pragmatic mother to write that letter. Or the one that must have preceded it, now her motivation had become clear. It was hard not to dwell on 'what ifs' as I quickly showered, stuffed the last bits into my bags and made my way downstairs.

The house was silent, as I'd have expected this early on the morning after a family wedding. I took a sheet of Beanie's colouring paper and scrawled a brief note of my own, tucking it behind a sunflower fridge magnet.

Thank you, for everything.

I'm so sorry for how it ended.

I hope the review helps make up for it,

Emmie

A week after I'd nearly passed out riding Barnie's rental bike up the coastal road, I whizzed down the curves towards Port Cathan and on towards the airport while barely breaking a sweat. It helped there was nothing else on the road other than a milk van, the postman, a couple of runners and a delivery truck. And that I stopped at Dahlia's, where they informed me I was the first customer of the day, to fill up my Isle of Siskin travel mug with freshly ground coffee and buy a slice of chocolate cherry pie. I pressed on for another mile before stopping where I'd collapsed by the side of the road on my first evening here, this time leaving the bike propped against a tree (the smell was by now barely noticeable, unless you gave the saddle a big sniff) as I snuck into the meadow.

Reclining against my rucksack, I inhaled the heady fragrance of flowers, sea salt and dew-damp earth and blinked back the tears pressing behind my eyes.

I sipped my coffee, ate my pie and resolved to savour this moment.

The sky was a perfect, mid-summer blue, the sun a new penny warming the back of my scalp.

A family of rabbits whiffled around the hedgerow, while the bleating of distant sheep mingled with the squawking chirrup of siskins in the alder trees.

Yesterday had been one of the loveliest and most traumatic days of my life.

I had successfully catered a wedding.

I had worn a stunning dress and kissed a beautiful man in a treehouse.

I had learned things about my mother I'd never have imagined. Including how she'd broken her own heart for the sake of her husband and his family.

I had been lied about, and to. Insulted and falsely accused.

I had made a decision so brave, it made my spur-of-the-moment holiday seem trivial in comparison.

And then, hours later, I had unmade it, after losing the man I was falling in love with, only a moment after we'd really begun.

Did I regret it, my island adventure?

Perhaps, only time would tell.

I soaked it all up for another few minutes, then clambered back on the bike and headed for home.

33

'I still don't get why you snuck off like that,' Blessing said, for about the tenth time, as we sat in the tiny back garden of the cottage, watching the bumblebees flitting between the foxgloves lining my back fence.

When I'd left a week ago, the outdoor seating had consisted of a half-rotten, moss-covered bench with a broken back. Now, we lounged in matching reclining chairs with plump, stripy cushions that Blessing assured me she'd got for next to nothing from a preloved furniture website, on the basis that if we were going to live with the inconvenience of being in the middle of nowhere, we might as well be comfy. I had to agree.

'What else was I going to do? I had a plane to catch.'

'Emmie, your flight was at twelve-fifteen. You messaged me from the airport at eight-twenty.'

I wriggled on my seat, taking a sip of Blessing's 'signature weekend cocktail' as I tried to come up with a plausible answer. It might have been the extra splash of gin that persuaded me to simply go with the truth.

'The way they all looked at me, once they knew I'd been hiding who I was, I couldn't bear to face that again.'

'Pip, too?'

'Especially Pip!' I sank lower in the chair, flicking a tiny spider off my knee. 'He only came after me to double-check that I was leaving and apologise for his mum. He didn't once try to convince me to stay. He was so angry when he heard I'd been hiding the truth.'

'That can't be true,' she protested. 'You said his dad explained that he was the one making you keep it a secret.'

'Maybe. But he was also mad that I didn't tell him about the milk, or the other stuff. He thinks I jeopardised his sister's wedding because I didn't trust him.'

Blessing blew a raspberry. 'The only person doing that was his mum.'

'Exactly. It's a lot easier to blame a woman you barely know than your own mother.'

'He's not contacted you today?'

I shook my head. 'I told him not to. There's nothing to say apart from, "Sorry, that all turned out a bit crappy". Why would he bother when it's such a complicated mess?'

'Um, because you're gorgeous and awesome and totally worth it?'

'Clearly not, because the only messages I've got are from Sherwood Airport staff freaking out about how they can't live without Parsley's coffee or pasties. Not one of them has mentioned missing me.'

'Hmm.' Blessing looked pensive, before topping up both our glasses from the jug she'd balanced on the wooden crate temporarily acting as a garden table.

'Seriously, though, you have to feel proud of yourself. For someone as untravelled as you to catch a plane on the spur of the moment, find yourself a place to stay, make friends, get invited to a hen do and a wedding. Have someone offer you their airport business! I'd never have had the guts to buy the ticket in the first place, with no hotel waiting for me on the other side. You are one fierce woman hiding behind that sad little ponytail.'

'What?' I spun my head around to face her. 'You were the one who badgered me into it!'

She beamed. 'Yeah. I had a feeling you'd do okay. And look what happened – instead of slaving away in that giant aluminium shed, you're here, with me, enjoying Blessing's sunshine happy hour, the world at your feet, endless possibilities just waiting for us to smash the hell out of them.'

'I am. And I'm very grateful.' I held up my glass. 'Here's to being unemployed, completely messing things up with my two-year crush and having a whacking great fine to pay for my defunct business.'

'Cheers.'

As we whiled away the rest of the day, chatting about ideas for the cottage, idly discussing grandiose plans about a future business and where we'd go for our first joint holiday, the island began to fade into something of a distant dream. Now I was surrounded by oak trees, squirrels rustling in the summer leaves, the extraordinary events of the past week already started to settle into the story that Blessing assured me we would laugh about one day.

My life was here, for now at least, and there was something wonderful about being with someone who'd known me for longer than anyone, in the place I'd always been, while so aware that things had changed forever.

For that, if nothing else, I would be forever grateful to the Isle of Siskin.

* * *

Saturday, we both slept in, ate scrambled eggs with leftover guacamole and sour cream for brunch and then got down to business.

Not actual business yet. We'd agreed a weekend off before we started making serious plans about that. In the meantime, there was a cottage that needed a makeover even more badly than its owner.

Blessing had been sleeping in my bedroom, as using Mum's felt wrong before I'd sorted through it. The only issue with this being that her promise to bring the 'bare essentials' with her until we'd redecorated the larger bedroom included so many bags, cases and piles of random clutter there was only space in my bedroom for one person at a time.

I'd slept on the sofa the past two nights, despite Blessing forcefully trying to insist I had my room back. I'd eventually convinced her that the sofa was infinitely preferable to squashing myself in with her stuffed-animal zoo, risking a bruised shin or broken toe if I needed to negotiate the slalom getting to the bathroom in the middle of the night.

Today, Blessing had driven to the nearest DIY shop. She had initially been shocked to hear that I'd never done any painting, until I asked her to name a room in the cottage that looked as though it had been decorated in the past quarter of a century, and she had to admit that my lack of experience made sense.

While she stocked up on paint, rollers, brushes and whatever else we might need, I started clearing out Mum's wardrobe and chest of drawers, separating clothes into rags and things worth donating to the local clothing bank. It didn't take long. Neither did sorting her two pairs of shoes.

From there, I quickly binned the scant remaining toiletries, and her cheap, plastic hairbrush. She had a few more utilitarian items lined up on top of her chest of drawers, which I relocated elsewhere in the house, including a box of tissues, nail scissors and packet of painkillers. I also moved a hot-water bottle, the small suitcase containing a washbag and, unsurprisingly, very little else.

I replaced the letters in their original box along with the photograph and dried flowers, and moved that downstairs for now.

By the time Blessing returned (with a distinct whiff of McDonald's fries clinging to her T-shirt), I was done. Under two hours and the room was emptied of anything reflecting the woman who'd slept there for three decades. I stood there for a while, feeling a sudden rush of grief for, not only the mother I'd lost, but any chance to discover who else she'd been. The letters had helped fill in some missing pieces, but the thirty-seven years prior to those were a mystery that, thanks to her disdain for sentimentality, I would never find the answers to.

'That's not quite true, though, is it?' Blessing said, when I expressed this while in the process of dismantling the old MDF wardrobe.

'What do you mean? If there was anything stored anywhere else in the house, I'd have found it by now.'

'But she isn't the only person who can answer those questions. Contrary to the rumours, she wasn't an android built in a lab. And despite being the toughest, most independent person ever, she didn't bring herself up.'

I sat back, wiping the sweat off my face. Who knew unscrewing screws was such hard work? 'You mean her family?'

'I mean *your* family.'

'You know my birth mum died when I was tiny.'

'Yes, but what about your grandparents? Her aunt, whatever you want to call her. Did your mum have brothers and sisters?'

I frowned. 'Which mum?'

Blessing looked up from where she'd been working on a door hinge. 'Either.'

'I don't know.'

'Okay, so what do you know?'

'I know Mum decided none of them were worth knowing. She left strict instructions in her "death folder" not to invite any of them to her funeral.'

We put down our screwdrivers and sat back against the dusty wall.

'Did she explain why?'

I shrugged. 'She used to say that the only limit to her family's depravity was their own laziness.'

'What does that even mean?'

'Kennedy, my mother, had been to prison a couple of times.'

'How did she die?'

I leant my head back until it rested against the wall. 'I'm not even sure. As I got older, I assumed it was drug-related. But we never talked about these things. I learned very young not to try. I know Nell's and Kennedy's mums were twins.'

'So they're likely to have been close?'

'And likely to have also died. Mum's birth certificate says her mother was eighteen when she was born, so they'd be, what, in their early nineties now?'

'Do you want to know if you have a family out there, somewhere? Who they are, what they're like? Whether they love reading and dreaming about adventures in far-flung places? Because you definitely didn't get that from Nell.'

'I don't know. I used to fantasise about Kennedy, invent a personality that explained why I was so different from Mum, but as I got older, it felt less and less relevant. I thought about it when Mum died, obviously, but while Kennedy was still only a name on a piece of paper, it was easy to put her out of my mind. That time was hard enough without stirring all that up.'

'Of course. So, what about your dad?'

I shook my head. 'That's a mystery that will never be solved. Short of doing one of those DNA tests and miraculously finding a paternal match.'

'Sounds like you've thought about it.'

'And dismissed it. Whoever he was, he either never knew that the mentally ill, drug-addicted woman he slept with had given birth to his child, or he didn't care. I have no desire whatsoever to know more about a man like that.'

'Fair enough.'

My mind kept drifting back to our conversation as we cleared out the dismantled furniture, wiped down the walls and prepped the room for painting. I kept coming back to the same question.

What's the worst that can happen if I contact my family?

Once we'd eaten a bowl of pasta while Blessing introduced me to her favourite gruesome crime box set, and then four episodes later said goodnight, leaving me to get comfy on the sofa, I made a rough mental list of the answers.

They might turn out to be as bad as Mum said – in which case, I'll simply walk away.

They might reject, or dislike, me. But if they don't want to give me a chance, then that's their loss, not mine.

I might find out a load of awful things about Mum. Which I can live with. Whoever she was before, the woman she was for her last twenty-four years is what matters to me.

I might love them. And they love me, too. Maybe Mum exaggerated, or perhaps they had a questionable past, but have become great people. In which case, we have to grieve all those lost years.

And the best that could happen?

I'd have a family. A place to belong. People who cared. Who could help me understand Mum better, why she was that way. Why I wasn't.

I decided that maybe I should do some tentative investigating. I would proceed with caution. Protect myself at every step. Expect nothing.

I'd start soon. Maybe once the decorating was finished, or the new business had got under way.

Was it a little pathetic that when I opened up Instagram, dilly-dallying about whether to start searching for other Browns and Swans, I instead found myself scrolling through Iris's wedding photos, heart scrunching up as I zoomed in on Pip, the devoted brother sandwiched between four sisters with a huge grin on his face?

And, then – *oomph*.

There I was, fairy lights glinting off my mussed hair, Aster's dress swishing flatteringly, eyes dancing as I walked across the grass, Pip's hand in mine. The photograph had caught us exchanging animated glances. He was laughing, completely at ease, as if we'd strolled together countless times before.

I looked... happy.

Together, we looked like a couple utterly in love.

I put down my phone and watched two more episodes of the crime box set before I calmed down enough to even pretend to try getting to sleep.

34

It was when I moved the creaky old bed away from the wall that I found it. A dusty grey cardboard folder, tucked in the inch-high space between the floor and the divan bed base.

Inside were photographs of a baby who must have been me. In a couple of the pictures, I was alone, in my pram and lying on a picnic blanket. In others, Mum was there, cradling me against her chest or sitting me on her knee in front of a cake with one candle on it. The rest featured other people too – women who all looked like older or younger versions of Nell, and a few small children.

This must be the family Nell refused to have anything to do with. Yet she clearly hadn't decided that until I was past my first birthday. What had happened?

After soaking up the images, I found the answer in an envelope inside the folder. It contained the court papers granting legal guardianship of Emmaline Swan to Nell Brown, dated a month after my first birthday. Fascinated, I read the statement about how Kennedy Swan had requested that the cousin who had already been caring for her daughter should be given parental responsibility. The formal assessment confirmed what Mum had told me, that Kennedy had a lot of problems, as well as two prison sentences behind her, but it was the rest that floored me.

> Ms Brown clearly cares deeply for Emmaline. They have formed a strong bond during this first year of Emmaline's life, and Emmaline sees Ms Brown as her mother. Concerns have been raised about Ms Brown's ability to raise a child, considering her own family background, but she has worked hard to address these by taking a significant amount of time off work to attend courses and educate herself on healthy parenting. She has also cut back the hours of her business, at considerable financial loss, in order to minimise the need for external childcare. Furthermore, she has abandoned her plans to open a second food outlet, being unwilling to take on the risk when responsible for a child.
>
> Ms Brown has argued vigorously that she is able to protect Emmaline from any safeguarding issues surrounding her family while maintaining those relationships. However, the wider concerns detailed in section 4.2 mean that the guardianship shall only be granted if Emmaline has no ongoing contact with either her maternal grandparents, Ms Brown's parents, or her aunt and uncle. Ms Brown has therefore agreed to cease all contact with her family in order to preserve the placement's confidentiality.

And so it went on. There were other questions raised, about how Mum would balance a business and a child as a single parent, what would happen if the kiosk failed. How she would handle any future relationships with men. It was a rigorous grilling, and Mum's answers were always the same. I was her priority now. Basically, she'd do whatever it took to make it work, and be the best mum that she could be.

Section 4.2 was missing, but that wasn't what mattered to me. I had always known that Mum made the usual sacrifices that went hand in hand with parenting. Those that, like most children, I'd taken for granted a lot of the time. But reading how she'd chosen to slash her income, abandon her dreams of expansion – to stay single! It also explained why she'd put so much into Parsley's, into sticking to what worked. She'd sworn to give it her all, so she had.

Above all, only a few years after losing the love of her life, she'd given up her family. For a child who wasn't even her responsibility.

I felt overcome by the enormity of what she'd done for me. I sobbed as I realised the true reason why she'd struggled so hard with allowing herself to be vulnerable, let alone happy. My heart shattered at the injustice that I'd never be able to tell her how grateful I was.

I decided then that, one day, when I felt strong enough, I would find Nell's family and show them that her sacrifice was worth it.

When Blessing found me applying the first coat of white paint later that Sunday morning, she took one look at my blotchy face and threw her arms around me, ignoring the roller dripping onto the carpet as I collapsed into a puddle of yet more tears.

* * *

Once I'd wrung myself dry and was insistent that I needed to stop thinking about it for now, we decided the best solution was a late brunch in the village café, accompanied by a long conversation about what else we'd like to do with the cottage, before heading back to apply Blessing's choice of teal feature wall. For some reason, the second coat took longer. Possibly due to my housemate insisting we stop to dance when one of her favourite songs came on, and this being her 'top tunes' playlist, so that meant basically every track.

We finished late afternoon, had a break for coffee and cookies and then started sawing furniture into manageable-sized pieces and feeding the bits to the fire pit Blessing picked up at the same time as the loungers.

'Look at us.' Blessing sighed once blisters forced us to give up on the saw, and we feasted on cheese and crackers in the warmth of the flames. 'Two weeks ago, I was climbing out of a bunk bed covered in ancient My Little Pony stickers, kicking my way through Honour's dirty school uniform to bagsy the shower, and now I'm here, with my bestie housemate, living like an actual adult, without Dad hovering over my shoulder lecturing about sharp blades, forest fires and the correct protocol for cleaning paintbrushes.'

'I think this is the first time I've genuinely relished making my own decisions, without second-guessing what Mum would have thought. Well,' I corrected myself, 'apart from the vegan pasties.'

'It was the pasties that kick-started this whole thing,' Blessing mused.

'You know what, it was before then. That day I overslept, something inside me shifted.'

'What made you sleep through your alarm for the first time ever?'

I added another section of bedpost to the fire, debating whether or not to admit the truth.

'I was dreaming.'

'Oh?'

'About the island,' I added sheepishly.

'Girl,' Blessing said slowly. I didn't have to look round to know she was raising one eyebrow, mouth curling up. 'Have you messaged him yet?' she asked, after a long minute of what I pretended was companionable rather than a loaded silence.

'Nope.'

'Still thinking about him?'

I showed her the Instagram picture.

'Oh, Emmie.' I did look at her this time. Her voice was so uncharacteristically gentle, it knocked me off guard. 'You really did fall in love.'

'It's only a photo.' I quickly took the phone back and stuffed it in my jacket pocket.

She said nothing, reaching over and taking hold of my hand, kindly not acknowledging the escaped tear.

Blessing was right. We were doing great. Brimming with plans and possibilities.

I had to figure out how to stop feeling as though a big fat chunk of my heart was missing.

* * *

We spent the next few days building flat-pack furniture, adding soft furnishings and other finishing touches before moving so much of Blessing's stuff into the room, it was virtually impossible to see any of the new décor. We then painted my room in a soft golden yellow that was the exact same shade as the Hawkins Farm winter barley. Meaning it was my own fault when, that first night back in my old bed, I dreamed about blue skies, shimmering meadows and the squawk of gulls swooping over the Irish Sea.

By Friday, we were so full of half-baked, half-bonkers business ideas that a formal meeting couldn't wait any longer. We set up my laptop, Blessing's iPad and two pristine notebooks on the largest worktop in the pasty kitchen, perching on our stools with giant lattes and cinnamon whirls from Middlebeck bakery, feeling about as bad-ass businesswomen as we could get.

Blessing kicked things off. 'Okay, if time, money and talents were completely limitless, what would you do?'

'I had wondered about seeing if there were any pitches going at local markets.'

She wrinkled her nose. 'To do what?'

'Sell pasties.'

'If time, money and talents were unlimited, basically meaning that you could do absolutely anything you wanted, you'd sell pasties on a market stall? In which case, what was the point of closing Parsley's?'

'Because I didn't want to work inside all day. What would you do with all this unlimited everything?'

She flicked a few braids over her shoulder. 'Initial thoughts... I'd form a circus troupe. Open a spa-hotel for pets. Set up a cookery school for ex-female prisoners. Become a Hollywood agent.'

'I have no idea how to do any of those things. I have no interest in doing them.'

'Neither do I, especially, but the point is we start with nothing off the table, then narrow it down to what sparks your interest, seems worth exploring. It's called blue-sky thinking.'

'Blessing, you know I've worked at the same place doing the exact same thing forever. I grew up living and breathing one basic food item. You might need to start a little more down to earth.'

'Fine.' She straightened her shoulders and took a bite of pastry, undaunted. 'Let's try a different angle. What do you like? What *does* spark joy for Emmaline Brown? Apart from dreamy thoughts about island farmers with great hair.'

It was a cheesy start to the discussion, but soon made it clear that Blessing had been busy while I'd been away, reading, listening to podcasts and even attending a couple of online seminars on setting up a new business.

After winding our way through starting our own organic chicken farm, via cooking vlogs, party planning and a detour into painting and decorating, we ended up near to where I started.

I wanted to keep baking, but was determined to have more flexibility, fresh air and to bring things into the twenty-first century.

And so, Parsley's Pasties became Sherwood Street Food. My inheritance money was enough to buy a second-hand food truck. A modest loan from Blessing's parents would cover the remaining initial outlay, which was minimal thanks to Parsley's. We would keep selling drinks and pasties but also experiment with specials including nachos, mini loaded Yorkshire puddings and, my favourite: individual portions of Siskin pot sausage. I spent hours perfecting new recipes, completing all the legal and health and safety admin and other practical tasks such as finding out how on earth to manage a catering business that moved. Blessing put herself in charge of publicity and marketing, including creating a website and the most important task of finding us places where we could sell the new food.

I'd thought running an established business was hard work. It was nothing compared to setting a new one up. Once we'd completed the first, major task of buying the truck, the rest of the summer was full-on, to say the least. But I had a partner – one who listened, collaborated, was eager to try new ideas *and* believed in modern technology.

I loved every second of it.

On the first weekend in August, we opened our hatch door at the Robin Hood Festival, Sherwood Forest's busiest event, which would be held over the next four weekends. One of the organisers had been a regular customer at the airport and snapped up our last-minute request the same day Blessing emailed them.

We spent most of the festivities with a queue weaving in and out of the trees. Robin Hood, Maid Marion and almost all the Merry Men became regular customers. Little John even gave us a shout-out during the big battle with the Sheriff of Nottingham's soldiers, crediting our pork and mustard Yorkshire pudding with fuelling his winning moves.

'These are heavenly,' the woman officially acting as Marion said after biting into a vegetarian pasty – it turned out her real name was also Marion, and she was married to the person playing Robin. 'Would you be interested in supplying my restaurant? It's on a campsite, not far from here: Scarlett's?'

Would I be interested in supplying one of the most popular restaurants in the area? I double-checked that Blessing's younger brother, Ben, who happened to be as charming a salesman as his sister, and far more skilled in the kitchen, was happy to keep being employed with us for the foreseeable future, and arranged a meeting for the following week.

Blessing also wangled an interview with a reporter, Bea Armstrong, who featured feel-good stories on the local news. As well as sticking to Mum's commitment to support Nottinghamshire businesses, we'd signed up to provide autumn work-experience placements for pupils at a local alternative provision school, Charis House, that happened to be run by Bea's parents, and also where her fiancé worked. After someone made a meme of her amusingly enthusiastic response to tasting pot sausage, it caused our website to crash under the number of enquiries.

We hired Blessing's sister, Honour, who was starting a university course in the autumn, so was delighted to be earning some proper money up until then, and redoubled our efforts on workdays, while ensuring we fiercely protected two days off each week.

We said yes to the enquiries we liked the sound of, and no to those that we suspected would be more stress than we cared to take on.

We were living the dream. Spending at least a couple of days every week enjoying the outdoors at festivals, weddings and other events, not an air-conditioning unit or harsh strip light to be seen.

Well, *a* dream, anyway.

Did I still dream about the Isle of Siskin?

Far too often. Possibly not helped by my occasional – or should that be embarrassingly frequent? – peeks into island goings-on via their social media pages and online newspaper.

Did I miss the barley fields, the quaint harbour cottages, and how naturally the islanders all lived in each other's pockets?

Did I yearn to have been there for the Sunflower Festival, selling my pasties, dancing an island jig and then strolling back to wherever home was beneath the stars?

Did I ache for Pip, wondering what he was doing, whether he'd found someone else to watch the sunset with, or if he still thought about me?

Absolutely. All of the above, and more.

But I also vowed to appreciate how far I'd come in the past few months, how, after the most unexpected turn, I'd ended up somewhere exhilarating, and been able to take some other brilliant people with me. Most of the time, I kept that vow.

35

On the last weekend in August, I was hit with another plot twist. Sherwood Street Food was starting to settle into a rhythm. We'd spent the summer smoothing out kinks, streamlining systems and had a steady yet manageable number of events booked in for the autumn. I'd barely found any space in my head for anything other than ensuring we had the right stock for the new recipes, supervising our staff and planning, prepping and providing the best street food in Nottinghamshire, but had found the odd afternoon or evening when I felt prompted to do a few quick online searches for my family, in the hope and fear that I might have one out there somewhere.

I got nowhere in looking for Nell's parents, which I wasn't surprised about as they would have been ninety-three and ninety-five, were they still alive. I tried my birth mother, Kennedy Swan. She'd died long before social media, online news or obituary websites, but I had little else to run with. After a few evenings fruitlessly investigating with the information from my birth certificate, I had hit nothing but dead ends.

Then, as the crowds dwindled towards the last hour of the final day of the Robin Hood festival, and we sent Honour off to fetch us all ice creams, a man approached the food truck.

'What can I get you?' I asked.

'Um.' The man was about my age, maybe a couple of years older. He looked out of place for the forest in a smart shirt, bow tie, and royal-blue corduroy trousers. He removed a blue bucket hat to scratch a head covered in very short hair, shifting from side to side. 'I'm not sure.'

'We've not got much left, if that helps. No pasties, but there's some no-cheese nachos and a venison taco. Oh, and the caramel blondie is fabulous, if you'd rather something sweet.'

'Actually.' He put the hat back on, bobbed his head up and down a couple of times and glanced around the clearing, looking painfully uncomfortable. 'I'll be back in a minute. I just need to...'

Then he hurried jerkily across the grass, around the side of a stall selling herbal soaps and candles, and disappeared.

'Was it something you said?' Blessing, who'd been cleaning up behind me, now squinted after him.

'Perhaps he had his heart set on a pasty.' I shrugged it off, turning my attention to packing up.

'Um, hello again.'

I straightened up from where I'd been stashing away paper napkins, wooden forks and other bits and pieces. The man was back.

Only, with him was...

Oh, my goodness.

For the first, bone-jarring second, I thought it was my mother.

Then I noticed the woman's petite frame, and for the next, adrenaline-pumping few moments, the incoherent thought spinning around inside my skull was that it was me.

A future me. This person was well into middle age, although

there were distinct streaks of reddish blonde amongst the grey of her shoulder-length layers.

She appeared equally shocked, green eyes round, mouth hanging slightly open.

'I told you, Mum. It's her.'

'And who would that be?' Blessing asked, not unkindly, as she took hold of my clammy hand.

'Is it you?' the woman asked, voice quavering. 'I saw the interview, on the news, and it was like seeing a ghost. I couldn't stop thinking about it. Then Owen here – he's my son – showed me your website, where it says about your story, and the pasty place. I thought, well, there might be more than one Emmaline Brown in the world, but there can't be that many of them with a mother called Nell, who happen to be the spit of my sister.'

She trailed off, blinking rapidly as she shook her head in disbelief.

'This is my mother, Dawn Swan. Her sister was Kennedy Swan,' Owen added, enunciating carefully.

It felt as though the food truck had flipped upside down, and I were hanging there, suspended in time and space and unable to do anything but scrabble to right myself again.

'We knew Nellie had taken on Kennedy's daughter,' Dawn went on, talking quickly now. 'But then they decided we weren't allowed to keep in contact, and, to be honest, they were right. I was that sorry to hear Nellie had died, but, given that we weren't allowed to know anything more about you, we wondered if you'd never known about us. I thought it best to see you in person, so I could be sure before overturning the pasty cart, as it were. I didn't want to be putting two and two together and making an imaginary long-lost niece. Sorry, I mean second cousin. But I just knew it was you.'

'First cousin once removed,' Owen corrected her.

'Either way, we're family. That's clear in every inch of her face.'

I clutched onto Blessing's hand for dear life. 'I am me. I mean, I am her. I... I don't think I mind if you call me your niece.'

'Oh, Emmie.' Dawn stretched up to try and reach me through the hatch, but all she could do was pat the counter. She dropped back, face contorted with emotion until Blessing hastily opened the side door to the truck and bundled me out.

'Oh, my precious girl.' Dawn pulled me against her, and, perhaps resorting back to nature over nurture, my arms flung themselves around her in a way that they'd never embraced Nell. Our heads rested together at the exact same height.

'I can't believe we found you,' Dawn cried.

'I can't believe you came searching for me,' I sobbed at the same time.

'If the looks weren't enough, it was when you tipped your head to the side and smiled. I nearly fell off the sofa, seeing that. Kennedy, my mother, Auntie Polly – all the Swan women do it. I had to come.'

'I've been trying to find you too.' I sniffed, prising myself away before I got snot on her T-shirt. 'I mean, not you. All I had was Polly and Clive's names, and Kennedy's date of birth and old address. I couldn't find anything and had no idea where else to search.'

'Nell really never told you about us?'

I shook my head. 'Not in any detail, no.'

'And what she told you wasn't pretty, I'd imagine. She'd begged her mum and mine to sort themselves out, prove the courts wrong, but they refused, said you'd be better off being adopted by strangers. Nellie was so angry.'

I said nothing, which was answer enough.

'She was always determined to do better than us.' Dawn pulled out a wodge of tissues from her shorts pocket and handed me a couple, using the rest to blow her nose and wipe her face. 'It was so hard to lose her – and you – but she knew it was what Kennedy wanted. She did it for both of you. And clearly did a stellar job of raising you. My niece! I'm Auntie Dawn! As far as I'm concerned, that cancels out every rotten thing she'll have said. About us, and to us.'

That statement made her start crying again. I'd not stopped yet, so there we both were, weeping all over the place while Blessing handed Owen a free blondie and a coffee, and the last few stragglers from the festival tried to pretend they weren't gawking as they skirted around us towards the exit.

In the end, my business partner took charge.

'Look, this has been a lot. Why don't you swap numbers, and, once you've had a bit of time to process things, arrange a proper meet-up, somewhere you can talk?'

After exchanging details with fumbling fingers, Dawn accepted her son's – *my biological cousin's!* – proffered arm, and allowed him to steer her to the exit.

'Whew, Emmie. That's a biggie.' Blessing went to hug me, but, fearing it would cause me to disintegrate into complete mush, I instead took her hand and gave it a quick squeeze.

'At least I know I'm not the only one in my family capable of expressing emotions,' I said, followed by a semi-hysterical giggle, which ended up with more crying, and Blessing giving me the hug anyway, seeing as I couldn't really get any mushier.

We'd planned to celebrate the end of the festival with a takeaway – no more proper cooking for at least a day or two – and a gory thriller that Blessing insisted I would love as much as the others she'd badgered me into watching. I hadn't especially enjoyed those, to be honest, but felt it was the least I could do after crying on her all through packing up and the drive home.

Instead, my friend insisted on us scouring the Internet for references to Molly, Dawn and Owen Swan.

'They might have seemed fine for those few minutes, but a court wouldn't have made your mum disown them without very good reason.'

We found nothing for Molly, or more surprisingly for Owen, but it turned out Dawn was a social media oversharer, and I soon had a family tree sketched out, including Dawn's three ex-husbands, two of whom definitely seemed to fit Mum's definition of a 'Negative Influence', her twin daughters and their partners plus assorted children. According to their profiles, the twins were a year older than me. There were photos featuring Owen's twenty-first birthday from seven years earlier, meaning that Dawn had borne three children in two years. There were also posts about another boy who had died from congenital heart disease. I put together more pieces and worked out that Dawn had been a couple of years older than Kennedy. Molly, their mother, had been almost forty when she had her second daughter, accounting for the twenty-year age difference between Kennedy and Nell.

My conclusions from all that research were basic.

I had a family.

They mostly lived in the same Derbyshire town, under an hour's drive away.

Most of them appeared – on the surface at least – to be respectable members of society. Dawn worked for Victim Support, and one son-in-law was a paramedic.

I couldn't think of a single good reason not to see Dawn again.

* * *

I waited until Monday morning – like someone trying not to seem too keen for a second date – and invited my mum's cousin, who I still felt strange referring to as my auntie, for lunch at a country pub exactly halfway between us. After a short back-and-forth, we arranged to meet that Thursday. Penny, one of the twins, would join us along with her baby and two-year-old. Layla, her sister, would be working at the Waterstones bookshop in Chesterfield. I felt almost giddy when Dawn mentioned that her daughter was a 'total bookworm'.

Her initial pronouncement had been playing in my head like a lullaby ever since the festival.

Either way, we're family.

I had no expectations that the Swans would be perfect.

But I was theirs. They were mine.

I had to hope that getting to know my new family would help me stop obsessing about the other family who'd made me feel as though I belonged.

So far, it was looking optimistic – clicks onto Hawkins and Isle of Siskin accounts had dropped to a mere one squillion per day. Prior to meeting Dawn and Owen, it had been at least twice that.

What I really wanted to do was knock on the farmhouse door and ask for Pip, then walk with him along the cliff-top externally processing my thoughts on how you meet a family for the first time, what you talk about, whether I should feel angry or cautious, or allow myself to feel hopeful and happy. To hear his advice on what degree of 'lowlife criminal' I could tolerate in my relatives, or whether I should accept them at face value, and simply enjoy hanging out with people who shared, not only my genes, but also my love of reading, and, judging by the photos, my taste in fashion, food and sappy films.

Apart from Blessing, he was the one person I trusted to understand my heart on this.

Why was it that, despite filling my new life with good things –

a thriving business, new social life with Blessing, working on the cottage, a whole new family to consider – none of it seemed to shake that feeling of missing something?

Missing someone.

36

On Thursday, I arrived at the pub a few minutes late, thanks to a delayed delivery from my butcher and roadworks on the A38.

'Flippin' heck,' Penny shrieked as I approached the corner table they'd squeezed around. 'You were right, Mum.'

She jumped up, flung her arms around me and held on until I was in danger of asphyxiation. Thankfully, at the point I'd have to rudely entangle myself or risk passing out, she let go, holding me at arm's length, eyes shining, face in a huge grin.

'I thought Mum was kidding herself, to be honest. What are the chances of spotting someone that looks a bit familiar on the news, and her turning out to be Kennedy's Emmie? But there's no mistaking it. Look!'

She pointed to her rainbow-striped trainers, laughing. Mine were identical, apart from being a couple of sizes smaller. They were one of the first things I'd bought since ditching the Parsley's Pastics uniform. Penny definitely had Nell's Viking-esque stature. Her hair, worn in a high ponytail, was more auburn than fair, with dark-brown eyes and a broader mouth than mine or her mother's, but everything else, including the way she tipped her head to one side while she spoke, was all Swan.

She introduced me to her baby, Riley, and his big brother, Milo, currently under the table refereeing a fight between a shark and a Tyrannosaurus Rex. Dawn gave me a nervous hug, and we all squashed in around the table, which was laden with plates.

'The boys were famished, so we ordered already,' Penny said. 'We're all mad for cheesy chip butties, so thought you'd probably like them, too, seeing as it's a family tradition. Bags of brown sauce and a squirt of salad cream.'

I'd never tried a chip butty. Mum didn't allow factory-made sauces in the house, let alone brown sauce or salad cream. But seeing as it was a family tradition, I overlooked the twinge of resistance to another person ordering for me, knowing that this was meant as a welcoming gesture, not a mother dictating her daughter's taste, and dug in.

Okay, so I didn't need to share everything in common with the Swans. The Brown in me still held some sway.

'You hate it, don't you?' Penny laughed, handing me a menu after watching me hesitate over a second bite.

The temptation to lie was strong, but the desire to be able to be myself with these people, and not be judged for it, was stronger.

I ordered a noodle bowl.

* * *

I'd been so nervous about the lunch, whittling about my rubbish social skills leading to awkward silences, or whether we'd even like each other, despite trying to remind myself that if we didn't get on, at least we'd tried. In the end, we all had so many questions that there was barely time to take a breath, let alone leave a lull in the conversation.

I asked, as tactfully as I could thanks to hours of overthinking it, why I'd not been allowed to have any contact with them.

'It was the right decision at the time,' Dawn said, with a dejected sigh. 'Our mums were branded our estate's female version of the Kray twins, back in the day. I mean,' she rushed on, noticing my look of alarm, 'nothing so bad as them two, but they were women who, shall we say, were flexible with the law when it suited them. You can't earn a living through low-key drug-dealing, ripping off businesses, or lying, cheating and scamming without backing it up with a bit of violence now and then. We were brought up with no boundaries, in constant fear of what might kick off next. Nell learned to control what small things she could, terrified of ending up like her parents. She was forever making more rules and routines for herself.'

'She said most of the family had been in prison.'

'The Swan twins served time together, and on their own. They were never honest about how long or how often, but I eventually figured out that the Great-Aunt Doris they kept going abroad to look after for months at a time was about as real as their insurance claims.' Dawn shook her head in despair. 'Kennedy followed in their footsteps, only she helped herself to too many of the drugs she was selling. Your grandad – no, hang on...' Dawn shook her head '...Nellie's dad – Clive Brown, I don't know if you want to call him your grandad or great-uncle, but anyway, he served six years in Nottingham Prison. My dad, Tommy, he spent most of his life too drunk to be of any use to the family business.'

'What about you, then, Mum?' Penny asked, before I could pluck up the courage.

Dawn sighed. 'As a youngster, I didn't have much choice when Mum told me to deliver a package here, lie to the policeman who was, of course, always trying to frame them. But I saw what it was doing to my sister, so I found myself a fella and got the heck out of there. The problem was, he turned out to be worse than any of them. Only time he kept his fists to himself was when I was pregnant. So, I had Gareth, Owen and then the twins, before Mum found out and sent him packing.'

'Is that why you couldn't take me in?' I asked.

'Because I had four kids under four, one of them with a life-limiting disability, another neurodiverse in ways that no one could begin to fathom in those days? Or because my husband was violent and controlling? Both, darling. Not to mention that any child would be better off far, far away from the lot of us. That's why I told Kennedy not to fight social services. I was that relieved when she agreed to give you up. Although it hurt her so much, she took off straight after.' She wiped her eyes with a paper napkin. 'I'd been waiting forever for the call to say she'd died, but losing my baby sister still broke me.'

'You turned it around in the end, though, didn't you, Mum?' Penny said. 'Once you got rid of Louis, it was all good.'

'It was,' Dawn said, nodding firmly. 'We'd lost Mum a while before, and Auntie Polly was living in a home, retired from all that nonsense. So, after waster number three, I decided I was done with men, and retrained as a Victim Support worker, in the hope I could make some amends on behalf of the Swan family and associates. I've got three upstanding kids, five fabulous grandkids. And a niece I'm so proud of, I could burst.'

'I'm sorry Mum never fought to give you another chance,' I said.

'I am, too. And I'm sorry I didn't try harder to let her know I deserved one. But we had no idea where she was. Last we heard, she'd got married and moved to some island.'

That started a whole new conversation, which lasted until my brain was so full, if I stayed any longer, I'd be too drained to drive home.

I left with an invitation to Milo's third birthday party, in a couple of weeks' time, where I could meet the rest of the family. This felt like a sensible length of time away, and there were always phones and Facebook in the meantime. I had no hesitation in accepting an invitation to go to a party on my own and meet a load of strangers who were also relatives. The last couple of hours had been a lot. But I had the same trainers as my cousin. Dawn was obsessed with cooking, baking desserts for anyone who'd eat them. They told me Layla read travel books and had a whole scrapbook full of dream destinations for when her children were older.

These were my people, and I left with the absolute certainty that the only thing I had to fear was missing out on the chance to be a part of them.

* * *

Before we knew it, autumn was well under way. The forest was adorned with a crisp rainbow of reds, burnished orange and gold. Some mornings were so chilly, our breath blew smoke signals into the cobalt sky as we loaded up the van. On others, we scuttled back and forth dodging puddles, praying the rain stopped so that we'd sell at least something that day.

The summer season had rounded off with Nottingham Goose Fair at the end of September, a travelling funfair spread over a large city recreation site where half a million visitors swarmed between every kind of ride, game and food stall imaginable. It was a horribly hectic ten days of constant noise, flashing lights and endless hungry customers, but the gruelling shifts meant we were entering the quieter months with a healthy bank balance and a sense of growing optimism that we had created something special.

Following that, Blessing and I took a much-needed week off to recuperate and reassess how the business was going.

Our conclusion? It was going brilliantly.

For the rest of the autumn, our plan was to rely on our weekends at the Sherwood Forest Visitor Centre along with two days a week in bustling markets, plus the now regular supply to Scarlett's restaurant and a couple of local cafés. We had four weddings spread over the next three months, and would be at different locations for five days straight over the week of Bonfire Night at the beginning of November, after which the Christmas markets and fairs started.

During our week off, I invited my family over for a damp barbecue, because there was no way they'd all fit in the house. This did require pausing more than once to brush off a twinge of guilt at what Mum would say to her garden being invaded by Swans, but I refused to let that taint the afternoon. It was my home now, and increasingly, I found it easier to accept that there was nothing wrong with wanting to do things my own way.

Hosting family was tiring and slightly stressful, yet heartwarming and exhilarating at the same time. We still had so much to learn about each other, and despite the many poignant similarities between us, the differences at times seemed stark. I didn't expect any of them to become a new best friend, but I found a family who were interested in me, who were keen to offer help and support – even when their opinions did tip into overbearing – and who rapidly decided they loved me with the same fiery fervency they adored each other.

It took some adjustments, having a whole load of people who cared. I wasn't used to daily group WhatsApp conversations about poorly children or a special offer on beef at the supermarket.

Someone asking how my day had been, or what my plans were for tomorrow.

It was wonderful and irritating, comforting and disconcerting all at the same time.

Chatting it through with Blessing on one of the rambles through the forest that we'd instigated to combat all the extra calories from taste-testing, I decided the only way I'd coped with all this change was due to my altered pace of life, which included time to process, talk and decompress on our precious days off.

'That's the only reason I'm not bullying you into saying yes to Beagle Boy,' Blessing said one Sunday afternoon, as we crunched through piles of fallen leaves, acorns and chestnuts, the autumn sunshine dappling the path between the trees.

'Saying yes to what?' I retorted, feeling a flush of colour that had nothing to do with the fresh air. 'He's not asked me anything.'

Beagle Boy was most definitely a man, not a boy. Probably somewhere in his thirties, he walked two beagles through Sherwood Forest every Saturday, stopping for something to eat before heading home. Over the past few weeks, he'd progressed from a quick hello and the odd comment about the weather to longer conversations spanning our recipes, local news and whatever mischief the dogs had got into that week.

'Only because you won't put him out of his misery and take the hint. "Any plans for the rest of the weekend, Emmie?" "What kind of food do you like to eat, when someone else is cooking?" And you shut him down every time. Which is fine,' she added, quickly, as I began to protest. 'Like I said, you've had more than enough going on lately. But one day, he's going to bite the bullet and ask you out. Might be worth thinking about your answer, because if he catches you off guard, who knows what you'll end up saying?'

'I'm not interested in Beagle Boy,' I said, with a reasonable amount of certainty.

'Not interested in him yet, or at all?' Blessing asked. 'Or should I say, not interested in him, or in anyone who isn't a hot farmer living in the middle of the Irish Sea?'

My spluttered attempt at a reply only provided more impetus to keep going.

'Because, last I heard, you told that farmer to leave you alone.'

'Which he has, so I don't know why you're dragging him up again.'

'Emmie, if you don't like some random dog walker, that's your prerogative. Even if he does have a cute smile and the rare ability to partake in a two-way conversation rather than waffling on about himself all the time. But if you're holding back on even considering whether you might like someone because you can't let go of Pip, then you need to do something about that.'

We slowed down to dodge around a giant puddle of mud.

'Of course I'm not over Pip. I don't know how to switch off my feelings for him. I can't just not like him any more for no reason.'

'No, but you can move on. People get over exes all the time. It's not easy, and it might take a while, but the first thing you do is stop obsessing over every Instagram account that might provide the tiniest titbit of tenuous information about them. You block them, or anything to do with them. Especially when you've got no one else in common, so the only possible excuse you have for cyberstalking them is to fuel those feelings.' She gave me a sardonic look. 'Don't think you're being subtle, Miss Devotee of Siskin News.'

'Do you think I'm a total loser?' I asked.

'No.' Blessing caught my sheepish expression. 'No! I think you had a two-year crush on a really good guy who clearly liked you too. He's now intrinsically tied up in a massively significant moment in your life. You'll inevitably have trouble letting him go. What I'm asking is, are you still sure that you want to?'

'I'm not sure I ever did want to.' I gave a dejected shrug. 'I'm no expert, but I've been on a steep learning curve about love in the past couple of months. I genuinely love Pip, Blessing. I wasn't simply swept up in holiday romance when I told you I was *in* love with him.'

Blessing stopped.

'Then you've got two options. Either do whatever it takes to get over him, or whatever it takes to, I don't know... *get* him.'

'Get him?'

She flapped her hand at me. 'You know what I mean. Figure out what you want most. If it's worth it, you'll find a way to make it work.'

'I'm really not sure I will.'

'Pah. Have you forgotten the challenges Team Sherwood Street Food can overcome if we put our minds to it?' We'd reached the stile leading to a clearing in the forest with a café where we always stopped for coffee and a cake. 'Think about it, and let me know which option you choose.'

* * *

After that conversation, it was hard to think about anything else. I'd dismissed any possibility of a life including Pip after the horrendous end to my stay on the island. I still had the letters painfully demonstrating how love was not always enough. I wouldn't contemplate starting anything that would result in Pip eventually having to leave the farm.

I wouldn't settle for a long-term relationship conducted from separate landmasses. Again, I had the evidence for how incompatible that was with farm life.

So, while the thought of option one felt like ripping through my guts with a potato peeler, option two required uprooting this fledgling shoot of a fabulous life to a place where I'd be judged and unfairly labelled.

Around and around I went as I rubbed flour and fat between my fingertips, sizzled different meats in our giant skillets and ploughed through a dozen other tasks as we prepped for the bonfire events. It didn't feel cowardly to shy away from reinserting myself into the fallout from a family's festering wounds. It felt wise, and healthy and like the best kind of advice Mum would have offered.

I loved Pip. But there were plenty of other good, kind, fascinating people out there.

I messaged Blessing one morning while standing in the queue at the wholesalers.

> I'm going with option one
>
> Send help as necessary

She replied, a few seconds later.

> Beagle Boy?

37

I blocked every site I could think of relating to the Isle of Siskin, and buried myself even deeper in work, what had become weekly lunches with my cousin Layla, plus some or all of her three kids, and even joined a local conservation group (I was the youngest member by at least two decades, to Blessing's disappointment, but they were all welcoming and I loved spending my day off scooping gubbins out of ditches or counting crayfish).

Blessing sprang a short break in Rome on me, as it was 'the least islandish place we could fly to for under a hundred quid'. We spent two full days exploring the standard tourist sights, researching ideas for new recipes and mastering the art of afternoon siestas. I even accepted a chaste kiss from one of the many men who flirted with us at the hotel bar, and flew home feeling as contented and positive as I'd been since my first holiday.

Heading to catch the flight out, we'd been held up by a traffic accident so had sped through the airport with no more than a gleeful wave at the familiar faces. We could only ogle the new juice and pretzel bar from a distance as we scrambled to reach Gate One before it closed.

However, on our return journey, it would have been rude not to say hello to some of the colleagues we'd spent years working with. Giddy with holiday vibes, we bought a smoothie each, one cheese and one chocolate pretzel, and headed over to see who was hanging around at the food court.

Barb soon appeared, briskly informing Blessing that her hair clearly didn't suit the Rome climate, before launching into a lengthy rant about the third assistant manager since Blessing. She was flabbergasted at the previous two's ingratitude in resigning after only a few days, spurning the decent salary, flexible shifts and Barb's expert input.

'Can you imagine?' she asked, at least three times, until Blessing snapped and told her that, having stuck it out for thirteen years, she didn't have to imagine why someone wouldn't want to be criticised, controlled and complained at all day.

After making a hasty exit from the food court, we bumped into Gregory.

'Ah, Emmie. Very good. You got my message, then?' He shook his head. 'If you want to follow me, they should be in one of the filing cabinets.'

'Um, what should?' I asked as we hurried after him.

'The mail. I would have forwarded it on, but, well, I didn't get around to it.'

After opening and closing a few drawers, he handed me a pile of envelopes held together by an elastic band. A quick flick through revealed most of them to be business junk mail, so I could understand why Gregory hadn't prioritised posting them on. There was a letter with my insurance company's logo on it, but they'd also emailed so I hadn't missed anything important.

And then, tucked inside a catering catalogue, was a handwritten letter, addressed to the more informal Emmie Brown.

'I'll read it in the car,' I said, seeing Blessing's eyes go round.

'Let's go.'

* * *

As soon as Blessing had pulled out of the airport and hit the main road, I opened the envelope with trembling hands. I knew all too well that a letter could change everything.

Dear Emmie,

I know you asked me to let you go. You said we can't be friends, and I understand that. I don't think I could ever spend time with you and not want more. But I couldn't leave things the way they ended. Violet said I seemed angry with you. That's not true. I was very, very angry with Ma. I was mad at Da for the secrets and lies. I was devastated that during what I'd thought was a perfect week, you'd been going through all that alone. I felt like a fool. Which made me furious at myself.

And all those things piling on top of each other stopped me from saying what I needed to that evening. Which is that I'm so sorry, for all of it. I'm sorry if for one moment you felt unwelcome here. As if your history, my family's mistakes, meant you couldn't stay.

What should have been the best adventure ended up a trial by Hawkins jury.

I don't know what else to say, except that I have missed you every day since you left. Everything feels off without you. My sisters can't bear my grumpiness any longer and have ordered me to do something about it.

I won't ask you to come back, not if it risks you being hurt again.

If you don't reply to this, I understand, and I won't try to contact you again.

But I needed to tell you that I'm sorry.
And I meant everything in the treehouse.
I still do.
Pip

I dropped my head onto the glove compartment with an agonising groan.

'When did he send that?' Blessing asked, after I'd read the letter aloud.

I checked the date at the top. 'August. About a month after I'd come home.'

'Then it wasn't a knee-jerk reaction. What are you going to do?'

'Ugh. I've been working so hard at moving on.'

She gave me a side glance.

'Okay. I've been starting to do a teensy bit better. And this doesn't change anything, does it? He's still there, I'm here. His mum hates me. I'm evil mainlander Nell's daughter.' I swallowed. 'But it was kind of him to apologise. It's nice to know he doesn't blame me for any of it.'

'No reply, then? Pressing on with option one?'

'Option one.'

* * *

In the first week in December, we set out to another event, which Blessing had booked at the last minute and vaguely described as a family celebration. Due to my attention being on avoiding the potholes on an unpaved country lane, it was only as we reached the farm gates that I spotted the banner.

'Is this a sick joke?'

'Um,' Blessing said. 'They said to go around the side to the back field. Someone will be there to meet us.'

'Okay, what I meant to say is, have you booked us a graduation party for the course where the man I'm trying my utmost to get over has just graduated from?'

The sign read:

Congratulations Agriculture Graduates

She squirmed in the passenger seat. 'There are loads of different agriculture courses. Grad parties are a whole new potential revenue stream. This one will be full of hungry young farmers, so they paid extra. I couldn't turn it down.'

'What happened to us only doing bookings we're both comfortable with?'

'Sometimes comfort is overrated.'

I pulled up beside a large outbuilding and found the university website on my phone.

'The only agricultural graduation ceremony is today.'

'Yes, but this is for the bachelor's degrees, not post-grad courses. I think you're probably safe.'

'And if I'm not?' I squeaked. 'I thought the Siskin Islanders were meddlers. This is a whole new level of butting in.'

'Okay, I'm sorry,' Blessing started, before backtracking. 'Actually, I'm not. What's the point of a best friend if we can't meddle when necessary? The whole social media ban isn't working. Maybe it wouldn't be the worst thing ever if you saw him face to face.'

'How could that possibly help?' I whined.

'Closure,' she said, firmly. 'He's only a man, Emmie. Perhaps you need to remind yourself of that.'

'Well, I hope you'll be okay with picking up the pieces if this all backfires.'

'Naturally.' She pointed through the windscreen. 'There, that must be Joel. Let's get to work.'

* * *

Once a giant bonfire had been lit, the graduates and their families began to arrive, frequently leaving the warmth of the blaze to wander our way in search of food. It was fair to say that it wasn't our finest evening.

Or, more accurately, it wasn't mine. I was a total wreck from the moment I'd turned off the engine and clambered out of the cab. Spilled drinks, dropped pasties, incorrect orders. When the first stream of guests had eased off, Blessing tried reassigning me to the non-customer side of the operation, keeping me facing away from the hatch so I couldn't agonisingly scan every single partygoer as they emerged from SUVs, taxis and pickup trucks, but it didn't help. I was a shaking, quaking, lovelorn bag of anxious nerves.

I didn't know whether to wish Pip would turn up so the torture could be over and done with, or if it was better to not see him, hopefully producing a different sort of closure that might be equally helpful.

* * *

It showed how keen Blessing was to infiltrate the graduation party market that she took a load of pictures of my stricken face as I put together a carton of nachos and posted it on our social media accounts.

In the end, after three hours of serving loaded fries, pasties and cakes to increasingly rowdy guests, I began to relax.

'He'd be here by now, if he was coming,' I finally conceded, slumping against the counter as fireworks whizzed and wailed in a field behind us.

'There you go, then. All that stress for nothing,' my business partner pronounced. 'Maybe this shows just how silly it is to let a man you never want to see again hold such sway over you.'

'Hmm.'

Maybe. But when, a few minutes later, a minivan screeched around the side of the farmyard, kicking up gravel as it came to an abrupt stop, my heart lurched for the hundredth time that evening.

The door opened, and one of my nightmares came true when my sworn enemy sprang out.

'It's her!' Rosemary yelled, holding onto a wide-brimmed, cream hat to stop it blowing off her head. 'Violet, you were right. It's Emmie!'

Then, before I could duck behind the counter, choose an appropriate weapon or make a run for it, the other van doors opened and the rest of the Hawkins family tumbled out.

I vaguely registered sisters, their children and grandmother along with Gabe and his brother. But, of course, my eyes could only lock on one man.

Pip was in the suit he'd worn for Iris's wedding underneath a heavy wool coat. He took three steps towards the food truck, then stopped.

If I'd been in any doubt, made any progress in my mission to get over this man, seeing him standing there blew that illusion into oblivion like the final firecracker exploding above us.

* * *

'Emmie?' Pip's voice was full of wonder.

'Pip. Hi.' Mine, on the other hand, sounded as if it had been generated by an early AI prototype.

'We saw you on Instagram,' he said, as if that explained what on earth he was doing here.

'We were at the airport, about to get on the plane, when Auntie Violet found it,' Flora said, breathless with excitement.

I stole a quick glance at Blessing, whose knowing grin confirmed that she'd deliberately posted the images in the harebrained hope this would happen.

'We've been looking for you *everywhere*!' Jack added, jumping up and down so that his flapping coat revealed the bare chest underneath. 'We even had to go to the actual Sherwood Forest, because Auntie Iris saw a food van on the website and thought it was you.'

His auntie shrugged. 'A reviewer said it was the best pasty they'd ever eaten. Who else could it be?'

'We're only there at weekends,' I said, still in shock.

'That explains it, then.' Violet nodded, cradling a baby in a puffy snowsuit against her chest.

'Why are you here?' I asked, because it still wasn't any clearer.

'To find you!' Beanie squealed, clutching her grandad Gabe's hand. Most of her face was hidden by a giant bobble hat, but I couldn't believe how much she'd grown.

'We're probably going to miss our plane now, but Grammie said we all had to come or you wouldn't listen to her,' Jack added.

'Is an adult going to fill Emmie in, or are we leaving it up to my kids to convince her?' Lily asked.

'Feel free to explain everything,' Blessing replied.

Lily shook her head. She looked gorgeous in an A-line, turquoise coat and matching boots, her dark hair gleaming.

'It's not up to me. Emmie knows how much I love her. It's for

Pip, Ma and Da to put the rest of us out of our misery by making this right.'

'Philip?' Rosemary asked, tentatively.

'No, Ma.' He went over and took her hand, drawing her closer to the food truck. 'If you say what you need to first, the rest of you can still catch the plane. I can follow on later, if Emmie is kind enough to spare me a few more minutes.'

'Right.' Rosemary straightened her hat, tugged at the belt on her matching jacket, pulled up her handbag strap and tried valiantly to look at me.

'Shall we find somewhere quieter?' I asked, dying to get this over with as quickly as possible so she would go, and I could hear from Pip.

'No.' Rosemary straightened up. 'They all know why I'm here. Which is to tell you that, you see… I'm sorry.'

'Okay.' *Was that it?*

'I behaved abominably.' She stopped, screwing up her face as though holding back a sneeze, before shaking her shoulders and pressing on. 'Appallingly. There's not much more to say, really. I was consumed with some sort of jealous madness. But I'm on medication now, and having lots of help. It's working. I haven't spiked anyone's milk jug in months.'

She gave a weak laugh, which was greeted by a grim silence. 'Too soon?'

'Yes, it's too soon,' Violet gasped.

'Anyway, what I needed to explain, apart from how sorry I am, is that if you came back, looking to spend more time with Philip, I won't stand in your way.'

'Rosemary.' Gabe spoke for the first time, his tone sharp enough to make me flinch.

'What I mean is, you would be very welcome. I would very much like the chance to get to know Nell's daughter properly. We can talk about it, about her, if you like. Or not, if you don't. Stay for a holiday – we'll cover the cost. Or forever. I completely respect and support whatever you decide.'

'Okay, that's probably enough, Ma,' Pip interrupted, glancing at me for confirmation.

'Um. Thank you,' I said, grateful for the hatch imposing some distance between us while I tried to think. 'I appreciate you coming here to tell me that. And I'm sorry you've been unwell.'

'Thank you,' Rosemary said, face scrunching up again. 'That's very gracious of you.'

'What time's your flight?' Blessing asked pointedly.

All the adults quickly checked their phones and watches.

'We can just about make it if we run,' Violet said.

'Is that...?' Gabe asked me.

'Yes. Please go.'

And so, in a flurry of kisses from the sisters and children, the briefest of introductions to baby Colin, a wink from Gabe and firm nod from Aster, they bundled back in the minivan and disappeared as quickly as they'd arrived.

All of them, that was, apart from one.

'Look, you two need a proper conversation, and it's freezing out here. Go on and find somewhere inside while I pack up,' Blessing said, her tone leaving no room for arguments.

'Is that okay?' Pip asked hesitantly.

'Well, you're here now, so it'll have to be,' Blessing huffed as she opened the truck's door and shooed me out. 'Go on, I want to get back before the roads ice over.'

* * *

Rather than trespassing inside the farm, we trudged through the field and found a bench on the far side of the bonfire. Most of the guests had either left or retreated indoors, so we were able to talk freely. If only we were bold enough to say anything.

'I still can't believe we found you,' Pip said, eventually breaking the silence.

'I can't believe you were looking,' I added, ducking my head. All my memories of Pip were bathed in sunlight or balmy summer nights. Sitting here, the dying embers no match for December's bitter chill, Pip being here felt like a dream.

'Honestly? I've been searching on the Internet for weeks.'

'No joy?' I disguised my ripple of delight with a cold-induced shiver.

'You're a very elusive woman.'

I gave a shy smile. 'I've never done social media. Even if Mum hadn't conditioned me into thinking it was trash, I've not had enough friends and no family to keep up with, so there didn't seem any point.'

'I tried the professional networking sites, even joined a couple to get proper access. I couldn't find your business details anywhere, let alone you.'

'We have a new business. As you can see. And although I've always gone by Brown, my legal surname for professional activities is Swan.' I shuffled close enough to give a playful nudge, relishing the warmth of another body. 'What else did you try?'

'I started hunting pasty shops, cafés, event catering, anything else I could think of.'

'Even though I'd asked you not to?'

'I wasn't planning on coming to find you in person. I just wanted to know where you were. If you were okay. I promised in my letter that I'd not pester you.' He sighed. 'But it turned out my sisters had other ideas. They were obsessed.'

'I only got the letter two weeks ago.'

He turned to look at me. 'But you read it?'

'It helped, knowing you didn't hate me. Trying to get over you was harder because I couldn't stop wondering if you blamed me for everything. At least I could let that go.'

'You were still trying to get over me? A couple of weeks ago?'

I shook my head. 'A couple of minutes ago. As soon as I drove up and saw that banner, I morphed into a gibbering wreck.'

'And now?'

For a long moment, the only sound was the crackle of twigs, the faint thud of a disco bass from inside the house.

'It's lovely to see you. And I'm pleased your mum has got some help. But things have moved on since the summer. Blessing and I have worked so hard to get the food truck up and running. We share a house. Her brother works for us. I can't simply disappear off to an island because I feel like it. We've got bookings for the next few months.'

Pip reached up and gripped his neck. The familiar gesture made me want to cry. I'd thought the island had changed things – made me believe it was possible to follow my heart, choose *me* for the first time. But it wasn't just me any more. I thought again about how Mum might have felt, taking on the responsibility of someone else's baby, with no one to help her and everything weighing on the success of her little kiosk.

'And you won't start a relationship with me if it can't go anywhere.'

'How can we, when we know it'll only break our hearts?'

Pip was quiet for a moment.

'Would it make any difference if I said that I love you?'

I closed my eyes, as if that could lessen the impact of those words.

After I'd been dreaming about this moment for so long, now it only hurt more that it was too late, too impossible to change anything. Maybe someone stronger, wiser, braver than me would choose to make the most of every moment, and deal with the future when it happened.

But I'd spent too long rereading Mum's letters, weeping over what Nell Brown had lost, bearing the brunt of how the scars shaped her forever.

This brand-new, fledgling me was still too fragile to handle whatever Pip could offer.

I leant against his shoulder, neither of us bothering to hide our sadness.

'I love you too. And I'm glad that you came. All of you. I will never be the same because of you and the island, but right now that's mostly for good reasons. Let's not start down a path that will inevitably ruin that.'

We talked for a while longer, but I needed to get home, and Pip would have to hurry to make the last flight to Siskin. In the end, Blessing insisted on driving him to the airport, despite the frost forming on the roads, and we spent a precious hour squeezed together on the bench in the cab, too forlorn to say much more.

'Okay?' my friend asked as we exited the airport drop-off zone.

'I will be.' I managed to almost sound as if I meant it too.

38

'Pack an overnight bag,' Blessing barked, bursting in my bedroom at 5 a.m., which by the middle of December was two hours earlier than I usually woke up on non-event days.

'What?' I mumbled, bracing my eyes against the sudden glare from the light flicking on while noting that she'd at least had the decency to bring a mug of tea.

'Last-minute booking, but it's a bit of a trek so we'll need to stay overnight.'

'What?' I asked again, dragging myself to a sitting position. 'How is that going to work?'

'The client is providing accommodation. I've checked it out; it's all good.'

I accepted the mug. 'Can I point out the small matter of what food we're going to sell?'

'I'd be alarmed if you didn't.' She plopped down on the empty side of the bed. 'The Christmas market at Hatherstone have cancelled because a snowstorm's been forecast for Wednesday. Which is even better reason for us to not be here. That leaves enough ingredients for today, if we top up on a few fresh items on the way.'

'We've still got to make everything.'

'Nope. After you crashed out last night, when I took the call, Ben came over. We have a truckload of pastry, fillings, and pot sausage all prepped and ready to go.'

I took a long sip of tea, hoping the caffeine burst would help me to come up with any other holes in Blessing's ridiculously last-minute plan.

'Come on, the short notice means a premium rate. Besides, it'll be an adventure. Who knows what might come of it?'

'I don't know...'

'Too late for that, they've paid a deposit. I'll see you downstairs in twenty minutes. Oh, and pack enough for a few nights. We might decide to make the most of the cancellation and hang around for a bit.'

* * *

Due to having spent the vast majority of my life within the same county, I accepted Blessing's explanation that we were heading to a small village near the Welsh coast, given that any more details would do nothing to enlighten me. Although this sudden booking wasn't standard, and an overnight was new, we'd worked together long enough for me to trust her on this. After all, she reminded me, what was the worst that could happen?

I trusted her so much that I still didn't click when we drove past the sign for the ferry port.

It was only when we turned off into the queue of waiting vehicles that I realised.

'Where are we going?' I demanded. Although I knew she'd

never be so thoughtless as to book an event on Siskin, my jangling nerves needed it confirmed.

'Isle of Man,' Blessing said, with such an air of nonchalance, it should have aroused suspicion. 'I didn't tell you because I thought you might be weird about going to an island. But this one is completely different. It's got tens of thousands of people, a proper town, and half-decent Wi-Fi for a start. Look, the ferry's a good three hours and we have to stay in the truck, so you might as well catch up on some sleep.'

More fool me, I accepted the eye-mask and blanket she offered and made myself comfortable.

* * *

I woke up as we bumped down off the tiny vessel and into a port that, with a jolt, I immediately knew all too well – even if it had been transformed with Christmas lights twinkling through the fog.

'What the hell?' I whipped around to face Blessing, anger igniting inside me with a ferocity only matched by the irrepressible burst of joy at seeing Port Cathan again.

'Yeah. I lied a bit.'

'Why would you do this?' I said, voice shrill. 'You know that going to hang out on my not-even-ex's island is not a "new adventure". It's the complete opposite. How could you possibly think this was okay?'

I chuntered on for a few more frantic minutes while we inched along the queue of vehicles exiting the port gates before finally pausing long enough for Blessing to answer.

'We aren't going to hang around for a few days. I lied a bit about that, too.'

'What are you talking about?' I asked, debating whether I had

time to jump out of the truck and run back onto the ferry before it set off back to Wales.

'I reckoned three months would probably be long enough. To decide whether we wanted to stay permanently, that is.'

'Can you see that this is really not the time to be cryptic?' I had to grip my head to stop it from spinning.

'Okay. Fair enough. We're relocating Sherwood Street Food to the Isle of Siskin. On a semi-temporary basis. I've rented us a totally cute cottage on the seafront and secured enough bookings to see us through the next couple of months.'

'What about all our bookings *in Sherwood Forest*?'

'I sorted them. All apart from the weddings. We'll have to drive back for those.'

'My house?'

'Ben is looking for somewhere. His experience with us got him the manager's job at Scarlett's restaurant, and his mate, Jay, wants to move in, too. Jay's a teacher, so his income is steady and they'll pay proper rent. I mean, if you don't mind. They might even want to buy it, if we decide to stay.'

'You've never even been here before!'

'Yeah. When I visited home for a couple of nights, the week after the grad party, it was here. My new home.'

'You can't do this. You can't decide to simply move me and our business to a whole new place. It's ludicrous. And way beyond controlling.' I was aghast. Appalled. Secretly... a little excited?

'Or...' Blessing's voice was soft '...what's ludicrous is you still spending all those hours looking at websites and accounts you supposedly blocked months ago. Still in love with a man who loves you back. An *exceptional* man. Who lives in a place you not that long ago decided to try living in for a while, because you loved it so much, and then changed your mind because of some overblown loyalty to your best friend, despite her being perfectly capable of making her own decisions.'

'You should have talked to me about this first,' I managed to whisper through my strangled throat.

'Yeah, well. I couldn't be bothered with the weeks of arguing back and forth until you eventually gave in. This was way more fun.'

'I've only packed four pairs of knickers.'

'Pip says he'll drive us back next week in his big truck to fetch what else we need.'

'Pip knows about this?'

'Look.' She nodded towards the windscreen.

I glanced forwards, blinking until I could see past my stupefaction to the gates, now only one van in front of us.

There was a crowd of people waiting, as I'd have expected on the island, where anyone coming home or deliveries made were a big deal.

What I would never have expected as Blessing pulled to a stop right in front of them was that some of those people held a banner with the words, *Welcome Emmie and Blessing* painted on it, and that the others were waving, cheering and grinning at us.

I sat there for a long, shell-shocked minute. In the end, Blessing got out and started hugging people and saying hello, shrugging and smiling in response to their frequent glances over at where I remained, frozen.

Eventually, Pip broke away from the gaggle of people, came right up to the cab and opened the door.

'Emmie. I gather you're a wee bit surprised.'

I couldn't even turn to look at him. 'I slept through the ferry.'

'I hope waking up here was more of a dream than a nightmare. Do you need a hand getting down? Or shall I come up?'

I held out one hand, and as his wrapped around mine, it

released something inside me. The rough warmth of the farmer's palm, riddled with callouses and scars of old nicks, felt as familiar and comforting as my own bed, or the texture of floured dough beneath my fingers.

Comforting, familiar and yet brimming with potential that zapped a thrill up my arm and straight to my heart.

I twisted around to face him, the anticipation plain across his features. He reached up his other hand, and I half jumped, half fell into his arms. Lifting my chin to meet his gaze, I found more than I could have hoped for in those gentle eyes.

'Thank you,' I said, because it was all I could come up with.

Then, while I was still too shocked to hold back, I stretched up onto the toes of my boots, and pressed my lips against his.

I perhaps should have been embarrassed that we embraced as long as we did, me clinging onto his jacket as my fingers turned to ice, him wrapping his arms around me in a futile attempt to brace against the freezing gusts blowing in off the sea as we kissed. I didn't care about the cold, the crick in my neck, his family hooting and hollering behind him. I'd spent six months missing this.

When we finally broke apart, chests heaving like a scene from *Bridgerton*, mouths grinning, eyes dancing, Pip bent to rest his forehead against mine, and whispered the only thing that mattered.

'Welcome home.'

* * *

Later that day, after we'd unpacked my one small bag, and the giant suitcases Blessing had snuck along without telling me, Pip picked us up and we headed over to the farm for a welcome gathering. It turned out the pasties and pot sausage Blessing and Ben had prepped was for our own party. We ate squeezed into the farmhouse living room, dining room and kitchen. Just about everyone I'd met previously was there, plus plenty of others I hadn't. We sang Christmas songs, accompanied by Richard's accordion, and a couple of people found space for a dance, while the enormous fireplace crackled and the children dozed under blankets or curled up in laps.

'Care for some fresh, island air?' Pip asked, once the guests began to disperse.

'It's a bit late to watch the sunset.'

'Aye, but the full moon over the water is just as bonny.'

Bundled up in hats, gloves and thick scarves, we strolled along the footpaths, gripping tightly to each other as we slid down the steps to the beach. The sky was like nothing I'd seen before – there wasn't a great deal of ambient light in Sherwood Forest, but out here was a whole different depth of darkness. That was, apart from the moon, and more stars than I'd thought possible.

Pip stood behind me, arms wrapped around my torso.

'I've missed that sound.'

'What, silence?'

'No, the sea!'

The air was still, so the waves were gentle as they broke upon the icy sand.

'I guess I don't much notice it any more.'

'There's a lot you islanders take for granted.'

'Oh?'

'Family, friends and all those shared memories. Knowing who you are, and where you belong. Whichever genius invented pot sausage.'

Pip smiled, and in the moonlight, his face looked cast in silver. 'You know I love it here. I try not to take it for granted, but without you, it felt a lot harder to appreciate.'

'Well, I'm here now.'

'I thought about leaving,' he said, after a while.

'What?' I turned to face him, still pressed up close so we could share some warmth.

'I'd even lined up an interview for a farm manager job at a place near you.'

'Pip, you couldn't! I love the forest, but there's nothing there for me any more. It would make no sense for you to move.'

'Well, we can both be very grateful that Blessing turned up, so we can give this a try, first.'

'No.' I pulled away so he could see how much I meant this next statement. 'I'm not an islander, so I don't take what you have here for granted. I'm thrilled to have some genuine family now – that's a whole other story – but I can visit them, and they'd love to come here. This place is it for me. I'm planning on a lot more overseas adventures with Blessing. Maybe one day with you, if you can get away from the farm, but this is my home now. My safe harbour. Where I'll leave a legacy for my children.'

Pip's smile grew until it filled his whole face. 'Our children?'

'The ninth generation of Hawkins. Flora really needs a cousin so she can stop stressing about having to run the farm.'

'Are you sure? You've kind of been swept into this.'

I nodded. 'I've totally been swept into it. But that's because Blessing knew it's what I wanted. My whole life has been spent trying to please another person. Doing things her way, following her plans and dreams. Being here, with you. This is what I want. It's my choice. And I couldn't be happier.'

'I love you, Pasty Girl.'

'I love you too, Hot Farmer.'

As we kissed, and watched the moonlight dance upon the water until we were so cold we had to turn back and head for the farmhouse, I knew that Nell Brown would be pretty happy to see how things were turning out for her daughter, too.

ACKNOWLEDGEMENTS

I finished the first draft of this book the same month I celebrated ten years of being a published author. So, it is with huge gratitude that I want to acknowledge everyone who has played a part in this story so far.

Firstly my agent, Kiran Kataria, and editor, Sarah Ritherdon. I would not still be writing if it wasn't for the faith you have in my books. Boldwood Books continue to be 'simply the best' publisher – the care, enthusiasm and expertise they provide is extraordinary.

Many people have been kind enough to aid my research over the years. For *Have I Told You Lately*, big thanks to Pat and Esther Lynn, for your farming expertise and honesty while showing me around Hockerwood Park, including 45,000 free range chickens!

Thanks also to the Cornish Pasty Company for kindly answering my questions.

A million thank yous to everyone who has helped me reach the mind-blowing number of one million books. For those who have bought, borrowed, reviewed or blogged about my stories – thank you so much for helping this wild and wonderful dream come true. If you've contacted me through social media, or my website – it genuinely encourages me to get writing; do keep in touch! And for anyone who has mentioned in person that they've read one of my books, then apologies for my awkward response. After ten years, I still find it strange that other people are reading about these characters who live in my head!

All my friends and family who have cheered me on and celebrated with me – I love you, and couldn't have done it without you.

For Ciara, Joe and Dom – raising children who have become such awesome adults will always be my best work. Asher and Bella – I am so very blessed that you trusted me to be a part of your story. George – you will always be my happy ever after.

Finally, I want to thank God, to whom I owe everything. If there is any wisdom, truth or joy in the words I write, it is all thanks to Him.

ABOUT THE AUTHOR

Beth Moran is the award winning author of ten contemporary fiction novels, including the number one bestselling *Let It Snow*. Her books are set in and around Sherwood Forest, where she can be found most mornings walking with her spaniel Murphy.

Sign up to Beth Moran's mailing list for news, competitions and updates on future books.

Visit Beth's website: https://bethmoranauthor.com/

Follow Beth on social media here:

- facebook.com/bethmoranauthor
- x.com/bethcmoran
- instagram.com/bethmoranauthor
- bookbub.com/authors/beth-moran

ALSO BY BETH MORAN

Christmas Every Day

A Day That Changed Everything

Take a Chance on Me

We Belong Together

Just The Way You Are

Let It Snow

Because You Loved Me

Always On My Mind

We Are Family

Take Me Home

Lean On Me

It Had to Be You

Have I Told You Lately

BECOME A MEMBER OF

THE SHELF CARE CLUB

The home of Boldwood's book club reads.

Find uplifting reads, sunny escapes, cosy romances, family dramas and more!

Sign up to the newsletter
https://bit.ly/theshelfcareclub

Boldwood

Boldwood Books is an award-winning fiction publishing company seeking out the best stories from around the world.

Find out more at www.boldwoodbooks.com

Join our reader community for brilliant books, competitions and offers!

Follow us

@BoldwoodBooks

@TheBoldBookClub

Sign up to our weekly deals newsletter

https://bit.ly/BoldwoodBNewsletter

Printed in Great Britain
by Amazon